The Book of Change

The Book of Change

Eileen Chang

張愛玲

《易經》英文原著

香港大學出版社
Hong Kong University Press

Hong Kong University Press
14/F Hing Wai Centre
7 Tin Wan Praya Road
Aberdeen
Hong Kong
http://www.hkupress.org

Hardback ISBN 978-988-8028-19-1
Paperback ISBN 978-988-8028-20-7

British Library Cataloguing-in-Publication Data
A catalogue record for this book is available from the British Library.

Printed and bound by Liang Yu Printing Factory Co. Ltd., Hong Kong, China

Introduction

David Der-wei Wang

Eileen Chang (1920–1995) arrived in Hong Kong from Shanghai in the summer of 1939 and enrolled in the University of Hong Kong. Chang had hoped to study in England, but the outbreak of the Second World War foiled this plan. But war interfered with her studies anyway: the Japanese invaded Hong Kong on December 7, 1941, the same day they launched the attack on Pearl Harbor. After eighteen days of resistance, the British colonial government surrendered on December 25. The University of Hong Kong shut down in the aftermath of the surrender; all students were forced to evacuate.

Like many other students who came to study in Hong Kong, Chang found herself stranded on the island in the subsequent months of the Japanese occupation. During this period, communication with mainland China and other areas was interrupted and travel became extremely hectic. Chang had to take on clerical and nursing jobs in order to make a living. Eventually, she was able to secure a seat on a refugee ship to Shanghai. When she finally made it home, it was already the summer of 1942.

This Hong Kong experience was a turning point in the life and career of Eileen Chang. Before she went to Hong Kong, Chang was a runaway, estranged from her father and stepmother as well as her biological mother. By comparison, Chang's student life at the University of Hong Kong was a happy one; it all came to a sudden halt because of the war.

The Japanese takeover of Hong Kong represented a cataclysmic moment in history and for Chang, it taught a lesson about the brutality of war and the gratuitousness of any human attachments. This lesson would prove to be all the more poignant after she returned to Shanghai and witnessed the transformations of the city now also under Japanese occupation. It was at this juncture that Chang decided to begin her writing life in earnest.

Therefore, it comes as little surprise that Chang should derive much from her Hong Kong experience when writing her early stories. The most famous piece is *Qingcheng zhilian* 傾城之戀 (Love in a fallen city, 1943), a novella about a romance between a divorced Shanghai woman and an overseas Chinese playboy against the background of wartime Hong Kong. The couple starts their affair with selfish motives respectively, but ends up finding true love in each other because of the fall of Hong Kong. Thus, a historical catastrophe serves unexpectedly as a romantic catalyst, turning a rendezvous into a lifelong marital pact. As Chang wryly observes, thousands of lives perished during the war, as if only for the purpose of making one mediocre couple's romance possible.[1] Such a bemused look at the contingencies of history and human fate would become a constant theme of Chang's writings. To that end, Hong Kong takes on a metaphorical dimension as a city where changeability and normalcy, individual desire and societal fate interact with each other in a mercurial way.

Equally noticeable is Chang's essay "Jinyu lu" 燼餘錄 (From the ashes, 1944). This is an extraordinary piece in Chang's *oeuvre*, not only because it provides a firsthand account of life in Hong Kong right after the Japanese invasion but also because it casts a unique view of the meaning of war and life under war. Under Chang's pen, the fall of Hong Kong did not bring about remarkable deeds of sacrifice or heroism so much as it revealed the cowardice and selfishness of humanity. Chang is quick to tell us that she is one of those people her essay sets out to satirize: first shocked by the disorder of the war, yet becoming accustomed to the new order of life in a short time. She describes herself as indifferent to the accidental deaths in the air raids and absent-minded on rescue missions; what concerns her most is food. Moreover, she calls attention to people's grotesque behavior and "bizarre wisdom" prompted by the instinct to survive. Mixing black humor with self-mockery, her exposé is both scathing and hauntingly nonchalant, such that it gives rise to an effect of muted festivity.

1. Eileen Chang, *Love in a Fallen City*: "Hong Kong's defeat had brought Liusu victory. But in this unreasonable world, who can distinguish cause and effect? Who knows which is which? Did a great city fall so that she could be vindicated? Countless thousands of people dead, countless thousands of people suffering, after that an earthshaking revolution...Liusu did not feel anything subtle about her place in history." Karen Kingsbury's translation, in *Love in a Fallen City* (New York: New York Review Books, 2007), 167.

And yet, Chang also is aware of the fact that although this behavior appears inhuman, it is only too predictably human. Behind her portrait of the anomalous manners and morals during wartime looms a deep pathos about the limitation of humanity. This is a *luanshi* 亂世 or a moment of historical catastrophe, as she calls it elsewhere, a time when all core values dissolve and human endeavor becomes meaningless. Her writing, accordingly, is nothing but a feeble, belated testimony, rescued from "the ashes." Hence the famous conclusion of "From the Ashes":

> The vehicle of the time drives inexorably forward. We ride along, passing through thoroughfares that are perhaps already quite familiar. Against a sky lit by flames, they are capable nevertheless of shaking us to the core. What a shame that we occupy ourselves instead searching for shadows of ourselves in the shop windows that flit so quickly by — we see only our own faces, pallid and trivial. In our selfishness and emptiness, in our smug and shameless ignorance, every one of us is like all the others. And each of us is alone.[2]

For readers who are familiar with Eileen Chang's writings in Chinese, the storyline of *The Book of Change* may first impress as an English-language fictional rewrite of "From the Ashes." We have discussed in *The Fall of the Pagoda*, Chang's penchant for rewriting in bilingual and cross-generic terms. *The Book of Change* provides yet another example. Chang wrote the novel in the late fifties as if intending to revisit her wartime experience in a different linguistic and generic medium. Almost all the events in "From the Ashes" are adapted into this novel, and episodes are even expanded to discrete, full-length chapters. By taking up the form of the novel, Chang presumably sought to release the dramatic power inherent in her biographical essay. However, from a critical perspective *The Book of Change* may not read as compellingly as "From the Ashes." Although the novel format allowed for more dramatic latitude in terms of narrating her wartime ordeal, as a literary text, it fails to evoke the same kind

2. Eileen Chang, *Written on Water*, trans. Andrew Jones (New York: Columbia University Press, 2005), 52.

of psychological and moral intensity that made "From the Ashes" such a complex reflection of and on the war. Missing are the subtexts that made the earlier essay a modern classic: the tension between historical catastrophe and everyday trivia, nationalist calls to arms and individual desire for survival, and the ubiquitous threat of death and youthful insouciance.

Nevertheless, *The Book of Change* does tell us something else regarding Chang's life and creative vision. For one thing, it reveals for the first time Chang's ambivalent relationship with her mother; it also brings to light how Chang manages to return to Shanghai months after her entrapment in Hong Kong. These additional details help enrich the context of "From the Ashes," pointing to a different direction in Chang's "plotting" of history and personal memory.

The Fall of the Pagoda, one might recall, had been conceived as the first part of *The Book of Change*. Lute, Chang's alter ego, is a sensitive, unhappy girl growing up in a decaying aristocratic family. Lute's mother, Dew, leaves her husband and children to pursue a free life overseas, and by the end of the novel, she has returned to Shanghai as a self-styled socialite. After a falling out with her father, Lute finds a temporary shelter at her mother's apartment and prepares to study in England at the latter's suggestion.

The Book of Change takes up where *The Fall of the Pagoda* leaves off. Composed of 22 chapters, the novel starts with Lute's initiation into her mother's flamboyant lifestyle in Shanghai, followed by her change of plan to study in Hong Kong instead of England due to the war, and her brief reunion with her mother on the colonial island. This portion of the novel covers ten chapters, and it ends with Dew's departure for India on the eve of the Japanese invasion.

The Book of Change devotes its final chapters to Lute's journey home. At a time when maritime transportation was mostly suspended, Lute first finds it almost unlikely that she will return to Shanghai. But through a case of mismanagement at the hospital where she works, she "persuades" her superior to find a few seats for her and her classmates. She ends up boarding a ship authorized by none other than the Japanese Commander-in-Chief in Hong Kong, Rensuke Isogai, for sending refugees with connections or means back to China. As Lute notes, passengers on board include such celebrities as Mei Lanfang 梅蘭芳, the superstar of Peking opera.

From this brief summary, we can now better gauge the relationship between "From the Ashes" and *The Book of Change*. Whereas "From the Ashes" concentrates on Chang's experience of the war at its most intense, *The Book of Change* offers a prolonged narrative about Lute's struggle for survival. Whereas "From the Ashes" relates how Chang is shocked to an epiphanic revelation of the war and its nihilist thrust, *The Book of Change* "domesticates" Lute's apprehensions by literally encrusting the war with familial concerns. While Lute has been deprived of parental love since childhood, Shanghai remains the space she feels endeared to and readily calls home. *The Book of Change* begins with Lute's departure from Shanghai and culminates in her return to Shanghai. Both thematically and formally, this circular journey is in contrast with the symbolism of total meltdown suggested by "From the Ashes."

The above observations become more significant when we examine the novel's title, *The Book of Change*, in the framework of an allusion. Chang no doubt draws her inspiration from the esoteric Chinese classic, the *Yi Jing* 易經 or *The Book of Change*. In the novel, Chang narrates a scene in which Lute, working at a makeshift hospital, discovers a heap of discarded books, and she "hopes to find a copy of *The Book of Change*":

> It was philosophy based on the forces of *yang* and *yin*, light and darkness, male and female, how they wax and wane, grow and erode, with eight basic diagrams by which fortunes could be told with tortoise shells. She had never read it. It was the most esoteric of the five classics and not taught in the classroom because of its obscurity and more important, its mention of sex.[3]

Chang herself has never been known for her knowledge of the *Yi Jing* either. By adopting the classic's title for her own novel, Chang inevitably prods one to ponder her motivations. She may intend to capitalize on the classic's exotic appeal so as to win her prospective readers' attention; to construe Lute's or her own fate in light of ancient wisdom; or to launch a subtle attack on her former husband Hu Lancheng who has taken pride in being an interpreter and practitioner of the *Yi Jing*. These possibilities aside, I argue that, vacillating between the appeal of

3. Eileen Chang, *The Book of Change*, 230.

Orientalism and a divinatory contemplation of personal life, Chang seeks to elicit from the (title of) *The Book of Change* a philosophy of writing, one that both testifies to the transience of life and plays with the transformative power of fiction.

To begin with, in view of the rich implication of the word "change" of *The Book of Change* in the Chinese original, *yi* 易, which could denote transience, simplicity, transformation and transaction, among others,[4] Chang may very well have brought it to bear on her own multifaceted experience. Although the novel is structured around the fall of Hong Kong and the heroine's return to Shanghai, by the time Chang began the project — the late fifties — she must have already been conscious of the unpredictable changeability governing all forms of retrospective writing. By then, Chang had experienced first-hand another national crisis: the fall of China to the Communists in 1949. This new crisis forced her to flee Shanghai for Hong Kong in 1952, via a reversal of the route she took ten years earlier, when she escaped Hong Kong. After a three-year sojourn in Hong Kong, she emigrated to the United States. During this period, Chang had two romances. Her clandestine marriage with Hu Lancheng ended in 1947; and in 1956, she met and married Ferdinand Reyher (1891-1967). Finally, writing in America in the late 1950s, Chang was an author twice removed from her homeland while struggling for a career in a language other than her mother tongue. Looking back at her adventures since 1938, she had every reason to sigh over the changes she had been through and contemplate the meaning of the changeability of one's fate.

At a deeper diction level, the title of *The Book of Change* as Chang uses it points to the paradox of change inherent in temporal flux and human vicissitudes. Scholars have pointed out that when change is understood as a constant factor of cosmic movement, of which human ups and downs are only an integral part, a different implication arises: change yields a perennial, repetitive pattern, thereby implying unchangeability.[5] As Lute comments, the ancient text teaches how "the forces of *yang* and *yin*, light and darkness, male and female" "wax and wane, grow and erode." It is the mutual implication between apparently opposing forces,

4. Cheng Zhongying 成中英，*Yixue bentilun* 易學本體論 (Theory of benti in the philosophy of Yijing) (Beijing: Beijing University Press, 2006), 3-34.

5. Ibid, 5, 29.

and the cyclical, dialectic pattern thus coming into existence, that manifests the Way of change. For all the complexities in interpretation, this Way should inform a simple truth that is accessible to everyone.

Accordingly, time should not only signify linear flow but also a "spatial flux," in which change and no change, exchange and interchange, interplay with each other and give rise to multiple configurations. This leads to the third level of implication of "change." That is, as a force that disturbs the status quo, change always contains an unceasingly transformative — generative indeed — momentum. Hence "production and reproduction is what is called (the process of) change" (*shengsheng zhiwei yi* 生生之謂易).[6] Change constitutes the basic principle that enacts the cosmology of life. It is in the context of this metaphysical tradition that one comes to appreciate the nonconformist aspect of Eileen Chang's penchant for rewriting. Repetition, as she would have it, indicates neither a dull duplication of that which is extant nor a return to the starting point. Rather it refers to a subtle dis-placement of the origin, a phantasmal re-presentation of the identical.[7]

To return to "From the Ashes" and *The Book of Change*. One discerns an array of reciprocal relations between the two works, such as autobiographical testimonial and fictional account, trauma and its displacement, history as prescience and history as hindsight. These elements make of each other's premises and attributes, generating new and unexpected meanings. Above all, the fact that Chang chooses English to rewrite her wartime experience calls attention to the chameleon nature of language as a vehicle of remembrances of things past. Accordingly, one can talk about an exercise of isomorphism in Chang's treatment of time, history, and language. With the fall of Hong Kong as the subject, "From the Ashes" casts an eschatological spell on humanity while *The Book of Change*, as its title suggests, projects a return and regeneration of life, for good or ill. Chaos and contingency are after all underlain by persistence and rejuvenation.

---

6. *Zhouyi* 周易, "Xici shang" 繫辭上, *Chinese Text Project*, http://chinese.dsturgeon.net/text.pl?node=46908&if=gb&en=on.
7. Gilles Deleuze, *Difference and Repetition*, trans. Paul Patton (New York: Columbia University Press, 1995). Also see J. Hillis Miller's discussion of repetition as an aesthetical principle of fictional creation, in *Fiction and Repetition* (Cambridge, Harvard University Press, 1982), chapter 1.

As suggested by Chang's *The Book of Change*, the concept of *change* continues to manifest its power in her writings of subsequent years. In 1976, Chang completed the draft of her Chinese novel *Little Reunion*. The novel is meant to be a full account of Chang's life from childhood up to her divorce from Hu Lancheng; as such, it completes what Chang had tried to do with her two English-language biographical fictions, *The Fall of the Pagoda* and *The Book of Change*. Interestingly enough, the narrative of *Little Reunion* is framed by Chang's (or her heroine's) recollection of her Hong Kong experience, particularly the Japanese attack on Hong Kong that coincided with her final exam day at the University of Hong Kong. Such a structural arrangement makes *Little Reunion* a chiasmic counterpart to *The Book of Change*, which, as discussed above, frames Chang's Hong Kong experience with her Shanghai memories. As such, the mutual contextualization of Shanghai and Hong Kong provides a spatial analogy to Chang's rumination on the poetics of change and interchange in a cyclical way.

* * *

The Book of Change opens with the initiation of Lute into her mother's world: "Lute has never seen an artichoke before." As it is, Lute's first "encounter" with the exotic vegetable at Dew's dining table is ripe with symbolism. For Dew, the artichoke conveys the taste "of Paris," her beloved city, while for Lute, it embodies the alienated relationship between the mother and daughter: something whose heart one gets to one leaf at a time and yet may find unpalatable in the end.

In a way typical of Eileen Chang's ironic style, this "artichoke" incident serves as a mock-heroic prelude to a novel that chronicles a girl's search for adulthood amid a historical disaster. Just as Dew and Coral, Lute's aunt, are engaged in the art of eating artichoke heart, the war is looming large. "Fighting may break out anytime," Dew notes. But even before the war befalls her, Lute is already witnessing the breakdown of all values on the home front.

The estranged rapport between Lute and Dew had been touched upon in *The Fall of the Pagoda*, but as Chang herself admitted, the relationship was mostly limited to the view of Lute as a child. Now an eighteen-years-old girl, Lute is ready to unpack the layers of her mother's psyche. Lute has left her father's house for good, only to find herself a misfit in her mother's apartment. She is awkward at social gatherings, to the point where her mother calls her a "pig." As she gradually peels away the layers of mystery of her mother's elegant circle, she becomes increasingly amazed by the seediness of gossip and scandal. She overhears that her mother and aunt may have been in a lesbian relationship; her aunt goes to bed with her cousin; her mother is dating more than one non-Chinese boyfriend at the same time; and more stunningly, her uncle Pillar is not her real uncle but a changeling bought from a beggar couple.

Judging by her self-centered lifestyle and capricious attitude toward her daughter, Dew may come across as a textbook example of the "evil mother." But a closer reading suggests that her changeability corresponds to the theme of *The Book of Change*. A victim of traditional marriage, Dew wants Lute to acquire a new style of life, but she also entertains the prospect that she may capitalize on her daughter's future marriage. She never hides her snobbishness with regard to things new and foreign, claiming that she is able to appreciate China more because she is able to adopt a foreigner's perspective. Chang refers several times to the agency of the "female" principle in the novel, citing the common wisdom of *yin* versus *yang*. To that end, her mother ought to be a role model. Both aloof and pragmatic, both persistent and unpredictable, this female principle as embodied by Dew, as Chang would have it, can ignite one's survival instinct wherever least expected. But it can also hurt because of its being free from any *man*-made decorum.

We thus come to the first turning point of the novel when Lute is unexpectedly awarded a private scholarship from her history professor Mr. Blaisdell. She brings the good news and money to Dew, only to arouse the latter's suspicion that she had exchanged her body for a monetary reward. Worse still, Lute later discovers that Dew gambled away all her scholarship over a mah-jong game. This leads to the falling out between the daughter and the mother. With Dew squandering away her scholarship, Lute feels she has "paid back" her mother's investment in her. She no longer "owes" Dew anything.

As such, Chang gives the implication of "change" an economic twist: as one of the glosses for the Chinese original *yi* 易 suggests, change means not only interchange or exchange but also transaction (*jiaoyi* 交易).[8] In view of the tension between Lute and Dew, one finds that where ethical and emotional binding short-changes, the calculus of give and take sets in. The mother's selfishness and the daughter's pragmatism read like a nightmarish supplement to the conventional feminist view of mother-daughter bonding. Nevertheless, Chang would have retorted: Isn't such an instinct for exchange/transaction germane to an understanding of our capacity for self-perseverance, something that particularly helps validate the female principle of survival and self-sufficiency?

When Lute bids a bitter farewell to Dew at the end of Chapter 10, she has unknowingly learned a most important lesson from her mother — the importance of being *not* earnest. With her mother's lesson in mind, Lute is able to quickly acquire the necessary self-interest and independence to survive the worst moments of the fall of Hong Kong. Indeed, she could not have obtained her tickets to Shanghai had she not exercised her shrewdness and calculation. In actual life, Chang never saw her mother again after a brief reunion in post-war Shanghai. In fictional accounts, however, she would continue to reenact the love-hate relationships between the mother and the daughter till the end of her career.

* * *

In the middle chapters, the novel is focused on the fall of Hong Kong in 1941. Lute and her classmates are nervously preparing for their finals in the morning when they heard the news of the Japanese attack. Instead of fear and panic, the students are excited. They know little of war, while the cancellation of the exams, followed by the shutdown of the school, means an unexpected escape from the routines of life. Some immediately start to worry about a proper wardrobe as they seek a safe shelter from the bombing. Chang describes the students' untimely jubilation in an indulging manner, for she knows that in a few days, they are going to be tested by the trials of starvation, exodus, and death. Even then, however, Chang is skeptical that the students have the capacity to learn from this harsh

8. Ibid., 10–11.

experience. Chang does not hold the residents of Hong Kong in high esteem either. For her, this colonial island "had never seen war, not even the Opium War that created the city." It merely serves as a space for showcasing the naiveté, cowardice, and selfishness of human beings at a time of drastic change.

Such a cynical attitude frees Chang from the formulaic discourse that would come to dominate modern Chinese literature during the Sino-Japanese War. She observes the responses of people around her with wonder, discerning in them a striking mixture of horror and humor. One such example is Lute's friend Bebe Sastri,[9] an Indian girl who was also from Shanghai. Bebe ventures out to a cartoon movie in downtown Hong Kong in the midst of a bombing raid, and bathes and sings in the dorm while a bomb drops on a neighboring dorm. Lute herself is no better off. Upon hearing the surrender of Hong Kong to the Japanese, she and several other classmates eagerly await the first opportunity to leave school so as to search for ice cream, completely undaunted by the prospect of stumbling over corpses scattered in the streets.

There is one time that Lute meets the threat of death face to face. In Chapter 14, Lute goes downtown by tram to register as an Air-Raid Precaution volunteer, only to be caught in an air raid. Together with other passengers, she jumps off the tram and barely finds a shelter before the bombs fall. Immediately after the ordeal, she realizes that she would have been killed had the bombs landed on her side of the street. However, what truly strikes her is the fact that even in the midst of bombing, the sky is as bright and blue as ever, and that the now empty tram stands still in the middle of the street, filled with pleasant sunshine. Moments after the bombing, the tram is again filled with passengers; everything quickly returns to the regular track. Lute is suddenly hit by an awareness of her desolate circumstance:

> The bombing moved away. She took the same tram home. Walking up she suddenly realized that there was no one to tell it to. Bebe was gone. And not just in Hong Kong but in the whole world, who was there?...She would tell Aunt Coral someday although she would not expect her aunt to be greatly

9. This character is based on Chang's best friend during the time, Fatima Mohideen, a girl whose father was from Ceylon and her mother a native of Tianjin.

> stirred to hear that she had nearly got killed. Bebe would miss her if she had died but Bebe was always happy.[10]

This sense of transience and gratuitousness is compounded by the news that Lute's history professor Blaisdell has been shot dead, not by Japanese soldiers but by friendly fire. Professor Blaisdell, one might recall, was the professor who gave Lute a private scholarship. Up to that point Lute had never cared much about her history class; she now learns her lesson at the cost of her teacher's death.

Despite the threat of death, what truly concerns Lute is daily survival. Food becomes the most pressing need. Lute observes the irony that the fear of food shortage increases her classmates' appetite; moreover, food rationing creates a new economy of smuggling or hoarding of private supplies; and that numerous food vendors pop up right after the fall of Hong Kong. In one episode at the hospital, Lute and other fellow nurses bake a tray of dinner rolls one night by using the coconut oil otherwise good only for making soap. They have a wonderful snack together despite — or because of — the patients dying amid incessant groaning and screaming just a few feet away.

Lute also observes that romance proliferates during wartime. People fall in love for the sake of either seeking protection or simply to fend off loneliness. As Chang narrates, these romances would not have formed during peaceful times. When the desire for companionship and the desire for convenience are conflated, the libidinous drive of human beings finds an unlikely alliance with an anarchist impulse. Adultery, co-habitation, and abortion all become understandable. After all, this is a time of chaos, a moment in which the extraordinary has become the ordinary. In Chang's view, in order to survive such a time, people are driven to grasp at anything that is tangible. Physical intimacy, like food, becomes a poignant index to convey the primordial need of humanity.

But what Chang wants to explore is not merely the ethical or political outcome of the war; she impresses us more with her inquiry into the *economics* of the war. At a time when all values break down, Chang tells us, people become more rather than less calculating. Food and sex, accordingly, are as fundamental to human needs as tokens of exchange, facilitating a wide range of motives from

10. *The Book of Change*, 181.

survival to opportunism. Chang's novella of the forties, *Love in a Fallen City*, provides a most compelling example in this regard. But if *Love in a Fallen City* still valorizes the residual axiology of true love in the time of war, *The Book of Change* brings the transaction of food, sex, marriage, and ideology, among others, down to the level of day-to-day negotiation. However devastating, the change brought by the Japanese occupation is quickly naturalized by people in exchange for a more manageable form of existence.

Bearing this insight in mind, I argue that Lute is able to adapt herself to the status quo thanks to the experience she has had in living with her father and mother respectively. Since childhood, she has been immersed in the abacus of human relationships, and she learns to become supersensitive to money after moving to live with her mother. The fall of Hong Kong creates an "ideal" venue where Lute puts her knowledge of change, and exchange, into practice. Ultimately, she manages to leave Hong Kong by striking a deal with her superior.

The Book of Change ends happily as Lute makes a safe return to Shanghai. But this narrative closure is clearly tongue-in-cheek because Lute manages to overcome her obstacles not by any socially recognized virtue such as patriotism or heroism but by an investment of bad faith at the right moment. While this may be the price Lute has to pay for growing up, I suspect that Chang entertains a deeper layer of cynicism. Coming to mind is the theme of *Love in a Fallen City*, that thousands of lives were sacrificed gratuitously in the war as if only for the sake of consummating one mediocre couple's romance. Likewise, the dénouement of *The Book of Change* insinuates that for all the mishaps resulting from the fall of Hong Kong, at least one girl prevails. Lute's triumph is predicated on nothing more than the law of untenability of human constancy. This paradox drives home the dialectics of (ex)change of Chang's novel.

*　　*　　*

Thus far, we have discussed Eileen Chang's *The Book of Change* in light of her personal and fictional experience as well as her paradoxical tribute to the ancient classic of the same title. I argue that by invoking the title *The Book of Change*, Chang sets in motion an endless interplay of thematic axes such as depth and surface, obscurity and simplicity, history and autobiography, philosophical rumination and fictional experiment, and most intriguingly, change as transformation and change as transaction. As a way to conclude my reading of the novel, I call attention to a specific derivative tendency arising from Chang's writings in mid-twentieth century.[11]

In my discussion of *The Fall of the Pagoda*, I introduce involutionary poetics as a principle of Change's writing, by which I mean a narrative practice that replaces a linear, progressive sequence with an inward turn to itself. With *The Book of Change*, I argue that on top of the involutionary inclination, Chang is playing with a *derivative* poetics. Derivative, in the sense that her narrative does not emphasize originality so much as a capacity of continued, figurative replacement and transformation, thereby subverting any claim to authenticity. To repeat, Chang's *The Book of Change* is both a re-configuration of the "traces" left by "From the Ashes" and a preview of *Little Reunion*, her tell-all fictional memoir. Moreover, insofar as the novel is a belated spin-off of Chang's earlier writings, it generates its own splits and doubles. Chang's *The Fall of the Pagoda*, now published independently, is originally part of *The Book of Change*.

Chang is also conscious of the derivative inclination of her writing, to the extent of elaborating on it at both structural and conceptual levels. As early as the second chapter of *The Book of Change*, Lute encounters Zeng Pu's 曾樸 (1872–1935) *Niehaihua* 孽海花 (A flower in the sea of sins, 1907), the most famous *roman à clef* in early twentieth century China. A panoramic exposé of late Qing politics and history, Zeng's novel won enormous popularity in part because the text is replete with thinly-disguised representations of contemporary figures, incidents, and anecdotes. The guessing game became so much of the reading experience that a glossary appeared to help readers identify the characters and their actual counterparts. For instance, the romance of Lute's grandparents (or Chang's grandparents, Zhang Peilun 張佩綸 [1848–1903] and Li Juou 李菊藕), which is otherwise not available in orthodox historiography, is featured in the novel.

11. For more definitions of derivative aesthetics, see my discussion in *Fin-de-siècle Splendor: Repressed Modernities of Late Qing Fiction*, 1849–1911 (Stanford: Stanford University Press, 1997), 76–80.

Lute's discovery of *A Flower in the Sea of Sins* prompts her to launch a parallel survey of (family) history and its fictitious doubles. She is so fascinated with the phantasmal duplicities arising from the novel that she concludes

> These were people she could admire. She admires her mother and aunt but they came and went, more like friends. Her grandparents would never leave her because they were dead. They will never disapprove or get angry, *they would just lie quietly in her blood and die once more when she died.*[12]

For readers familiar with Chang's oeuvre, the italicized part of the quote reappears, in Chinese, in Chang's autobiographic photo album *Duizhao ji: du laozhaopian* 對照記：讀老照片 (Mutual reflections: reading old photographs, 1992).[13] In other words, the way in which Chang recycles a textual line from one work to another parallels her effort to resuscitate a family line from one generation to another.

This example also intimates the thrust of Chang's "self-writing" as a life-long project that stems as much from her confessional urge as from her desire for self-fictionalization. Through Lute's story, Chang seems to suggest that if she could learn her family history from nowhere but a novel such as *A Flower in the Sea of Sins*, it makes equal sense that she could write her own experience back into fictional forms.

The circular, derivative inclination in Chang's writings has at least two more models. It is well known that Chang was fascinated by Han Bangqing's 韓邦慶 (1856–1894) *Haishanghua liezhuan* 海上花列傳 (Singsong girls of Shanghai, 1892) a courtesan novel based on its author's own adventures in the pleasure quarters of fin-de-siècle Shanghai. Han's novel has never been popular. But Chang likes it because, against the generic tradition of the courtesan novel, it downplays the glamour of the demimonde, presenting instead an ambiance full of mundane goings-on and mediocre personalities. Hence a forerunner of modern Chinese realism. Both *The Fall of the Pagoda* and *The Book of Change*

12. *The Book of Change*, 20.
13. Excerpts of "Mutual Reflections: reading old photographs" were translated by Janice Wickeri under the title "Reflections: Worlds and Pictures" in *Renditions*, number 45 (Spring 1996), 13–23.

bear the imprints of *The Singsong Girls of Shanghai* in ornamenting (family) history with everyday trivia while discerning a total desolation underneath any human pursuit of vanities.[14]

In turn, *Singsong Girls of Shanghai* derives its structure and characterization from Cao Xueqin's 曹雪芹 (1724?–1763) *Hongloumeng* 紅樓夢 (Dream of the red chamber, 1792), the *magnum opus* of classical Chinese fiction and the ultimate source of Chang's inspiration. Chang first came to read the *Dream of the Red Chamber* at the age of eight; as early as 1934, she attempted to create a modern version of it in *Modeng Hongloumeng* 摩登紅樓夢 (Modern *Dream of the Red Chamber*).[15] The masterpiece's exposé of an aristocratic household in decline must have struck the young Chang as similar to her own family's fate, let alone its stress on the ephemeral nature of youth, femininity and dream, and vertiginous interplay of attachment and transcendence.

More pertinent to our concern is the fact that, as she grew older, Chang became increasingly conscious of the pain and pleasure in Cao Xueqin's continued revision — rewriting — of his manuscript throughout his life. Cao Xueqin "worked on it for ten years, in the course of which he rewrote it no less than five times (*piyue shizai, zengshan wuci* 披閱十載，增刪五次)" while leaving it unfinished in the end.[16] The *Dream of the Red Chamber* is a project that ceaselessly transforms itself along with the development of its author's life. To that effect, it is a *Book of Change* of its own kind.

Therefore, it may not be a coincidence that when rewriting her life stories in the last four decades of her career, Chang was engaged in two parallel projects at the same time. She translated *Singsong Girls of Shanghai* from the Wu dialect into Mandarin Chinese, and from Chinese into English; she undertook a close reading of *The Dream of the Red Chamber* by means of textual analysis, philological verification, and biographical research, a project later published as *Hongloumeng yan* 紅樓夢魘 (The nightmare of the *Dream of the Red*

14. See my discussion in *Fin-lde-siècle Splendor*, 89–101.

15. This novel is a playful parody of Cao Xueqin's masterpiece. It was aborted by Chang after composing the initial chapters and has never been published.

16. I am using David Hawkes' translation, *The Story of the Stone*, volume 1 (New York: Penguin, 1973), 51.

Chamber, 1977). These three projects (creation, exegesis, translation) cannot be separated from each other; rather, they form an intertextual, cross-generic, and translingual network, pointing to the multiple terms of Chang's derivative poetics.

Upon completing her Mandarin translation of *Singsong Girls of Shanghai*, Chang sarcastically observes, "Whereas modern Chinese readers had overlooked *Singsong Girls of Shanghai* three generations in a row, Eileen Chang had closely read the *Dream of Red Chamber* as many as five times in recent years."[17] Implied here is not merely Chang's critique of the fate of two masterpieces but her idiosyncratic agenda of writing and reading. Moving from English (*The Book of Change*, *The Fall of the Pagoda*) to Chinese (*Little Reunion*), from fiction to pictorial representation (*Mutual Reflections*), and from translation to critical annotation, Chang takes writing as a continuum of metamorphoses. She harbors little "anxiety of influence," next to nothing of any "politics of interpretation." She would have sneered at these as symptoms of Western poetics. When she conflates exegesis with creative writing, she reenacts the subtle hermeneutic circle of "relate/transmit" (述) and "create" (作). When she engages in translating her own and others' works, she would not align herself with "translingual practice," a theory haunted by the fear of incommensurability in meaning and power, but instead finds an analogy in "changing fashions," an exercise enacted as much by political motivations as by gendered, intimate desires and material innovations. *Gengyi ji* 更衣記 (A chronicle of changing clothes, 1944), it will be recalled, is Chang's Chinese translation of her own "Chinese Life and Fashions" (1943), and one of the earliest examples of her bilingual writings.[18]

17. "張愛玲五詳《紅樓夢》，看官們三棄《海上花》." Eileen Chang, "Guoyuban Haishanghua yihouji" 國語版《海上花》譯後記 (Afterword to the Mandarin edition of *Singsong Girls of Shanghai*), in Chang, trans. with annotations, *Guyu Haishanghua liezhuan* 國語海上花列傳, volume II (Taipei: Huangguan chubanshe, 1995), 724.

18. Chang wrote her English essay "Chinese Life and Fashions" in 1943 for the English-language journal the *XX Century*. She translated and revised the piece for a Chinese-language magazine *Gujin* 古今 (Past and Present), retitling it "Gengyi ji" 更衣記 (A chronicle of changing clothes). This piece was later included in Chang's collection *Liuyan* 流言 (Written on water). See Andrew Jones's triangulated translation into English of Chang's translation into Chinese in *Written on Water*, 65–77.

To that extent, translation or *yi* 譯 can also be taken to resonate with the broader, epistemological dynamics of change and exchange, *yi* 易.

* * *

In this essay I have described the metamorphosis of *The Book of Change* in detail so as to stress the tortuous path Chang took in writing it. I argue that *The Book of Change*, as its title implies, epitomizes a writing project that cannot stop transforming itself until its author's life comes to an end. Each incarnation of this writing project points to Chang's changing attitude towards her early experience as well as her renewed tactic of storytelling. As such, Chang writes as if undertaking her own *A la recherche du temps perdu* (Remembrance of things past). She demonstrates that the "things past" are not locked in the passage of time, waiting to be retrieved, any more than they are active ingredients in one's memory, ever ready to interact with things that are happening in the present.

Conventional wisdom has it that Chang's creativity suffered a precipitous decline after leaving China in 1952. This may be the conclusion if one defines creativity narrowly in terms of originality, novelty, and iconoclasm, notions that are the byproducts of the age or Romanticism and high modernism. But a project such as *The Book of Change* encourages one to reevaluate Chang's creative output. At a time when most Chinese writers tirelessly explored the new and unprecedented in the May Fourth brand of the modernist spirit, Chang opted to dwell on what many a critic deems decadent and ideologically problematic. She points nevertheless to a genealogy where revolution is underlined by involution, and revelation presupposes derivation. And it is not till a new century that we finally come to realize that where most of her fellow writers performed the least modern of modernities, Chang managed to bring about the most unconventional of conventionalities.

1

Lute had never seen an artichoke before. Her mother had got to like them in France. After she came back she would buy one occasionally in the Seymour Road market, the one place in Shanghai that had it, cook it herself and sit down before it, a beautiful woman contemplating her favorite cactus plant, plucking a leaf here, a leaf there. Each petal was inserted between her lips for a moment before it was set down on the side of the plate.

"This is how you eat *artishu*," she said to Lute and went on eating with a severe expression, her big eyes lowered, the cheek hollows deepened, the mouth pursing for the nibble. It tasted of Paris and she could not go back.

Lute looked away. Showing too much interest would seem as if she wanted to try some of it. Her aunt Coral said half laughing:

"What's so good about it?" She had also eaten artichokes in Europe.

"Oh, it's good," Dew said shortly, secretively.

They made a strange household. Miss Yang, Miss Shen and Little Miss Shen, the succession of amahs were told when they came. They were foreigners' amahs, smart girls who alternated as factory workers and taxi dancers, had seen the world and were equal to any irregularities. If there were any confusion they kept it to themselves. Miss Yang was the pretty one, Miss Shen the one with glasses and a figure. No, they were not related, they said smiling with an air of mystery. Little Miss Shen was taller than them both, gawky and seeming as much a newcomer to the flat as the amahs themselves. Later they heard from the elevator man that she was Miss Yang's daughter. Miss Yang was divorced. Miss Shen worked for a foreign *hong*, so was out most of the day. Miss Yang was the difficult one. None of them stayed long. Dew and Coral did without rather than draw on the amahs recommended by their relatives. Privacy was hard to get in the Orient and their relatives were curious. After divorcing Lute's father Dew had continued to live with his sister. The two had always championed each other against the family.

"They're lovers," Dew's brother Pillar said laughing. "That's why Miss Coral doesn't want to get married."

Back from Paris Dew had insisted that Lute's father carry out an old promise put down in the divorce contract and send Lute to England to study, which precipitated a crisis. Lute had to run away to her mother.

"Just watch, Lute is not going to marry either," Pillar said. "Somehow no one wants to get married after being with our Miss Dew."

It was said that they paid more for an apartment than others for a whole house, yet did their own house work. Why? If not for fear of servants talking?

Lute did not see how they could afford to move to a bigger and better apartment in the heart of the foreign settlements furthest away from the Japanese encirclement. She understood her mother had come back only because she could no longer afford to live abroad. She herself had made matters worse by landing on her. The lessons with crammers were horribly expensive. Her aunt was also hard up ever since losing the lawsuit against Uncle Prudent and had to get a job. But it was always exciting to watch her mother furnish house. Dew got angry when Coral worked after hours instead of coming home early to help with the decorating.

"Here I have to do everything," she said to Lute who was no help. "Left it all to me. Her job is so important. So anxious to please. When it only pays fifty dollars a month and she owes me a thousand times more."

She paced the room littered with fabrics, wires, carved panels, glass panes, her Egyptian appliqués, paint buckets, the small rug she had ordered copied from a Picasso abstract.

"And do you know why your aunt owes me money? It was not borrowed," she lowered her voice, "just taken. My money left in her care because of the changes in the market. Just took it without a word. All I have. Why, she wants my life!"

Lute looked aghast but went instantly blank inside with a suspension of judgment. She liked her aunt.

"A friend of mine was so angry. 'This is stealing,' he said. 'She can go to jail for that.' " Dew narrowed her eyes imitating the intense whisper in English, her swan's neck arched forward suddenly snake-like.

"But why did she do it?" Lute asked.

"Because of your Cousin Bright of course. Speculating to raise money for his father, getting in deeper and deeper. Naturally when you love someone you want to help him, but taking other people's money!"

Incredible as it was about her aunt and Cousin Bright Lute believed it at once. Her aunt's voice on the telephone came back to her, talking to Bright she now realized, subdued and husky, almost a whisper, but giving way now and then to an uncontrollable irritation. So this is the aftermath of passion. And she had thought them such a perfect example of platonic friendship between man and woman. She had said so the night she sat with them on the dark veranda. The silence that followed had puzzled her which was why she had remembered. She had been thirteen. It had never dawned on her that her aunt could possibly be in love with anyone that counted as a nephew. Besides they were not the kind to fall in love. Even now she never thought of speculating whether they were already lovers the night on the veranda. Blank areas surrounded the people she liked, making the greater part of the picture as in the old paintings. It was a kind of spaciousness in human relationship which she took for granted.

Her mother was saying, "How I have told her and told her, love is good as long as you don't cross the line, the minute there is a relation of the flesh it's all spoiled. Otherwise even when it ends sadly, when you meet again some day, many years later even — ai! how wonderful it feels. But not if there has actually been anything. She would not listen, so now she's broken-hearted and broke, and her reputation gone, although I've kept quiet — what for, I sometimes wonder. I'm the deaf-mute who swallowed a bitter herb and can't tell about it. I didn't even tell your Uncle Pillar. He and your Aunt Pillar will be unpleasant to her and spread it all over town. I never told your Aunt Fisher but I'm sure she knows. She hates your aunt because of Cousin Bright who's just like her own son. She blames it all on your aunt — naturally since she's older than he. Aunt Fisher wouldn't have anything to do with her at all if not for me. It's me she comes to see."

"Why live together still?" Lute mumbled tentatively.

"To save money of course. For her a good address helps at the office, so they will feel they have somebody from a different class."

Lute was perplexed. For fifty dollars a month they want a stenographer and a grand lady too?

"There's also this, relatives will laugh if we're to fall out now, after standing by each other all these years."

"Is she going to pay back the money?"

"Of course she says she will when she sells her houses, but they're all tied up. The way things are now in Shanghai nobody knows when they will ever be sold. When I came back I thought I was going back as soon as possible. I never knew I was going to be stranded here. And now I have you. You know what your father is saying? 'It's she herself that pulled the brick loose that fell on her own feet.' Just the sort of thing he'd say. The reason why I had to have you continue your studies is because you're no good at anything else. All my friends advise me against it. One friend told me," and she repeated in English, again with narrowed eyes and arched neck, "'You're a fool. Keep your money,'"

Lute herself had doubts about going to England on her mother's money but it was another thing to have other people tell her mother she was wasting her money.

"People can't understand why I must send you to England. I can let you get a job here. But you're not the kind who will make good in an office. People say why don't you marry her off. I can —"

You can? Lute thought indignantly. After telling me all my life to think for myself, be the new woman?

"But I don't like those arranged introductions," Dew went on. "Because when you meet somebody that way you're not in a normal state of mind, do you understand me? It's not like meeting people under ordinary circumstances, then you can see them as they really are."

What has this got to do with me, Lute thought. Those half old-fashioned matchmaking dinners and movie parties, maybe they're useful for some people, not for me.

"Then people also say: what if she falls in love before she finishes studying? True, you may meet somebody in England. With young girls of course, the first man she meets is always, oh so wonderful," she said with bitter repugnance.

"I won't," Lute said smiling.

Dew averted her head. "It's no use your promising."

"No, I just know," Lute said smiling. "Besides I feel very bad as it is about so much money being spent. I've got to earn it all back."

"Money by itself is nothing. I've never cared about money, even now when I'm suffering so much on its account. Not like your aunt, even as a young girl – you wouldn't have thought it of her, so blunt and gruff, as if she knew nothing about these things. When the property was divided she had already got her share when this package of gold leaves turned up, said to have been set aside for the daughter's dowry. In the old days daughters only got a dowry, no inheritance. Naturally you can't have both. Well then an elder said since this was something the mother had specially put aside for the girl, let her have it. Another said since she already got her share she should divide this with her brother but not their half brother. Your father was shy. 'Let her have it,' he said. Of course I said nothing. And she just took it without a word. That's her. It showed in other ways. When she got praised for some little thing that was my idea, whether it was a pattern or design or a suggestion of what was the best present to give, and people said 'So clever of Miss Coral,' she just calmly took all the credit without a word. Ai-yo! I heard so much about you Shens – hoy, the Shens! Every time I said no my mother threw it in my face. And what did I find when I was married? Your father's underwear was ragged at the collar, the bedsheets were dirty, the pillowcases smelled of saliva. With your Aunt Prudent keeping house even laundry soap was short and sheets were seldom changed. Your old amah looked after your father then, dared not say a word of course – frightened to death. I had to give her my own money to buy soap and the cloth for underwear. Your aunt was fifteen. She took a liking to me and was always coming in to chat. Your father hated her so much. Even I, not that I wanted to be alone with him, it got so that even I thought her a nuisance. They were such an odd pair. Your grandmother was to blame. She shut herself up and her two children with her and just drilled the books into them. And what good did it do? To this day your father memorized all the time like crazy and took opium and morphine, and your aunt became a thief."

All the disgust she had fought down and the pain she had borne to make herself a dutiful wife and sweet sister-in-law had boomeranged after all these years exploding into a thousand petty spites. Lute was appalled at the price of virtue. Still walking back and forth Dew wailed wrinkling up her face half laughing:

"Ai-yo! how could anyone do such a thing and still sleep at night! To my way of thinking, even on your deathbed you can't die in peace, to have such a thing on your conscience."

Lute remained silent, incapable of sympathy, having been indicted along with her aunt. Her mother did not take it amiss, thinking it was family loyalty that would not let her say anything against an elder.

"Hold this up for me." Dew stood a glass pane up for retouching.

It was over.

When Coral came home half an hour later they chatted preparing dinner with no more than the usual strain. Lute was anxious that there be no change in her manner toward her aunt that might show that she knew. It was easy since she really felt no different toward her. As for Bright, being unable to see him as a lover she could not see him as a betrayer either. He was just the small quiet college student that she embarrassed every time she stood up in the same room with him now that she was nearly a head taller.

But she seldom talked to her aunt these days. As neither spoke much in front of Dew, Lute was ashamed to open up when her mother was not around, as if afraid of her. Before Dew returned they used to talk quite a lot. It was her aunt who had taken her step by step into the past although the process had spread over years through a mutual lack of interest. As a child of course she had no particular desire to know about older people. Coral on her part had always declared half laughing:

"I'm the worst person to ask. How can I remember other people's business? I never pay attention when I hear these things," to show she was no gossip. Unbeautiful and unloved when she was growing up she looked back with no nostalgia. But her unenthusiastic telling made it all the more real. It seemed the locked courtyards were right next door, the unused rooms yellowed by a dead sun, where the ghosts talked and went about in days like any other day. Lute grew to like the past, comically old-fashioned, sad because it was gone and with an overall dusty coziness to burrow into. In the future an airplane might come and fetch her at her window and she could imagine herself stepping out over the ledge into a mild yet withering sunlight that turned her into an old woman so she could hardly lift a limb. But the past was safe even when it was cruel to its own people.

"Huh! in those days!" was a frequent exclamation of Coral's in an affronted tone. It went without saying that everything had been forbidden.

Lute was no good at figuring out relationships. Only quite recently had she learned how she was related to Aunt Fisher and Cousin Bright. Uncle Fisher-in-Snow was her grandmother's nephew. Bright was not Aunt Fisher's son although he called her mother.

"Who is Cousin Bright's mother?" she finally thought of asking one day after running into him at Coral's.

"A slave girl. Concubine Yen's slave girl." Coral impatiently jerked her head away at the end of each sentence as if she had told enough. Her voice was low and husky as always when speaking of Bright, almost like after weeping. "Concubine Yen beat her when she found out. After the baby was born she took it and sold the mother."

"Uncle Fisher didn't say anything?"

"He was afraid of her. She was his favorite."

"Does Cousin Bright know where his mother is now?"

"How would he know? He thought Concubine Yen was his mother. Until Uncle Fisher didn't want her any more and Cousin Bright pleaded with him and cried. Uncle Fisher said to him, 'Don't be a fool. She's not your mother.' And he told him. After that he hated her. He's so angry when Aunt Fisher asks her to stay with them every time she comes."

"Comes from where?"

"Peking. Uncle Fisher won't have her in the same town. She gets her allowance only if she stays up north. But she's always coming to Shanghai trying to see him. He wouldn't see her."

Lute could imagine he was difficult to see. She herself had never seen him.

"But Aunt Fisher's house is always open to her. Aunt Fisher explains, 'Embarrassing, you know.' Still there's no need to be so chummy – put her up, small as their house is, and dine and chat together. Of course Concubine Yen makes up to her now, 'Taitai! Taitai!' never off her mouth. In the old days how she bullied the *taitai*. Bright won't greet her. She comes after him, Little Master this and Little Master that. And Aunt Fisher scolds him: after all she looked after you when you were a child. As if she doesn't know what that woman did to his mother. She's like this. Cousin Bright finds it difficult to care for her although she really treats him like her own son."

"Is Concubine Yen still beautiful?"

"Bald now. Wears a wig with scalloped waves. Uncle Fisher avoided her as soon as her hair started to fall out."

"I've never come across her at Aunt Fisher's?"

"You may have. She's still very trim in a black gown. She was here after Uncle Fisher *chu la sheh*."

That was what they called it, *chu la sheh*, had an accident. Lute did not hear of it at home and all Coral had said was:

"He's being held for mishandling public funds."

Lute had heard it mentioned that he was in the Bureau of Shipping. Once or twice her father and aunt had spoken of him in a mysteriously inhibited tone, half awed, half sneering:

"Have you seen Fisher lately?"

"No. Not for some time now. Have you?"

"Me neither. Well, he's a rich man now." Elm Brook snickered. "Rich" was euphemism for "influential" which implied collaboration with one of the bandit governments that succeeded the dynasty.

"I heard he's trying to raise some funds. Hard up as usual it seems."

"There's not enough money in the Nationalist government to keep him going," Elm Brook chortled.

"Hoy, him!" Coral made a disgusted face. They both expelled shivery breath through half parted teeth.

The overtones of the short exchange made no sense to Lute. She did not know that no Lo was supposed to work for a republican government. The Los and their relatives sat home nursing their names. The dynasty had fallen and the dynasty was the nation. One lived in retirement and threw himself away on wine, women and opium, all was appropriate as long as it was tinged with sadness. He saw himself as a patriot who was scoundrelly in every other respect, none of which really mattered. There was no greater sorrow than the death of the heart. Lute never realized that her father had this ready-made excuse for idleness.

Some of his cousins were more restive. Up north the Sixth Shen had come out and graced a warlord's cabinet. The Eighth Shen followed suit. But the name could only be used once. After the fall of the Peking government they were secure in the foreign settlements of Tientsin, their fortunes made, their political virginity lost. In the south Marquis Lo took the plunge with the Nanking government. Twenty years after the revolution his name was still an asset. Of course it had been such a polite revolution with every care taken to leave the Manchu imperial house its face. The abdicated emperor still reigned inside his palace with pomp and ceremony on a yearly stipend from the Republic. Newspapers referred to the last dynasty as Sueng Ching, the Abdicated Ching. This graciousness and confusion finally came to an end with the new start in Nanking, the true heir of Sun Yat-sen's revolution. This time it was really going to be different. Yet in the course of a few years once it had settled down it had welcomed this link with the past. Marquis Lo got his appointment. His photograph was in the newspapers. His given name Fisher-in-Snow was a word picture in itself. A long article told the history of the coastal shipping monopoly, a pet project of the first Marquis, and praised the singularly apt choice of the founder's grandson for his successor as head of the bureau.

The grandfather was again mentioned in the news of the embezzlement case, more prominently displayed this time, headlined in most newspapers to the dismay of the relatives.

"The old daddy is dragged in again," Coral said.

The Marquise had lived on a small allowance apart from her husband with no share in his glory. Now she went to his rich uncle, fell on her knees and banged her head.

"Kowtow, Bright," she told her husband's son, "beg Granduncle to save your father. Kowtow to Grandaunt."

The old couple pulled her up trying to comfort her, hinting that they had disapproved of the government job all along. The fat Marquise with Bright in tow went from door to door kowtowing to all their relatives. Bright loved his father as much as she did but he hated this especially when it was no use. No one helped.

As Lute knew nothing about the others it did not seem strange that her aunt should take it on herself to help get the Marquis out. But as time went on it turned out to be a long project and she had seen in the newspapers the astronomical number of Yuans owing, more naughts than you could count. Coral had a ready answer for the unspoken question which she had no doubt given to many other relatives:

"After all he was Grandmother's favorite nephew," she said referring to her own mother. "She said he's the only sensible one. Of course I'm fond of him myself. He's very good to talk to."

"Is he?" Lute said surprised. He was such an invisible man.

"Oh yes," Coral said curtly in her conversation-ending way.

Lute seldom heard about her grandmother. Dew used to like to tell about "Your *wai-po*, maternal grandmother." There was the story of the besieged widows, *wai-po* and the concubines. But the few times when the other grandmother was mentioned she had kept silent with a small sour smile. Lute now knew why she did not like the mother-in-law she had never met, aside from her being her mother-in-law. She had heard too much about her before her marriage and afterwards had found herself cheated.

Lute knew her grandparents as the pair of ill-matched portraits hung over the table of worship every feast day in her father's house, the oil painting of a seated man and the head photo of a woman. She rather liked those pictures and was glad they were not stereotyped ancestral portraits. He was full-faced and shiny orange with down-slanting eyes, sitting with one foot forward, poised to go. She was forbidding, Buddha-like, a pearl in the middle of her brows on the bandeaux. But Lute had never really thought about them until one day she picked up a book from her father's smoking den and took it downstairs to read. It was a new historical novel.

Her brother came in.

"Grandfather's in it," he said in his usual quietly satisfied tone when he had a piece of news for her.

"What? Where?"

"His name is changed, I can't remember to what. Something that sounds alike."

"What is Grandfather's name?" she asked smiling.

It was disrespect to say a parent's or grandparent's name. Still one was supposed to know it. At times she seemed almost to flaunt her ignorance. Just because she could visit Aunt Coral and write to Mother she would make out she was amphibian, belonging to both worlds and more to the new than the old. He did not look at her as he mumbled Shen Yu-fung. She was his elder. They searched in the thick book together.

"Master Hill!" their stepmother's amah yelled down the stairs. He was wanted in the smoking den.

"Ann-nnh?" he answered loudly, nasally in a forced voice, being accustomed to speak in whispers. The exasperated questioning note seemed to say "What now?" to show his sister he was not servile in spite of the scoldings and beatings. He rose briskly in his over-large blue gown and went out of the room in long strides, confident that he was just wanted for some errand.

Lute skimmed through the pages with a pounding heart. Who was Grandfather? The mandarin who seduced the boat girl? Or the scholar in love with a beautiful young actor?

The story of the novel went from man to man. The last character Wong went to a funeral. There was an usher for each guest, two for an official above the third grade, four for a cabinet member. Wong saw four ushers advance to meet a new mourner at the sounding of the clapper. Expecting a minister he saw instead an official of the fourth grade indicated by the bright blue porcelain hat knob, swaggering in with his plump moustached face held high and toes high.

"Who is that?" Wong asked his friend.

"Don't you know him?"

He told Wong about Sheng. Only a few years back Sheng had just passed his finals and got a post in Peking. He was so poor he had an elder brother pretend to be a servant and the two took turns toting his bedding roll to the capital on a carrying pole. He vegetated in his out-of-the-way office. After eating sesame cakes for lunch one day, feeling dry in the mouth and still hungry he thought of those big officials fattening on graft while he could not even afford a decent lunch. It was within his rights to speak out so why not? He sat down and wrote a memorial, naming three viceroys and implicating two ministers. The cases he made were plausible, the classical allusions apt and biting. The Dowager Empress thundered with rage. Demotions, suspensions and investigations followed. Thus encouraged, Sheng sent in a memorial every morning and a secret folder every night, always instantly effective. He even took on the internationally known Marquis Lo, then premier, citing ten cases of graft and arrogance. Lo got a reprimand and lost his special privileges: "Strip off his yellow jacket, pull the three-eyed peacock feather off his hat," the imperial edict read.

Sheng was strongly for war when trouble started with France over Indo-China. Annam, Tonkin and Cambodia, China's protectorates encroached on by France, appealed for help. Opinions were divided at court, some said China was in no position to fight, others like Sheng argued that China had to make a firm stand this time. The Dowager Empress demanded that France evacuate Tonkin. War broke out. Sheng's many enemies said:

"Let Sheng go since he's so keen."

Sheng himself volunteered to go to the front. He had talked so cogently on war the Empress trusted him.

"Anyway his spirit might be just what we need," she said.

He was appointed special commissioner to oversee the army and navy. The navy was entirely in the hands of the Fukienese, a coastal people used to boating. The Fukienese officers could not stand Sheng but acted humble and humored him along. The Chinese navy engaged the French off the Fukien coast near the port of Keelung in Formosa. Terrified by the roar of the cannons Sheng fled back to the mainland and ran miles in a pouring rain with a brass basin over his head. The news of defeat followed on his heels. He immediately sent in a memorial censoring himself, asking to be punished. The Fukienese put all the blame on him. The Empress was going to have his head but settled for exile to Manchuria and permanent disbarment from public service.

Premier Lo bore him no grudge.

"He's a pity," Lo said. "He was no fighter, he should have been kept home as a critic."

Lo helped his family and sent him gifts of wine, books and a fur gown for the Manchurian climate. After several years when the humiliation of the war with the

French had worn off a little Lo spoke for him and got him back from Manchuria. But the Empress was so angry with him he was politically finished. Lo hired him as secretary.

Coming to Lo's office one day he caught a glimpse of a beautiful girl fleeing from the room.

"That was my little girl," Lo said. "No manners. Don't mind her."

Sheng in turn apologized for intruding. Sitting down he saw a piece of paper on the table. A title jumped at him, "Thoughts on Keelung". Shocked and mortified he picked it up. It was a poem.

"Looking south toward Keelung I weep,
I heard the commander rode back alone..."

The tone was bitter but not unsympathetic. When Sheng finished reading it his tears were rolling down.

"My little girl's scribbling has dirtied a poet's eyes," Lo said smiling.

"Forgive me, I cannot help feeling moved at such kindness."

"She's just learning to make rhymes."

Sheng complimented back and the talk turned on other things. But Lo's attitude about his daughter had him puzzled and stirred. At the risk of offending his only friend and patron he asked a mutual acquaintance to be matchmaker. He was a widower twice over. Lo said yes. Lo's wife was distraught.

"Your daughter has no takers, you old fool? Any number of suitors you turned down, kept her at home till she's twenty-two, people are saying Let's see what kind of a match he's going to make for her. So now you give her to a forty-year-old jailbird with a son her age."

The old couple quarreled but the younger couple got on well after marriage. They settled in Nanking to be away from Peking's politics and built a garden. Lo had given his daughter a dowry that set them up for life. Sheng was grateful to his marrow.

Lo never gave up trying to get him a new start. The allied army of eight foreign nations brought on by the Boxers' Rebellion occupied Peking and refused to talk peace. The only Chinese whose word they could trust was Lo who was eighty, sick and long out of favor. A stream of imperial edicts came to him from the northwest border where the court had fled, cajoled and commanded, invoked the last emperor and promised him a free hand in all dealings. When Lo finally got on the way he suggested Sheng among others to help with the negotiations. The Empress did not object.

Lo arrived in Peking and took up residence in a temple. It was a difficult job picking up the pieces. He died in the temple just after the treaty was signed. A few years afterward Sheng drank himself to death, just past fifty.

Lute asked her father, overjoyed, "Is it true about Grandfather in that book?"

"All nonsense," Elm Brook snorted.

"That was not how he came to marry Grandmother?"

"First of all she never wrote that poem. And his running into her just like that. In those days that was just not possible."

"But Grandfather did fight the French?"

"You'll find out all that if you'd only read Grandfather's collected works. – Read all day long and never a serious book," he muttered smiling exasperatedly.

This last she took as a pat on the head. No use asking about the brass basin. He would get angry. She was not afraid of him except for a physical wariness as for a runaway locomotive with his endless rolling walk in circles, his snorts and toots and smoke, cigar when he was up from the opium couch dressed for the day in T shirt and pajama pants, a blind look at the back of his glasses.

She supposed the basin had been a good substitute for a helmet under fire, then when her grandfather got on shore he had kept it on during the marathon run because it was raining. It would seem at a time like this one would not be worrying about getting one's pigtail wet, but she had seen a gang of northern coolies running for cover when it started to rain. She could tell they were northerners from their cries of alarm and calling to each other and laughing exclamations of relief when they huddled under a fence leaning on their carrying poles. They were not used to water where they came from. Her grandfather had also been a northern farm boy.

Elm Brook talked about the novel to several relatives who had brought up the subject. He sounded pleased and excited correcting its inaccuracies and was soon deep in the welter of the politics of the 1880's which Lute could not follow. Ordinarily he never mentioned his father, feeling unworthy. It had fallen to his half brother Prudent Pool to print all their father's poems and essays, correspondence and memorials, distribute the books among relatives and set his own sons to study them. Lute looked through these, floundered among the obscure classical allusions and was put out by the conventional grovelings and hosannas at every reference to the throne. His poems of the specially difficult Kiangsi school were turgid with amassed allusions. All his letters talked politics and never privately. It was impossible to get through the proprieties to the real man. She was sorry not to be able to know him a little better through his writings when he had written so copiously. He was so near and yet inaccessible. Her father would simply say she did not know enough classics.

"You never saw Grandfather?" she asked her old amah.

"No, Old Master had passed away when I came."

"Tell me something about Grandmother."

She thought for a moment.

"Old Taitai used to like to go and walk in the garden. In those days ladies walked with two of us holding them up by the elbow, their feet were small. But when she heard the peach blossoms were out, or the pear blossoms were out, she must go and see."

"What else?"

After thinking hard she said, "Old Taitai saved on everything, even candles and straw paper."

Straw paper was a scraping rough yellow toilet paper of the cheapest kind. Lute found it hard to reconcile this with the beautiful rich girl. She must have got frightened as a widow with money, seeing it go. For a while Lute was speechless, desolated by the picture the old amah had made, like stone horses of an ancient tomb standing in tall weeds in the wind at sundown:

"Can't you remember anything else?"

"I remember, but what is there to tell?"

"What did you use to talk about when Father and you talked about Grandmother? When he called you in to cut his toe nails and chat."

"Things come up as you talk. I can't remember now."

The next time Lute went to see Coral she asked her aunt.

"On yes, I've seen the book," Coral said. "The poem about Keelung was made up. Grandmother never wrote it. In fact Grandfather wrote all of her poems in those duets that they were supposed to have written to each other."

"Is the rest of it true?"

"The war with the French is true. When we were children we were told to hate the French. We were also told to hate the Fukienese, they were all cunning and treacherous."

"Grandfather had no money until he married Grandmother?"

"Yes, he had always been poor."

"Was Grandmother nice to Uncle Prudent?" Lute could not see her as a stepmother.

"She was very severe with him. He was already grown up and married when she came over, still he was very afraid of her."

"He robbed her children after she died."

"After inheriting his share of her money." Coral was silent for a while. "That's why I feel since all our money came from the Los it's only fair that I should help Uncle Fisher," she said half guiltily with a little laugh. "The only thing I was sorry to see go was our garden in Nanking, there were some really beautiful things there."

"Is it still there?"

"Now it's the Legislature Building. The Nationalist government bought it."

"Do you remember Grandfather at all?"

"No. Even when Grandmother died I was still childish. I just remember she had white flesh with sometimes a red spot on it, not a mole, actually a blood vessel had burst there but it looked lovely against the white. I used to press my face against her body and fondle her." The amorous smile in her eyes behind the glasses startled Lute. "I've always hated Grandfather because I got my looks from him."

"But why? You don't look alike. Besides I thought he was quite good-looking in the portrait."

Coral shook her head slightly smiling tight-lipped. "I'm said to look like him."

"You have fine features really. If only you can see your face without glasses."

"Near-sighted eyes don't look nice without glasses. No light in them, no spirit."

"They don't suit you."

"I'm glad enough to have them. There was Seventh Cousin who came up from the country and saw a pair of glasses for the first time. He put them on and said, 'Why, there're really so many stars in the sky. I always thought they were cheating me.' "

"I heard this before. Father used to tell it."

"We died laughing."

"I can't imagine you and Father having family jokes."

"We were never really chummy. For one thing he was four years older and that made a lot of difference then."

"Why was he so afraid of Grandmother?" Lute had heard the old amah laugh at how frightened he was.

"She drove him hard. A daughter is different. She spoiled me I suppose and dressed me as a boy. The fact was I'd rather be a girl but was too shy to say so."

"Did she think it was cute?"

"She was against bound feet. Maybe she wanted me to be spirited and independent. I think she wasn't happy with her lot. She couldn't have had much feeling for Grandfather."

"The novel said they were very happy together," Lute said dismayed.

"Of course in those days you did as your father said and looked happy about it."

"She must have admired him though."

"Certainly. She'd take her father's word for it."

"But she was sad after he died?"

"Of course. She died herself at forty-six. She wouldn't see anybody and was called arrogant and eccentric. Like dressing your father in girls' things."

"Why did she do that? Because the gods are more jealous of boys?"

"Y-yes, and later when he was growing up I think she also purposely wanted to keep him shy, so embarrassed by his clothes he would avoid the other boys. She was so afraid he would go bad."

"She didn't mind Uncle Fisher."

"A nephew is different. And she always said Fisher wouldn't be like this if only he'd study books a little more. He was the only one she would see. He was so handsome and dashing, I remember the time he came just before going to his first post in Peking."

Lute thought, if that was what she liked she could not have really loved Grandfather. The real love and understanding had been between the two men, the father and son-in-law.

"She said when Grandfather was alive he had also liked to talk to Fisher and had been happy that his father-in-law at least had one good grandson to carry on. A pity he wouldn't study a bit more."

She had quoted her husband just as Coral used her as excuse. "He was Mother's favorite nephew." The fascination with the same man passed on to the daughter after thirty years had dragged her into ruin. Unable to work this out Lute just felt a stirring of antagonism against this worthless marquis her aunt was trying so hard to rescue. Girl knight that she was she had made no attempt to deliver Lute and Hill from their stepmother.

"I only have this one photograph of Grandmother when she was young." Coral got out her album and opened it at the first page.

"Oh," Lute whispered. "How beautiful."

"The other is her mother."

The older woman was seated on a porch against carved latticed doors. The girl stood with a hand on the chair back, the summer silk of the wide garments falling down straight, the tiny slippers lost in the shadows under the trousers so that she seemed to float without feet, tall and slender. The full young face under the zigzig central parting was like an egg standing on its larger end. There was just a faint smile on her lips but the almond eyes were surprisingly laughing, almost sarcastically. What about? The photographer burrowing under the black cloth? Just the giggles coming on at having her picture taken?

"Who took the picture?"

"In those days it was always a foreign photographer called into the house."

"How old was she then?"

"Eighteen."

Four years before her betrothal. Her laughter pained Lute. She had the right to expect more from life than that political wreck and the little time they had together, then the solitary garden, bitterness and middle-aged death. What was more natural than that she should take a liking to a charming nephew, one of the few men she could meet to speak to in all her life?

"Why are you so interested?" Coral suddenly asked with a curious smile.

"Because I read about them in a book."

"I always thought your generation ought to be looking to the future instead of looking back. We've suffered enough from it, the next generation should be different."

"It's just this suddenly coming upon them in a book."

These were people she could admire. She admired her mother and aunt but they came and went, more like friends. Her grandparents would never leave her because they were dead. They would never disapprove or get angry, they would just lie quietly in her blood and die once more when she died.

Also the discovery had come just when she desperately needed something. She hated what was happening at home to her brother and old amah but could do nothing about it until she grew up and had no idea what she would do then. Her mother had trained her to look to the West. But her mother had been away for years and the West had disappeared with her down the horizon. Here suddenly all the gold and colors of the Orient had opened up before her even if there was no going in the painted wall.

The sea route was again open now that her mother was back and she herself was going to England. But it was no longer the foreign countries she had known of as a child. Dew pictured it gloomily for fear of getting her hopes up for a good time.

"Students mostly live on bread and cheese. But too much cheese is bad for you. Students wear nothing but a blouse and skirt, a sweater when it's cold. Students never get to see anything. We laugh so much at those returned students talking about Paris or Vienna. As if they know."

The dreary round trip would take her back to a provincial Chinese university.

"Lots of them now in the interior. You can always get a good teaching job," Dew said.

Still Lute was proud of going. She's going to England, was the first thing Dew told relatives upon presenting her, to make it clear that having a daughter with her was just a temporary arrangement, otherwise embarrassing. Dew was just now reading that historical novel which had come out when she was away and had been read by all their relatives.

"This is just story-writing," she said and added with a sigh, "To think what stories I can tell, if I ever get to write them."

She would be shocked if she had guessed how much Lute's grandparents meant to her. Lute had lived with her father long enough to know what it was like to find comfort in the past when it was not even your own past. It had aged her and joined her to her country, the most memory-ridden in the world. Her father walked around the room all day memorizing his old lessons in a torrential chant. Even the endless pacing like a caged animal turned out to be copied from his mother's father the premier. A good habit his mother had said and he should do likewise, fifty turns around the room after each meal. The premier had kept it up even in the midst of battle at the head of an army against the Taiping rebels. Much as Lute abhorred her father's inaction she had also been under the spell, that air of autumnal lethargy in his house. Even when it had killed her brother in the same way it had nearly killed her. She did not have a doctor either that time she got pneumonia when she was locked up in the house.

Her first history lesson with her first tutor had begun with the founding of Chou Dynasty after Shang was overthrown. Two brothers, Bai-yi and Shu-chi, clansmen of Shang, had refused to go over to the new dynasty. They went up a mountain and ate weeds rather than eat the grain of Chou. They were starved to death on the Sheu-yang Mountain. After the tutor explained the text Lute had burst out crying. He was nonplussed, having no idea he was such a good storyteller and rather suspecting a ruse to stop the lesson. He waited not saying anything. Her brother sitting beside her sharing the book tried not to notice, evidently thinking she was showing off again. She continued to blubber, so the tutor read on to the next page punctuating as he went with an ink brush dipped in vermillion. She was sorry for the two brothers and saw them picking weeds all alone on a yellow grassy mountain in the setting sun. It took a streak of perverseness to pit one's will against heaven. It was the same as when you cried and the more you were told to stop the more you had to go on until you were hoarse and swollen. As it came back to her now she thought it had been a premonition of the loneliness of those who went against the drift of the world.

She had read a research article by Dr. Hu Shih in another book she picked up in the smoking den. It set out to prove that Laotze had come from the last people of Shang who after the fall of Shang had made a living on their knowledge of old traditions and priestcraft, turning into hereditary priests but careful to keep out of the administration's way. So centuries after the death of those two brothers their clansman Laotze taught the clan's wisdom of survival with constant admonitions to be frightened, keep to the wall and walk fast, always beware of trouble. In the eternal struggle between *yin* and *yang* he apparently believed *yin* the female and passive would win most of the time. Lute thought, he did triumph over Confucius although officially he was never worshipped by the state. There was more of him than Confucius in our mentality. He was our only prop through all the disasters in history.

3

It was Mother's Day, Lute read in the newspapers. She looked in the window of a flower shop. Giving flowers would be the kind of gesture her mother understood. She liked the *shao-yao* best, the big oval flowers related the peonies but not as highly valued, called the peony's slave girl. The deep pink petals made many layers of ruffles around the egg yolk center. Of the half dozen arranged in a vase there was one that was the largest and most perfect. She studied it for a long time before she went in and pointed it out.

"How much for just that one?"

"Thirty cents," the man said smiling, already leaning forward to pick it out.

It was much more expensive than she had thought. Thirty cents for a single flower and a slave girl among flowers. But by now it seemed nothing else would be more fitting for her mother who even looked like it.

"I got this for you, Mother," she handed Dew the flower in tissue wrapping.

"It's very lovely," Dew said smiling, surprised.

"Oh, it's Mother's Day today," Coral said half laughing.

"Put it in a glass of water and put it over there. It's broken at the stem," Dew murmured.

A wire reinforced the stalk which broke right under the flower's great head. Lute was thunderstruck, a rush of blood booming in her ears. She had never thought of looking at the stalk. How could she have been such a fool as to be taken in like that? After all Dew had said about being careful with money.

"It's broken!" she wailed.

"It doesn't matter. Put it in water," Dew said gently.

"But it won't last!"

"It will."

For once she said nothing about carelessness and forgetfulness. The flower bloomed on her bedside table for days.

She had an English friend named Hennings, a lanky red-faced young businessman who was learning Chinese. He often asked her to accompany him to the new legitimate stage dramas and she would explain the dialogues to him. All the new plays were patriotic historical dramas about China's struggle against barbarian invaders with transparent references to the Japanese. The theaters were packed, the actors were stars overnight, the audience booed the traitors and applauded every stirring speech, thrilling to the strange freedom of Shanghai with the Japanese breathing down their necks on all sides. Hennings served with the International Volunteers. After duty he called to take her to see him play water polo. Dew chatted happily with Coral as she dressed.

"Always water polo. This time they're playing the American Marines."

"I never could hear Hennings," Coral said. "He mumbles and swallows half the sentence."

"No, he starts laughing in the middle of it and drowns out the last half. A bad habit. The Chinese say it's unlucky never to finish a sentence."

"The English all talk like that. They can't all be short-lived."

"How foreigners sweat. Did you see his shirt?"

"The khaki is black down his back."

"Go and talk to him."

"He doesn't like me."

"He gives people that impression sometimes. But he's a real friend."

"The English are, once they become your friend."

"Poor Hennings, he's really a good man," Dew said wistfully. "Watch out," she reached behind Lute to peel a handkerchief off the wall tiles and press it to her perfume bottle.

The three were as cozy together this minute as when Lute was a child, each in her usual place, Lute watching her mother get ready to go out, Coral standing by to chat. Lute had crowded into the bathroom to get out of the line of vision from the living room door.

"Anybody comes, just say I'm your aunt," Dew had told her once.

"It wouldn't be so bad if she's not so tall," Coral had said laughing.

"Hennings is all right, he knows."

Was he the one that had advised her against sending her daughter to England? Perhaps any real friend of hers would, Lute thought. She liked all her mother's men friends and was glad Dew looked so young. It made life seem longer and kinder, not the way Dew had always represented it, beautiful today, withered and dead tomorrow. All the same young people should be considerate and make room for their elders in this as in other things. Of course men friends were just the same as women friends. Only old-fashioned people jump to conclusions at the most ordinary associations between the sexes. On the other hand Lute had the impression that her mother had been in love many times even before her divorce, only she did not believe in affairs. "Love is holy," had been the slogan of her generation when they first discovered love and the West. Now it was already different. Love had been conceded its proper place in life but had changed in the transplanting. Dew complained of this while supervising her nieces' courtships.

"You really got yourself into it," Coral said.

"All because their mother wanted me to introduce returned students to them. It has to be returned students. And now their father complains to me, 'I heard them chasing around in the parlor, I got worried. Mr. Fong was there with the eldest. I walked past the door and saw him with his hand in her gown and the buttons unfastened under the armpit. I really got desperate, I yelled.' Yelled what, I asked. 'Just yelled,' he said, 'I was really desperate. I suppose I called for the newspapers or something, then I got the youngest to go in and sit with them.' "

"How times change," Coral said. "Pillar used to be a demon himself, now he's a guardian of morals."

"It's the girls' fault of course. A man may be let into the house without coming into the parlor and bedroom. There's a limit to be set at every step."

"I'm a bit shocked myself to hear them talk of marrying somebody big and tall," Coral half whispered laughing and grimacing. "Mr. Fong not big enough. For girls to talk of bigness!"

Lute was puzzled. What was so indecent about preferring a big tall man?

"We Chinese don't understand love," Dew said.

"That's why people say once you have loved a foreigner you never go back to a Chinese."

"Chinese men also don't like a woman who's gone round with foreigners."

"Sailors' girl she's called."

"A good thing I don't want to get married again."

"Chinese don't marry divorcées anyway."

"Yes, a virgin, that's all they know. Like my slave girl Sunflower, not even pretty, how Pillar begged me for her. My Nanking cousin also asked for her. Really wicked, these people. As long as it's a young girl."

"There are old hands who are said to prefer older women."

"That's only with singsong girls, that's different. Ordinarily there's never a young girl with no taker. The French say young girls are insipid. A woman doesn't really get to have personality until after thirty."

After thirty, Lute repeated hazily to herself. What use was personality when life was over? She wasn't thinking of her mother who was an exception. But suddenly with this glimpse of a land of everlasting youth in France, as she looked at her mother leaning forward into the mirror over the wash basin Lute had for a moment a stifled feeling of the everyday world of China closing in all round, the more one wanted to get away. For the first time she had some idea of why her mother always spoke of being stranded here in her own country.

Still she never connected this with the name Philippe that Dew often mentioned to Coral. As time went on she spoke of him more and more freely.

"Oh, you should have seen my Philippe," she said laughing. "So handsome!"

"He's the law student?" Coral asked idly with the air of having been over all that before.

"Yes, but he's drafted now. They all have to do military service."

"For how long?"

"Two years. He's so afraid there will be war, he's sure he will be killed. When I left he said he would never see me again."

Another time she said in a hard voice, "With these things of course, once you leave it's finished."

Lute took a long time to see that her mother was separated from a man she loved and mired here, a creditor forced to live with two debtors. She alternately raged against Lute and unburdened herself to Lute about Coral.

"Here I am, stuck, unable to move a step, and why? Supposed to be for your sake, but what for really, come to think of it? Hai-yo," she muffled a sigh and turned away murmuring to herself, "Say no more."

Her profile and cheekbones were rocklike above the pyramidal neck and fragile shoulders. Still nobody knew how much longer her beauty would last. Maybe she could never face Philippe again with the same face. It made Lute miserable to know she was the cause of it.

Every time there was a letter from France Dew got her French dictionary out. But when she wrote back she asked Coral for English words.

"I have to write in English, my French is not good enough."

Sometimes she told Lute to fill in a word for her. She would cover half the page with a book, the other half with another piece of paper, showing just a line in the middle. After working on it for a spell she would lock the letter in a drawer. Whose curiosity was she forestalling? Her daughter's evidently since she told Coral everything. Lute never thought this far, just did not like it and looked away every time she locked it, wincing in anticipation of the jangle of keys.

She locked the drawer before going to her brother's house to play mah-jong but forgot to take the key out. Lute came in the room and saw the key in the lock with the key ring dangling from it. Suddenly her misery welled up and overwhelmed her. If I have done wrong I want to know just what it is I've done, she told herself, turned the key and opened the drawer. Two blue air letters were lying on top, Philippe's in French which she could not read, Dew's in English which she glanced over hurriedly. It began:

"Philippe my darling,

I got your letter two weeks now and wanted to write to you at once only I was so busy, so many things to do, sew and not yet finished doing the apartment, not even the time to study my French, you would scold me darling. I miss you so much my darling. How are you keeping? ..."

and ended with "Heaps of love and a million kisses from your Dew".

The row of crosses at the bottom Lute took to be the marking off of a new section, only there was no more space. It did not sound like her mother but the words seemed to mean more because they were going to fly a great distance, almost like a telegram. She put it back quickly and locked the drawer looking around terrified.

"We Chinese don't think anything of opening other people's mail," Coral had remarked once and Dew had said to Lute:

"Your father used to like to read our letters," and laughed warmly deep down in that hollow-chested way she had of laughing at Elm Brook.

Now that Lute had proved herself to be as bad as her father, somehow one guilt canceled out another and she no longer felt so bad about Philippe.

She had passed her examination but still could not go to England.

"Everybody says fighting may break out any minute," Dew said.

Lute only had a vague impression of the Nazis and Austria and Czeckoslovakia. When time came to book passage her mother would know.

"Better get the passport ready," Dew said.

It was difficult for inhabitants of Shanghai the Lone Island to get passports from Chungking. Dew entrusted the matter to a cousin's husband, M.H. Cheung, a former official who had not followed the government to the wartime capital but still had connections there. The day the thin little black book arrived Dew was very pleased.

"So quick," she said, "I really should ask the Cheungs to dinner. M.H. was certainly quick about it."

"He didn't act the mandarin with you," Coral said.

"I can't get over how you people still say mandarin," Dew said laughing. "Even in joke. After all we're a republic now."

Lute's crammer thought she might still make up for the missed semester next spring. By spring she was still waiting along with the rest of the world for the war.

"Can't go now," Dew said with a slight shake of the head.

"No?" Lute said smiling, hiding her eagerness.

Dew dismissed the question with another impatient little jerk of the head, looking away, her face set.

"The more I look at Lute the more I wonder," she said to Coral. "I don't know how she's ever going to get about alone."

"You never can tell, maybe when she has to she can."

"Aunt doesn't care," Dew said later to Lute. "It's not her worry."

Her temper grew worse.

"Don't have the teapot facing me," she cried looking up as Lute set the cups and saucers on the table. "I hate most of all to have that spout stick in my face."

Lute turned the spout toward herself. Never having read Freud she had no idea what it might suggest. With a stretch of imagination it could be likened to a rearing snake or a dinosaur's neck ending in a lipless laughing mouth. Dew saw her studying it.

"Turn it to the side where nobody's sitting."

Lute turned the teapot again. It was just one more thing to remember and being more bizarre made it easier to remember.

"I asked the Cheungs to dinner on Friday together with the Wus," Dew said to Coral.

She had known the Wus in France. Leonard Wu studying medicine there had fallen in love with Tina Hsia, an art student. He already had a wife in his home village. They came back to China together and he was now a surgeon at a big hospital but had not yet succeeded in getting a divorce.

"Do the Cheungs know that they are not married?" Coral asked.

"No, they only know each other through me, and I'm just asking the four of them because I owe them all a dinner."

"It just occurred to me. You know Mrs. M.H., the typical mandarin's lady."

"She's never been like that with me. I must say she's always been good to me."

"She even puts up with her husband admiring you."

Dew laughed. "She tells me so importantly: even M.H. praises you. As though it's the final proof and verdict."

"Old-fashioned wives don't mind as long as they're sure you won't have anything to do with their husbands."

"I should have invited them long ago, only the recent wedding spell wore me to a frazzle." Her eldest niece had married Mr. Fong. "Ai-yo! Chasing all over town buying dress materials and still no pleasing Big Miss. I don't know why I did it except that they themselves know nothing about these things."

"When's the next one getting married?"

"I know you must have had enough of it, all the fuss and the Yangs dropping in here all the time."

"No, the only thing I mind is those wedding nerves. I come home from office and find a girl weeping on my bed. It's not very restful."

"You just can't stand people. If you live alone not even a ghost will haunt your door. Are you going to be here on Friday?"

"Do you want me to be here?"

"It will seem funny if you're not. After all we're living together."

"All right, if you think I should."

"I know you don't like the Cheungs."

"I don't particularly dislike them."

"You don't like Tina."

"Ayee-ee, that Tina!" Coral made a face.

"I think she's pretty," Lute said.

"Ayee-ee! What taste."

"Tina does look cheap sometimes," Dew said. "In Paris for a while she was going to the bad. A good thing about Leonard. I'm always telling her not to quarrel so much even if it's sweet to make up in the end."

"You're always up to the neck in lovers' quarrels," Coral said.

"I don't know why, the minute there's trouble they come running to me."

"If you can run and tell somebody then it's still not real trouble."

"Different people act differently."

"What I can't get over is you don't mind it — not as if you don't have enough of that sort of trouble yourself," Coral mumbled laughing slightly embarrassed.

"Well, can you come home early Friday to help get things ready?"

"All right."

Coral was cagey about all Dew's friends, not knowing whether they had been told about her taking the money. While she guessed that they had all been told by now she could never be sure of a particular person's reaction.

"I can't let you face this alone," Bright had said before Dew came back.

"This is between me and her," Coral had answered, "nothing to do with you."

"I can't very well take this attitude."

"There's nothing you can do. Your father has just come out, everything is in pieces."

"He feels so badly about you. And he doesn't know about Dew yet."

"Better tell him before he hears from elsewhere. I can't stop Dew from talking."

"Are you going to tell her about us?"

"I'll have to. Hard enough to explain as it is."

"In her anger she'll spread the story."

"You didn't use to think it was such a crime."

"It's just Father. He thinks so highly of you."

They managed to quarrel without touching on the real issue. Now that his father was out it became plain to both of them that he would never go and tell his father he was going to marry an aunt. Spoil everything just when he was cutting a figure as the faithful son who had turned out to be so capable? The Marquis no longer scolded him every time he saw him and had actually begun to lean on him.

Bright and Coral had never spoken of marriage. Once he had asked:

"Why don't you marry?"

Although they had her apartment to themselves they always whispered together as if there were somebody in the next room. Thinking he had said "Why don't' you marry me" she answered archly:

"You never asked me."

A slight pause and he repeated smiling, "No, I said why don't you marry."

They both had enough poise to pass over this. Not long afterward they slept together which showed she was not trying to trap him into a proposal. Also because her body was lovelier than her face it seemed to be the only reality that could break down the myth of their being aunt and nephew, on different levels of the family tree. The rescuing of his father went on, the two of them working side by side not really hopefully but like the legendary Yu Gung, Old Mr. Foolish, who did not like to have a mountain outside his front door and shovelled off the earth day by day. Finally Yu Gung opened the door one morning and found the mountain gone. It had grown nervous and flown away in the night to dump itself down in another province. Except in this case it fell on top of her. While waiting for Dew to come back she often thought of killing herself. What she minded most was the way that they had ended it, with Bright looking like a plain cad and she a fool.

At Friday's dinner she was sure Dew had told Tina Wu everything. Probably Mrs. Cheung too. She hoped not, Mrs. Cheung was overbearing enough without having anything on you. M.H. Cheung was at least a man of the world. If he knew it would not show. But unexpectedly M.H. snubbed her pointedly, turning away when she was in the middle of a sentence. Coral tried to laugh at him, telling herself it is the most unrequited lover who is most liable to get indignant on the loved one's behalf, angry at the way everybody else treats her. Bald and oval-headed M.H. looked like an egg standing on another egg. He was making an effort to talk to the Wus but having studied in America instead of France owed allegiance to a different country. Also M.H.'s stay in America was a long time ago. They could not discover a single common acquaintance in either the old or the new continent. M.H.'s wife unbent as far as her roundness permitted but could not find much to say to Tina either.

"Oh, Dew!" Tina kept wailing chidingly in a honeyed tone and now and then even "Oh, Coral!"

Her tanned face shone like a gold dish, the eyelashes heavily black-coated. Her flouncy dress looked hot and her hair looked hot. Her perfume smouldered. Dew wore her hair like a cap with a black fox border over the deeply shadowed cheeks and eyes. Both striking, both in Western clothes, she and Tina were such contrasts they were showy together and made the room seem crowded. Lute hovered trying to be self-effacing, an elongated adolescent with a short bob. She helped put the jigsaw table together to form a plum blossom. Dew had cooked a soup of a whole ham and chicken in an earthen pot. The other dishes she had ordered from a restaurant.

"Go get another chair," she said.

Lute hurried into the other room but there was not a chair left. She looked in the hallway and kitchen. All the chairs had already been taken to the living room. She would have to go back and ask her mother what to do when she was so busy with the guests. Instead she tried to move an armchair. Maybe it would go in the door. It was heavy but she was used to plunging into all kinds of manual work heartily. To hang back would seem as if she still looked down on labor as they did in her father's house. She half dragged, half pushed the upholstered chair across the thick carpet maneuvering it a foot or a half at a time. To her relief it just fitted through the doorway. She was easing it into the living room when she heard some gaspings.

"What are you doing?" Dew said coming toward her.

"There's no other chair."

"How on earth did you think of this?" Dew half whispered furiously.

"Won't it do?"

"What made you think of it?" Dew hissed.

Lute smiled and strained to back it out of the door. Passage through the uncarpeted hallway was comparatively easy except for the painful squeaks that showed her mother's floor was being scratched. Dew followed the juggernaut into the other room.

"Don't pull the carpet, you'll pull everything down. Now who would have thought of such a thing?"

She stared, still incredulous, as Lute moved it by jerks, half lifting it.

"Pig!" she said, turned and went back to the living room.

Lute heard the sound of something smashed to bits inside her. The only other time her mother had ever called anyone pig that she knew of was long ago, before the first time she left China. Sitting at her dressing table with Lute standing by, no higher than the table, she had been angry with Sunflower for something.

"Pig!" she cried and slapped her. "Now kneel down. Kneel for me."

Sunflower propped her hand on the dressing table and knelt down holding herself erect. Lute was amazed how tall she remained chopped off from the knees. She looked ludicrous. Lute threw her head back and started to bawl.

"What is this for?" her mother asked half laughing. "What has it got to do with you?"

Unable to answer she just opened her mouth wide and let go.

"All right, all right, stop it. Get up," Dew said to Sunflower and got up herself and walked away.

That time she had won but that was long ago.

She went along with her mother and aunt to see the Marquise one evening. The Marquise had moved into a small alley house ever since her husband's arrest. She kept many cats. There was a faint smell of the cats' pan of ashes. The little white room under the dim light depressed Lute. To make up for it she exclaimed over the first thing she saw on the desk, a spotted bamboo ink brush with an ivory tip.

"Take it," the Marquise thrust it at her smiling.

"No, no really," Lute said mortified, "you keep it, Aunt."

"Take it, take it."

"I don't need it, I use a pen."

"Take-it-take-it!"

"Take what Aunt gives you," Dew said.

"Busy, Miss Coral?" the Marquise spoke to Coral for the first time, with ill-concealed sourness.

"Very, but it won't be so bad once I get used to it."

"She works late at the office every day," Dew said.

"And you? Been playing mah-jong?" the Marquise said.

"No, not lately."

"A pity we're three short of one. Lute doesn't play."

"Count me out today," Coral said.

"Another day," Dew said. "How's Bright?"

"Bright is out," the Marquise said shortly, then added, "He's got a job now with the Bank of China."

"That's good," Dew said. "You've gone thin."

"That's good too." She gave a mirthless snort. "I was fat enough to sell by the pound."

She looked changed in a baffling way. Behind her rimless glasses the face was yellow and lumpy like a peeled roasted chestnut.

"You've been well though, haven't you?" Dew said.

"I was poorly a while back."

"Are you still going to the same doctor?" Coral said.

"Yes, Dr. Kwan."

"It's the strain you've been under," Dew said.

"I don't worry," the Marquise said with another mirthless snort. "What good does it do?"

"That's right, that's what I tell myself. What's the good of worrying, hai-yo!" Dew sighed.

"Play mah-jong?" the Marquise whispered like a temptress. "I'll find a fourth."

"No, not today."

"I'll phone for somebody."

"No, really, we'll be going soon."

"You're staying for dinner."

The dinner table was laid in the area at the top of the stairs. Instead of a cook she just had her amah Old Lin do the cooking. Old Lin who was not old came upstairs in the middle of the meal and stood by the banisters. She was a sulky comely widow whose round face was slightly pockmarked. She had worked here many years and the Marquise was very afraid of her.

"How're the peas?" she asked.

"Very good," the Marquise said, "but Old Lin," she cooed ingratiatingly, "next time put in just a touch more soya sauce."

"Hm," Old Lin said. "It's tasteless."

"No, no, it's because those peas are naturally sweet so they need a little more soy. Tender, aren't they?"

"Yes, very good," Dew said.

"I didn't dare put in too much soy," Old Lin said. "Salty is too salty again. It's difficult when you can't try it."

"Old Lin is a vegetarian and there's pork in this," the Marquise explained.

"And she still cooks so well," Dew said.

"Anyway this is better than have a cook dip his whiskers in everything you eat," said the Marquise.

They were back in the room after dinner when Old Lin came in to say, "Taitai, Master is here."

The Marquis dropped in once a month to bring his wife her allowance. A man servant had used to deliver the hundred dollars but the Marquis had come in person ever since his release. He only stayed a few minutes in the parlor to inquire of his wife if all went well but it had become a little ritual that squared him with his conscience, apparently wakened by adversity.

The Marquise got up.

"Let's all go downstairs."

Dew exchanged glances with Coral. "Maybe later, after you've talked."

"Come on, come on."

So they all went down, Lute trailing behind, excited to be seeing her legendary uncle at last. It was difficult to realize that this man was the ruination of her aunt and her mother too.

He got up when they came in and bowed slightly, the movement exaggerated by the concave sweep of the limp silk gown hanging on bones. Shockingly thin he looked like a tall old woman with drooping eyes, the pale aquiline face clean shaven but unscrubbed, glowing waxlike, the hair parted in the center and plastered down making two thin black pieces to cover part of the high forehead. He was one of those people who kept to the styles of their youth. Lute had plenty of time to look him up and down as she was not expected to take part in the conversation. His feet were especially archaic, in white socks and round-cut black gabardine shoes rimmed by thick white cloth soles. She wondered where these shoes could still be bought. Were they made at home? The only place where she had ever seen them was in a shop window displaying burial clothes in the styles of the last dynasty. Hearing him speak was a further shock. He had the amahs' country accent. All the other Los had dropped it but he saw no reason to change anything about himself. He was thanking Dew and Coral for helping him.

"I can hardly take any credit," Dew said. "I wasn't' even here."

"You've been just as kind. Such heroism coming from such fragile women, it kills us men with shame. I've always admired you two most among all our relatives."

"Not much to choose from," Coral said.

"Ha ha! You're right there. All right, just say I admire you two most of all. Where's Lute going to school?"

"She's going to England," Dew said.

"Excellent. Excellent. Follow in Mother's footsteps. You know, Miss Coral, I can never get over the difference between you and your honorable brother. It's often the case nowadays, *yin* is strong and *yang* is weak. No wonder our country is in such a sorry state."

"Every time that happens we always manage to blame women for it," Coral said.

"Ha ha ha! 'The beauty that topples a city and wrecks a nation'. True. True. Always blame it on women."

It was roasting hot in the little parlor but he seemed not to mind. The fan he carried remained folded.

"Bright is not home?" he addressed his wife for the first time.

She cleared her throat and clasped her hands tighter in her lap. "Kmm. Bright has gone to the Wongs'. Kmm."

"Have you been very active lately?" Coral asked him.

"No, I never get out except to the *luang* meetings."

"I've never seen one," Coral said.

"They're silly but just for something to do."

"What's *luang*?" Lute whispered to Coral. She had long given up on the transmigration of souls, eternal life with variety. But she still remained hopeful for a chink or leak in a supernatural system that might betray its existence.

"Like a Ouija board," Coral said.

"Just a handbar on top, with a stick down below to write on the sand in a tray," he explained.

"Is there anything in it at all?" Dew asked.

"Well, it all depends on the chief operator. Two people guide the handbar but it's up to him to interpret the scrawls."

"Gods descend on the *luang* and prophesy, is that it?" Coral asked.

"They don't always prophesy, they may just address a poem to somebody in the audience and make him write one back in the same rhymes."

"I heard you can even flirt a little when it's a goddess," Coral said.

He smiled. "Sometimes the *luang* punishes a person for having disrespectful thoughts and makes him kowtow."

"Have you ever been punished?"

"No, not yet, fortunately," he mumbled smiling with downcast eyes. He was old-fashioned enough to keep to the disrespectable portion of womankind and always drew the line with a gallant flourish.

"Have any of the predictions come true?" Dew asked.

"That I can't say. There's one immortal that keeps dropping in, though unwelcome. He never would predict the future, just writes bad poems. Press him too hard and he will answer: Off now to Tienmu Mountain — an appointment with Laotze to view the foliage." His guests laughed. "Why not drop in one day for a look? To us it's just a place to meet. Nowhere to go and nothing better to do."

"You're being too modest. I heard you're coming out of your hermitage," Coral said.

"No, no such thing. Why, where did you hear this?"

"Now who was it that said this? A bit of it just scraped past my ears."

"It's out of the question. With my health in this state I can't follow the government to Chungking even if they would have me."

"Aren't they trying to make you take charge close at hand?"

"You mean the Japanese? No, no. With the country in this state and my health like this, all I want is shut the door and live out the rest of my days in peace."

"What if people won't let you alone?"

"No no, seriously, nobody approached me. The Japanese are not that desperate, ha ha."

"With your prestige?"

"What prestige? Maybe I still have a few friends who say So-and-so is not as bad as he's made out to be. But even they can't defend me if I get mixed up with the Japanese. No, that's not for me. No."

The Marquise was silent throughout. From time to time she cleared her throat rumblingly. But after he was gone she seemed happy that he had stayed so long and talked so much to her visitors. When they returned upstairs Dew said:

"He looks very well."

"Yes, he seems well," the Marquise said.

After a slight pause Coral asked, "Who is it now, still Number Nine?"

Number Nine was not the ninth concubine but the number she had been known by in the singsong house.

"Yes, she seems to last," said the Marquise with a snort of laughter.

"She must be getting on," Dew said.

Coral said, "She wasn't young when she came to him. Already retired for the second time."

"Bright can't stand her," the Marquise said. "He has to see her every time he goes to his father. Me, she and I are river water and well water, we don't come up against each other. It's not like with Concubine Yen before, together in the same house. Even then I had nothing against Concubine Yen. She was there before I came."

The Marquis had been a widower with three concubines when he married the Marquise. To show he was earnestly making a fresh start he had disbanded all except Yen the favorite.

"She lasted the longest," Coral said.

"I remember when I was a bride she kowtowed to me and I was going to bow back," the Marquise half whispered smiling, once again a frightened young daughter-in-law imparting confidences. "But would they let you? Two amahs had me by the arm one on each side, held me up stiff as a board. They'd had instructions from home to see that I started out right. Keep the concubine down. So afterwards everybody said how proud the bride was, wouldn't unbend an inch.

Mr. Fisher was angry but he didn't show it because I'd only just come. A few days later Concubine Yen came over to get acquainted. The bridal chamber had a whole row of those carved transoms. 'It's hot,' I said, 'open the window.' There happened to be no amahs around, so Concubine Yen took the rosewood stick leaning on the wall and pushed a transom open. After she went back to her own room she cried and cried. She had been told to open the window just like a servant. Oh, how she cried. Mr. Fisher was angry but he did not say anything to me."

His visit this evening had stirred her up. She had a need to explain how things had come to be like this. She continued with titters and confidential half winks and bobbings of the head:

"They told me Now is the time to make a stand, later will be too late. Not a full month yet and he would scarcely speak to me. I didn't know what to do. After all they were there to advise me. I was all by myself except for those amahs from home. So I quarreled with him and tried to kill myself, I ran my head against the wall. Who'd have known the building was so old? The wall came down."

Coral said, "Yes, I remember hearing them say the bride was so strong, when she lost her temper she just gave a push and the wall came down."

"I thought you got on well with Concubine Yen," Dew said.

"That was later. She finally saw that I meant no harm. When Mr. Fisher got a post in Peking he took both of us along. I was so happy to get away. Be on your own instead of living with in-laws. Once out of the house Concubine Yen felt free not to stand on ceremonies with me and I didn't mind, I wanted it like that."

Dew laughed. "You're really a model wife."

"No, it was just that I'd made up my mind I wanted to be with him. After all a woman's lot is with her husband. Then one day my brother telephoned. There were telephones already. Ours was in Concubine Yen's courtyard and the servant who answered was sassy. My brother said 'I want to speak to Taitai.' 'East Courtyard Taitai or West Courtyard Taitai?' he asked. My brother got angry: 'That's a fart! There's only one Taitai and I want her on the phone.' 'Come get her yourself, I don't know which one you mean.' 'I won't speak to you, I'll just settle with your master.' And he rushed over to see Mr. Fisher and slapped him. Concubine Yen was with him and also got her ears boxed. After that I couldn't very well stay on, I had to go back to my mother-in-law."

"The world is full of busybodies," Coral said.

The Marquise said smiling, "That's why sometimes I thought if nobody else had butted in maybe we wouldn't have come to this."

"If only people would mind their own business," Dew murmured.

The Marquise glanced across the room where Lute was playing with the cats.

"That time he was ill," she whispered. "The only time he came back to live. I looked after him. He stayed in for months. I always thought if only I had a child. I wanted one so much. But Bright's room was right next to ours and he was about thirteen, fourteen. Of course he felt embarrassed with a half grown son next door."

"Isn't that ridiculous blaming Bright," Dew said to Coral after they got home. "As if any man who wants his wife would be stopped by a thing like that."

"He used to tell people, the Fat One wants it very much," Coral said.

"These men. His own wife!"

They thought Lute was asleep while they were still in the bathroom.

"Always 'the Fat One', even when she was just buxom."

"She had a sweet face. They're just made up too differently."

"The way she talks, it was always somebody else's fault."

"If anybody was to blame it was the Chows, they married her to him and then started her off on the wrong foot."

"This was the first I ever heard her say anything against her own family. She never would hear a word against them."

"The funny thing is the one person she hasn't got a grudge against is Concubine Yen." Dew laughed.

"They're still great friends when Concubine Yen comes to visit. 'She's pitiful now,' she says."

"To listen to her that time they lived together in Peking was the best years of her life."

"She doesn't care as long as she can be with Mr. Fisher."

"I wonder if there's anything to that story about a man they played mah-jong with."

"What man?"

"Concubine Yen was said to have thrown them together."

"Yes, I seem to remember there was some talk."

"You can't tell, if anybody made a move at Mrs. Fisher she might get foolish," Dew said.

"I don't know, maybe she was just trying to act sophisticated. In those days it didn't take much to start people talking."

"I wonder what really happened. Most likely it was just Concubine Yen trying to make a fool of her for fun."

"Can't tell," Coral grunted.

"I never dared ask her. Don't underestimate Mrs. Fisher. There are things she never will speak of."

"I was surprised she talked so much tonight with me there. I know she hates me."

"She was a bit strained in the beginning but warmed up later."

"Because Mr. Fisher came."

"The way she puts the blame on everybody makes me nervous to think of us talking to him and leaving her out."

"She never has anything to say when he's around."

"She looked so embarrassed, painful to watch."

"And clearing her throat all the time. I couldn't stand that kmm — kmm —"

"What I dread most is to play mah-jong with her. The way she rocks from side to side when she's worried. The minute she loses she starts to sway, and the more she sways the more she loses."

"She used to be a good loser. She never had any money in those days either."

"She was such fun."

"She's changed ever since Mr. Fisher got in trouble."

"But she always was in a terrible hurry, like getting up at midnight when we were going to see sunrises on North Peak."

"And waking everybody up."

Lute remembered going with them to North Peak on West Lake. In the evening the Marquise had taken her along on a little walk outside their hotel to buy persimmons. There was something unpredictable about the Marquise that made it more exciting to go out with her than with any other grown-up. At ten years old Lute already had to walk slowly to keep pace with her half bound feet, now let out, waddling in embroidered slippers. She kept up a soothing murmur half to herself:

"The persimmons are good here. But where are they? You like persimmons? They're just in season. Now where are the stalls? Should be lots here on this block. Or have we passed them?"

The lights had just come on, not enough for the wide streets of Hangchow. Lute thrilled to the dank autumn air and strange dark city but she sensed a dissatisfaction in the Marquise. She could see now she would rather have anybody but a child with her. There was nothing grandmotherly or even very motherly about her. Had she ever been in love with anybody beside her husband? Lute wished she had. As it was all her wants and drives were channeled into the one man intended for her so that she remained staunchly, legitimately, ridiculously in love with him all her life. China's realistic attitude toward sex was for men only. Women were the scapegoats who redeemed the world by their virtues. Lute had read Lu Hsueng on the men who never fought back at bandits and foreign invaders, yet cried disgrace if their women did not jump into wells or moats fast enough to escape rape, going into the water in droves like lemmings. The woman's lot in the midst of all the hedonism around her was like the poor in a land of plenty, more unbearable perhaps than in a strictly puritanical country. But all that was more or less past, Lute thought. The Marquise was already a relic. She never realized that her mother was only ten years younger, but that was the decade that made all the difference. She had the head of her cot against the wall with the refrigerator on the other side. She could hear it chugging away, engine humming, dishes rattling. It was as though she was already on the ship to England, leaving China's sorrows far behind.

When the refrigerator stopped working Dew was saying half laughing:

"I don't know how you could have asked a man a thing like that — whether he's going to turn collaborator."

"I heard it from Autumn Crane."

"Autumn Crane may be thinking of asking him for a job."

"It could be. After Manchukuo he's dyed black already, it won't hurt to jump into the dye pot again."

"Why don't you speak for him? Surely he owes you that much."

"How can I, when he denies it so thoroughly?"

"He all but swore. Do you think it's the truth?"

Coral just grunted.

"He must be very hard up just now. Could he be flirting with the Japanese?"

"Who can tell about him?"

"Bright may know, only he's never around any more."

Water hissed loudly in the silence. They stopped talking and Lute fell asleep.

A week later the Marquis broke into the headlines again in even larger print than at his arrest. Lute heard the news before it came out in the papers. Coral had just returned from the office when the telephone rang.

"Hello? ... Yes," she said shortly in a low voice, waiving all identifications and greetings, which meant it was Bright.

She listened reservedly. "Um ... Um ... Yes ... How is he now? ... Um ... Why don't you ask her doctor if she can stand it? ... Of course she'll blame you for keeping it from her. What do her people say? ... I just got home this minute ... Why not telephone the Chows, see what they say, then at least you can refer back to them ... Of course you must be all confused just now ... Of course ... All right."

She hung up.

"Fisher got shot," she told Dew. "He's in Paolung Hospital."

"*Mon Dieu*, who did it?"

"They don't know. Two gunmen. They got away."

"Is he badly hurt?"

"He's unconscious."

They spoke in whispers.

"So there is something to the talk about him and the Japanese."

"It looks that way."

Everybody knew collaborators were afraid of assassinations.

"Have they told Mrs. Fisher?"

"That's the problem. She's ill again. Bright doesn't dare tell her with her heart trouble."

"She'll be so angry when she gets to know. She was already so hurt being kept in the dark about things when you people were trying to get Mr. Fisher out."

"This time I have nothing to do with it."

"What if anything should happen to him and she never got to see him?"

"That's why Bright is in a fix."

"I shouldn't say such a thing but I was thinking he hasn't been here all this time but the minute something happens he runs to you for help."

"That's what I thought too. Only I've done so much already, I might as well be helpful to the last."

"Of course you know your own business best. I was only thinking."

The inhibitive air of disaster in the house stopped Lute from asking questions. She had to wait for the next day's paper. She felt no concern, just excitement. The antithetical headlines nicely balanced the three bullets in his body to the two gunmen still at large. The account began delicately in classical prose:

> "Fisher-in-Snow Lo, former Commissioner of the Bureau of Shipping and Commerce, who had been accused of embezzlement of government funds, which case had just closed, was fired at by two gunmen upon leaving a house on Medhurst Road yesterday afternoon at half past four. The ground floor of the building is occupied by the Forest of Zen, a vegetarian restaurant. On the second floor is installed a dais for *luang* and Lo being a devotee attended the séances every day without fail. Leaving after the meeting yesterday Lo was on the point of stepping into his car parked by the curb when a man in white Western shirt and yellow khaki trousers darted up from behind and fired several shots at him in rapid succession. Lo immediately fell down lying in a pool of blood. Another man in white shirt and navy blue trousers rushed out of the doorway of the next house and fired at Lo almost simultaneously. Both escaped, taking advantage of the confusion, racing off in the direction of Avenue Road. When the policeman on duty arrived at the scene he drove back the spectators and summoned an ambulance which took Lo to the Paolung Hospital emergency ward. Lo's chauffeur who was not hurt and several other eye-witnesses were taken to the station for questioning ..."

It went on to describe the grave state he was in, followed by a resumé of his antecedents, his grandfather, his own career under the abdicated Ching and in the present government his term as Commissioner which ended under a cloud.

"Ever since his release Lo has lived in strict retirement at his residence on Seymour Road. But it is feared that the attempted assassination has a political background. There may be spiders' threads and horsehoof prints that can be traced."

There was a blurred photograph. What looked like a spattering of tar all over was shockingly like blood except that the spots were too black to belong in the picture. It could be any man in a Chinese gown lying on the ground alongside a car except for the one archaic foot that came out quite clear, jutting up at right angle, white stocking set in the round arch of the cloth shoe.

Coral came back from office with the news that the Marquis had died that afternoon. Bright had called her at the office.

"Who did it, they still have no idea?" Dew asked.

"It's the Blue Clothes Society," Coral whispered shortly.

"Blue Clothes Society?" Lute said.

"Chiang Kai-shek's secret service."

All three fell silent at the disgrace of being killed for being a traitor. To Lute it even added to the drama and the awe and desire she had for all big things happening.

"How do they know?" Dew whispered.

"It's just guessing. But it looked like the work of Blue Clothes. They must have followed him for days and known his habits."

"Couldn't it be the Japanese?" Dew said. "If he'd taken their money and then became coy?"

"They wouldn't have given up on him so quickly. It couldn't have gone on very long. He's only been out this long."

"Who'd have thought he'd come to such an end. With all their prophecies the *luang* never foretold this."

"It's true that his eyes leaked light," Coral lowered her voice guiltily as she did when she was ashamed of still believing in this kind of thing.

"How? Leak light?" Lute asked.

"The eye-white shows around the black."

"That's bad?"

"They say it means a cruel death."

Bright came the next evening with the latest pressing problem. The body was now in the funeral parlor. But where to go from there? A hasty cheap burial would confirm the slur on his name. The only thing was to put off burial indefinitely, for years if necessary, a not uncommon practice, until there was enough money for suitable grounds and monument. It would also be easier to raise money after the scandal had died down. But which of his homes should house the coffin? The concubine Miss Nine had a large house. But the Chows always looking out for the rights and prerogatives of the Marquise insisted that it be taken to her house. She had been so much put upon all these years, she should at least have him when he was dead. Number Nine would see reason or get her ears boxed like Concubine Yen. Bright pointed out that at the Chows' advice the Marquise had not been told about the assassination. What if she was to come downstairs and see the coffin? The effect of the sudden shock might be serious.

The Chows countered that Number Nine having come from a singsong house could not be expected to stay virtuous for long. Who could tell what carryings-on might take place in front of the coffin in the parlor? The deceased had suffered enough without further outrages. The only other alternative was parking the coffin in a temple for a small annual fee. But there was no telling what his enemies might do if they wanted to make an example of him for propaganda purposes. The Chows had no need to cite cases in history of "whipping the corpse three hundred strokes of the lash". A temple was a public place. With just one caretaker the coffins were left practically unguarded.

After the coffin was taken to the Marquise's house the question of the funeral came up. A large one would attract too much attention and perhaps invite trouble. A quiet one would seem furtive. Bright again had to come to Coral for advice. They settled on a small funeral in a downtown temple hiring the minimum number of monks for the Buddhist service and no Taoist priests. The excuse would be the Marquise, who could not be told on account of her health and might get wind of it if there was a big to-do. He also had to buy advertising space in newspapers for the obituary announcement but not in the paper the Marquise subscribed to. Specially printed cards were sent out to all acquaintances. The standard phrasing which specified that the head of the house "ended his longevity in the main bedroom" had to be altered.

"I should ask Uncle Elm, I heard Uncle Elm likes to help at funerals," he said. His eyes were red with weeping and lack of sleep but he had got his wry manner back now that he and Coral were friends again.

Lute happened to be by. "He does?" she exclaimed.

"Yes, he knows all the burial rituals. He wants to see that the correct things are done."

Lute was momentarily seized by a chill sympathy and fright. What her father found to do out of his lifelong inaction! This was something that did not cost him anything and made him feel important, a custodian of tradition on the one occasion in life where old rules were still observed unquestioningly and gratefully obeyed when pointed out by an authority on hand. Still his enthusiasm brought snickers behind his back.

"Why don't you ask him?" Coral said.

Bright answered, "He'd just think it's an excuse to borrow money."

Number Nine would not help with the funeral expenses, she was angry that she could not have the coffin in her house. If the Marquis had received money from the Japanese when he was alive Bright knew nothing of it and Miss Nine claimed the same. He had come across Japanese callers once or twice at the house but had placed no importance on it at the time. As he negotiated daily with Number Nine the Chows said behind his back that he was fawning on her because she had money. The remark might be taken to mean more than it did on the surface since he had a record for incest. The Marquise was also angry with him for never being at home when she was sick in bed. Badgered on all sides he had no one to turn to except Coral.

There came gaps in their conversation when he was afraid that Coral would talk about herself and face him with her misery. But Coral managed to put him at ease. She wanted this to end gracefully just so that she could think back without feeling ashamed. He even got to confide in her that the Marquise wanted to see him married. Worried about her own illness she had told him it would make her happy if he would get married while she could see it. He never went out with girls but relatives would make introductions. He said there was not enough money. Of course she did not know his father had just died, so marriage was out of the question. She thought he was just putting her off with excuses. Poverty had never stopped anyone from getting married. She thought it was still because of Coral.

"All I ask is that you don't get married in Shanghai," Coral said smiling. If he did she would have to go to the wedding.

He promised.

"The fact is I'll have to resign at the bank. It's a national bank. I have to wait a bit so it won't be too obvious. I'm thinking of going north, only it's impossible just now with Mother sick."

"Are you going to look for a job in the north?"

"I've already been offered a job to take care of the ancestral temple."

"How? Keep it in repairs or look after needy clansmen?"

"Yes, I'm a needy clansman myself. At any rate that will give me time to look around."

"And you have plenty of relatives out there to make matches for you."

"Now is not the time for that, without even rice to eat," he mumbled smiling.

"What kind of a girl would you like to marry?" She did not know why she should inflict such pain on herself. Just to be nonchalant in the Western manner? No, it was also that they had found each other after what seemed a lifetime of being orphans in other people's courtyards, and had nursed each other with their flesh and each had encouraged the other to be free and natural and selfish. Even now she felt a kind of exultation that he was able to be entirely honest at last with another human being.

"She doesn't have to be pretty. Somebody like Lute I thought, who's very young and doesn't know anything."

"That's natural, you've worshipped your father long enough, it's your turn to be worshipped," she said smiling.

"It's not that I want to be worshipped, I just have the idea that might make me feel responsible and give me the push to start out fresh and try to make a living."

"I never knew you liked Lute."

"Yes, I've always liked her."

Dew was polite when he came but kept out of the way. Lute also. But Lute had a strange forgetfulness about her aunt and Bright. It was difficult to remember that they had been lovers. It was people's typical attitude toward members of their family, between parents and children and brothers and sisters, the persistent feeling that the other was naive and rather inept in matters of love and sex, and always a readiness to believe that there had never been anything of the sort.

5

The top of the apartment house was meant to be a public veranda but it seemed nobody liked to use it. The squared-off chimneys and the big concrete blocks which served unknown purposes made stark shapes against the hard blue sky. Lute always went up there with a book when her mother had a friend coming to tea. Lately it had been a French army officer, a Captain Boudinet. She had opened the door for him once. He stood there not speaking with chin pressed down on his white uniform, very like the plaster bust of Napoleon on her father's desk but handsomer. She firmly gave him not another thought, even after the tea when she came back to the room smelling stale and of cigarette smoke. It was good for her mother to be in love. Love was like cigarettes, all right after twenty, sophisticated and becoming after thirty but wrong before twenty unless it was for girls like her cousins who had to find husbands because there was nothing else they could do.

It was pleasant up there on the roof except that the aridness of concrete and sky always made her thirsty. She sat reading on a concrete stump, not thinking, yet

certain things made themselves evident, standing around her on the empty floor, low squat geometric shapes so silent they were wordless even in her mind but nevertheless there. Once she had wondered why her aunt still lived with her mother when it had become so painful. Why was she doing the same? Why did she let her mother sacrifice herself and keep reminding her of it? This waiting for the European situation to clear. Martyrdom postponed was worse than when it was taken at one shot. She ought to go out and get a job and support herself. She was almost eighteen. The matriculation certificate was at least as good as a high school diploma. No, but she could not pass up the opportunity to go to England. Then don't be so thin-skinned, she told herself, don't suffer and do nothing about it, it's despicable. The more you suffer the more shame on you. We're ruining each other, we weren't such people before. Don't ruin her altogether. Jump off the roof and let the earth slap the life out of you. She did not look down at the sidewalk seven storeys below but it was there, minutes away, just another concrete block only flattened out, no less real than all the other silent shapes squatting on their haunches around her casting their shadows in the late sun. You who were greedy for endless incarnations, even one life is too much for you, she said to herself or would have if she had the words.

She could not figure out how much her mother had already spent on her. It kept growing in her mind, nebulous and astronomical, almost like what the Marquis had embezzled. She did not know how she could walk out now, or was that just an excuse to go on like this? But what would Dew say if she were to tell her she no longer wanted to go to England? What would all their relatives say who had thought it was madness to educate a girl to begin with? And her father and stepmother? Jump off the roof and the pavement would slap her deaf to all that they might say.

The fact remained that her mother helped her and she was ungrateful and did not love her any more. She was not like Cousin Bright who adored his father for being the man that he would never be. The relationship between parent and offspring, half identification and half antagonism, as itchily wobbly as loose-fitting false teeth, both she and her mother were not used to it. It's a sin against human dignity to prostrate one's self before another person. It's often part of love but then many things connected with love are sins. Maybe she was against it only because she had never loved her mother enough, and now was disillusioned like a theater devotee admitted backstage. It was not fair, she knew.

What horrified her more than the tantrums was how little it took to make her mother happy. A marked-down dress, a phone call from Hennings or Captain Boudinet and her voice would become quiet and sweet even when speaking to Lute, sometimes with breathless girlish titters. Were women so cheap? Like in the amahs' Buddhist jingle:

"In life just don't be born a woman,
To the end of her days her joys depend on others."

She tried not to feel this way. There was the old saying: *Eng yuen fung ming*, settle your accounts of gratitude and hatred cleanly. She would revenge herself on her father and stepmother as she would one day repay her mother. She had promised herself a long time ago she would take revenge and must carry it out if only to prove she would pay her debt to her mother. She would make a cartoon or anyway a drawing of the goings-on at her father's house, the beatings and imprisonment while the police refused to interfere because of the war across the Soochow Creek. She would send it to a newspaper. Who knew but it might lead to a raid on the house for opium.

To make sure that it would come to the attention of the Settlement police she would send it to an English language paper. She modeled it on a Buddhist painting she had seen that told a story through continuous action across a long scroll. The same nightmarish figures appeared again and again. The great Chapei fire burned on the north bank of the creek outside the house. The picture was called "Hostilities South of the Soochow Creek". The longest paper she could find was still not long enough, she had to do the scroll in two sections and write a note to the editor to explain. She sent it to the American paper that Dew and Coral subscribed to, so if the picture came out she would see it.

Every day she turned the pages with thumping heart. Three weeks went by and she gave up hope. It was a good thing she had not told her mother or aunt. Her only dread now was they would know if the picture was sent back to her. She had not asked for it back but they might just be officious enough to return it. She rushed to answer the door every time in case it was the mailman.

The letter came on a Saturday when Dew and Coral were both home. The newspaper editor who signed himself Howard Coleman said the drawing would come out next Sunday and hoped she would not mind it being cut into four sections. He enclosed ten dollars and asked her to drop in for a talk.

"That's wonderful," Coral said. "When did you paint this?"

"It's just an ink drawing."

Dew looked pleased but said nothing.

"It sounds like he may offer you a job."

"Tell him you're going to school in England," Dew said.

"I can work while I'm waiting to go," Lute said.

Dew quickly brushed this aside with a slight shake of her head and batting her eyes unsmiling.

"I don't know any Americans," Coral said reflectively. "I always thought I wouldn't like to work for them, they pay better but you can get fired any time."

"Even if she wants to work this is not the right work for her," Dew murmured in a tone of dismissal.

"I wish we knew somebody who knows these American newspapermen. It just happens there's nobody around who does," Coral said half to herself.

"I don't like Americans," Dew said. "Oh, they get friendly fast enough. Call you by your first name, put an arm around you and make jokes."

"And you still don't know where you stand with them," Coral said. "You never can tell about the Americans. They're the inscrutable occidental."

"Do they have all those newspapermen here to cover the war?"

"They're always writing about bars and being drunk."

"Did they make up the name Blood Alley? It's not Chinese."

"Either they or the sailors."

"Badlands, that's another name they made up."

Lute listened for some turn of the conversation that might still make it all right to work for a newspaper. To be a staff cartoonist, that was suddenly everything she had ever dreamed of. But her mother was probably right, she wouldn't know how to behave with these people. She had just scored a point with her mother by selling a drawing. Don't spoil it now.

"Do I have to telephone and say I can't come?"

"Better write him a letter. Tell him you have to go away to study so you can't take a job."

"He never mentioned a job."

"Aunt will help you write it." Sensing her disappointment Dew added, "It will be wonderful of course if you can make a career of painting, only this is a difficult country for painters. Ask Tina. All the artists who studied in Paris came back here, not one can make a living by painting."

"Unless you can get known abroad," Coral said.

"That's something you can't count on."

"There's more of a market for Chinese style paintings," Coral said.

"You can't tell about these things. Wonderful of course if —" Dew made a deprecatory little gesture. "But with a good British degree you always have something to fall back on."

"Mr. McCullough says the Victoria University in Hong Kong is a good college," Coral murmured her suggestion of a comedown looking away from both mother and daughter. "There you can get in without another examination."

"A pity about England though, after waiting so long," Dew said.

"He says it's very British."

"Well, wait and see. As long as so much time has already been spent waiting."

When Lute came down with headache and fever it seemed to have solved the lesser problem of what to tell the newspaper editor.

"Aunt can telephone for you and say you're sick and can't come to the office," Dew said.

Coral made the phone call. The drawing came out in a half page spread on the front page of Sunday's second section. Lute was still sick a few days later when Captain Boudinet was to come to dinner. Coral had arranged to go to a cousin's house for dinner taking Lute. Now Dew had to cancel her dinner with Captain Boudinet but he was not home when she telephoned. His Annamite servant did not know when he would be back. The Annamite did not have much French, nor did she.

"All he does is shout *Il est pas LA*!" she mimicked.

Not sure whether he had the message right or even got her number down she rang up every hour or so and kept running into him. After the fourth try she came into the living room where Lute was lying on the divan, to take her temperature once again but instead burst out:

"How you plague people. You live just to make trouble for people. I'm afraid of you now, yes I'm honestly afraid of you. Dread your getting sick and you get sick. It's no use doing anything for you. I should let you live or die by your own doing."

Lute was feeling filthy for putting a sick bed in the room she loved but at these words she shut her mind and hardened her heart. Coral came back after five.

"I've been trying to get Boudinet on the phone all day." Dew told her about the Annamite.

"So he's still coming," Coral said.

"I don't know. If he got the message he'd phone."

"Lute still has fever?"

"Yes. Funny it doesn't go down."

"It's been quite a few days now."

"I'll have to get Dr. Immelhausen to come and take a look."

Dr. Immelhausen came over on his way home from office. He was his usual cheerful self. Dew had a little talk with him in the hallways when he left.

"He says it's typhoid. I said where could you have got it? He said it was something you ate. And I told him we couldn't be more careful, it must be something you ate outside."

"I haven't been out for days."

"Well, what did you eat?"

"Nothing. Just what we've always had."

"Isn't that strange?" she appealed to Coral. "With all our precautions she should get typhoid. Pillar is going to have a good laugh. It's just as he says, they eat off the street and nothing ever happens but the more careful you are the more you get sick."

"It's a question of the power of resistance," Coral said.

"It must be something from outside."

"I'll get the medicines tomorrow before I go to office."

"The doctor says the most important thing is not to eat any solid food," Dew turned to Lute. "Not anything, not a morsel. Do you understand? The bowel will break," she whispered painfully ashamed as though it touched an indecent part of the innards. On second thought she added, "It's not a dangerous illness if you're careful."

"Any illness with a name is not good," Coral said lightly.

"Maybe you'll be more comfortable in a hospital. We'll see."

"Did he say she should go to a hospital?"

"Doctors always rather have you in a hospital."

The doorbell rang.

"It's Boudinet," Dew moaned.

"Already? It's not yet seven." But she waited for Dew to go to the door.

Dew came back with a basket of flowers almost as tall as herself.

"It's the people downstairs. They said this was delivered to them by mistake. They finally decided it must be ours, when it's all wilted."

"The elevator man brought it last Monday," Coral said. "He asked if there's a Miss Lu living here and I told him there's no such person. So he said he'd try the Levits downstairs."

"Why, here's a card. How could there be such a mix-up?"

"It's my fault. It just never occurred to me that Lute might get flowers," Coral sniffed defensively.

Dew passed the envelope to Lute. "It's from the newspaper."

"Very nice of them," Coral said.

Lute took the note out.

"Dear Lute,

Here's hoping for your speedy recovery.

Sincerely,

Howard Coleman"

She gave it back for her mother to read. Dew took it offhandedly, then bent shrewd eyes over it. A fold appeared above her eyes to make them look old.

Coral pulled the basket nearer the head of the bed. "This must have cost quite a few dollars."

She stopped, cutting herself short. Lute knew what she was about to say was instead of spending it on flowers they could have paid a little more for the drawing. She went on in a guilty murmur:

"What a pity it's wilted."

"I'm never much for sending flowers," Lute said. "It's a foreign thing."

Dew returned the note to her. "Here. Better thank him at once, it's been almost a week now."

"Yes, what will people think? As if you're offended," Coral said.

"You better telephone him, Coral. Explain there's been a mistake and tell him it's typhoid fever she has."

"I'll telephone right now, maybe he's still there. Newspapers don't keep office hours." Coral went out.

Lute held the note loosely, her hand resting on the bed sheet near the pillow. She did not have to read it again to remember every word in it. It seemed the supreme accolade to a lifetime's work. How impressed he must have been to send her this tall basket that must have looked a little ridiculous even when the flowers were fresh, as though she was a war hero dying of wounds sustained in "Hostilities South of the Soochow Creek". She looked at the dead dahlias with curled black claws, the chrysanthemums like dry mops, the gladioli twirled like paper napkins with just a touch of orange at the edge. Thundering joy came over her. Her face swollen full by fever shone like a gilded idol.

Dew had been straightening up the room, taking her time as though guessing that the minute she was out of the room Lute would read over the note again, perhaps to kiss it. She turned round and looked at her.

"All right now. It's not as if the flowers were for you."

Lute stared at her. It struck them both that the remark was insane. There was a pause while Dew decided not to explain. When she spoke again she was gentle and brisk.

"I'm going out for dinner but Aunt will be here if you want anything."

"Yew," Lute said.

Dew went out to the hallway. Coral had just rung off.

"What did he say?" Dew asked.

"Nothing. He said he was sorry it was typhoid."

"Where she got it from I'll never understand."

"You want to telephone Boudinet again?"

"First you telephone your cousin. You can't go tonight. With Lute sick we can't both be out."

"Are you going out?"

"I don't know yet."

"Oh — if Boudinet turns up you may go out for dinner."

"Yes, and Immelhausen has also asked me."

"Just now when he was here?"

"Yes, he said he'd take care of Lute's hospital bills if I had dinner with him tonight."

"Very gallant."

"At his house."

"Oh. Well, are you going?"

"I've known for a long time that he doesn't mean well."

"And now he's taking advantage of your distress."

They both felt a little embarrassed. Dew did her face in the bathroom while Coral leaned against the doorway.

"His house is on Avenue Petain," Coral said, riffling through a memorandum file in her mind. "He's never married."

"Who knows, he may have a wife in Germany."

"He's been here more than thirty years!"

"Even then. Nobody knows anything about him."

"Why, he must be seventy," Coral tittered fearfully.

"Foreigners don't age."

"The Fourth Miss Hsu used to go to him."

"Was it tuberculosis?"

"Yes. He never takes you seriously unless you're actually dying," she said.

"He is the cold hard sort."

"If you don't come back am I to call police?"

"I don't know yet whether I'm going."

"What did you tell him?"

"I said I would think it over. I made him promise not to telephone."

"To make him worry a little?"

"Anyway call up your cousin. There has to be somebody in the house with Lute."

"I wish I could have let her know earlier," Coral went to the phone.

"This Lute is a real trouble maker," Dew said with a soft laugh.

Coral was a little shocked because Dew had always had strong views against mixing money with love. But then Dew would say: Whose fault is it that I'm in such straits? Besides she was sacrificing for Lute which put a different complexion on it.

Boudinet called up in time for Dew to cancel their dinner before she went out. She took Lute to the hospital the next afternoon and got her a private room. Dr. Immelhausen made his rounds a little later when Dew was still there talking to the nurses. His manner had become expansive like a host in his own house.

"Aha!" he said to Lute. "Comfortable? Yes? See how patient she is, always with hands folded over her heart —" he copied the posture and cast his eyes up in a saintly manner. "So quiet, never moves, such a good patient."

Lute smiled and flattened her hands so they no longer showed under the bedclothes. Illness was a bore but there was no choice except to wait it through. She never had any doubt that this would pass like the others she had had. At night she was alone in the painstakingly blank white room with nothing to look at and not even a bright light to see it by. A woman's voice groaned all night in the next room. All sounds had been carefully shut out except these moans. Toward dawn it became unbearable. Is she dying? Lute thought. No, experienced voices seemed to answer, people don't die so easily. Her brother had died but that was different. Anything was possible in her father's house with his smoky cavern of a den where he and his specter-like concubine lay and cooked over their opium lamp until finally his second wife the spider woman had come out of the mustiness. Here it was normal life outside. Sick people groaned and moaned, that was all. Sure enough, the sound ceased at dawn when the business of the morning began, washing and taking medicines.

"Who is in the next room?"

"A young girl. The same age as you," the young nurse said surprised, "the same illness too."

"She groaned the whole night, I couldn't sleep."

"She died this morning," she murmured unwillingly, to stop the complaint.

"What?"

"Her bowel broke." Her face darkened with a wounded frightened look. "It's very painful. But your case is different," she added quickly. "Here is – not like yours, you're lucky."

Lute was a little frightened at the coincidence. She did not like to be classified wrongly and be put in this incubator of death with little compartments in rows. Only this egg would not hatch. This one was a stone. She made herself as invulnerable as in her father's house. For two months she withstood the doctor's favorite joke, mimicking her hands joined over her chest. At last he had a new one.

"Ah, Friday, the big day. On Friday we can eat. I am counting, I am watching the calendar."

Coral brought chicken soup on Friday. The next day Dew brought chicken rice gruel. They had taken turns coming. She heard the Marquise was very ill. After she came out of the hospital they took her along to see the Marquise on a summer night. Death was much more real in the little house than it had been at the hospital. First they passed it on their way up. The light was on in the parlor so they had looked in. The small hot room where they had talked with the Marquis a year ago had been turned into a kind of chapel with candlesticks and incense pot and spirit tablet on the scroll table against the wall. His raised coffin was placed at right angles with the table making a T. The black-painted box had a cheap high gloss. The head panel receded like the bow of a boat giving an illusion of motion, of forging ahead. An old red blanket was thrown over it, the way a horse blanket covered the middle of a horse. A prayer cushion on the floor made it feasible to pay respects to the departed at any time. Along the other walls was still room for the rosewood chairs, the small tea table with the ash tray on it, the sofa and armchairs in their cloth covers. The room gave off a mixed feeling, both homely and sinister. She found it hard to get it into her head that it had been like this for almost a year now, sitting down here unknown to the mistress of the house, an unexploded bomb.

"Lute should kowtow to Uncle," Dew whispered.

"Maybe later," Coral said. "Nobody around."

Old Lin came halfway down the stairs to meet them, her eyes red and swollen from weeping.

"How is Taitai?" Dew whispered.

"Seems a little better." But her tears fell as she answered.

"She never came downstairs in all this time?" Coral asked.

"Hai-ya, so many times she wanted to go down, and why not? She was much better in the spring. The trouble I had holding her back."

"It must have been hard on you, Old Lin," Dew said.

"That's the truth, Miss Yang, I lived with my heart dangling and my gall strung up."

The house still smelled of cats' ash pan. This was her house that she was leaving and the man she loved was in his coffin downstairs. It seemed to Lute death means more this way.

The wife of one of the young Los came to the head of the stairs at the sound of their voices.

"I thought it was Bright," she whispered.

"Who else is here?" Coral asked when the greetings were over.

"Everybody."

"The Chows here too?"

"Everybody is here."

"How is she?" Dew asked.

The young woman pulled her a step aside, for no purpose except to emphasize the secrecy. "There's talk of pouring on joy."

That was the last resort, for the son of the house to get married so the flood of joy would flush the death out.

"What does Bright say to it?" Dew asked.

"That's the trouble. He won't. Aunt has wanted this all along."

Coral said nothing and the other two avoided looking at her.

"It must be difficult too to find anyone in a hurry," Dew said.

"Plenty to choose from, but he won't."

"Where's Bright? Is he out?" Coral spoke up to sidetrack the conversation.

"He went to look over coffins. The Chows thought it wouldn't hurt to pour it on."

That was another kind of pouring, the last desperate measure, purposely seeking ill omens, fight poison with poison.

"Is her mind still clear?"

"Very. She's waiting for someone."

"Waiting for Mr. Fisher?" Dew whispered.

The nephew's wife nodded. "Sick for a whole year now and he never came."

"She never suspected anything?"

"No. Never mentions him. She hates."

Out of respect for her elders she did not say "hates him". In the moment of silence that followed they felt the hate spreading over them all.

"Actually it may be just as well to tell her now," Dew said.

"That's what I say. They're talking over this right now in there," she jerked her chin toward a back room. "Tell her and put her heart at ease. But the shock, and it's touch and go just now, who dares push her?"

"What does Bright say?" Dew asked.

"Bright won't say anything one way or the other. It seems to me he has no shoulders for responsibility. After all Aunt Fisher has brought him up as her own son. Now is the time to act like one."

Dew said pacifyingly, "Bright has his difficulties too. He's the son and his mother's life is at stake."

"That of course. But this is for him to decide, he's the son as you say."

"We'd better go in now," Coral said.

Old Lin had gone into the sick room first for a look and was now standing at the door waiting for them. They went in while the young Mrs. Lo went back to the others.

The only light in the room was a table lamp dimmed by a makeshift shade of folded newspaper. Medicine bottles gleamed around the lamp. A stick of incense stood in a cup on the far side of the room scenting the stale air with a quiet old temple smell.

"Better today, Mrs. Fisher?" Dew asked.

"Ai," the Marquise whispered nodding slightly on her pillow.

"We don't want to tire you with talking, we just came over to see how you are," Coral said.

"With autumn coming on you'll mend fast, it's been a terrible summer," Dew said.

"Glasses."

Old Lin put on her glasses for her. The thin gold frame was now too wide for her face. The deepened lines around the nose soured her slight smile.

"I was ill myself," Dew said. "Lute just got out of hospital and Coral had a rush of work, or we would have come long ago."

"The office is short of hands with the foreigners gone on vacation."

What's all this, Lute thought, instead of the one thing she wants to know and will make the difference of heaven and hell.

"This room too hot for you?" the Marquise said faintly.

"No, no, your room is cool, it faces south, doesn't it, Coral?"

"Southeast, isn't it?"

The Marquise showed her coldness by being listless. Her eyelids drooped behind the glasses.

"We'll go now, we'll come and see you another day," Dew said.

The young Mrs. Lo was waiting for them outside. She took Dew and Coral by their arms.

"Uncle Chow and Aunt Chow said to ask you to come in, they want your opinion."

"How can we speak up? What rights have we here?" they both said.

But they let themselves be propelled into the conference room. Lute followed. She had never seen the Marquise's brother and his wife but had met all her nieces and nephews and their wives, both the Chows and the Los. The brother, grizzled and bewhiskered, said to Dew and Coral:

"Now you two ladies are her good friends. Do you think we ought to tell her?"

"We can't very well say anything, we're outsiders," Coral said.

"Especially me, not even related," Dew murmured referring to her divorce.

"We're also outsiders," the brother said. "We're Chows, she's a Lo."

"You're her own people, Uncle Chow," said a Lo. "Whatever you decide nobody will dispute."

"It's a matter for you Los."

"She's always trusted you most, Uncle Chow."

"She belongs to your family, I can't take the responsibility."

"It's not for us to say. We're of the small generation."

"Bright isn't back yet? He's the son. It's up to the son."

I'll sneak out while they're still arguing and go and tell her, Lute thought. I don't care, I don't belong to the caucus here, I'm nobody. I owe it to her, she's good to me, even now she was thinking of me and went so far as to speak to me over my mother's head. I'll go back to the sick room, there's nobody there except Old Lin and I'm not afraid of her though Aunt Fisher is.

But she was also a little frightened of Old Lin who had the might of right on her side in protecting a dying person from intruders. She was also afraid of disturbing the near dead, already half out of the human state into the ancestral and holy.

Dew and Coral were taking their leave. There was still time to rush in there and tell it before anybody could stop her. But what would Dew say? Things were bad enough without her shaming her mother in front of all their relatives. Everybody would say she was a crazy girl and no wonder her father had treated her like that. She followed them out. At the head of the stairs she had a feeling of frustration like jabbing with a weightless finger, unable to poke through a thin sheet of paper. A few steps down if one would just lean over the banister the coffin was in sight and yet the Marquise would never know, just as if the other death had taken place a year after her own or a hundred years later, it would make no difference. Eternity had sealed off these few stairs.

Lute did not see the Marquise again but went to her funeral in the temple. To the end no one had told her. Dew did not go because the Shens would be there.

"I wonder if your father has been and gone," Coral said to Lute, "I've run into him before at relatives', we just ignore each other, but I'm not sure how he's going to act if he sees you."

There was no funeral service, just a table of worship set up at one end of the great hall where the mourners drifted in throughout the day to kowtow to the dead. Bright kowtowed back behind the mourning curtain. While waiting their turn Coral chatted with the guests standing around. Lute saw her Cousin

Maple, one of the older boys at the house of her two uncles in Tientsin, so regimented that she never quite knew which one was his father. In Tientsin when she was little he had been in his teens, already looking much the same as now, tall and dignified with tortoise-shell glasses over long pink cheeks and speaking just as seldom. Once his grandmother had him take Lute and her brother to the bookstore and let them choose whatever they fancied. Lute's old amah went along and made sure that they did not ask for anything. Maple looked over a number of paperweights and compasses, mechanical pencils, instruments that glittered under the glass counter like science fiction gadgets in Lute's eyes, with a shifting crystalline light. She was disappointed that he also ended with buying nothing. He grunted so curtly to the obsequious sales clerk who had probably recognized the cabinet minister's son, Lute wondered why he was offended. He was married now by family arrangement, one of his father's political alliances. His wife turned out to be slightly deaf. He did not complain. But he was determined to break away from home. He found a bank clerk's job in Shanghai and took his wife with him so they could be on their own. Coral was very impressed with him.

"He seems to combine the new and old morals," she said. "Too often it's the other way round, they want to divorce the wife their parents got them but they want to live on their parents."

He and his wife and Autumn Crane were standing in a little knot. They greeted Lute but the two men went on talking.

"Bright is going up north as soon as he winds up things here," Autumn Crane was saying.

"Oh, is he?"

"How is it over there?"

"The north is not like before. Japanese all over the place."

"Sixth Master keeps very much to himself?"

"Father never sees anybody. Even then trouble seeks you out."

"Japanese making trouble?"

"Mostly old subordinates coming to borrow money."

"Lucky the Ministry clerks are still not like ex-officers, they don't carry guns."

"Some have guns too, the old house guards, and some are ganged up with Japanese ronins."

"Do you know if my father has been here?" Lute whispered to Maple's wife.

She smiled vaguely and did not answer. She stood solidly with joined hands, short and handsome, slightly buckteethed. Lute was bewildered. She should not have asked about her father. But it was no news her leaving her father even if they disapproved.

"She has trouble with her ears," Maple turned round and said embarrassedly.

Lute could never remember his wife was half deaf. She could not remember such things about people. Maple had told her before to raise her voice when speaking to her. Again she had forgotten. She felt contrite at the pained look on his face. He evidently minded very much about his wife's hearing.

"I was just wondering," she started in a loud voice, then became conscious of the dark hushed temple around them and finished in a mumble, "if Father has already been here."

"I haven't seen Uncle Elm. Have you, Uncle Crane?"

"No, I haven't."

Coral was coming toward them nodding greetings. Maple did not seem to have seen her. He turned and walked away. Lute thought it was odd but did not pay much attention to it. His wife mumbled "Aunt Coral" and Coral exchanged a few words with Autumn Crane.

"Come on, it's our turn," she told Lute.

They went up and kowtowed one after the other, then Coral got them a lift from one of the Los and they went home.

Dew was going to the Cheungs to play mah-jong on Saturday. Lute woke her in the morning crossing the bedroom. She spent the rest of the morning trying to get back to sleep and got up at noon angry.

"When I don't get enough sleep my eyelids don't fold right," she said. "And just happens to be today when I'm going out."

Coral came back. After Dew had gone out in the afternoon a strange peace descended on the apartment. It was a lovely sunny day with autumn in the air. The eerie sense of peace and quiet was so pronounced even Coral got restless.

"I feel like eating dumplings," she said suddenly.

Lute was about to offer to go and buy some when she remembered that Coral was still hard up although she had got a raise.

"I'll make some," Coral said. "Do you feel like dumplings?"

"I love them. Aren't they difficult to make?"

"No, not difficult."

"We haven't got anything for stuffing."

"Just use sesame butter and sugar."

"It sounds good." She helped eagerly to get everything out. "There's no yeast."

"It doesn't have to have yeast."

"No?"

"No, it's all right without."

Lute sugared the sesame butter and stirred it. "I've never had a sesame butter dumpling."

"Neither have I. Never made dumplings before," Coral said half to herself with a guilty little laugh. "No idea how this will turn out."

"It doesn't matter. I like dumplings."

The deep rich quiet of the house continued to butter her ears. Even the dishes did not clatter.

"I can never remember Cousin Maple's wife is deaf," she said. "The other day I again forgot to raise my voice to speak to her."

A hurt look came over Coral's face.

"He cut me. I don't know why."

"What? I thought he was so nearsighted he didn't see you, it was dark in the temple."

"No, he deliberately snubbed me. And I was so nice to them when they first came, helped them to find lodgings and everything. I thought he was the best of the lot among the younger generation."

"But why would he want to do a thing like that?"

"I don't' know. As it is I've avoided most of our relatives after the lawsuit so I won't put them in a difficult position if they want to keep on the good side of your Uncle Prudent. Even Aunt Fisher, she was so sorry having to give up Uncle Prudent. 'A pity. A nice house of relatives,' she said."

"Did she say that?"

"Certainly. This was one of the things that chilled me."

"I never knew."

"She was frightened to death when you broke with your father. Didn't dare say a word about it. She never asked you after you got out, did she?"

"No."

"I really shouldn't be saying this so soon after she died."

As she talked Lute slowly came to realize why Maple had acted that way. He must have heard the scandal about Bright. Coral knew why, she was just talking to cover up. Had she ever wondered whether Lute knew? She probably thought Lute was the one person Dew had not told. Lute would not have it in her to pretend living together all this time.

The steaming pan was boiling, letting out white steam. Coral turned on the tap too big, running water into the mixing bowl. It splashed on her glasses. When she took them off to wipe them Lute saw a jagged white line on her left eyelid.

"Is that a scar?"

"That's where your father hit me with an opium pipe."

Lute was stunned. "When?"

"The last time I went."

"When you came with Uncle Crane?" The first day she was locked in her aunt had come to the rescue. She had heard the voices shouting on the stairs.

"Certainly. He jumped up from the couch and hit me with the big pipe, broke my glasses. I had to go to a hospital and have several stitches sewn."

"I didn't know," Lute whispered.

"A good thing no splinter got in the eye, I could have gone blind."

"You never mentioned it."

"Didn't I? I must have told you when you first got out."

"No."

"I suppose in the excitement I forgot."

Lute thought if it had been her mother she could not forget to tell her.

"I never noticed it," she said weakly.

"It seems nobody ever noticed."

Coral did not sound happy about that.

The dumplings looked small and greyish when they came out of the steaming pan. Without yeast they were not puffed out the way they should.

"This stuffing is delicious," Lute said.

"Yes. They're all right," Coral said.

Lute liked them. The leathery unleavened dough and her enjoyment of it combined to make up the taste of poverty. We're poor, she thought. Tears came to her eyes. Coral chewing abstractedly did not notice.

6

England and France declared war on Germany just before school opened after the summer so Lute still had time to enroll at the Victoria University in Hong Kong and get in at the last minute. Dew had arranged for her to go on the same ship with Bebe Shastri, an Indian girl who had been taking lessons from the same crammer and was going to the same college. They spoke over the telephone but did not meet until they sailed. Dew and Coral came to see Lute off. Tourist class passengers could not have visitors on board. They looked around the hot bright wharf and saw the Indian family.

"Are you Bebe?" Coral went up to her. "I'm Lute's aunt."

The father wore a fez, the mother a bun and European dress. The brothers were internationalized, no different from the smart Eurasians or Portuguese around town. Bebe held the red carnations from her brothers against her high bosom. She was small with a gold baby face and big Indian eyes. She made the introductions and everybody shook hands all round.

"Lute doesn't know anything, Bebe will have to look after her," Dew said. She spent the next quarter of an hour cultivating the Shastris just as she had the hospital nurses when Lute was sick, to make sure she would get special care. Coral took down the address of Bebe's father's silk store. Then the Shastris started to take turns kissing Bebe.

"She seems like a capable girl," Dew stepped aside and whispered to Lute. "It'll be a great help to have somebody with you." Aloud she said, "All right, you'd better be going. Be careful now."

"I'm going, Mother. I'm going, Aunt."

"Good luck," Coral said and put out a hand.

A bit taken aback Lute shook her aunt's hand. The gesture struck her as being so English it seemed comical between them. She could hardly keep from laughing out loud as she turned and followed Bebe up the gangplank.

After they had found their cabin Bebe said:

"Let's go out and wave."

"No, I'll stay here for a while. You go," Lute said.

"Don't you want to see them?"

"They'd be gone."

"How do you know? Come out and see."

"No, they won't be there. It's too hot on the wharf."

"All right, I'll call you if they're still there." She went out.

Lute took a few things out of her suitcase and put it away. A huge blast of horn filled the air, the world coming to an end in a great moo. She looked out the porthole at the yellow Whampoo, the sampans scattering now. The ship was moving. Shanghai was pulling heavily away, every strand of the bonds between them that she had not known were there now tugging at her heart. She regretted not having known it better but she loved it without having seen what it was really like, the way people in the old days had thought of their betrothed, and the way most people loved their country. Weeping she heard Bebe come in and did not turn from the porthole. Bebe did not say anything. Lute could hear her straightening her luggage.

"How we've really got going," she said after a while. "Feel it?"

"Yes."

"We're still on the river though. Do you want to go out and look?"

"Yes, Let's go."

"Have a carnation. Just tuck it in your button loop."

"Thanks."

"I'll fix it for you."

"Have you always lived in Shanghai?"

"No, I was born in Singapore."

"Really? Can you speak Cantonese?"

"Yes."

"That's wonderful, I can't, I didn't know what to do when we get to Hong Kong."

At dinner Bebe asked the steward to change her pork chop.

"It's my religion, we don't eat pork."

The steward took her plate away.

"I'm Moslem," she told Lute.

"You must have a lot of trouble eating in China."

"Oh, I always ask first."

After dinner she again offered to teach Lute to play chess.

"Please don't. I'll never learn."

"I just thought to pass the time. Well, shall we walk around?"

The ship was small and in the night the China Sea did not look big. Standing at the rails Lute said to make conversation, "I don't know anything about Mohammedanism."

"It's Islam, or Moslem, not Mohammedan. We don't worship Mohammed."

"We have Moslems too, but only in the northwest."

"Well, it's been said about Chinese Moslems, that they're only Moslem in not eating pork."

"Just that has caused riots."

"Yes, the Chinese can never understand why anyone wouldn't want to eat pork."

"In the end you know what they say? They say the pig is the Moslems' ancestor," Lute whispered giggling.

"It's an old law that came from sanitary reasons. These things always have a practical reason."

"But ... what about having four wives?"

"I knew you were going to ask that. Actually nobody I know has more than one wife. My mother says she won't mind if my father takes three more wives, but he doesn't."

"Isn't it dangerous just to depend on a man's conscience?"

"It's not conscience, since our religion allows it."

"Doesn't that make it still more risky?"

"It's all up to the individual. It's also a matter of custom, in some parts of the world they have harems just as the Chinese have concubines."

"It's not legal any more."

To Lute Islam was an exotic racial thing, not of the spirit. As Bebe went on talking about their principles and their tolerance in incorporating part of Christianity, Lute's mind began to wander. Finally she asked:

"Do you think you just believe because you're born into it?"

"Oh, we're all born into it. We don't make converts."

"That's a great thing. I dread missionaries."

"Yes, you can't talk to them about Christianity, they'll just try to convert you."

"The Christian heaven is so dull. I've always wished I could believe in reincarnation. It's so ideal, live forever and have variety."

"Only it's so obviously wishful thinking."

"But theirs is also, except it's not my wish, and it's just as difficult to believe."

"You're not supposed to believe in a religion just because you don't want to be finished when you die."

"Do you really believe in the Moslem paradise with the houris? That's only for men."

"You can't take it literally. The Koran was describing something to those desert tribes in terms of things they could understand, cool running water and black-eyed houris."

"There is also the modern Christian idea that life is just a moral gymnasium, we're just here to train for the life after death. I think that's horrible."

"They're afraid to live," Bebe said. "They're the kind that teach school after they graduate and never get out. I liked school but I wouldn't want to be there all my life."

"But you're taking Medicine, it's so long. Seven years did you say?"

"Father wants one of us to be a doctor and he won't let me go to college unless I study Medicine. Father's like that."

"Do you want to be a doctor?"

"In a way I also want it. I'm interested, and I think I'll make a good doctor."

"Y-yes, I imagine you'll be very good."

"None of my brothers wanted to go to college. They were in a hurry to go into business."

"I certainly would if I were good at it. I don't believe in college."

"Then why are you going?"

"Because I'm no good at anything else."

"Now you're being afraid."

"Yes, I am," Lute said after a moment of thinking.

"It's no use being afraid. Life has to be lived," Bebe said but her voice had turned so small and bleak it was no comfort.

The next day they were far out at sea. The little Norwegian ship pitched badly. That night they had Chinese dinner, five dishes shared by a table of four. A woman at their table who spoke only Cantonese had been talking to Bebe, glad to be with someone who spoke her dialect. It happened that all the dishes seemed to have pork in them.

"Can't you ask for something else?" Lute said.

"Is that beef chow mein?" Bebe asked with a controlled expression.

"I don't know. Take a look," Lute said.

Bebe shied away from the proffered spoon. "Is it pork? I can't stand the smell."

"Pork has no smell, not like beef or mutton."

"You're just used to it."

Bebe concentrated on the chow mein after the steward had verified that it was beef. But the Cantonese woman also liked the chow mein best. Her chopsticks returned again and again to the dish.

"Is it rocking so badly?" Lute noticed Bebe swaying from side to side in her seat.

"Don't you feel it?" Bebe said swinging like a pendulum.

"I don't know. I've never been seasick."

"You're a good sailor."

The Cantonese woman got up suddenly and hurried out, a handkerchief pressed to her mouth. Bebe stopped rocking and finished all the chow mein.

"A thing like that," Lute said laughing later, "how do you square it with Allah?"

"I was just fooling, I didn't know she was so susceptible."

"Once you believe in a god like a father you'll try to get round him like getting round your father."

"You try getting round my father."

"I always thought nothing is bad as long as you're frank to yourself about it."

"That's worse, to know it's bad and still do it."

"Hypocrisy is better?"

"Certainly, there you at least have some standards and principles."

"I don't believe in those things." It made her think immediately of her stepmother.

"My father always says it's the clever people who need religion most, because without it they can do so many bad things. But if you're dumb then it doesn't matter so much if you have no scruples because you're not liable to do much harm anyway."

Lute smiled ruefully, unwilling to be classified among the inane. But she could only say, "That's like the Chinese saying, those who have claws are not given wings."

"Yes, nature has a sense of balance."

Perhaps it was true that there were only two kinds of thinking people in the world, the unsentimental incompetents and the clever wicked sentimentalists. Bebe said as though in answer:

"My father is a sharp businessman but he's a good man. He was a millionaire three times."

"He's in the silk business?"

"He does all kinds of other things on the side, real estate, investments. He didn't lose his religion through all his ups and downs. He's always angry with us for not knowing more Arabic. The Koran is in Arabic. He has a terrible temper. Mother's very good, she lets him scold. But sometimes she gets mad too, we all do, only we take turns to lose our temper. We're very happy at home."

"Really?"

"Yes, we are really. I know what Chinese families are like sometimes, we have Chinese girls in our school. But we are really happy."

"I believe you."

At bottom she did not believe it, but after they had been a year at the university hostel she had heard more about the Shastris, mainly about the father, until it became believable.

"My father came to Singapore as a young man to learn his business. He said when he first came he had seen Chinese women come into the shop and they were very beautiful, but how they spit! He said to himself, I'm not going to marry a woman who spits."

"My father likes to tell the story of the man who thinks he is a teapot. He puts a hand on his hip and leans over the other way. 'I pour,' he says and you know he is round in the middle just like a teapot and his arm is short —" she put her own short arm on her hip and slowly tilted her hour glass figure.

Lute laughed and laughed although she had read this before in the *Reader's Digest*. She could not see Mr. Shastri reading the *Digest* and this added to the joke.

"You were so funny when I first met you," Bebe sometimes said with a small sour smile that looked as though she was holding something in her mouth.

Lute wanted to ask how, but just smiled instead. She could guess at the implied horror and distaste, rather similar to her own feelings about her brother. Bebe seemed to assume that she was different now and took credits on herself for it. She did not think she had changed any. Good marks and having Bebe for a friend gave her more confidence but she remained the same inside and out, still straight and thin, her face a full Mongolian oval with vague eyes so impassive they seemed colorless, only the eye-whites showing blue against her pallor. Bebe was going home for the summer. She also wanted to very much although it was out of the question. She wept all day when Bebe started to pack.

"All right, I won't go," Bebe said. And when Lute seemed stupefied, "I'll stay with you," she added shortly.

"No, no, please go."

"It makes no difference to me really. I'll have just as good a time here."

Lute did not know how to explain that it was not because of her, much as she would be missed. It was just Shanghai and had nothing to do with her mother and aunt either though they happened to be there. In fact she did not like to think of landing on them again even for just a couple of months. But there would be Shanghai, that big flat characterless city where even the rickshas were dirty brown instead of red with green hood as here, intended by the British to be colorful. When she thought of Shanghai it was more of the crowds of people she had lived alongside of for a lifetime without getting to know. They were the world and life itself while Hong Kong was like a depopulated tropical island neatly laid out for some sort of project. Brief excursions downtown showed dingy old arcaded houses with little cafes advertising curried dewlap rice in the smeared windows. Shanghai had worse slums but they were just rubbish in a big river. The evening before she left she had looked down from the apartment house roof. The mass of misty lights stretched out flat as a board tilted up slightly against the lavender sky. A speechless regret emptied and blew out her heart. She still had not known then how much she belonged there.

Her mother had written to explain needlessly why she had better not come. Besides she herself was leaving Shanghai. Lute thought Coral had probably returned the money so she could travel again, though not to Europe with the war.

She rang up passing through Hong Kong and came to see Lute. All the girls had gone home, Bebe also at Lute's insistence. The Catholic nuns who ran the dormitory had arranged for Lute to stay on for the summer free of charge, knowing she was poor. In return she was to help correct papers for the convent school. She was proud of the chance to show people she had a beautiful mother and was sorry the other girls were not there to see her. Sister Dominic, a big Portuguese woman in a starched Dutch cap, showed them around the house. They came out from the basement.

"It's very lovely." Dew said. "Now I have to be going."

The three of them started down together, pausing to look at the great stretch of sea all round. Flowers in embossed blue pots were placed at a regular distance on the balustrades all the way down to the road. Out in the open air Lute thought Dew looked a little worn in her turquoise shirt and slacks. It must be her new towering hair-do that was too severe. The image of her mother seemed to be cut out and superimposed on the pale blue sea, just as the potted coxcomb flowers had always seemed to her like cut-outs, their dark red frills in their detailed nearness so unreal against the distant sea.

Sister Dominic was talking to Dew in the offhand, uninterested manner she reserved for visiting parents who were not prospective patrons.

"Where are you staying?"

"Repulse Bay Hotel."

Lute had heard Repulse Bay Hotel was the most expensive one in Hong Kong. She tried not to look at Sister Dominic whose heavy face was without expression.

"Come and see me tomorrow," Dew turned to Lute. "Telephone first, ask for Room 319."

"Is it very far?"

"There's a bus."

"Yes, the Repulse Bay bus will take you there," Sister Dominic said, brusquely it seemed to Lute.

"Well, I have to be on my way," Dew said and mumbled, "A car is waiting below," in a way that stopped the others where they were instead of following her to the bottom steps and having to be introduced to whoever was in the car.

Sister Dominic said goodbye and waddled up the steps. Lute stood there a little longer rather than go up with her with that embarrassment between them.

7

The Repulse Bay bus dropped her on a neat macadam road with greenery massed on both sides in fernlike close-knit clumps. The still, close air was loud with cicadas. The road led to the door of a long pale yellow building, dark and spacious inside with no elevators.

"This is really nice," she said looking around the big chintzy hotel room with the bright blue sea filling three quarters of the window.

"I like it," Dew said. "We were going to stay at the Gloucester but this is much better, and with a lovely beach."

Who was she with? Lute did not ask. She did not ask after her aunt either. Her mother might not like it although presumably they had parted friends.

Dew had gone back to the bathroom mirror and Lute took up her old position by the door. In the brilliant afternoon light on white tiles she was shocked to see her mother's shoulder blades protruding through the transparent orange nightgown. She could not wear

a thing like that. On her it looked tawdry instead of sexy. This was so unlike her, always the faultlessly dressed copper-faced mannequin.

"Oh, I saw that little Indian girl, what's her name?"

"Bebe."

"She telephoned, so I asked her to tea. She's a smart girl."

"Yes, I like her very much."

"Just don't let her dominate you. That won't be good."

"No, I won't," Lute said smiling.

Peering into the pools of her mirrored eyes while rubbing a lotion on her face, Dew gave her little talk on health, omitting the one on education since Lute did well in her studies. For the first time she had enjoyed writing to her mother reporting all the marks she got.

"Have you other friends? Beside Bebe?"

"No."

"Classmates?"

"They're all gone for the summer."

"Don't you write to any of them?" A slight hesitation showed she meant boys.

"No."

"I came with your Uncle and Aunt M.H. Auntie Tina and Dr. Wu are also here."

"Oh! They're all here?"

They were dismissed in a murmur, "They're going to Chungking."

Lute did not ask where she herself was going. Evidently not Chungking.

"I heard your father is hard up. They gave up their house and moved into two rooms, then into one. Then they said, Why pay rent? So your stepmother went to your Uncle Prudent's house and asked to let them live in the attic."

"What?" Lute gaped half laughing.

"So they moved in."

"Cousin Stallion said yes? It's him now, isn't it? Aunt Prudent is dead too?"

"Yes, Stallion and his wife are in charge now."

"And he let them in?" Even as a teenager Stallion had been smooth and elusive, Lute had noticed before she was old enough to know he was wary of poor relations.

"He had to I suppose. After all if your father didn't turn against his own sister your Uncle Prudent would have lost the lawsuit. And wouldn't have left Stallion so rich. Hai-ya, there's you Shens for you!"

Lute could see her stepmother going on that errand, slim and smart in an old black gown, her hair slicked back for the flat bun low on the back of her flat head, the big rectangular eyes smiling on the pale rectangular face. She would be asking for no more than her rights, having of course seized on some big principle such as mutual help and closer family union in a time of national crisis. No reference to the lawsuit.

"Your father didn't get much for betraying your aunt, making that separate settlement out of court. That was his capable wife's doing too, she put him up to it. Now at least she got him the attic for a last installment. Hai-ya, really, retribution comes quick these days!"

Lute thought, Stallion probably did not dare offer them a loan instead, there would be no end of that.

"How they have come to this already I just cannot understand. Gave up their car, their house, and no children, just the two of them. Even gave up smoking, both of them. Opium had gotten too expensive. Of course his land is in a bad district — Japanese and Communists taking turns there. But what happened to the other things he had? It just goes to show what I've always said: education is more reliable than inheritance. I have no money to leave you, I can only give you an education so you can support yourself." She droned on.

Lute was shaken inside, her last refuge gone. Although there was no possibility of her ever going back to her father there had always been more sense of belonging there than with her mother who had made it so clear that she and her brother had understood even when they were children, that they had no claims on her.

"And your stepmother so shrewd," Dew was now saying. "What did it get her? Hai-ya, come to think of it, what she did to your brother. Deliberately passed him tuberculosis and never got him a proper doctor. I feel bad about the time he ran away from home and I made him go back. I couldn't help it." Her voice had turned hoarse. "There's you and it's already more than I can manage."

Lute had always blamed herself about her brother. From the very beginning after her stepmother came when they had first started on him. She did not know what she could have done but she would have known if she had really wanted to badly enough. Instead she had only thought if only she had money she could pull him out and remake him, putting it all on the lack of money which was the natural state of somebody her age.

For one thing she could have been more feminine with him instead of trying to talk to him man to man. He had been susceptible to girls. It was painful how normal he remained. At some early stage he seemed to have taken an assessment of himself and the world and decided he could do worse than sit tight and wait for the money. It turned out he had miscalculated the rate things changed. He did not live to see the end but at fifteen he had seen his father carefully put away a business letter unanswered until finally the piece of property was foreclosed. Paralyzed by fear. She had known their father to be afraid even when she was a child. He had seen the change coming, picking up speed. He was farsighted in his way and being afraid had hastened it.

"I told him to go and have an X ray, I had it all arranged," her mother was saying. "And would he go? Avoided me ever since, as frightened as a little ghost before the king of hell. I talk to you people about health, talked until my lips were torn and your ears were callused. Did anyone ever pay attention? Now you know."

A knock on the outside door and the bellboy came in.

"That's the tea," Dew said and Lute was surprised to see her gather herself in, even pinching her mouth to make it smaller. "Is he gone?" she whispered and peered out to make sure before emerging in her orange nylon gown.

She poured tea and offered Lute buttered toast from the covered silver dish. Mrs. M.H. Cheung looked in.

"Are you busy?"

"No, there's only Lute here."

"Ek, Lute. How are you?"

She showed Dew a piece of dress material she had bought. "Have you seen Tina after lunch?" she asked.

"No."

"I was telling M.H.: Don't let's play mah-jong any more. Wasn't that embarrassing the way they quarreled, each blaming the other for throwing away the wrong tile."

"Yes, they've got into this bad habit. Anything starts off an argument."

"But isn't it embarrassing for bystanders?"

"That's nothing compared to what I go through, with Tina running to me crying every time."

"Dr. Wu doesn't look it but he does have a temper."

"It's still his divorce problem that's bothering them. His parents say: We only know this one to be our daughter-in-law. She served us these many years when you were abroad, doing your duty for you. Who dares turn her out?"

"That's often the case."

"Too common nowadays."

"But she's all set now. The minute they get to Chungking she's the Resistance wife. Nowadays Resistance wives are recognized."

"That's what I tell her. I said Why does he take you with him if he wants to leave you?"

"She says he's leaving her?"

"Just her imagination. She's getting so that she's jealous of me even."

They whispered with suppressed giggles.

"I don't blame him if he sees you side by side with her making her look cheap. I can never get used to the way she takes food from his plate."

"You noticed that too? And straightening his tie in public."

"Just when he was talking to you."

"Leonard's fault too. He did it on purpose."

"But why? To pick a quarrel?"

"Yes, on purpose. That's why I tell her it's bad to quarrel so much, it gets to be a habit."

"We're not going to play mah-jong again tonight, are we?"

"I don't know. They were talking about a boat restaurant."

"Anyway we'll meet you in the lounge."

After she had left Dew asked, "What time do you have dinner at the dormitory?"

"They'll keep it for me until eight."

"Do they have plenty of hot water for baths?"

"No, only cold water in the summer vacation."

"Then bathe here. The bath towels are changed every day, there's always one I never use."

After her bath Dew said, "There's still time to take a turn outside. You should see their garden. Wait till I get dressed, I'll show you the way."

They went down the dark paneled corridors and raffia-carpeted shallow stairs, a veranda on each floor draped with purple wistarias. On the lawn they took a stone path between shrubberies that breathed coolness now that the sun had gone down. Lute did not see much of the garden, she was too full of the odd sensation of having her mother walking beside her and not going anywhere, just walking with her.

"Don't tell anybody about Tina. It's not nice to talk about people behind their backs. It's different with Auntie M.H., she can't help knowing, traveling together and all."

"I won't talk."

"It just goes to show what I have always said: Don't have relations with a man no matter how in love. Look at Tina, and she's a capable girl, don't underestimate Tina. Even then it's come to this. I'm just telling you so it'll be a lesson to you."

"Auntie M.H. doesn't like her?"

"Ai-yo, don't start me on that now. Both complaining to me about the other. I'm so sorry now I got up this party. It's just for convenience. M.H. has connections. And the Wus were thinking of doing some business as everybody does nowadays. Of course being a doctor makes it easier for him to get penicillin and such, there's a terrible shortage in the interior. They'll fly back and forth between Hanoi and Kunming, I'm going to Calcutta first, but they'll be a great help. I've never been in business before. Now because of you I have to think of making some money."

Lute had heard of the *dan bong*, traders running the blockade of the Chinese interior, a new profession open to men and women, rich and poor. The lowliest were no more than peddlers that fought their way into third class trains, bribing their way past stations and Japanese sentry posts, got slapped and kicked, the women mauled and sometimes required to sleep with a gendarme or inspector. Some of the amahs went into the business. The high-class *dan bong* traveled on those air routes still open to Free China. The ladies who smuggled in embargoed goods were old hands anyway at not declaring things at the customs. But Lute was in ignorance and awe of all business and had some idea of the risk for outsiders trying to get in.

"I feel so bad about spending your money, Mother," she said smiling. "I wish I were not such a drag on you. I don't matter really, I'll never be anything worth sacrificing you for."

Dew seemed taken aback although she did not stop walking or turn to look at her. When she spoke a moment later she kept her eyes on the landscape the way she always addressed the mirror.

"I don't like the way you talk, as if I have more right to live than you. My life is over. I always come and go by myself, now I begin to realize it's hard for a woman to go about alone. Nobody had real feelings for you as you get older."

Lute heard this with dismay. Even the most individual and lasting woman finally becomes no exception, defeated by the human nature of all mankind.

"A friend used to tell me, you should have somebody to take care of you, you're too good to look out for yourself. But I just couldn't take his advice. Now I've finally decided to let somebody take care of me. It's also on account of you."

Lute slowly took in the piece of news in its disagreeable wrapping. So she was going to Calcutta to a man who had loved her for a long time. It was tender and sentimental even if she had never loved him. Lute did not mind being blamed for this too like going into the smuggling business but there was nothing she could think of saying that would not sound inconsiderate. Who was he? Somebody nice certainly since he had been so patient and faithful. If she so much as said she was glad, it would seem to confirm the assumption that she would like to have a stepfather contribute to her support. She supposed he was a foreigner. For a moment she saw a tall man whose face she had never seen before, red-necked above his overcoat in the clothes-hanger mirror in some unknown dark foyer. Further speculations would be prying. Suddenly her mother seemed almost gone already. Although still walking by her side she had turned precious and evanescent, just a dissolving puff of perfume, the more so as Lute could not turn to look at her.

"I've never given in to money before, no matter how it made me suffer. I've had it offered to me. And just take your Uncle Pillar, I can have all his money if I want. This you're not to tell anybody. Your Uncle Pillar was a beggar's child."

Nothing about her relatives could surprise Lute any more but this was new. Uncle Pillar a beggar boy!

"Don't ever tell anyone."

"No, I won't."

"They were famine refugees. The baby was born as they begged their way along, only a few days old when Sister-in-law Hu went out and bought him."

Among the stable of half retired amahs at Pillar's house Lute seemed to remember a neat moon-faced amah addressed as Sister-in-law Hu in their polite way. But she had been around only when Lute first came to Shanghai. Later she had gone back to the country.

"She was frightened to death bringing him in. Clansmen had been watching the house day and night for months. They had said all along it was a false belly. Everybody was searched going in and out. Sister-in-law Hu put the baby in a basket and put layers of cakes on top, covered with a piece of cloth. One of them turned the cloth back and took a look. I'm dead, she thought. They were all ready with big sticks and stones, going to break down the door, kill the widow and the concubines for cheating them out of their rights, throw everybody out and take everything."

"What if it turned out a boy was born? What would they do with this one?" Lute asked, the truth only now dawning on her. They had kept the newborn daughter and added a son to make twins. It was imperative that the deceased had a *yi fu tze*, son of the belly left behind.

"They'd keep him, probably let an amah adopt him. They wouldn't drown him in a bucket. But he certainly wouldn't live if he was discovered on the way in. He didn't make a sound though. Sister-in-law Hu began to wonder when she got in the courtyard. She didn't dare look, there were clansmen up the walls and in the trees. She thought he must be smothered to death. When she finally looked he was fast asleep. That's why she always said he was blessed, fated to be the little baron."

"Does he know?"

"No, it's kept from him. Sister-in-law Hu was well set up for life of course. Mother must have rewarded her afterwards, and Mother's last words were she was to be specially looked after."

"It's just like the Peking opera about the eunuch smuggling the prince out in a food box."

"Now you're not to fight Uncle Pillar for the property," Dew said, already regretting letting out the secret.

"Me?" Lute said astonished. What had it got to do with her? Her mother's was not hers. Even her mother's claims were a little ridiculous after more than half a lifetime, when Uncle Pillar had squandered his money and brought up a big family on it as well, to sue for what was left on the evidence of an old amah who was most likely dead. "I'll never do that."

"I know you put a lot of importance on money."

"Only to earn it, not to take it from our own people."

"Now you know he's not."

"To me he's always my uncle."

"I just thought of warning you because you Shens sued each other. You have your father's and your aunt's examples before you."

"That's different, they were revenging on Uncle Prudent."

"I'm just telling you in case some day, who knows, if you're really hard pressed for money."

"No matter how poor I'll never want to take anything from Uncle Pillar." Lute was still trying to smile.

"I'm just telling you."

They walked in silence. Lute remembered so well the first time she had heard this story of the clansmen's siege, at nine when her mother had just come back from England. The talk after lunch was the pleasantest half hour of the day. The table had been cleared. There was fruit in the dark red porcelain bowl with a pale sunburst. The green tea was settling in the glass, still too hot to drink. The fruit peels in the plates were beginning to smell stale but nobody felt like getting up. The siege of the widows had been a part of all this like a piece of family tapestry, wonderful though hard to believe that her mother and Uncle Pillar were old enough to have come out of a legend, the twins whose birth had raised a siege. It was sad to have the tale improved upon after ten years when everything else had deteriorated. Then to have this new twist added in an appendix in which she found herself in the story, as much a villain as the clansmen!

"You'd better go now if you don't want to be late for dinner," Dew said and they parted at the hotel entrance.

8

It was night when Lute got back from Repulse Bay, cut across the university compound and uphill toward the dormitory. Emerging from the steps on to the motor road she saw the searchlights in the sky. They were the only signs of war time. She liked them, they satisfied an impulse she had never followed, of doodling on any large empty area. She had heard of sky-writing but this was the only instance she had seen where men could draw chalk lines around the moon. Tonight there were three. From here it looked like all three were in Kowloon but they could have just as well come from warships in the bay. They swung around, crossed, fanned out, paralleled. An impatient teacher's hand wiped the blackboard clean with a flick of the brush, too quickly, before the diagrams were understood. The sky was exactly the slate grey color of a blackboard filmed by chalk dust and with the same wavy surface. The war was not felt at all in Hong Kong. Certainly it was never mentioned in the classrooms except when a lecturer was absent, gone to military drills as all Englishmen had to.

"Well, children, I have to go and play soldiers again," Mr. Blaisdell had drawled, his cigarette seesawing between his lips. "Terrible nuisance really, leaves us very little time to get through the Renaissance. Of course there are two schools of thought about this. You for instance are not sorry, I can see you're glad."

Two of the lights were on again. One beam rested its tip on a cloud. She could now see there were clouds, invisible before in the black night, piled like the fat multiple petals of a flower. The tip of the searchlight made a pale spot on the grey cloud and did not move. Watching it was somehow intolerably frustrating, made her heart itch like a fingertip just touching it.

She climbed the last lap up the cement stairs cut in the dormitory's stone foundation. Walking up the portico steps she rang the bell and waited, looking out toward the sea. The city lights lay low under the blackness of the bay. Over on the other side Kowloon's green street lights were strung out like a bead necklace marking the horizon. But the upper two thirds of the entire vista was the chalk-striped sky. The next minute she was struck in the face by an illumination that lit her up from top to toe in the small portico painted cream color with bulbous columns. It took her a moment to realize it was the searchlight from across the bay. It remained fixed on her as she stood petrified, enshrined. What on earth they thought they had found she could not imagine. The light snapped off, or merely swerved off, the effect was the same. In the darkness she half laughed soundlessly, her body still saturated with light. She would never be the same again she thought. The door opened behind her.

"Thank you, Sister."

"Your dinner is set out for you. Call Sister Celestine when you finish."

She headed for the basement but had to walk carefully, get adjusted again to the measurements of the hallway after experiencing the immense reach of light striking from afar.

"Come back," Sister Dominic beckoned with an inclination of her massive head. Doubling her chin to look down, she extracted a letter from her starched bodice and handed it to her.

"Oh, it's registered."

"I signed for you."

"Thank you, Sister."

Her glance at the envelope had shown it to be addressed in English in an unfamiliar hand. Who could have written her such a long letter in English, so thick it bulged out square? No, it had a book inside. A small book, long and narrow. An odd shape. Maybe a dictionary. Who would ever send her anything unless it was a dictionary? She did not open it on the way down or even look to see if it was local or from Shanghai.

She turned on the light in the basement. There was her dinner on the refectory table covered by an inverted soup plate. Before she sat down she opened the letter and stared down at the big wad of well-worn ten dollar bills. The letter said:

> "Dear Miss Shen,
>
> I am taking the liberty of writing to you, having heard that you applied for a scholarship without success before coming here. There is however a grant for the sophomore with the best average marks which I am certain you would get next year, which would take care of all tuition and dormitory fees until graduation. In the mean time allow me to present you with a small scholarship of my own which would see you through until next summer. I do not wish to be thanked and must insist on being taken at my word. I may add, although it is perhaps looking too far ahead, that I have every confidence you would win the fellowship for postgraduate work at Oxford if you keep up this work.
>
> Sincerely yours,
> Gerald H. Blaisdell"

The words pounded remotely in her ears like surf. She should have recognized the sprawling handwriting but she supposed he wrote more carefully on blackboard. She counted the money with cold fingers and had to do it twice before she was sure it was eight hundred dollars. The searchlight had found her again in the cellar. Still standing leaning against the table she read the letter once more and this time it sang. Oxford! She was going to Oxford after all by a devious route and this time she really wanted it because it was something she herself had earned. Education was security her mother was always saying, and now it seemed there was money coming even before she had finished studying. As in an old poem often quoted to spur scholars on:

"In books there are houses of gold;
In books there are girls like white jade."

She put everything back in the envelope. It shook her strangely that the stack of old smelly banknotes with an elastic band around it had been crammed so carelessly into the envelope, the flap half unstuck, showing a trust in the Hong Kong post office as well as all humanity that she had never known. He did not bother to change it into larger notes either. She pulled her chair out and sat down to eat but for a while just rested icy fingertips on the lukewarm soup bowl that covered the plate, grateful for the warmth that made this more real. No, she would not go and telephone her mother right now. For one thing Dew would be out. Even if she happened to be in Lute did not want to talk about it over the phone. Sister Dominic being Portuguese from Macao spoke Cantonese but not Mandarin. She was so sharp however she was sure to connect the excitement with the letter. While Mr. Blaisdell did not ask her to keep it a secret, why else did he send cash instead of a check? He would not like any kind of talk. It was just a good deed but it was to help a girl. She remembered some of the girls said he was eccentric and did not get on well with the Dean. He should have been made a professor long ago but somehow was not.

She telephoned Dew the next afternoon as she had been told to, thinking, if she tells me I can't come today then I have to tell her over the phone, I can't hold it another day. Dew told her to come.

"I got this letter from our history lecturer," she said as casually as she could.

As Dew was reading it she unwrapped her newspaper parcel and took the money out.

"He gave me a scholarship of eight hundred dollars."

"I don't understand," Dew said. "Is there such a scholarship? Why is it his to give?"

"No, it says here, next year there will be a scholarship I can get, but this is his own money."

"You can't take money from people," Dew said with an embarrassed little laugh.

"This is different, he just wants to help a needy student."

"How can you take people's money just like that?"

"But he's so good about it," Lute argued desperately, afraid she would be made to return it. "He doesn't even want to be thanked."

Dew was silent. Lute folded up the newspaper she had wrapped the money with. The stack of ten dollar bills looked gross now, as thick and long as a bar of laundry soap. It must remind her mother of people who gave a dollar's worth of pennies to street singers to make it seem more.

"Where shall I put it?"

"Leave it there," Dew said carelessly.

Lute left it on the table and resolutely kept from giving it another look although her instinct was to rush it to the bank vault, the most precious money in the world. The letter and envelope she put away in her purse. Dew might still want to send back the money. A good thing she didn't think of asking for the address. If she asked for it she would just have to try again to talk her out of it.

Dew was packing things back into a trunk, not her own clothes but the kind of exquisite miscellany that she had always had.

"Here, you might help me a little. Pass me that piece over there. The other one. Right in front of your eyes." She walked over quickly and got it herself.

Their old irritation with each other came up again. Lute found the only thing to do was to stand around showing a readiness to help but letting her do all the work herself. Dew although disheartened still sought to make it a demonstration of the art of packing:

"The most important thing is to fill every space. There! See? So they won't tumble loose and get crushed."

"Is that fur?"

"That's beaver." She held it up. "You may look if you like, just don't handle them, this Hong Kong weather is cruel on things."

"That's a lovely color."

"That I got because it's cheap." She started to show the whole lot. "People really pay for these things when there's a shortage of everything. That silver piece now, that really cost money."

She had gone on a shopping spree under cover of business. If she could not sell it she could always make use of it herself, there was always this to fall back on. But Lute was instantly ashamed of the thought. It was just her disappointment over her mother's reception of her big news. What had she expected? Her mother had always been old-fashioned about parental modesty, never to appear impressed for fear of her getting conceited. But she was no longer fascinated by her mother's things, they seemed fussy. Was her mother's taste changed or was she catering to the Chunking market? It was always easier to buy for other people. As in buying gifts, the stores were full of what seemed just the thing for somebody else.

The telephone rang. Dew took it.

"Hello? ... Ah, Tina. I was just putting the things away ... Yes, they turned up, but you know how it is, they love it but the minute they hear it's for sale it's this or that and they don't want it after all ... Never mind, it will bring more in the interior ... Yes, come over, I'm not dong anything."

Tina came with long hair swinging down her back over the flared flower skirt.

"Lute!" She wailed chidingly. "Oh Dew! she looks just like you now."

Dew smiled, seeming to be looking for an appropriate remark. A pent-up anger in Lute made her speak up smiling, surprising herself, "Please don't say that. It makes me happy of course but Mother will feel so insulted."

Dew was about to speak, then checked herself.

"Why?" Tina drawled uncertainly. "Of course she's glad that you look like her."

"Sit over here, I'll finish in a minute."

"I can't wait to tell you about last night, I died laughing."

"I knew there was going to be talk." Dew laughed her low excited laugh.

"Mrs. M.H. said, 'Who's that officer?' They saw you at the bar."

"A foreigner and a soldier," Dew said with mock horror.

"M.H. never said a word. Who was he, she asked and was it the same one as the one on the beach. Was he English? 'How should I know?' M.H. said. She said 'Can't you tell by his uniform?' He didn't answer."

"Old returned students like him are more old-fashioned than anybody else."

"What had it got to do with him? So ridiculous too the way she kept goading him."

"Ai-ya, Tina, it's hard to have friends nowadays. Friends speak one way in front of you, another way behind your back."

Whether or not Tina took it as a hint that she herself was no better, she did not stay long after that.

"I'll change and go to the beach," Dew said to Lute. "Come along, you ought to see it."

"I can't swim."

"You don't have to swim. Just find a place to sit and look around. It's supposed to be one of the most beautiful beaches in the world."

They set out together, Dew in a bat-winged sulfur yellow wrap. Lute wondered uneasily if her mother was making another effort to come closer like yesterday when they had walked and talked in the garden which only ended in mutual exasperation. Or did she think it was time that Lute should learn to be a little more sophisticated?

They stepped down a short incline from the highway and there was the untidy-looking sand. Lute looked around bewildered. Old brown shacks stood on stilts in front of evergreen bushes and barbwires. The big trees with scarlet blossoms called the flame of the forest stood way back out of the picture as though afraid to get their feet wet. Scattered all over were knots of people sitting on towels on the rumpled pocked sand, pale yellow like sawdust. She could see the backs of people sitting under big umbrellas like peddlers with nothing to sell when the country fair was nearly over. She supposed most were foreigners although there were a few Cantonese men, women and children pottering serious-faced at the water's edge. The sea was not as blue here as when it was out of reach. Even seen from the ferry boat it was a brighter blue.

"There's a lot of mosquitoes here," she explained, having to stop all the time to bend and scratch. Stooping down she could not help seeing her mother's stick legs, all straight from the knees down, atrophied by the binding of the feet. She had never noticed it before when her mother had seemed completely beautiful. A pair of white beach slippers hid the humped feet but looked a little clumsy like rain boots. She tried not to look. They were the same kind of feet whose every step gave birth to a lotus flower. The ancient compliment probably referred to the tip of a little red slipper coming out of the skirt at every step like a lotus petal on the floor. Here in the glare of the seaside and at the extremity of thin bare legs they were the cloven hoofs of Pan.

"They're sandflies, not mosquitoes," Dew said.

"Oh. No wonder they're called sandflies."

"They're small but they're worse than mosquitoes. Here, you can sit on this rock, nice view from here."

"Lute sat down and again had to scratch apologetically. "I'm terribly bitten."

"Don't scratch, it just makes it worse."

"I should have put on stockings to come here."

"Sit a while anyway, then you can go if you want to. The bus stop is right across the road. I'm going over there."

Dew jutted her chin vaguely seaward and turned and walked off, taking off her beach coat. Lute had a glimpse of a low-out white swimming suit with half hollow, half padded cups shown up startlingly against the pale sand before she waded in. Lute was so put out she watched the rest of the scene with no comprehension at first, her mother wading, an impersonal small figure now that could be anybody, and a waist-length man rearing up from the water or coming forward to meet her, Lute had missed seeing which it was. A sense of taboo switched her eyes away instantly as in reflex action. She had only had time to see it was a foreigner with wet brown hair matted over his forehead, a youngish face, rather long jutting chin and hefty white torso. By the time she looked back she had lost them successfully in the crowd.

The sandflies kept biting and she felt conspicuous sitting here scratching her legs under the slit gown. She got up and walked away slowly in case her mother should happen to be looking this way and would think she was prudishly hurrying off.

The next day she found Dew in bed, telling M.H.'s wife:

"I didn't get a wink of sleep. Tina came knocking at my door so late. This time Leonard was going to murder her."

M.H.'s wife laughed. "It ought to be easy for a surgeon."

"She was really scared."

"Did she sleep here?"

"Sleep! By the time she talked herself out it was ten o'clock in the morning."

"It was late enough when you people broke up. I didn't even hear M.H. turn in. Who won?"

"Tina and M.H. Didn't he tell you?"

"He's not up yet. How much did you lose?"

"I was the only loser. Leonard came out about even. M.H. is on a winning streak lately."

"That's why he wouldn't let me play for him. How much did you lose?"

"Eight hundred."

"That's quite a lot for mah-jong."

"It's those new-fangled tiles they put in."

The words eight hundred hit Lute dully, with no meaning at first. Wasn't that what she had brought yesterday? Why couldn't her mother at least lose seven hundred or even eight fifty? She found herself remonstrating with a god she did not believe in: Please, your joke is not funny. How was she to look Mr. Blaisdell in the face again, and he not even getting a professor's salary. She now saw that her mother had not wanted to tell how much she lost but after a moment of hesitation had told it anyway, tossing out the figure lightly, not looking at her, as though saying: There, see how far that goes.

"I can't stand this much longer," Dew was saying.

"Nobody can have a good time with the two of them at odds like this," M.H.'s wife said.

"Won't even let you get enough sleep."

"I was asking M.H. when we're leaving here."

"The sooner the better. Only my lizard skins are not ready yet."

"What lizard skins?"

"The batch I bought."

"Oh, the crocodile skins."

"Lizard. They're cheaper and the colors are lovely, nice for matching handbags and shoes."

"They ought to sell in the interior."

"That's what I thought, and Hong Kong is the place to get them made."

They went shopping and dropped Lute in town where she took a bus back.

The next day Dew was busy. The day after Lute called up to say she had to stay home to correct papers for the convent school. When she next came to the hotel nearly a week later there was a change in her manner. She no longer cared what her mother said or did. It was not any decision she had come to, just a realization of having come to the end of something, a closed door or a wall inches from her face so she could smell the faint odor of dust, blocked and slightly asphyxiated but with a sense of solidity and rest, knowing this was the end. She had first felt that the day her mother said I lost eight hundred.

9

Summer was long and brilliant in Hong Kong. At Repulse Bay Lute heard no talk of leaving. She stayed away as much as she could. Her mother began to notice and seemed angry at first, then suspicious.

"Have you been to see your teacher? What's his name, Blake?" she asked conversationally.

"Blaisdell. No, I wrote him a letter."

"How can you just take people's money and not even go and thank them?" Dew murmured half laughing embarrassedly.

"I can't just go to people's house."

"No, of course you have to telephone first."

"He has no telephone."

"No telephone? He told you?"

"No, but I heard he doesn't want a telephone in his house."

"Why? He sounds like an old philosopher. About how old is he?"

"Maybe forty."

"Is he married?"

"I don't know, I heard he lives alone."

After a pause Dew said, "How much salary does he get, that he can afford to be so generous?"

"They're supposed to be well paid compared to local people."

"Where does he live?"

"Stone Bay Road, it says on the envelope."

"Where is that?"

"I don't know. It must be very far."

"Next time we go for a drive we'll take you there so you can thank him in person."

Lute's voice rose. "But that's exactly what he doesn't want. He'll be so annoyed."

"He was just being modest."

"No, he really meant it."

"How do you know?"

"Because he is like that."

Dew said no more about it.

"I had a dream last night," she was talking to M.H.'s wife one day as she brushed her hair. Lute was also there. "I dreamt I was in the bathroom, I looked around and thought, where did all this blood come from?" She squinted worriedly at the mosaic tiles, acting it out. "I took a rag and started to mop up the floor. And ai-ya, I thought, why it's all over the place, on the wall, the pipes, everywhere. What happened? I thought."

M.H.'s wife laughed sitting on the bathtub rim. "It all came from this crying murder and running to you for help in the dead of the night."

"It must be. What else could it be? Such a strange dream. I was mopping, mopping and suddenly I found this brown paper parcel stuck behind the door. I dared not open it."

"The body cut up by the surgeon," giggled M.H.'s wife.

"I looked up and saw Lute was standing at the door. So I said, 'What on earth is this? Who's been in here?' Lute did not say anything and looked the way she always does, stiff and expressionless."

She had talked without once looking at Lute but Lute sensed her puzzlement and hurt. Sitting outside looking into the bathroom she turned the same blank face toward her mother. How did she come into this nightmare?

"Then? Then what happened?" M.H.'s wife asked.

"Then I said to Lute, 'What's this here? We can't just leave this here, the room boy will be coming in a minute.' Even as I was talking I could hear a pounding at the door and a rattling of doorknob."

She gestured with the hairbrush. The hotel was so quiet one could hear the faint boop-boop of the bristles half sucking on silken bouffant hair and in the distance the whirr of a lawnmower. There was a lot more to the dream but Lute had lost track of the story. No more mention of herself. But she had the feeling that for a moment there her mother had been afraid of being murdered by her. Her mind was instantly a tumult of protests: I never want her to die, all I want is to keep away so as to stay alive and sane. She's always going away anyway. If only she enjoys the time she spends with me instead of just wanting me to benefit from every minute of her company to make up for lost time and appease her conscience. She doesn't like me and I don't like people who don't like me.

M.H.'s wife wondered if he had wakened from his nap. She went back to their room. There was silence after she left. Lute stood at the nearest window looking out, ready to come to the bathroom door if Dew spoke. Dew often scolded her, in front of Mrs. M.H. too but there was nothing in her present behavior she could be scolded for.

She always stayed for tea and bath. Today she did not know how they were going to sit through tea together.

"Sister Dominic told me to go back early today. They're all going to the convent later," she said.

Dew inclined her head slightly with averted eyes.

She bathed before leaving and was just reaching for the towel when the door was flung open with a bang. As though breaking into a locked room Dew charged in angrily to get something from the glass shelf, a lipstick or tweezer, but looking sharply at her. She checked the impulse to cover herself with the towel in a convulsive movement that would seem guilty, but she could not be more indignant if it had been a stranger. Standing frozen in the water, chilled by the sense of exposure, in her mind she had a moment's full view of herself, wide thin shoulders, boyish breasts and long plump legs, the waist no thicker than a thigh. Dew slammed the bathroom door going out.

So her mother thought she had given herself to her history teacher for eight hundred dollars and she could perhaps tell by looking. The old stories were full of ways of telling. Some could judge by a girl's eyebrows, whether the hairs held together or sprawled. Lute could not get over how her mother always thought well of herself and yet instantly suspected the worst of everybody else. She cleaned the tub and got herself in hand. But when she came out she was still so angry the anger stood thick and solid outside her. She could feel the heavy wall alongside her cheek, not quite touching, and hampering her elbows and knees like clumsy armor. She was sure her mother could see it. But Dew did not look at her as she went.

Things continue when you think they can't. She came again several days later and it was like before, no better but no worse.

"A strange thing happened the other day," Dew said to her one afternoon at tea with lowered voice. "Somebody went through my trunks."

"What?" Lute cried, relieved at the chance to marvel and sympathize. "Is anything missing?"

"No, nothing was taken."

"That's odd."

"It was no thief. It was the police." Dew said boredly.

"Police!"

"When you didn't telephone I wondered if anything had happened at your end, if you were followed or warned off or something."

"By the police?"

"It's war time. They're suspicious."

"Of what? — Spies?"

"What else? They see me, a woman by herself, who's traveled a lot, who makes friends with foreigners and may seem mysterious."

At her mother's own description of herself Lute suddenly realized that she did look exactly like a Chinese Mata Hari.

"Which trunk was it?"

"This one."

Lute looked at it with awe.

"I was out and when I came back at night I noticed some of the things in the room were not the way I had them before. Strange, I thought, the boy had done the room in the morning. I opened the trunk to get something. I can always tell when somebody has touched my things even when everything has been put back in place."

"It's just clothes in there?"

"Also letters, photographs, all the odds and ends."

Photographs – Lute thought uneasily of the endless packages and envelopes holding stacks of snapshots of Dew's tiny lone figure posing against the coasts of Java, India, the Mediterranean, Shanghai, Hangchow, Macao, Tsingtao, Peitaiho.

"The hotel won't do anything about it?" she said uncertainly.

"I didn't speak to them. They won't tell you anything anyway if it was the police."

"What does Uncle M.H. say?"

"I didn't tell any of them. No use getting them alarmed. The only person I told this to was an English army officer, just to see what he says."

That was the man in the sea that she had seen.

"What did he say?"

Dew shrugged slightly. "He thinks I'm supersensitive, I must have imagined it."

"Is he connected with the police?"

"No, he's regular army. But the police may think I made friends with him to get information out of him. For all you know he may suspect it himself. I asked just to test him."

"Did he seem to know anything about it?"

"Hard to say. When you know a person all you know is his face, not his heart."

Dew was much given to these proverbs in verse that an amah Lute remembered used to declaim. Her last quote heaved out with a suppressed sigh reminded Lute of what she had said another time that as a woman grows older nobody has any real feelings for her.

"One of the reasons I didn't tell the others was there's too much gossip around here. So I was at sixes and sevens these days with nobody to talk to, and not a word from you. Such queer things happening one after the other, even you acting so strangely. I was thinking perhaps I made a mistake with you, telling you all the time where you did wrong instead of being polite to you like your aunt, letting you go your own way because she didn't care."

Habit made it the natural thing for Lute to hold her tongue once her mother got on this tack. But this time was a little different. Something was expected from her, some protestation of devotion. In what terms neither of them could imagine. Still Dew waited.

When she spoke again her voice was a little hoarse. "Just as someone who has helped you, it seems to me you ought to feel something in return, even if it was a stranger."

I would be grateful if it had been a stranger, Lute thought. A stranger had no obligations of any kind to me.

"I do feel it very much, Mother," she said smiling. "I told you how it's on my conscience. Although it's no use saying it now, I will return all the money."

How she had dreamed of handing her a boxful of roses with bundles of money underneath. Her mother would like that.

"I don't want any money from you," Dew raised her voice. "Money means very little to me. Even now hard pressed as I am I've never thought of investing in you hoping to — to —" she gestured helplessly and got the unthinkable words out with a little laugh, picturing herself as an old lady, "to live on you one day. But just between human beings people have feelings for those that have helped them. Thinking back I treated my mother right, I don't deserve to be paid back like this."

The chain had broken, Lute thought. It has lasted thousands of years but has to break some time, somewhere along the file of generations bound to one another by filial piety, that one-sided love, each professing a religious passion for his parent while understating his own weakness for his child. It's unfortunate when you happen to be the link that broke and what you gave to your mother is not returned by your daughter. It would not have mattered so much if you could have gone on touring the Western world, young and well-loved. Now that you feel you can no longer love with honor you want to come back, and are shocked everything is not the way it was in your mother's day.

"Ai-yo," Dew sighed, talking more and more like the amahs of her childhood in Nanking, "I get to wonder what sins I committed in my other lives, that I never finish paying for. I thought I've gone through enough but things still keep coming up, undreamed of things. Even you acting like this. Why? Surely you can be frank with me. Cruel as the tiger is, it does not eat its cub."

Another ringing quotation of peasant wisdom. Lute was perturbed herself but could not help thinking it was funny coming just now.

"I know your father hurt you very much, but you've always known I was different, I talked reason with you even when you were little."

No! Lute wanted to shout, outraged at the presumption as of a mere acquaintance talking as if he knew all about her. Father never hurt me. Because I never adored him.

She had missed what else her mother said. Now it was about her aunt.

"I don't know what your aunt told you about me."

"Aunt never said anything."

"It isn't that I keep things from you. There are things that you were too young to understand. As you know I've always believed love and the body are two different things, relations of flesh only spoils everything. I never wanted it. It's the others. They force me."

She started to cry. Her mouth dropped open, a small black gap in the earth brown mask of the unmade-up face that appeared longer and narrower than it was. Lute was too embarrassed to feel any shock. Still it was a surprise. Her mother had always advocated chastity so insistently with such conviction. Oddly enough even now in the confusion just after the thunderclap Lute never for a moment took her for a hypocrite. She preached what she really believed in. After her divorce she had left books and magazines behind in a wicker trunk that Lute had discovered on the unused top floor and had dug into with great joy. There was the complete translation of Arséne Lupin and an old historical novel called "The Unofficial History of a Goddess", which she had heard her mother mention more than once in recent years as one of her favorite books. The goddess was Chi Sai-erh, the beautiful sorceress of Chingchow who led a rebellion against the emperor. At fifteen, already conscious of her destiny, she had to submit to her parents' wishes and go through with an arranged match. She gritted her teeth and withstood the wedding night but made a pact with her husband afterwards. Since she had broken her body on his account and lost her chance for immortality he must not touch her again but he could take as many concubines as he wanted. After coming to Hong Kong Lute had been reminded of the Sorceress of Chingchow by the Cantonese amahs. Many of them had taken vows never to marry but sometimes a girl was betrothed against her wish. Rather than having her family break their word she went through the wedding ceremony and lived with the bridegroom for a few days, then ran away to find work in the city and never had anything to do with men again. She had preserved the family honor by proving herself a virgin. There could be no suspicion then that she had run away with a lover. It was an old custom in the country around Canton, the only way women had of escaping blind marriages and mothers-in-law. In other provinces without this outlandish custom there would seem to be no way out except learning magic and leading a rebellion against the emperor. Dew had also had to marry in order to prove she was a virgin. Malicious gossip was bound to make out that she was against the match because of some other man, her mother had argued while pleading with her.

"She wept to me, what could I do?" Dew had said explaining her divorce to Lute, going back to how she had got married.

Lute had not understood then but she did now seeing her mother cry. Although the chain had broken it still paralyzed her with a prickly feeling all over. The most reliable person in the world was crying, the sky had darkened and was about to fall, just as if she was still a child. She misunderstands, Lute thought, she thinks it's the men that turned me against her. I must tell her I don't think that way at all. Lute thought like the books she read, Shaw and Wells, except that to her the question of chastity was purely academic. If it concerned herself or somebody really close to her she might see it the Chinese way but in her mother's case she was purely rational. What difference does it make if she has affairs? Who is there for her to be faithful to, she thought. But how am I to tell her that it isn't this at all. Then what is it? I just don't like her? No, it's better to let her think it's this. Being Chinese she will think it's only right that I should feel this way. She'll be resigned. There is a beauty and dignity in seeing one's self as a sinner.

To keep from looking at her mother her eyes had rested unseeing on the wall mirror with varnished curlicues. With a start she recognized the face in it as her own, the high arched light eyebrows, blank almond eyes set wide apart and soft narrow nose. Dew did not notice her happy discovery. Deprived of her usual shield, the bathroom mirror, she addressed the space above her teacup. As to herself Lute knew she kept her eyes on the cold ageless ivory figurine's face in the mirror in order to remain cold. She could not stand the weeping and still less her own condemning silence, becoming more painful every minute. She hated to be misunderstood and longed to say, I'm not like that, I'll never judge you, besides you're right in everything you do, except sometimes toward me and that's only because we should not be together. Tell her the truth, never mind if she understands. She's cleverer than you. If you can't find the right words say something anyhow. She's suffering.

But Lute could not speak. The past had turned to stone and was spreading too quickly to the present, freezing her to the connected blocks and shapeless things. She felt it coming on around her mouth. Even if the lips would move the head was mindless rock. In despair she told herself it wouldn't last much longer, her mother would stop crying knowing it was useless, they would speak of something else and the moment would be gone forever. But it was unbearable, Dew sobbing in abandon, her mouth hanging open in her thin face leaned against a half fist, elbow on the table. Lute stood up and ran out of the room.

She downed the long brown passages in one gulp, impatiently swallowing the stairs. A white uniform ducked, holding a silver tray high on one hand. She must slow down. What would people think? The bellboys could easily find out which room she had come from. But a fury of gaucherie had her in its grip and she could not stop running. The same raffia-carpeted passage again stretched out before her with the same vista of draped purple wistarias coming at her fast. It was like being pursued in a nightmare, absurd as it was to think of her mother chasing her through the hotel corridors calling for her to come back.

At last she was out under the sky, knowing she had behaved abominably but too relieved to care. At least it was over. Running away like that she must have seemed the picture of shocked innocence, which was just as well. Let her mother think what she wanted. It was the only way. It was over now and she could trust her mother never to bring this up again. The sun was down but it was still bright when she walked to the bus stop. It must be getting dark in the room where Dew sat crying, she wouldn't have got up to turn on the light. No, she would have gone to wash her face long ago, maybe as soon as she herself had left. She wouldn't just sit there, people don't do things like that. But even on the bus she wanted to go back to that room. Probably nobody there now.

The bus jolted to a stop on a lighted street. They were already in the city. She looked out at a cotton padding shop where the stuff was fluffed out. The door was wide open because it was hot. Overhead lights shone down on a dais where the men beat the cotton with the cotton bow, a springy flat-pole they carried on one shoulder with a string running from end to end. Three of them stripped down to short pants stood half stooped and shifting nimbly around the raised floor. When they plucked the string the cotton flew in the air, they shuffled around seeming to dance to the music of the toneless twanging. Their slender golden torsos glistened with sweat. She could hear the faint bong-bong-bong-bong of the strings as the cotton snow came down in the golden room. The picture lasted only for a few minutes but it moved her greatly.

"I'm still among people," she said to herself, not knowing why she was saying this and why it should comfort her. In the agony that shut her in a box like madness, anything that came through was merciful relief, infinitely beautiful and touching.

She made herself telephone the next day to ask if she should come. She knew her mother would act as if nothing had happened. Tina was there that afternoon trying on clothes. Dew rubbed sunburn ointment on Tina's back and discussed a movie they saw.

"You ought to see it, Lute," Tina said.

"Go tomorrow," Dew said.

"Yes, give her a holiday, Dew."

The day after Dew was not in when Lute rang up. The next morning Sister Dominic called Lute to the phone. Her mother was up early, she thought.

"Is this Miss Lute Shen?" a man's voice said in English.

"Yes, who is this?"

"This is police headquarters. Can you come over this morning, Miss Shen? There're a few things we want to check with you."

"What is it about?" she asked. Every time something happened she went hollow and calm.

"Just a matter of routine. You're from Shanghai? And your mother is visiting here?"

"Y-yes?"

"It won't take a few minutes. Can you get here before eleven?"

"Where is the police headquarters?"

"60 De Vore Road. Ask for Captain Johnston."

"How do I get there?"

"Let's see, you take Number Four bus, don't you? Then change to Shovel Bay tram."

"Where do I get the tram?"

She got detailed instructions from him before she hung up. The more stupid the better, she thought, although she had not been pretending. She telephoned her mother to ask what she should tell them. Dew was out again. At quarter past ten in the morning?

10

She walked into a large office on the second floor. A narrow-faced drab blond officer looked up from one of the fenced-off desks when she asked for Captain Johnston, then went on writing. A swarthy husky man also in khaki came up to her.

"Miss Shen? Come this way, please."

He showed her to one in a row of cubicles and seated her beside the desk.

How do innocent people behave when summoned by the police for no reason? Probably resentful and jumpy. But she must be overdoing it. The dark man glanced at her.

"It's just routine, a few questions to ask you. Would you like a cup of tea?"

"No, thanks."

"Just a cup of tea. We were going to have some ourselves."

"All right, thank you."

He rang the bell. A scrawny Chinese materialized, dressed in a white shirt like a clerk.

"Two teas."

The man disappeared without a word leaving a smell of bare feet in sneakers.

"You don't smoke, do you?"

He lit a cigarette himself. The blond officer sidled in quickly carrying himself like a furled umbrella.

"This is Captain Johnston. I'm Inspector Marevalo," said the dark man who looked Macaonese and could have been Sister Dominic's nephew with the same broad countenance and thick eyebrows and lashes. He did the talking and taking notes. Johnston merely sat in on the interview, a big notebook open in front of him. What could that be? A "file" on her mother? He kept turning the pages as if for reference. It could not be all about her? As Lute saw it upside down she could only see it was loose-leaved and typewritten. She was beginning to feel frightened and with it came an urge to laugh as though she was already telling about it afterwards, not to her mother who would be furious if she laughed but to somebody like Bebe or Aunt Coral. There was no getting rid of the feeling that this was rather a lark. She was used to trusting the police. She felt at home sitting at here and not more nervous than at an oral examination in school. Marevalo took notes like a bad student, laboriously, at random and very little. She wished he would let her jot it all down herself.

"How old is your father?" "How old is your mother?" And later to catch her lying, "Your father is older than your mother by how many years?" That would never confuse her. They were the same age.

She had qualms naming her mother's friends in Shanghai, Captain Boudinet for instance, was it really necessary? But isn't it always better to tell the truth especially when there is nothing to hide?

"Did you know Marquis Lo?"

"He was my uncle." Wait till Aunt Coral hears this. They even found out about him.

"How was he related to your mother?"

"He was just my father's cousin."

"But your mother knew him very well?"

"No, she seldom saw him."

"She must have known him well. Didn't she put up the money to help free him?"

"No, that was my aunt."

"But it was your mother's money?"

"Borrowed by my aunt."

How did they know all this? Dew would not have told them unless they had brought it up first. She had that sinking feeling of realizing an illness was coming on that was not the matter of a few days. She took a sip of the hot milky tea almost hungrily. Marevalo seemed jarred by her movement. Did he think her mouth had suddenly gone dry?

"Did he come often to your mother's house?"

"Marquis Lo? Never. The fact is we only saw him once."

"In your mother's house?"

"No, his house."

"She went there often?"

"No. It was his wife's house, he didn't live there."

Her only concern right now was not to say anything that would make her mother angry.

"Did you forward any letters for your mother? After you came to Hong Kong."

"No. The mail still goes anywhere from Shanghai."

"Did you forward any parcels to Chungking?"

"No."

"To anywhere else in the interior?"

"No."

He got up and sauntered out of the partition to stretch his legs or freshen up. But Johnston took over without losing a moment, referring to his big book.

"Marquis Lo was assassinated when?"

"I can't remember. – 1938."

"He never returned the money to your mother?"

"No, that was between my mother and my aunt."

To be more convincing she gave them the story of her aunt's love affair with the son of the Marquis. She was betraying no secret. Her mother was sure to have told them if the matter had come up, as it must have. Marevalo rejoined them. Neither took notes.

"So my aunt took the money without telling her."

"But they're still friends?" Johnston asked.

"Only outwardly."

"They still lived together."

"To save expenses."

"Your mother was hard up?"

"Yes."

"She has money now?"

"She hasn't got much money."

"She stayed at Repulse Bay Hotel. For over a month now."

"I suppose my aunt returned her the money."

"You don't know for sure?"

"No, I didn't ask."

"You seem to know very little about your mother."

"It's our sense of privacy."

"That's very unusual in a Chinese family, isn't it?"

"They were separated for years," Marevalo spoke up unexpectedly. They were like gangsters she had read about who work in pairs, one telling the other, "You be the red face, I'll be the white face." In Peking opera the warrior wears red paint while the cultured person is fair-complexioned. One of them would be fierce and threatening while the other is reasonable, almost siding with the victim against his partner. The grateful man breaks easily. Of the two here, Johnston being British naturally played the villain. Marevalo had Chinese blood in him and no doubt spoke fluent Cantonese although he did not use it today.

Johnston leaned back and let him take her over the same grounds again.

"Did you know any of your mother's Japanese friends?"

"She doesn't know any Japanese. She hates them."

"She doesn't mind Germans, does she?"

"She doesn't know any Germans."

"Do you know Dr. Immelhausen?"

Again the jolt of a familiar name. "He's just our doctor."

"Did he come often to the house?"

"Only when I was sick. I had typhoid."

"What is his full name?"

"I don't know."

Johnston questioned her again. And what was the difference between her parents' ages?

He finally closed his book saying:

"Thank you, Miss Shen, but we may have to talk to you again."

Lute gasped incredulously.

"It's very inconclusive," he said.

Marevalo said frowning with lowered voice, "We're very sorry. Security is a big problem here, with the war."

Lute was suddenly reminded of something that she was never quite sure of — the Japanese were right on the other side of Kowloon. Unlike the proud and publicized Lone Island of Shanghai, here nobody wanted to say anything about it except that it was safe, it was British. But wasn't Japan one of the Axis countries and England at war with the Axis?

"Of course you have to be careful," she cried sympathetically.

They both looked a little startled and suspicious. This was no time for her to be reasonable.

She had been in there three hours. She telephoned from a grocery store nearby. Dew was still out. She asked for M.H.'s wife.

"We called you but you were not in," M.H.'s wife said.

"I'm telephoning from outside. I can't get Mother."

"She's not back yet. They had her in for questioning. This is too ridiculous for words."

"I've just been to the police station myself."

"Can you come over? Talk after you get here."

She found M.H.'s wife alone in her room.

"It started yesterday when we went down to lunch. A police officer came up and asked to speak to us, so M.H. and I went with him to the lounge. Asked about our trip. Mostly about your mother. It turned out the Wus had also been questioned. We didn't see her at lunch so we called up and she was out. She was often out by herself so we just kept calling her room, not sure what to do. First thing this morning the man was here again. M.H. nearly lost his temper. Then we found out she hadn't been back last night. We really got worried. That's when we telephoned you."

"Where is she, he didn't say?"

"We didn't know at the time that she wasn't here. M.H. has gone to see the consul. Don't worry, it will all be straightened out, only it's so maddening."

Tina and Leonard Wu came in to find out if there was news. Seeing Lute they told their story over again. They had also been questioned a second time this morning.

"Now we've had a taste of a colony," Leonard said. "We Chinese say China is a half colony. Still there's a difference."

"It's true the British dare not act like this in Shanghai," M.H.'s wife said.

"They're highhanded enough in the Settlement but still not like this," he said.

"But of course. Hong Kong is theirs," Tina said.

"They must be jittery on account of the war," M.H.'s wife said.

"No matter what they can't treat friendly nationals like this," Leonard said.

"We would have left long ago," M.H.'s wife said, "but your mother said there's still work on the lizard skins not finished."

"You know your mother, Lute, she's never in a hurry," Tina said.

"What a trip," sighed M.H.'s wife. "Who'd have thought ...?"

"What did they ask you, Lute?" Tina said exasperatedly.

Lute repeated some of the questions.

"About the same as they asked us, eh, Leonard?"

Leonard Wu, small boyishly handsome and like a small boy too careful with his manners, already spoke more today than he ever did.

"Dr. Wu, do you know anything about this German doctor?" M.H.'s wife said.

"Yes, why did they ask about Dr. Immelhausen?" Lute said.

"M.H. was going to him but he went back to Germany," M.H.'s wife said. "At his age, after thirty, forty years in Shanghai. The Germans in Shanghai were lucky to be out of the war and not interned or anything."

"There was talk that he was suspected of spying," Leonard said.

"No wonder. So that's why they suspect Dew," M.H.'s wife gave a low cry.

"But isn't that silly?" Tina said. "Anybody could have been his patient." But her voice trailed away guiltily.

They fell silent, evidently inhibited by Lute's presence.

"M.H. didn't telephone?" Leonard asked.

"No, he didn't."

"The main thing now is to get in touch with her first of all," Leonard said.

"Leave it to M.H., he knows people," Tina said.

"M.H. doesn't know anybody in Hong Kong," his wife said.

"Still he's known. Not like us," Tina said.

"Of course he does what he can. Can't you think of some of her English friends? As M.H. said, we yellow faces are no use here, it has to be white faces."

"There's that Lieutenant Blackwell, but I don't know about him, haven't seen him around ever since this happened," Tina said.

That was the English army officer, Lute thought.

"No use if he didn't know her before," M.H.'s wife said.

"What about Hennings? We might send him a telegram," Leonard said.

"We don't have his address," Tina said.

"Send it to his firm in Calcutta."

"Is he in India?" Lute asked. It did not surprise her that he was the one that Dew was going to. It would be somebody like him.

"Yes, he's left Shanghai," Tina said.

"He can still vouch for her," he said.

"If only he's here," Tina said.

"Well, see what the consul says," M.H.'s wife said.

"The consul is the person to see," Leonard said.

"We'll know when M.H. comes back," Tina said.

The Wus drifted out.

It was a long afternoon, already getting dark when M.H. came back. He held up a hand, palm outward and shook it from side to side.

"Don't even mention it," he said to his wife before she spoke a word. "Maddening. The consul went to see several people. They talked officialese at him. War time and all that, and they just have her in for questioning, no need for lawyers."

"How can they hold people just like that?" his wife cried.

"They're at war."

"They're not at war with Chungking," she pointed out.

"They know Chungking won't care," he grunted annoyed at her. "What is a Chinese subject without backing?"

"But they know about you," Lute said.

"I have no influence, I haven't been working for the government these many years."

"But as long as they know about you here." What she wanted to say was "Doesn't it mean anything to have you vouch for her?"

"I can only tell them the truth," he said in a reasonable tone, "that we saw very little of your mother although we're relatives. Until this trip, and that was only because we happened to be going the same way."

"The fact is we didn't know a thing about all those things they asked us," his wife said.

"I didn't either," Lute said.

"Of course it's just a stupid mistake, all comes from lack of consideration for the Chinese," M.H. said.

"Where is she?" his wife asked.

"That's what the consul is trying to find out. He'll see the Commissioner tomorrow."

"Would you like a hot towel?"

He nodded. His wife went into the bathroom and ran the water until it was boiling hot. Meanwhile he asked Lute about her interview.

"Why don't you go back and ask them, insist you have to know where your mother is? You're not a transient here, you're a student at the university and that means something here."

"Oh, does it?"

"Yes, the university is quite a power on this island, it's an official institution."

"I'll go right now, in case they're still in the office."

The lights were on in the police station. Nobody stopped her going upstairs. There the deserted corridor smelled of stockingless feet in sneakers more strongly than in the daytime. The door to the office was locked. Was her mother somewhere in the house? The large old office building was deceptively homey under dark yellow light bulbs. Better not be caught wandering around. Still she stood at the office door stupidly turning the doorknob with her shadow on the grey unlit frosted pane. A policeman came down the passage, his footsteps loud on the dark brown floor with linoleum sheen. Johnston and Marevalo had gone home he told her, so she left.

She was by now so used to climbing the hill at night the way seemed much shorter. The familiarity was especially comforting tonight. Deep down she was convinced it was like any other mishap her mother had had traveling, the time her father seized the luggage before the ship sailed, the trouble with the visa when going ashore in New York. She could hear her mother and her aunt talking about it after it was all over, their outraged half laughing voices. She wished Coral was here, she was so good at rescues. She had got the Marquis out even when he was guilty. The *luang* had spoken to the Marquis in a poem about the dragon flying up to heaven aided by a storm. He was congratulated by the other devotees who had all heard rumors that he was going to head the new puppet government. A few days later he was shot down coming out of the house of the *luang*. Bright had told Coral there was this story going round. Lute pushed the Marquis out of her mind. Hadn't he done enough?

She had a feeling that M.H. had more to tell his wife after she was gone. The Chinese had a way of withholding information from old ladies and children, extending to all incompetents. She could understand the anger of the Marquise when Bright and Coral kept things from her during the rescue. But she could hardly blame M.H. for treating her as her mother did. Besides they probably judged her rightly.

Halfway up she passed the professors' houses, empty and pitchdark. She did not know where they could have gone this summer with the war on. Mr. Blaisdell was in Hong Kong. But she would not go to him for help. Something in her plunked down like a shutter blacking out the merest thought of associating him with her mother in any way. M.H. had said the university was a powerful institution here. What about the Dean? He lived in one of these little houses. He must be away. The Registrar? Or even the Chancellor, never seen except on speech days. Wouldn't her mother be angry if she went around spreading the story, trying to make them vouch for a woman they knew nothing about? At a time like this she could understand why the emperor's officials when faced with emergency generally had recourse to doing nothing. There was always more likelihood of being blamed for doing the wrong thing than for not having thought of the right thing to do. Leave it to M.H. Her mother trusted him. But she was going back to the police station tomorrow. That was M.H.'s suggestion.

Sister Dominic never said anything when she opened the door for her. But Lute had the impression that the police had been there to investigate her. Sister Dominic had probably telephoned the Mother Superior for instructions and was not going to ask her any questions. The Church would keep out of this.

11

She went again to ask Johnston and Marevalo where they were holding her mother. Unable to act the distraught daughter, all she did was to subject herself to another long interview in which they questioned her in relays. She told M.H. and his wife about it in their hotel room that evening.

"Don't go any more," he said. "There's always the danger of saying something wrong and making it worse."

He had been in town all day with little results. There was nothing to do but wait to hear from the consul. He looked rattled. When Lute apologized and thanked him again for his trouble he answered:

"I do what little I can, but it's difficult to be of help when you don't know much about it."

"Even I, not to say him," his wife chimed in, "your mother and I grew up together, we're like sisters, even I don't know anything about all that, the French officer and the German doctor."

"The strange thing is how they knew everything," he said.

"There's a ghost in this." His wife glared at him with her plump chin going up, then turned away boredly. Evidently they had been over this before.

"A ghost?" Lute said.

"How do you suppose they know so much about what happened in Shanghai?" she asked.

"I thought they investigated."

"Where could they have found out all that? She's not known to the police in Shanghai."

"Didn't they suspect her because of Immelhausen?"

"Who told them she knew him?" She held Lute's eyes in a fixed stare, almost accusingly. "Tell me if it isn't strange."

No, she did not name Dr. Immelhausen as one of her mother's friends — never thought of it — Lute told herself nervously.

M.H.'s wife finally said, "Who else but some nosey friend of hers who keeps a clear account of other people's business. Not like me — so hazy I didn't even know about this British officer, right under our nose."

Her husband looked affronted at the very mention of Lieutenant Blackwell and became silent.

"This one is also a bad one," his wife continued, "never came around once after this happened, just pulled his head in his shell. I won't be surprised if he's the one that started this. We've been followed everywhere we went this last month, I can tell from the questions they asked."

"But who was it that told them about Shanghai?" Lute asked.

"Think." M.H.'s wife glared at her with an upthrust of chin. "Who else is there?"

"Why would she do a thing like that?"

"Hard to tell with such people. Your mother sensitive as she is gets herself hated sometimes."

"You can't say things like that about people without proof," her husband said disapprovingly.

"I was only telling Lute."

"Do you think she went to the police?" Lute asked.

"That I can't tell. Your mother did say Tina knew all sorts of people. Getting to be a power in the French Concession when they were in Shanghai because she knew the French police."

"Really?" Lute said, out of her depth.

"Threw parties for them, invited them to the house." Looking away with an offended air she tossed back over her shoulder as if that explained everything, "She speaks French."

"Yes, they both do," Lute said.

"It probably didn't hurt Dr. Wu to have backing. He had his own hospital in the French Concession."

"All that was in Shanghai," M.H. said irritably.

"I just can't help getting riled, you running around all day at your age, begging favors from strangers. Even a dragon cannot fight local snakes. And other people sitting in the shade talking coolly. Lute, you should hear some of the things they say. It's only by comparison you see the difference in people's hearts. I shouldn't be blaming your mother at a time like this, but she seems changed to me ever since we came to Hong Kong. The truth is I was surprised at her sometimes. Look at these people she takes for friends, Tina, and that Blackwell. Nowadays with trouble all over the world it's not like ordinary times, it's dangerous not to look closely before you make friends."

Lute said nothing, thinking, I don't like it when others criticize her but don't I also feel superior because she has got herself into this mess? Most of us don't really get to know our parents until they are starting to crumble. Time is on our side against them. Just because we survive them we think we are the fitter to survive. Dew has gone far on her bound feet from one era to another without breaking her ladylike pace. She wants the best of both worlds East and West and is aggrieved when anything was denied her, a faithful daughter or devoted alien lovers. All lives are equal, Buddha said. Not just legally or even with regards to possessions and opportunities but in charm and beauty and cleverness, in every way in which human beings appear to differ. To Lute they are more alike than they seem and her sympathies were always with those that asked for no more than fairness, knowing they were going to get less.

She had gloried in her mother's pioneering divorce but had no real concept of what the marriage had been like. She had loved her home and even her father. Her mother's own brief accounts of how she had been forced to marry was the same story that Lute was to read a thousand times in contemporary fiction and no more real. Several years ago she had gone to see Coral one day when a distant aunt happened to be there. They had been talking about how they had first met at Dew's wedding.

"It's strange how some brides look beautiful and some not as good as on other days." Coral had said.

"How did Mother look?" Lute asked.

"She was beautiful," Coral said.

"She wore the palace aigrette, I wore the phoenix crown at my wedding."

"Some say it's not good to be beautiful as a bride," Coral said.

Lute had seen an old-fashioned wedding only once when an uncle on the Yangs' side got married. She went with her cousins Pillar's daughters who told her:

"It's going to be a real old-style wedding, flowered sedan chair and all. Real fun."

They did not have such weddings any more in the city. Even the most conservative family had what was called civilized wedding with the Wedding March and exchange of rings.

"What made them decide to have it like this?" Lute asked.

"The bride's family wants it. Fourth Uncle says he doesn't mind."

"Has he seen the bride?"

"Oh yes. It's an arranged match but they've met."

The grimy old house was decorated with scarlet and green sashes draped over doorways dangling hydrangea balls of puckered silk. The bridegroom was similarly ornamented with a scarlet cordon ending in hydrangea balls of like material. He was a rather tough-looking young man incongruous with his gown and jacket and elderly black satin skull cap. He smiled when he was teased and teased back when it was with a pretty girl.

"Just wait till it's your turn," he said to Pillar's eldest daughter. "Fourth Uncle will show you. It won't be long now."

"Look how pretty Fourth Uncle is. Ring the bell," she said and pulled at the silk ball.

"Not as pretty as you."

He seized her hand but she snatched it off and backed away glaring.

"Fourth Uncle is the worst. The bride will be here in a minute, and still so cheeky."

Her third sister who was thirteen like Lute stamped her feet and called out laughing:

"Hey-eh hey-eh hey-eh! Fourth Uncle, shameless! You're the bridegroom and still going after girls."

He gritted his teeth. "Little monkey, you're the worst."

He came at her threateningly. She ran and ducked behind Lute spinning her around.

"Fourth Uncle shameless!" she sang and streaked off.

"The little monkey," he muttered.

He was surrounded by another group of giggling guests.

"Laugh away," he said. "I don't care. I'm the performing monkey today."

"Hey-eh hey-eh hey-eh!" Lute's third cousin flashed by again singing, "Fourth Uncle shameless."

"I will catch you."

He chased her from one room to another bumping into guests and amahs. When he finally gave up she leaned panting against Lute.

"Fourth Uncle is bad," she said between her teeth but with a strange light in her narrowed eyes.

They milled around the house for hours. Finally they heard firecrackers outside the front door.

"The bride is here! The bride is here!"

The girls raced for the door. A small crowd had already gathered on the street looking and laughing at the flowered sedan chair.

"I didn't know these things were still for rent," somebody said.

"A real old curiosity now," another said.

The closed chair advanced, studded with baubles and tinseled spires, rows of worn pink tassels undulating against the red cloth walls. The four coolies set it down. Another round of firecrackers and two amahs came up to help the bride out. The piece of scarlet cloth that muffled her head hung loose over her face ending just under the neck, giving the impression of a chin sticking out. It enlarged the head and made her a red ghoul with a hatchet profile. She wore an embroidered ensemble of scarlet jacket and skirt under the monstrous head.

She entered the house with an amah at each elbow. The bridegroom joined her to kowtow to heaven and earth and his ancestors. She was ushered to the curtained bed and seated there, a demon in its shrine. The guests gathered around and made the bridegroom come near. Somebody handed him a scales stick. With a little urging he poked the stick under her headcloth and lifted it.

"Throw it on the canopy! Throw it harder!" a woman cried.

He thrust it up playfully and it stayed up.

The bride sat unveiled amidst a momentary uncomfortable hush of disappointment. Her plump face was somewhat large and long, vacant and thick-lipped. She did not wear a phoenix crown or palace aigrette, just a stiff new permanent wave. The bridegroom was made to sit down by her side and the joking started. But it was not as much fun as Lute's cousins had promised her. It was a dismal farce. She could not imagine her mother in it.

Her mother had a pair of wedding scrolls that she had seen on the wall when she was a baby in amahs' arms. Framed embroideries of *dwuan* script, the earliest hieroglyphs, like many-colored long-tailed birds on pale pink satin, they were the first words she had been taught to read but there were two characters she never could remember:

"Grace the chamber, grace the house, grace the —

Abound in blessings, abound in years, abound in sons."

These among many other things had been specially made for her dowry by commission to well-known embroiderers of the Shiang school. The equivalent of a small factory was set to work for her while she was still trying to get out of it. The parade of gifts arrived. The dowry went off in another parade. Each pageant made the inevitable day more ironclad with every nail knocked in. Finally she kowtowed to her mother and ancestors in farewell and was put in the flowered sedan chair, shut in the gently heaving dark box and expected to weep all the way. Firecrackers gave her a warlike send-off. The band walking in front made an exciting confusing music like a hundred flutes playing the same tune but not in the same time, the one just slightly behind the other. They had dressed her like a corpse in many layers of clothing and underclothes. Her head was muffled in the same red cloth that covered the face of the dead. The preoccupation with virginity made this the end of a woman. She was given over to fate, severed with her past and no longer had a future. The wedding bore all the marks of a human sacrifice, the honor, the terror and weeping. A popular phrase of the 1920's had been "man-eating ritualism". It was hard to see it that way now when the old rituals had become funny. The system was dead, so was Dew's mother for whose sake she went through with it. It robbed her sacrifice of all purpose but did not give her back her life. It no longer mattered what she did with herself.

Still she had minded what people would say except perhaps on this last trip after fretting so long to get away and bent on a last fling before marrying again. What was Hennings doing to help her? Did he get the telegram? Lute had asked yesterday and got a vague answer. Apparently after talking it over they had put off sending it, not sure whether Dew would mind having him hear about the other men involved. Perhaps Tina had advanced the idea and none of the others had wanted to risk getting the blame. I'm just as bad, Lute thought. There must be something I can do. Am I really such a useless fool? She lay in bed thinking over her conversations with the police, tormented by what she had said wrong, knowing even then that she was being evasive. Was that the extent of her responsibility, not saying anything wrong?

She was going to Repulse Bay after lunch but she called up M.H.'s room at half past nine in the morning to find out if the telegram to Hennings had been sent.

"272 no answer," chanted the Eurasian girl at the switchboard.

"Will you please see if they're in the dining room?"

"Hold on a minute please."

After a long time the singsong voice came back. "272 not in dining room."

She left a message for them to call back. What had happened now? Both of them out so early? She made herself wait another half hour before she rang up again.

"272 no answer." Then "272 not in dining room."

"Can I speak to Room 206, Dr. or Mrs. Wu?"

"One minute please."

Lute braced herself. Most likely it would be Tina who came to the phone.

"206 has checked out."

The ground underfoot hollowed out like a drawer pulled out noisily.

"Checked out? Do you mean they have left? When?"

"One minute. Hold on ... 206 checked out this morning at 10:15."

She got ready to go to Repulse Bay at once. The phone call caught her just when she was leaving.

"Is this Lute? She's out," M.H.'s wife said irritably as though saying "High time," so as not to seem overjoyed. "Come in the afternoon, she's resting now."

"Is she all right?"

"Yes, everything all right. Did you ring up earlier? We were in your mother's room. All right, so you'll be here around three."

About three o'clock she knocked at the door. It seemed a long moment before it opened a crack. Her mother's shrewdest face peered out darkly with the light behind her. Without a word she walked away in her white brocade dressing gown back to the trunk she was packing, half open like a giant clam standing upright. Lute closed the door.

"Mother," she murmured beaming weakly to show overwhelming relief.

"What an incredible business," Dew said arranging the lapels of coats hung in the trunk.

"At least it's over now."

"They have no right to hold me, war or no war, as I told them. They can't do things like that even in their own colonies."

"Was it — all in the station house?"

"Of course. They can't put me in jail just like that. Even then it can be counted against you next time you want visas to go anywhere, that's why I was so furious. I told them, you have no evidence whatsoever, you know you'll have to let me go in the end and it had better be now."

"Were they — polite?"

"Yes, they know they couldn't frighten me."

"You weren't uncomfortable."

"At a time like this does one still think of comforts? You realize how serious it was?"

She was clearly annoyed by Lute's smile and respectful inanities as if inquiring after an elder with an embarrassing disease. No matter how little feelings she had, at a time like this happy tears would not be out of place. Lute knew.

Dew went on talking, reiterating what she had said to the police but not what they had said to her. When it came Lute's turn to tell of her interviews she found herself skipping and gliding over things from a feeling that Dew did not really want to hear them.

"When was it you first saw them? Tuesday?" she interrupted looking straight at Lute for the first time today, from deep inside her heavy lashes.

"No, Wednesday."

The somber shaded eyes reflected, as though making some calculations. Counting the days? To see if it could be Lute who had unwittingly let out all that about the Marquis and Boudinet and Immelhausen?

"Is Tina gone?" Lute asked.

"How did you know?"

"I asked for her when I couldn't get Auntie M.H. on the phone."

"Hey-ya, such a joke. When I was back she burst in here and oi-ya! how she worried, she nearly died and Leonard was so angry with the British, they couldn't stand one more day in British territory, only they couldn't just go off leaving me here. Then something came up in Hanoi that couldn't wait, and now that I'm out they can leave with a clear conscience. I'm no fool, I don't need Mrs. M.H. to point it out to me, I know who set this wild fire on me. What I don't understand is how one can do such a thing without thinking ahead. Move your bowels behind the door — how long can you hide it? Unless the British just shoot me just like that. But when men want someone to die he does not die, only when heaven wants someone to die he dies. So you run off, but in this world nowadays I won't be so sure we'll never come face to face again."

"Did they go by plane?"

"Lucky there were still seats, she said. Probably booked beforehand. They were running out on me, Leonard must be afraid too of getting involved. I don't know if he suspected it was Tina's doing, how chilling that would be, a woman capable of that, always by your side. I thought I'd seen through friendship – hasn't your aunt done enough? Hey-ya, just to think nowadays even married couples can divorce, what are friends after all? But friend or no friend, to do such a thing – kill with a borrowed sword. Even Mrs. M.H. – she accuses Tina but what about they themselves? They told the police they knew nothing about me, it just happened we were traveling together, just as though I was using M.H. as a shield. It probably did me as much damage as anything else. We Chinese are so afraid the minute we have a name or position. A leaf falls and we fear it will break our head. Now they say they can't go to Chungking because of this trouble I had here. Such a joke! It wasn't as if I was convicted for spying – they let me go because they had nothing on me and just to save face told me the case was not closed. If there's still danger of being implicated, why we're not even traveling together from here on. It's just that M.H. is too well-known, she says, people are liable to pick on him. It's not for me to tell M.H. he may not be as important as all that. So they're going house-hunting, going to settle down in Hong Kong for the time being. All my fault. The strangest thing is everywhere I go I come across strangers who're so good to me, nurse me when I'm ill, spare me all kinds of trouble, get angry on my account, go out of their way to do things for me and so thoughtful they think of every little thing." Her voice stiffened with rising tears. "It's the people closest to me who treat me the worst, the nearer the more heartless. Ai-yo, say no more."

Lute said nothing. She was past caring, there was just the desolation of an end that seemed endless.

Dew went on packing. When she had buttoned down a flap she straightened up saying, "That's that."

She indicated the table with her chin.

"This letter from your aunt came day before yesterday. It's been steamed open, I can tell. Those few days I wasn't here they must have turned the whole room upside down. Maybe planted microphones. Your aunt says she has a friend now. Funny I thought, as long as I was there she had none, the minute I was gone she got one. Doesn't it seem like I was to blame? She just got a promotion too. Everything comes right the minute I go away."

Lute did not say anything and thought nothing either, allotting her aunt all the space she needed around her, not even wondering whether the man friend was Chinese or foreign, married or single and whether they were going to get married.

"Stand back," Dew said struggling to tie up her sewing machine like roping a steer.

It had brown paper wrapped around it. She was amazingly strong and wiry, still Lute felt guilty not helping. But it was impossible to poke a hand in without snarling up everything.

"I'm going to need this," she said. "The tailors are no good in the interior, or India either."

"Aren't they?"

"No," she jerked her head impatiently toward the far side. "I brought this back from France, never got a chance to use it in Shanghai. Lots of things I started that I could easily run up myself, and use right now, but there never was time."

Her things were scattered flowerlike around the room. The caravan was setting out again. M.H.'s room had the same view and furnishings, yet looked dismal compared to this.

"Here, hold this for me," she said. "Don't pull, just hold it."

There was a knock on the door. A bellboy brought in a padlocked high tin box.

"The lizard skins," Dew said after he had left. "I wouldn't have stayed here so long except to wait for those shoes and purses, and you know what they told me this morning when I telephoned the workshop? They haven't started yet, said they hadn't come to an agreement on the price and were still waiting to hear from me."

"How was that possible? Did they misunderstand?"

"They just want to raise the price, that's all. Bullying people from the outer provinces. So I said all right, never mind, give it back to me right away. I'm leaving in a few days."

She unlocked the box, carefully peeled a skin off the top layer and opened it out. It was exactly like a huge banana leaf, the same deep green color with the same veins and bulges, so beautiful Lute had a pang of heartache at the folding crease down the center, worn whitish. She could understand why her mother wanted to buy them.

"They're from Malaya," Dew said.

It was surprisingly cold inside the tight-packed box. Where did it get that cold dankness? From the monsoon rains of the jungle or the Hong Kong workshop?

"Can you get them made in India?"

"No, it's expensive there and no good. As long as M.H. is going to stay here I'll just leave it with them. If they have to leave they can always send it to your aunt, she'll get it made for me in Shanghai."

"Is Aunt still keeping the apartment?"

"Yes, half of it is still mine. I want a place to land my feet on when I get back."

She had brought so much luggage Lute had thought she had left Shanghai for good.

"My things are still there," she said to Lute's amazement, discounting her seventeen pieces of baggage. "Your aunt can't stand having anything around but I couldn't just throw everything away, it will cost money too to buy new ones. Although nowadays you never can tell whether anything is still yours. My things in Paris, the concierge let me move them to the cellar and promised to take care of them but with the war, who knows if they're still there."

She put out roots everywhere as if to convince herself she would be coming back. Lute supposed it assuaged the sadness of leaving but it also took away from the beauty of a wanderer's life. She would never just get up and go, she must threaten to come back any time so nobody dared forget her, and leave her things like a tail in the door.

She had talked all this time without looking directly at Lute, the best she could do just now for a confidante. When at last she had come to a stop and silence set in, although she had never expected anything from Lute she felt somehow disappointed, with a sense of loss. She sat not speaking, pressing her lips tight and pinching in her cheeks. With a shock Lute saw how she had aged. Just two, three days in a detention room could not have done it, it must have been the worry. Once the fugitive Wu Tze-hsu had had trouble crossing the Djao Pass and in one night his hair and beard had turned white and he was able to get through unrecognized. With her it was not grey hair or wrinkles. She just looked like a different person. She had gone much darker, perhaps a retroactive tan from the beach. She did not look Chinese, more like some of the smoky brown peoples of Southeast Asia who grew darker, thinner and ferocious-looking as they grew older. How was Hennings going to take it? No, she would change back as soon as she became happy. To Lute it was not a natural thing for her mother to age. Blackwell's betrayal must have hurt her even more than Tina's.

Her boat was to sail the next week. Lute came every day. M.H.'s wife was with Dew most of the time but they both seemed to have talked themselves out, clarifying their own stands during the incident without getting much understanding. M.H.'s wife was plaintive rather than aggrieved and did not want to hide all of it. Though properly solicitous she spoke shortly and her round mound of a face was one big pout. With Lute she was stiff and wary. She should not have said those things about Dew to her daughter. Lute had probably repeated them to Dew, if not about her affair with Blackwell. Maybe that also.

The last afternoon Dew stood before the big mirror pinning on a carved jade brooch. She was made up rosy beige, all the features carefully delineated. It had the effect of bathing her in a cruel light. She wore a black suit with pale green jade squares for buttons that matched her brooch. Lute had admired it before but now it seemed too flamboyant. Then she was struck by the way her mother was looking into the mirror, intently observant as always but this time with such a tragic love, pouring out the whole force of her personality into the eyes on the other side and the eyes had never been so huge and limpid black under the lashes or so blazing and commanding, as if she wanted to hold her own attention to the eyes alone so she would not see the waning face with the lower half partly missing.

"There's no point in your going to the wharf. The Cheungs will see me off," she said.

Lute saw them into the taxi.

"I'll telephone you, Lute, as soon as we find a place to live," M.H.'s wife called out peeping over Dew who was getting settled in her seat.

Dew put her face to the window but dropped her eyes. "All right, you can go now," she said irritably.

The car went off with a lurch. Lute stood on the driveway for a moment, unhappy but tremendously relieved.

It was still dark when Lute woke up. There was a peculiar silence in the Hong Kong hills once the pine waves had stopped. That was the old Chinese term for the wind in the pines but to Lute it was a wailing alien sound. Heard on the pillow it always reminded her she was away from home. There were not so many trees in Shanghai. Here every winter the pines roared all night. It sounded like a cold island surrounded by stormy seas. But toward dawn when the wind dropped and the cars stopped winding their silken spools uphill there was a period of thorough stillness undisturbed by cocks, not reared at this sea level. The expensive dead quiet sounded small as if it was indoors.

Every house here stood alone on a private mountain of masonry looking out to sea. The overblown foundation was to keep out the wetness. Gardens were planted on top like ziggurats. She reared up at once to shake off that painful word. She had loved ancient history and last year's medieval history. So did Mr. Blaisdell, she could tell from the way he pronounced

Chandrucupta Maurya, bouncing every syllable off his tongue with rhythm and relish. This year he had enjoyed as much the Japanese emperor's name, Tokogawa Ieyasu, the last pronounced Ai-ye-ya-su like the Chinese coolies' chant when they carry loads. But there weren't many colorful bits in modern history like Japan's first contact with the West. Wistfully he had touched on Lord McCartney's mission to the Manchu court and the tantalizing life of the first Western merchants in China trading through the eighteen hongs, restricted to an islet outside Canton, not allowed a peep of the legendary empire made famous by Marco Polo.

"I wish we could go into this more but there's simply no time," he had said, the cigarette seesawing between his lips.

No time. History examination would be in two hours. Last night going through her scanty notes she had found very little she could hang on to, as she had known all along, one reason she had put off studying. She gave up around midnight with the kind of common sense that desperation fell on: at least get enough sleep so she would have a clear head in the morning. Her head felt stuffy. She got dressed by the desk lamp.

"Lu-ute!" Bebe called from the opposite compartment.

"Yes, I'm up. Are you getting up?"

No answer. Bebe conscientiously gave her a shout every morning before her own eyes were open and then often fell back to sleep. Lute went over to see. Her head was muffled in the sleeping bag sent to her from Shanghai. Her mother had known sleeping bags would not be needed in the sub-tropics but this way her blanket could not fall off.

"Aren't you getting up?" Lute gave her a push.

The brown baby face looked startled coming out of the bag. Her family was from the part of India near Burma. "Hm? What's the time?"

"Half past six."

"I'm so tired."

She rolled over and hammered herself on the small of her back. She had such curves, if she slept on her back she got an ache at the hollow of the waist from keeping it in mid-air.

"When did you go to sleep?" she asked.

"Before one."

"That early? But you're not worried."

"Yes, I am."

"What are you having today?"

"History."

She pulled a lighted lamp from under her bedding.

"Why? Were you studying underneath there?"

"No, I used it as a hot water bottle," she laughed guiltily. "It was cold last night." She clamped it back on the bedpost and saw Lute in the light. "Are you really worried?"

"Yes, I hardly know anything."

"Really? You're not just saying that?"

"Oh, I'll pass," she said quickly.

But Bebe knew it was not just a question of passing. She knew about the eight hundred dollars Mr. Blaisdell gave her as a private scholarship.

"Maybe it's my fault, I shouldn't have dragged you out for walks and things but I thought it was good for you."

"No, it has nothing to do with you," Lute said smiling.

Bebe was still conscience-stricken. "You see I was always telling people you did well not because you studied hard. I hate to have you called a mug." She had gone to a British school in Shanghai where the studious "mugs" were abhorred.

"I told you you have nothing to do with it. I just didn't feel like studying."

"Yes, you studied very little, didn't you?" Bebe half whispered with a scared smile.

"I just don't like modern history. It's as dull as newspapers."

The closer it got the wider and more confused the scene, the story line was lost and so were the fascinating details. The historians wrote as though it was about powerful persons still living and were afraid of libel suits or worse. Of course this was only part of the reason. She had become self-conscious in history class. Bebe would never understand this and would just think she was in love with Mr. Blaisdell. Perhaps she was a little. She felt startled every time she saw him bicycle to school, red-faced above the piece of old blue Chinese silk he used for a scarf. In answer to her smile and nod he would wave briefly, keeping a careful balance on the bicycle that looked too small for him. He had a car, Ruthie had said but he got it just for his cook boy to go to market in. He had a beautiful white house full of Chinese antiques out in the wilds miles away from the university. He had been to Canton once with Professor Chow and gone to a famous Buddhist nunnery where the nuns were also courtesans. Professor Chow had told the boys in the class in a companionable moment, Ruthie said. The words dived in Lute's ears but she had no wish to know more. The important thing about him was his eight hundred dollars and the letter that came with it which had given her self-respect for the first time in her life. The next year she had won the other scholarship as he said she would. She had found a place among human beings, the desperation in her had quieted down and she had gone on to other things, fiction and catch-as-catch-can reading. But what would Mr. Blaisdell think of her, to be spoiled by such a small success.

Bebe reached for her biology book beside the pillow and Lute went to wash. The girls had not stirred yet on both sides of the corridor. Paula's light was on, she had been studying all night. The half door of the cubicle was hooked back to show Paula Hu sitting in bed in her scarlet quilted robe bending over a big book in her lap, balancing a skull in her left hand like a football player absent-mindedly holding a football. The green-shaded desk lamp underlined her hollow cheeks and the upslant of her eyes. She had a whole skeleton in the room, a thigh bone here, a forearm there. The smell of formaldehyde made her keep her door open.

An alarm went off in another part of the house, the chilling sound corkscrewing through the silence. Downstairs the nuns' heavy walking shoes were walking. There were shrill cries of "Soeur Celestine!" who was the Chinese sister that did the housework.

As Lute came back to her room the first thing she saw was the lamp sitting on the window ledge, the cream-colored glass globe burning weakly against the slate blue sea. She winced before she could go up and put it out. Her mother had bought it. How to face her mother now? Having missed school like most women of her day Dew had a passion for academic institutions and had taken pride in finding out every rule and requirement not in the syllabus. Hearing that each student was to bring his own table light she had bought one in Shanghai and packed it in Lute's trunk, risking breakage.

"The exchange is one to three," she had said, "so before you buy anything in Hong Kong multiply the price by three and it's not so cheap."

Bebe was bandying questions and answers across the partition with a classmate. They called out their questions forcefully but became mousy at once when it came their turn to answer. Lute could not bear those small sad voices as if husky from weeping and speaking perfunctorily, without hope and not expecting mercy. She opened her own notes. That duet of doom overrode all the other noises, doors swinging, banging, toilets flushed furiously, exhaustedly; girls yelling to each other going down to breakfast. To "eat their fill of battle rice," the phrase occurred to Lute, from *The Tale of Three Kingdoms*. She also needed strength just for the sheer physical labor of writing non-stop for three hours as she did last year. But this time what to write?

She collected her jacket, pen and inkpot, one of the things that had told Mr. Blaisdell she was poor. In a college for the heirs of Malayan tin kings and rubber barons she alone had no fountain pen and had to carry an inkpot to class.

"Aren't you getting up yet?" She stood at Bebe's door.

"I won't be a minute. Wait for me."

"I'd better go down first."

"All right," Bebe said with an injured air. "Margaret, ask me something quick."

"What is the endocardium and describe it."

Back came the small sad voice. "The endocardium is a serous membrane. It's inside the cavities of the heart and surrounds the chordae tendineae ..."

Lute hurried off to escape that sound.

The nuns were already saying morning Mass. She came downstairs past the open door of the parlor where the Sisters had their altar behind a partition. The murmurous drone of a small chorus same as every morning. Today it made her feel sickish. The false calm it spread lay flat inside her like that little puddle over the heart about to be thrown up. She went on quickly past the kitchen where the nuns' breakfasts were waiting for them, smelling of hot cocoa. The Latin chant followed her, it sounded like the last rites being said in a clean hospital room, the kneeling priest's black skirt spread on waxed floor.

The basement refectory was a remodeled garage with red tiles and big square pillars painted cream color. It seemed to her there had never been so many girls here nor so prettily decked out. It was because the local girls who usually went home were all present for once, the first morning of the mid-term examinations, and they were the most stylish in their *cheongsams* of imported pastel wools with printed patterns of parachutes, puppies and anchors.

"*Say lo*! *Say lo*! I die! I die!" they groaned in Cantonese tossing their ringlets bound back with gold striped plastic ribbons.

We had a tradition of being beheaded gaily, Lute thought: the prisoner's hair was plastered with glue to make two little horns with paper flowers at the base and he sang on the way and played up to the spectators. She sat down to her last meal.

Say lo, *say lo* was all she could make out of the Cantonese chatter. The Hong Kong girls were sophisticated and old-fashioned at the same time, coming as they did from hidebound families that were becoming rare in other parts of China. In Hong Kong the Laws and Precedents of Great Ching were still effective, the British ruling through non-interference with native customs. The law of the Great Ching or the Manchu Empire recognized concubines. Each of these girls had five or six mothers and one tyrannical father, prosperous businessman and aspiring knight of the British Empire. They had been sent to the dormitory to study in a quiet place away from the hurly-burly of life at home. The girls were lively and influenced by the heterogeneous women at their house. They were full of devilment and constant talk of boys but did not go out dating, still held in leash by their family. "Hong Kong weather, Hong Kong girl," and the weather here was especially unpredictable.

They were shouting history questions across the tables. They had surprisingly big voices for their small build. Mr. Blaisdell had said three Cantonese girls could make more noise than a roomful of northern students. Lute winced again. She saw Mr. Blaisdell talking, the doll-like blue eyes in his red face, the close-lipped smile on the receding mouth with the cigarette jerked up and down, the cleft chin curved out to catch the ashes. How long would it be before he read the examination papers and came to hers, shedding cigarette ash on it? She made herself stop. She knew from experience even the most dreaded things came and went in a commonplace manner. There was nothing unimaginable about it really, she would do badly, Blaisdell would be sarcastic in class, unless he was too angry, but he would never call her in for a scolding. Nothing unimaginable, just unthinkable. The day had finally come and stood before her like a mountain. There was no crossing it and no life on the other side.

Nearly all the local girls took Arts, considered the easiest course, just as all the girls from Malaya took Medicine. It was hardly worth coming this far for anything less than becoming a doctor. The course required seven years and even when the seven years were up the degree was often as elusive as Rachel. The seniors were middle-aged women in the other girls' eyes. They had already assumed the professional manner and rough language among themselves. On ordinary days they dominated the table with shop talk, guffawing over the professors' barbs.

"Man, that Richard Fong! you know what he did? Just to spite Eggleston." All the Malayans kept saying "Man" like jive talk.

"Man, that Eggleston is terrible. Yells at you for nothing."

"Richard Fong got bawled out for being late, so you know what he did? He threw a penis in front of the building."

"Peanuts?"

"No, man, penis."

"No, man!"

"Took it out of a preserving jar to throw it on the path in front of the Anatomy Building."

"He can get expelled, man."

"Sure."

"Does Eggleston know?"

"I don't know. The coolie swept up."

But this morning they ate in silence, seasoned soldiers who had learned the value of a hot meal before combat and in their faces the bleak look of veterans aware of their luck running out.

The two new girls from Malaya waggled their fingers violently as if to shake their hands dry.

"Hey-ya, I've never been through this before," said Angeline Ng. "We didn't even take an examination when we came here."

"No, we didn't have to," said Veronica Kwok.

"This time it's certain death."

"You're all right, with your brother coaching you."

"No, he didn't, he's taking his finals. He telephoned last night to ask, Did you study? Ai-ya, I thought, what if I fail? My brother nearly came to blows with my father for sending me to college," Angeline said smiling but her almond eyes turned small and hard on the pale round face.

"You don't have to worry. A senior coaching you."

"Never! He never did."

"For me it's certain death."

"You're still better than I."

The two had been rival belles in Kuala Lumpur. Here they were a little frightened of the other girls and hung together. Veronica was dark and slim. Her father owned a rice store. She had wanted to study medicine in Hong Kong mainly because Angeline was going.

"In Kuala Lumpur we would run into each other at the cinema," Veronica had said half laughing, "Angeline with her girl friends and I with mine — we weren't together much in those days, eh, Angeline?" she asked with genuine surprise. "We would wave and call out to each other, it's a small theater and the only one. If I happened to be wearing a Western dress she would run home and change into a Western dress. If I saw any of the girls wearing a *cheongsam* I would run home and change into a *cheongsam*. Sometimes we ran home three, four times before the show."

"You wear *cheongsams* too in Malaya?" Lute had asked.

"Not every day. People think you're stuck up if you wear *cheongsam* all the time, as if you're going to a wedding or something."

"We also have sarongs and Malay costumes," Angeline said, "very lovely, lace or transparent blouse, with embroideries and gold buttons."

"What do you wear most of the time?"

"At home we wear Chinese blouse and pants. Here nobody wears it except amahs," Veronica finished in an embarrassed murmur.

Despite their extensive wardrobes they had discovered they looked dowdy beside the Hong Kong girls. They went shopping together and called in a tailor to make *cheongsams* in the latest style. They spoke Cantonese but talked to each other in Fukienese, their people having emigrated from Fukien. Now and then one of them would fling a Malay phrase at the other and both would be convulsed. Veronica swished a handkerchief around and took a few swaying steps forward and another step back, singing:

"*Sa yong ah*! *Sa yong ah*!"

"What's *sa yong ah*?" Lute asked.

"*Sui ah*!" Angeline cursed doubled over with her hand clapped to her mouth.

Veronica had broken down with both hands on her knees. "*Ho sui eh*, those Malays."

"What does it mean?"

"*Sa yong* is lover," Angeline said.

"Well, that's how they dance." Veronica said.

"My father lives with a Malay woman," Angeline said. "They say she has a spell on him."

"Is it really true that Malays can cast spells?" Lute asked eagerly.

"Oh yes, some do. It is very strange you know, this woman. They say she must have a spell on him, otherwise why would he act the way he does? He lives in her house, never comes home and when he does he flies into a rage the minute he steps in the door. Everybody says it's so odd."

Lute could think of a reason but it was not possible to tell Angeline.

"One time he came home and saw me around, so he started to scold —"

"What about?"

"Oh, there was always something. One word went down wrong and he grabbed me by the hair and hit me," she said half smiling. Somehow from her tone it was clear that she already had a full figure then and her father must have seen how pretty she was and it added to her bitterness. "So he was hitting me and my mother came up with an axe and said, take it, kill all of us. He paid no attention, just kept hitting me, and she went at him with the axe and he ran. She chased him round and round the house, ai-ya!" she ended with a soft moan collapsing back gently on her bed as though exhausted by laughter.

"What happened in the end?" Lute asked.

"Oh, I took the axe from her. Ai-ya, how we died laughing every time we said, remember how you chased him around the house?"

"I thought he's not with that woman any more," Veronica said.

"He's better now. We saw her sometimes when we went out walking. She always sat in front of her house chewing betel nuts, you know the Malay houses, that stand on stilts. I would tell my little brothers and sisters not to look and to spit."

"The Malays are the worst," Veronica said.

"And the Indians. Remember that boy?" Angeline giggled. "*Ho sui eh*!"

"The one that turned cartwheels outside the convent?"

"Yes, so silly, hoping the girls would see him."

"They said he came for you."

"Never! Who said that?"

"They saw him follow your bicycle."

"Never. No such thing. Lucky the Sisters didn't get to hear of it." She turned to Lute. "The Sisters in our school were not like here. Here the Sisters are polite to us."

"We're university students now," Veronica said.

"In our school they watch you even when you bathe."

"Yes, what I hate most was the bathing."

"No bathtubs, just a cement pool, everybody goes in wearing a hospital gown that ties on at the back, and you wash yourself under the gown," Angeline said shamefaced, her pretty eyes again contracted and curiously rusty-looking. "And a Sister stands watch all the time at the edge of the pool, *ho sui eh*," she swore.

Lute could see the indignity of furtively soaping one's self between the legs while the nun stood above in full habit, her pair of walking shoes protruding at the pool's rim.

Angeline had that same look now sitting at the breakfast table staring hard-eyed into space, fingering the gold cross on her bosom. Veronica imitated the mock groans of the Hong Kong girls, "*Say lo, say lo*!" but she lacked that lustiness and volume that made the others sound as though they did not mean it.

Paula Hu sat next to Tamara Rabinovitch. They looked as trim as a pair of secretaries, Tamara in a grey flannel suit, Paula in a similar jacket over a wool *cheongsam*. Tamara was from Harbin, Paula from Shanghai. The Russian girl was tall with long golden hair in regular little waves. Paula's sharp little face showed no strain from her sleepless night. She kept a book in her lap reading as she ate.

"Is everybody down?" she called out in her brassy manner. "Today we wait for nobody."

"Yes, for once we're not going to be late," Tamara said. "The stationwagon leaves at eight twenty sharp."

"Eight fifteen," there was a shout from another table. "I'll still have to walk to Chemistry Building."

"Where's Bebe?" Paula looked around. "Isn't she up yet, Lute?"

"She'll be down in a minute," Lute said.

"Who else?" Paula said. "Where's Jade Ray?"

"Bebeshka is going to be late again," Tamara said.

Sister Celestine breezed in, willowy in her black habit, holding a pot high. She could be twenty or forty and wore round glasses with thin black frames under the big white winged cap.

"What's that, Sister?" somebody asked as she set the pot down importantly on the center table.

"This is from Flower King to you all." *Fa wong*, flower king, was Cantonese for gardener.

"What is it? What for?" several girls called out, then shrieked, "Sour pig feet!" when the pot lid came off and the odor became unmistakable. "Flower King's wife had a baby? When? Last night?"

"Boy or girl?" a senior said gingerly. She did not ask if a midwife had been brought in with so many doctors in the house. Well, practically doctors. Though of course it must be the Sisters wouldn't let them be disturbed the night before the examination.

"Boy," announced Sister Celestine.

"Flower King is so happy," the orphan girl Marie said grinning. She helped around the place.

"Hey, Ah Ma-lee, where are the plates?" When Sister Celestine felt affectionate she put the Chinese prefix Ah before Marie's name. At other times it was plain occidental Ma-lee.

Marie rushed out for fresh plates.

"What is it?" Tamara got up to peer into the pot.

Paula was also curious. "Why pig feet?"

"And hard-boiled eggs," reported Tamara.

"It's to give strength to the new mother," a Hong Kong girl said.

"Why give it to us?"

There were giggles.

"Just a Cantonese custom. You send some of it to all your friends and relatives."

"Oh, like giving away cigars."

"We only give red eggs," Paula said to Lute, then turned to Lilypad Chen who was from the northwest, "Eh, Lilypad?" with guarded chumminess. There were only a few girls here from non-Cantonese China but they were not banded together in the face of Cantonese exclusiveness. Paula always spoke more warily to Lilypad and Lute than to the local girls. Bebe did not count. She was Indian.

The pungent sweet sourness filled the room. As Sister Celestine helped dish out the sticky stew someone protested, "We're leaving in a minute, Sister."

"Just have a taste. It's goodwill from Flower King," Sister Celestine said.

"Hurry up, Jade Ray, we're leaving," Paula called to the girl who had just dashed in. "Hey, did you see Bebe?"

"No."

"This time we're not going to wait for *anybody*."

Jade Ray stood undecided for a moment with near panic in her large frame although very little showed on the pink-and-white moon face pushed flat against rimless glasses. She went and sat down in the only vacant seat in sight, diagonally opposite Lilypad, and quickly helped herself to omelet. The two never dined at the same table. They were the only two from the interior and stood out from all the others in their blue cotton gowns, the trademark of the national schools known for austerity and patriotism. Jade Ray cut her hair level to the middle of the ears. Lilypad had two pigtails. They never used cosmetics. Lilypad's only lapse was in last spring when she had bought a bright blue wool coat with red and white chalk stripes which she wore every day to classes through meals.

"With this coat on I look like a student of the Victoria University. With this coat off I don't look like a student of the Victoria University," she had said with a sardonic smile.

She had sculptured features half obscured by a dingy yellow complexion and dull hair that seemed clogged by all the sand and dust of the Yellow River Basin. She was an exchange student from Shansi. Like most northerners she smelled of garlic and the odor persisted after two years of the nuns' French cooking which never had garlic in case some of the girls would object. To Lute it was a nostalgic smell that reminded her of Dragon Boat Festivals when children were given garlic cloves roasted in oven ashes, still white and tender. Eaten at noon on that day it killed off all diseases of the coming summer. Lilypad did not have it on her breath. It hung about her hair and face and her room. Her new blue coat soon got it. No one ever mentioned it. She kept very much to herself. Once speaking of her family in Shansi Paula asked:

"Aren't they worried to have you go so far from home?"

"My father is glad I got away. The Japanese are in Shansi. Some of the students managed to get to Chungking, but there it's very much war time, even in the colleges. Not like here, my father said I could do some real studying here."

She ordered her own Chinese newspaper. Jade Ray also had her own newspaper. After school each read her paper waiting for supper down in the basement which everybody preferred to the parlor with its hushed proximity to the altar and old Sister Agnes the warden hovering around. The evening of the trouble between the two politically-minded girls, the garage doors were already closed. Sister Celestine was ironing in a corner. Lilypad leaned over the table and pounded, exclaiming and half laughing over the headlines: "They've reached Shiangtan!" She was always following the fighting crying out place names with more animation in her face than at any other time. Lute could never make out from her expression whether China was advancing or retreating.

As she ironed Sister Celestine prattled to Bebe with birdlike nods and bows, now lowering her voice, now sparing a busy hand to cup her mouth. Lute only understood enough Cantonese to make out the recurring words "Ah Ma-lee" and "black-hearted". It could not be Marie who was black-hearted since her name bore the prefix that was Sister Celestine's form of endearment. Lute was waiting with Bebe to get their baths for which Sister Celestine had to get the key from Sister Dominic to unlock the geyser and light it with matches she brought with her. Sister Dominic would rather have her trudge up and downstairs twenty times a day than leave it to the girls and have the house blown up.

"Sister, hurry up!" Bebe had a special whine for Sister Celestine. "Bath, Sister!"

"Just let me finish this piece, Ah-Bebe, I'm almost done."

Bebe took the empty tea-cozy and wore it on her head like a Cossack cap, tilted her chair back against a pillar, pointed a finger at Sister Celestine and sang:

> "Refrain, audacious tart, your suit from pressing.
> Remember who you are and who addressing."

She had acted Gilbert and Sullivan in school.

"Soeur Celéstine!" Sister Agnes screamed upstairs.

"Ai-nne!" answered Sister Celestine. If the other were in the room she would have mumbled "Oui, ma soeur" but she would never shout in French.

"I told you to hurry, Sister, and now they want you in the kitchen."

"Soeur Celéstine!"

"Ai-i-nne! *Lay la*, *lay la*, coming, coming."

"You'll get my bath first, won't you Sister?" Bebe called after her.

"All right, all right."

"What was she saying about Marie?" Lute asked.

"About how badly her husband's family treated her. Everything was so wonderful when Marie was getting married. Sister Celestine was so excited when the father-and-mother-in-law first came to look at Marie and brought the boy too. Such nice people, and the mother-in-law so fond of Marie, giving her a gold bracelet and a gold ring and the boy so quiet, already making good money. But now they beat Marie and took back her ring and bracelet, they live in a sampan and didn't even give her enough to eat."

"Is she going to get a divorce?"

"Poor people don't divorce. She's back here now and she's not going back to them."

"And they would leave it at that?"

"They are afraid of the convent."

"Marie looks about twelve, though I suppose she's much older."

"She's quite pretty except for looking like a potato. All the girls at the orphanage have figures like that. It comes from what they eat."

Bebe went upstairs. Paula came in and sat down to read a letter. The local girl Ruthie came looking for a dress, lamented that it was not yet ironed and started to iron it herself. When it happened Lute sat at the same table but violence always came too quick for her. Lilypad folding back her paper picked up a sheet of the other paper for an idle glance. The next second she tore it in two, muttering:

"Traitor talk. Why this is traitor talk."

Jade Ray stood leaning across the table pulling at the paper, hulking and busty in her bright blue sack gown.

"That's my paper. What right have you get? Give me back."

Without looking up Lilypad went on to tear the paper in four, doubled it up and strained to tear it into eight pieces. Anger darkened her dusty yellow skin and the eyebrows slanted up in two straight lines.

"Traitor paper. Why anyone would read such garbage I just can't understand. How anyone could write such nonsense, utterly without heart or liver."

"I forbid you to insult the Peace Movement," Jade Ray let out a surprisingly booming voice, suddenly imperious and mandarin-like. "Everybody has a right to his own opinion, and if you are so pro-Chungking why are you here? Why are you hiding behind the British?"

"What Peace Movement? These are traitors, running dogs of the Japanese."

"I forbid you to talk nonsense about things you don't know anything about."

She loomed large across the table to snatch back her paper or to strike, nobody knew, for by then Paula and Ruthie were holding her back.

"Never mind, Jade Ray, come on, no more. Come on, Lilypad, the Sisters will hear."

Jade Ray stalked out of the room with the rest of her newspaper. *South China Daily News*, Lute had noticed before but had not known it was a collaborators' paper.

"What was it about?" Ruthie said weakly, not really wanting to know, afraid to start it all over again.

Lilypad said nothing. Her noble cow eyes seemed more than ever to be on the sides of her face so that she looked toward the others but not at them. She did not want to preach patriotism to these British colonials. The ones from Shanghai were not much different. She had offered Lute her newspaper once and had been told smiling and as if boastfully:

"I never read newspapers except for the movie advertisements."

Lilypad had smiled back.

Some time after the quarrel it was whispered around that Jade Ray was Wang Ching-wei's niece. The news would have made more of a stir if they knew who Wang Ching-wei was. Instead it had to be explained at each telling that he was some important pro-Japanese personage now ruling in Nanking. It did not give the dormitory more distinction. A Hong Kong baronet's niece meant much more.

Ruthie was in Paula's room one evening when Bebe and Lute happened to look in. Lute had never seen the cubicle before with the skeleton lying around, Paula sitting on the bed with her feet tucked under the red robe, a book in her lap, a skull beside her pillow, a drumstick bone lying on the blue silk padded blanket.

"It's her family," Ruthie was saying quietly. "She's Wang Ching-wei's niece you know."

"Ehn," Paula gave an attentive grunt, smiling as before but a cautious stillness had come into her face. Her father was a lawyer in Shanghai the Lone Island surrounded by Japanese and was careful to keep clear of politics.

"You were there, weren't you?" Ruthie turned to Bebe and Lute.

"Where?" Bebe said.

"That day. Jade Ray and Lilypad. They haven't spoken ever since," Ruthie said.

"So that's what Sister Celestine has been telling me. I didn't know what it was all about," Bebe said huffily half laughing, brushing it aside.

"Nobody knew. We had no idea even when we saw it happen," Ruthie said.

"Ehn," "Ehn," Paula continued to smile and grunt acknowledgement looking from one to the other as they spoke.

"Come to think of it," Ruthie said, "Jade Ray seems such a tomboy but she's quiet about a lot of things. She never even said whether her family is in Hong Kong."

"She only has relatives here, she said," Paula whispered.

"Then where is her family?"

"I don't know."

After a short silence Ruthie teased Bebe about her boy friend P.T. Pan and Paula joined in.

"Isn't that odd about Jade Ray?" Lute said to Bebe afterwards. She did not know much more than the Hong Kong girls and only had a vague idea Wang Ching-wei was an important personage who seemed to have gone over to the Japanese.

"I'm not interested in these things," Bebe said with a closed face. The Indians of Shanghai also knew enough to keep out of politics.

In time Lute had forgotten altogether about Jade Ray and Lilypad. Especially today she had no eyes for the hidden drama at her table with the two enemies seated across from each other. She had an egg from the gardener's stew. Is that how the condemned eats a hearty breakfast, she wondered. Oatmeal, omelet, toast and coffee tunneled down to a strange hollowness in the stomach. And now the sweet sour egg. Nothing seemed to make any difference.

"Well, Lute," Ruthie said brightly, "I don't know a thing."

"I don't either."

"Aah, you don't have to worry."

"No, really. I didn't even take all the notes."

"You don't need them."

But Ruthie gave her a searching glance, evidently half believing her and embarrassed by her downfall. Lute was suddenly sorry she had spoken. She didn't have to be so insistent.

"*Say lo, say lo*!" Ruthie turned to another girl bouncing in her seat. "Tell me something about 1848. I don't know a thing about 1848."

The room was wide open to the sea with all the garage doors hooked back. The December weather was cool and crisp. Iron railings bordered the asphalt path outside. The sloping garden was not visible, dropped out of sight along with the city at the foot of the hill. From where Lute sat all she could see was the sky and sea, of the same pale dull blue-green like duck egg shell. Kowloon hazily ringed the horizon. A string of hump-backed islands to the left floated like a family of tortoises in the void. Other islands made other horizons further out. A formation of airplanes was flying in a V, as low and flattened out as everything out there but too dark and heavy for the eggshell monochrome. The hum came over the bay quite clearly. Some of the girls looked up from their plates.

"What's that?" Ruthie asked. There had been a thump, then another, not loud, but giving the heart a lurch every time like the sudden drop of an elevator.

"Maneuvers," a senior said. After a few more thumps she asked, "Did the papers say anything about maneuvers?"

Tamara snickered, "Who's got time to read newspapers with the examination on. Unless it's Lilypad and Jade Ray."

Neither answered because their names had been coupled.

Bebe rushed in with her school blazer slung over a shoulder and began to make a sandwich standing up.

"Look at you, Bebeshka, always the last," Tamara said.

"We're leaving right now, Bebe. Today we're going to be on time," Paula said.

"All right, all right. Is there a clean cup anywhere?"

At first nobody had noticed Sister Dominic coming in. She had stopped just inside the doorway, hands folded on her stomach, waiting for the talk to subside. She was the real manager here but being Portuguese and still worse, Macaonese, she was only number three here under Sister Agnes, French and Sister Clara, English. Her magnificent black eyes looked up from under the starched white cap with huge wings furled back like an Old Dutch Cleanser. Her big face was as usual playfully grim, the jowls pressed down hard on her bodice.

"The university telephoned," she said. Despite her commanding presence she always spoke in a low voice as if afraid of seeming vulgar. English was not her forte although she only had a slight accent. "Hong Kong is under attack," she continued evenly out of the squeezed jaws in her bowed head. "There will be no examination today."

She spoke especially low for the announcement. But there was only a moment's incomprehension.

"Attacked? Who attacked?" several girls cried out. Everybody was talking at once. "Are we at war? Sister! A war is on? Sister, what else did they say? Were those Japanese planes?"

"There is fighting going on," Sister Dominic said coldly, offhandedly, gazing up from under bushy brows. Behind her hovered another Dutch cap, Sister Celestine, whose staring bespectacled eyes looked like a single soya bean pickle left on a glass plate.

Lute was slower to understand than all the others. The waves of their shouts washed all over her once, twice, three, four times as over a rock. It could not be that she was saved? Just now at the sounds of the thuds after the airplanes rumbled by she had had a flash of crazy hope. Modest even in her madness she had not thought of bombs or war. Perhaps an oil explosion somewhere, some accident, but she did not want Mr. Blaisdell hurt and the questions had already been printed anyway. The hopelessness was apparent even in that split second of dreaming. But now it was here, it was done, the fatal day was arrested just when it was smoothly sunnily trolleying her to doom. Of course it would take a war to do that. She had sat through two wars in Shanghai. It was just a matter of staying indoors.

All the local girls were rushing upstairs to telephone home.

"No use trying, everybody is telephoning all over town," said Sister Dominic but no one listened.

"Sister, where's the fighting? Where did the bombs fall?" the others clamored. "Is Kowloon all right? What about the New Territories? Sister, Sister!"

"I don't know. That was all the University had said. Sister Agnes is trying to get the Convent."

"Ai-ya, those were Japanese airplanes just now?" Angeline wailed.

"What airplanes? Did you see planes?" Bebe asked and went out to look carrying her sandwich.

"Come back here," Sister Dominic said. "Nobody is going out. Bebe," she shouted from the doorway.

"Good," Lilypad said half to herself with a strange smile. "So they're attacking Hong Kong. The British were so afraid to spoil their good relations with the Japanese. Now they're getting it too."

Lute had not made a sound and had stayed exactly the way she was ever since turning around in her chair to face Sister Dominic, leaning sideways glued to the chair back, afraid that the least movement would betray the unseemly joy storming inside her.

Ruthie came back downstairs.

"Did you get through?" a senior asked.

"The line is busy, I tried several times."

"Don't worry, everybody's telephoning just now."

"You live in Kowloon?"

The other answered for her, "They have a summerhouse out in the New Territories. Ruthie, your family is not week-ending there?"

Ruthie started to cry. The others fell into frightened silence. The New Territories is where the peninsula joins the mainland.

"Don't worry, maybe they're trying to phone you. The whole city is on the phone, man."

"Jade Ray is already packing," Ruthie said. "Their car is coming for her."

Lilypad snickered. "I saw her get up and go out before Sister had finished speaking. So quick! She knew what it was all about. The snake knows the holes the snake made. Peace Movement indeed! This is more like it."

Nobody had noticed Jade Ray leaving the room except Lilypad who had avoided looking at her all through the meal. Now that she mentioned it Lute remembered seeing Jade Ray get up from the table with an alert expression on her moon face as if her name had been called.

"What good does it do though? Trapped, the same as everybody else," Lilypad said. "Bombs have no eyes, they fall on traitors too."

There was silence down the entire length of the refectory table with the pink marble top. For a moment the scene was like the Last Supper, a Flemish Last Supper because the barnlike pillared room was bright and cozy, the red paved floor shiny clean. In the background stretched the vista of sky and sea, meticulously rendered down to every motionless ship in the harbor.

Sister Dominic was yelling at the girls who had gone out to look. Bebe leaned against the iron railing still munching her makeshift sandwich, bending her head and twisting around to bite off a trailing piece of omelet from below. Veronica was pointing and telling her about the bombing she had missed. The gardener rested both elbows on the railing a discreet distance away.

When none of the girls paid her any attention Sister Dominic snapped "Veronica!" She was always more severe with Angeline and Veronica than with anybody else, knowing these two had been brought up to fear nuns. "Veronica, come in at once." Then lowering her voice with a little sidewise nod, "Come here," as if she had a piece of candy for her alone.

Veronica came sheepishly, her small mouth hanging open a little in a half smile on the milky brown face.

"Bebe. Tamara." Sister Dominic clapped her hands.

No answer.

"Flower King," she called out to the wiry little man. "Shut all the doors. Everybody inside!" She clapped once more and turned her back on them.

The gardener closed and bolted the garage doors. The girls took their time to wander back through the gardener's quarters.

"Everybody stay down here. Here it is like an air raid shelter, safest place in the house. Now, those of you who have a place to go to on the Hong Kong side, I would say go. In times like these it is always best to be with your own family or relatives. Understand, we are not asking you to leave. But our first duty is to look after those that have no home here."

Bebe complained as she came in, "Sister, the air raid is over."

"It is still on. Nobody goes outside until the All Clear is blown."

"How can they blow the All Clear when they never sounded the warning? It would just get people confused."

"Yes, why didn't we hear the siren? Unless it's been bombed out of order," Tamara said. "Funny, after all that practising, the first real raid and not a peep out of it."

"Soeur Dominic!" shrieked Sister Agnes.

Sister Dominic bustled out. There was a parley in French on the stairs. The minute she left the room Sister Celestine surged forward, black skirt rustling, rosary clunking.

"Ah-Bebe, Ah-Bebe, what was she saying? There's a war on? Japan is fighting Hong Kong?"

A senior said, "*Say lo*, *say lo*, Sister, the Japanese are coming."

"Don't frighten her," said another.

"Sister, there's no more coffee!" Bebe whined. "Sister will you get me some more coffee?"

"Who told you to be so late? Here, there's some more on this table."

"Stone cold, Sister!"

"Ai-ya, all right, I'll make you some. Flower King saw a bomb fall," she leaned over Bebe, a hand cupped over her mouth but talking just as loudly. She had a great admiration for the gardener. "He was out there pruning the bushes, he saw it come down and the explosion go up. He was wondering where that was, he thought it might be Stone Pool Inlet. So I said *say lo*, isn't that where Ma-lee's in-laws live? Those black-hearted people, they can't be getting their deserts so quickly?"

She stopped speaking when she heard Sister Dominic coming and made as if she was clearing the table.

"Hey, I'm not finished yet," Bebe pulled a plate of cold oatmeal toward her and reached for the cream pitcher.

"The university telephoned again," Sister Dominic said. "Professor Creeley wants all the medical students to stand by. From third year up. They will need you in the war hospital and the first aid stations."

"The poor Medicals," wailed the seniors. "Always more work for the Medicals."

But they had perked up instantly, doctors again. After Sister Dominic left there were loud discussions. The lilt of their Straits accent with its upswing at the end of every sentence sounded aggressive in itself. All the local girls had gone.

"It won't last long. The Japs don't know what they're in for. Sure, man, all the Tommies here, and the battleships."

"And the Canadians, the Scottish Highlanders."

"And Singapore so near. Hoy, Singapore! So many battleships there. The fort of the Orient."

"We were prepared for the Japs, only nobody thought they would dare. Sure we're ready for them. The Volunteers drilling all the time, all the professors going off camping, what do you think it was for?"

"It will be over in a few days. The British will have to finish them off quick. If it drags on there is the food problem. That's the one thing. Hong Kong is an island, all the foodstuffs come from the mainland. If we get cut off what are all these people going to eat?"

"Oh, Hong Kong is well-stocked. All that canned beef and canned milk in the government warehouse."

They are probably right, Lute thought, the war will be over in a few days, the university will open and go on with the examination. Does it seem unlikely? She no longer knew. The incredible had just happened. She had used up all her power of disbelief. She was so completely given over to pure bliss, she did not even mind these speculations of a speedy end to her happiness. The hedging it with conditions, the qualifying it only made it more real. The garage doors being closed the basement was lit only by the unbroken strip of frosted panes across the doors. The talk droned on cozily as on a rainy day when there was nowhere to go. She could listen all day. She moved over to a seat next to Bebe and settled down to listen.

"If this happened in Shanghai at least I have my family with me," Paula said between her teeth. "Shanghai was the Lone Island going any minute and Hong Kong was so safe."

"Yes, that's the worst thing, getting caught here all alone," Tamara said. She had been pretty silent. In Harbin the White Russians had learned to put up with the Japanese.

Veronica said, "I have never been in a war."

"Who has?" a senior said.

"Bebe, weren't you in Shanghai in '37?" Paula said. "Weren't you, Lute?"

When Bebe did not answer Lute was obliged to. "There was no fighting in our district."

"Not in ours either," Paula murmured as though it was a matter of course. Chapei and Hongkew were the poorer parts of town.

Lute wondered why Bebe seemed strangely preoccupied, sullen, almost as if offended, keeping at her oatmeal with her head lowered like an animal feeding.

"It seems the only one here who has seen war is Lilypad," a senior said.

There was a brief silence. Everybody was always a little afraid to get Lilypad started, not that she was much given to talking.

She smiled faintly. "Yes, it has followed me here. It serves me right for running away."

"What is it like — war?" the senior asked conversationally, but with qualms, none too eager for a foretaste.

"Well, war is cruel. It is also hunger, and always running away to a safer place."

The others looked uncomfortably at the leggy crusts broken off all round the bread, making square turns like knee joints. One or more of these brown legs curled up or sprawled indecently beside each plate. The table looked a mess in the wan light from the door panes.

"Well, let's hope this will be over quickly," a senior said.

"It won't last long."

They were back to their analysis of the situation.

Sister Celestine brought a pot of hot coffee for Bebe. She was very angry.

"Scolded me. Said I should have taken the headcloths in, that was pasted on the boards to dry. Big white patches, the airplanes might see, she said. How could I have gone out with Sister Dominic yelling at everybody to stay in?"

"Who scolded you?" Bebe said pouring coffee.

"The old one. *Tzeng na sui eh*! Hey-ya, scolded me."

Bebe never even looked at her as she talked, yet she came only to her although most of the girls spoke Cantonese.

"That Ma-lee is a bad one too. Lazy. Can't leave a thing to her and anything goes wrong I get the blame. I have to do everything myself."

"Sister will you get me some more butter?" Bebe whined.

"So Jade Ray is already gone. I had no idea, and already packed and gone. After all the washing and ironing I did, gone just like that."

Lute understood enough Cantonese to guess at her complaint. Once she had spoken to Bebe offering to do laundry for her at three cents a piece, to make some money to buy a wedding present for Marie. The nuns were not allowed to have any money of their own. This time it was a present for the gardener's baby. But Sister Dominic must not know. She had also asked Bebe to speak for her to Paula, Tamara, Margaret, Ruthie, Jade Ray and to impress on them the importance of keeping it a secret. Jade Ray must have forgotten to settle with her before she left.

Sister Celestine brought Bebe another pat of butter.

"I'm going up to sleep," Bebe said to Lute when she had finished eating.

"Aren't we supposed to stay here?"

"There's no air raid on. You want to stay here? I'm going up."

"I'll come with you."

Lute asked on the stairs, "How do you feel?"

"I don't' know," Bebe said wonderingly. "How do you feel?"

"Of course I'm very happy that there won't be any examination." She added hurriedly, "I know it's selfish, but I can't help being happy."

"Yes. It's very bad though."

"I know, but I can't help it."

"Yes, I know you're like that," Bebe said with averted eyes.

It was quiet upstairs. Most of the local girls were gone. Some were still telephoning downstairs.

"What do you want to do now? I'm going to sleep."

"Don't laugh, I'm going to study history, in case the war is over in a few days."

Bebe laughed. "Isn't that just like you? Come and study in my room."

"All right!"

"Take the chair, throw the clothes on the bed."

Bebe took off her dress. Her bra and panties were like white paint on golden brown wood. She got into her unmade bed.

"I should really clear the desk," she said. "Have you enough room?"

"Plenty."

"I'm so tired. Call me at lunch."

"All right."

Cream-colored partitions made up two sides of the cubicle. The other two sides were uncurtained windows. The sea stood high all round like flat blue panels. On a nail over the head of the bed hung the big hat of plaited split bamboo that she had bought jointly with Lute at a village fair outside Kowloon and painted bright pink and green. They had also painted pictures on the blue cotton veil stitched round the hat and spread out in a circle. Lute let Bebe have it on her wall. Her own room was bare of all decorations. Bebe had also picked pink-plumed reeds and stood them in the wastebasket in a corner next to her rolled up prayer rug. Her Koran lay on the window sill within reach of the bed. The little book's blue velvet cover had gathered dust but she did sometimes read from it sitting in bed shaping the Arabic strenuously with her lips.

More girls had come up. Veronica and Angeline were at the hallway wardrobe putting things away. Veronica ruefully flipped through her stack of brocade and silk gowns.

"I haven't worn any of these yet." Stepping aside to let Tamara pass, she asked, "Tamara, what do you wear in a war?"

Tamara shrieked with laughter. "Veronica wants to know what to wear for a war."

Veronica was a little riled. "I ask you because I don't know. I've never been in a war."

If only she had the complete notes, given a day or two Lute thought she could still catch up. She must not make a mess of her second chance. Of course if she was well-prepared, the war was sure to continue and there would never be an examination. The one way you could be certain that a thing would not happen was to be ready for it, so fate would have the pleasure of making all your preparations useless. She could not concentrate and had to read aloud. Urgently she murmured what amounted to an incantation for a long war. She read through Parliamentary reforms and colonial expansion but somehow it was difficult, almost as if the ink of the writing had already turned yellow, the meaning obsolete. No, it was clear enough but she had that curious baffling sensation, not so much eyestrain as an unidentifiable itch somewhere, of reading a document preserved in a glass case.

The siren sounded All Clear at three o'clock in the afternoon, apropos of nothing.

13

No bathing during air raids. Lute had never heard Sister Dominic sound angrier, shouting at the foot of the stairs:

"Bebe! Turn off the water. Shut the geyser, do you hear? Shut the geyser and come downstairs this minute. Be-BE!"

But she would not venture a single step up the stairway. Bombs were thudding all around and an upstairs window had broken.

Lute was in Bebe's room reading but not history notes, she had given that up. Aside from not having laid in a good supply of fiction from the library she was cozily settled down to wait it out. The two wars she had known in Shanghai each took about a month to run its course. Nobody spoke of it ending in a few days any more. At the gathering around the refectory table Paula had half whispered to a senior:

"It's said that Kowloon is already lost."

"Really?"

Another senior echoed the small cry. But as they turned frightened faces toward each other they came at

once to a tacit agreement that it was bad for morale. No more was said and it was never mentioned again. Lute for one still had the idea that the fighting was on the Kowloon side. It was difficult to tell cannons from bombs. She did not know that the sacred hill with the governor's house at the top was hit by cannons from the shores of the island. It just sounded like the bombs were falling closer. There had been a stretch of perfect sunny days. The city sloping down to the sea was a faded carpet being beaten. With every thud you could feel it giving way so the big stick did not fall as hard as it should and the softness closed around each blow, deadening the sound. Perhaps they were nearer than they seemed.

Behind the locked bathroom door the water continued to run, in an agonizingly small stream because it would not be sufficiently heated if turned on big. The thin jet plunged resoundingly from the geyser's high spout into the depth of the tub which Bebe seemed determined to fill. It took so long Lute began to feel on edge. Downstairs Sister Dominic turned on Sister Celestine.

"Why did you give her the key? Blow up the whole house ... She asked you. Must you do everything she tells you? You're a Sister, not a servant."

Lute tried to figure how a bomb fragment might touch off an explosion in a lighted geyser. The chemistry confused her, or was it physics? She thought of the amahs' warning: never take a bath when there is a thunderstorm. Her brother could but not she, nor the amahs themselves. The thunder god looking through the window would be angered by the obscenity of a female body and would strike. She wondered if Sister Dominic being part Chinese had something like this at the back of her mind.

Bebe was now splashing about singing "O Mistress Mine". The water was still running. Another window broke and fell tinkling far down.

Lute asked herself if she shouldn't go down to the basement? She did not mind the foul air and the talk but it was too dark there to read. If a shrapnel was to get her it would get her wherever she was, up or downstairs. One may rush into a haven only to meet one's death. That too sounded like the amahs but it was hard to think altogether differently from the amahs. She and Bebe bolstered up each other's foolhardiness. Bebe always wanted to come up and sleep, she stored up sleep like a camel water, could also go without it for long stretches.

Here Lute could read without ruining her eyes but she would go blind if a piece of window glass flew into her eyes. She should not sit close to a window but the room was so small it was all window. It was like being suspended in a glass bubble high over the sea. Bombs were busily punching holes in the world and time. Winds blew unobstructed from other seas and mountains, passing through her hair. Falling window glass tinkled like bells on the eaves of a pagoda. She felt foolish to be so exhilarated. At least she had her back to the windows to avoid the splinters although it seemed silly to worry about eyes in a time like this. "When the skin is no more, what is the fur to attach to?" an ancient scholar had said.

Bebe pattered out of the bathroom in her black kimono embroidered with yellow dragons and asked round-eyed in a stage whisper:

"Did you hear her scream?"

"Yes. She was really angry."

She doubled over laughing without a sound, a bit guiltily. "The way she screamed!"

"Did the bathroom window break?"

"No."

"I was afraid glass would fall in your tub."

"I just let her scream, I was singing."

"Sister Celestine got such a scolding."

"She must be frightened to death."

"Did she come from the country?"

"Somewhere outside Canton."

"Is she a farmer's daughter?"

"I don't know, her family must be well off. They all have to pay quite a lot of money to get in, you know."

"Like a dowry."

"Well, they're supposed to be married to Christ."

"Only they never see the bridegroom and have to live with in-laws."

"She's happy," Bebe said.

Lute had seen Sister Celestine playing with her collection of little holy pictures and swapping them with Marie's, very like those colored pictures in Chinese cigarette packages that the men servants used to give Lute when she was a child. Once she showed Bebe the doll's clothes she had made for a Madonna statuette she got. Lute somehow could not bear her kind of happiness.

"She has no worries," Bebe said. "At a time like this she knows she'll be taken care of."

It seemed to Lute like a high rate of insurance. War did not come often to Hong Kong, in fact never until now.

"The movies are still on, do you know?" Bebe said.

"Really? People still go?"

"I'm going. I'm crazy," she snickered pulling up a silk stocking.

"You're going to a movie?" Lute said in amazement.

"A boy asked me."

"Can you go in this air raid?"

"Oh, this will be over soon."

"How are you going?"

"I don't know. He's coming to fetch me."

"What's the picture?"

"I don't know. Some mystery. Probably no good but I don't mind, this may be the last picture for a long long time."

The thought silenced them both. Then suddenly anxious, Bebe said, "Do you want to go?"

"No," Lute said half laughing. "I was thinking of all the big pictures that were coming at Christmas time, we'll never see them now."

"Oh, we may still see them some day."

"It won't be the same. Somehow you feel differently about old pictures."

"We'll be old too."

"Yes," Lute said without conviction.

"Is my hair all right?"

"Comb it a little more at the back. No, more to the left. No, here."

Bebe combed and tore. The long black hair swelled bigger and bushier and still bigger, shapeless like thick smoke, until finally both she and Lute broke down laughing.

"The more you comb the more comes out," Lute said.

"Like the genie from the bottle and it can't be put back again."

"It's the new perm."

"Maybe it's a good thing I just got a perm."

"I'm sorry now I never got one."

"I must try and do something to your hair. Sister Dominic will have fits when I tell her I'm going to a movie."

"Must you tell her?"

"I have to tell her I'll be late for dinner. What shall I wear?"

"Wear the green sleeveless jacket."

Bebe clapped a hand over her month and dipped forward just once to indicate a collapse from laughter. She had made it herself from a piece of lime green wool, only enough for a sandwich flap held together at the waist with the top of two leather gloves so that the little black hands came from behind holding her snugly at the waist.

"No. Nobody will see it anyway. I won't even take off my coat."

"Please wear it," Lute said with anguish, feeling the pressure of war years sitting on the garment that would never see the light of day until it had become funny old-fashioned frou-frou.

"No, no I can't."

"What difference does it make if nobody sees it anyway?"

But Bebe settled for a two-toned sweater and leather-trimmed coat. The bombing had stopped.

"Bebe! Somebody to see you," Sister Agnes quavered from the entrance hall.

As a rule it was Sister Dominic who opened the door to visitors and shouted up her summons. She must be still angry. Bebe hurried down. Lute heard her calling, the melting whine back in her voice:

"Where's Sister Dominic? Sister Dominic! Sister will you keep my dinner for me?" as though she was trying to wheedle something special and outrageous out of her.

Dinner was dismal, lit by a single candle in the center of the long table. In the shadows of the big pillars the basement was like a burial chamber except for that thick living stench peculiar to Hong Kong house sealed up for months in the monsoon rains.

"Ai-ya, this soup has worms!" Angeline cried out.

"War is war. We mustn't be too finicky," a senior said.

"We don't have to eat worms," Tamara said. "At least, we'll finish the rats first."

"Where? I don't see any worms." The senior fished in her lettuce soup.

"Yes, there are," another said reluctantly peering in.

"Hey, Marie!" Paula called to the pantry in half playful horror. "Ai-ya, didn't you wash the lettuce, Marie? There are worms."

The orphan girl stood woefully in the doorway. "I did wash it, but it was dark in there and I didn't dare go near the window."

"It's all right, it's all been boiled," the first senior said.

"We're lucky to be still eating regular meals," Lilypad said.

"I asked Sister Dominic if they have any plans of moving back to the convent," Paula said. "She said oh no! It's bedlam right now at the convent."

Tamara laughed. "They don't want to take us with them."

Paula also laughed but added placatingly, "It's true they must be overcrowded. In war time everybody goes to the churches for protection."

"I don't know if the Japanese have any respect for the Christian religion. They're Buddhist, aren't they?" Tamara said.

"It may be more dangerous down at the convent than here, who knows?" Paula said.

"The danger here is too few people in the house," a senior said. "All girls. There's just the gardener."

"Ai-ya, say no more, I'm frightened to death," Angeline said half smiling, waggling her hands as if to shake them dry.

"Yes, the chauffeur doesn't even sleep in," Paula said.

"Sister was telling me how she has to take the stationwagon down every day to get bread," Tamara giggled.

"Why? Is bread so hard to get already?" a senior asked.

"No, this is the bread she gets from Lane Crawford that everybody likes so much. It has to be eaten fresh."

"Who was that, Sister Dominic?"

"And Sister Clara. They always go in pairs."

"Plus the chauffeur, that's three lives at stake every day," Paula said.

Why can't we eat rice? Lute thought. The first thing a Chinese householder would do in a war was stock up on rice and coal; if gas was used gas might fail. She knew that much. Keeping out of wars was part of her family history. The Shens like everybody else had fled to Shanghai at the fall of the dynasty. Since then they had shifted between the treaty ports of Tientsin and Shanghai keeping out of the warlords' way. After the warlords had come the Japanese who attacked Shanghai twice but never touched the Settlements.

She could see the two Sisters shopping downtown like a pair of policemen patrolling a vicious slum. The Sisters seemed excited by the war. The day of the first air raid they had cooked a fine dinner as though for a special occasion: kidney sauté, trifles with rum, followed by a sweet sour candy they had made from pomelo peels. Now they had settled into the war but still took the trouble to fry the canned meat loaf, mash and fry the potatoes. Lute felt it was time for everyone to eat less and was disgusted at her own appetite. It came from sitting around all day with nothing to do except wait for mealtime. The truth was everybody was eating more than ever before. If Lute had the habit of speaking up she would have proposed rationing. As it was it wouldn't make any appreciable difference if she alone held back and yet she did, after the second slice of the crusty bread the Sisters risked death to get. It really smelled wonderful.

Lilypad took a third slice defiantly and pushed the bread basket toward Lute. "Eat. Finish this. Eat while you can. Where do you get things like this these days? Huh-ya!" she sighed and spread a palm toward the dishes disgustedly. "This is not the kind of things you eat in a war. Huh-ya!"

She rarely spoke at dinner, hunched forward staring ahead with that bleak expression that separated her clay cow's eyes and set them way out on the sides of the face. She stayed in the basement all day and listened sourly to uncongenial talk. Now she dipped her head lower and fell to, seeming sorry to have broken her silence. She hiccupped after washing down the last of the crust with coffee and canned milk. Leaning her elbows on the table she suddenly held her face in her hands.

"You people don't know what it's like." She was weeping. "You people just don't know."

The others said nothing. Guiltily they went on eating the improper food.

Dinner was just over when Bebe came back looking furtive, wrapped in the aura of sin.

"Where have you been?" cried Tamara. "You didn't really go to a movie?" She whooped with laughter.

"C-razy!" Paula muttered. There were snickers all round the table.

"Who did you go with?" Tamara asked.

"A boy."

"Who? P.T. Pan?"

Lute knew of Pan only because Tamara and Paula were always teasing Bebe about him. Bebe's confidences were always a boy had said this and a boy had done that. It never occurred to her it might be Bebe's way of turning one or two into a battalion. Still Bebe was the most popular girl in the dormitory. The Hong Kong girls did not go out with boys. Tamara sometimes went out with one or the other of the Russian students. Then there was Paula's Mr. Yip and Lilypad's Mr. Tong. The nuns considered Paula as good as engaged to a boy in her class and did not murmur when every now and then they had to wait up for her to return by midnight. Lilypad had a family friend who came to see her regularly; she demurred when Sister Dominic referred to him as Lilypad's Mr. Tong.

"He's married, Sister," she said laughing.

But it was the only time Lute had ever seen her laugh or smile without looking cynical.

"Was it Pan?" Paula asked, while Bebe wanted to know if the kitchen knew she was back.

"It was Pan, wasn't it? C-razy!"

Nobody said anything more on the subject nor asked about conditions downtown. The movie-going somehow seemed to be a silly prank rather in bad taste at this time. Paula did not even tease Bebe about Pan taking her home, climbing the hill together in a total blackout. Bebe had always dismissed Paula's joshing with "Don't be silly." Once when Paula said she and P.T. Pan were in love, Lute had asked her afterward:

"Are you in love with Pan?"

"Don't be silly. He's so childish, he just thinks he likes me."

Lute had seen him, slender and shy, forelock slanting down a sweet mousy face. He had come from Malaya.

"Can you tell me why boys like to hold hands?" Bebe had said indignantly to Lute. "I mean what do they get out of it? Kissing I can understand, but holding hands!"

"It's contact."

"Well, isn't it the same as shaking hands? Don't we shake hands with everybody?"

"It's different when it's a person you love."

Bebe turned away. An oddly bitter look came over her face making it almost crafty. "According to Paula there's no such thing as love. You just get used to a man, that's all, she said," she ended with a slight sputter.

Lute thought for a while, daunted at the prospect. "I don't believe that."

"I don't know," Bebe said. "You don't know either."

Another time Bebe burst out indignantly, "Can you imagine a boy after being out with a girl might want to go to a prostitute?"

Lute was staunchly resolved not to be nonplussed. "That's understandable," she said smiling.

Yet she had been shocked to come upon Paula and Mr. Yip kissing. She came back to the dormitory after classes and they were sitting on the bottom steps looking very small in front of the stone foundation that rose skyward like an ancient fort. They had the peculiar distinctness of cut-out figures. Against the uneven grey of the massed stones Paula's thin little face seemed slightly flushed and almost muscular, the very substance of flesh and blood. Seeing someone coming she drew back at once with a soundless laugh and the man's arms fell away from her. Lute smiled at them blindly, no longer seeing them, and half ran up the steps. She had never seen anybody kiss except the moon-washed giant faces in a movie close-up and only foreigners, never a Chinese since Chinese films had no kissing. Here the picture was so small and clear and real and enacted by Chinese, it had shaken her up more completely than any pornography.

"Was the picture any good?" she asked Bebe at the dining table with lowered voice.

Bebe also answered in a half whisper, "You wouldn't like it. A mystery. Tut, what's it called? I can't even remember. But you know, the theater was crowded, people standing at the back and along the walls. Somehow the laughs sound different when you know there's an air raid outside. And coming out the lobby was dark, a little blue light in the ticket window, it gives you the eeriest feeling."

Tamara had gone up but she came back excitedly:

"The boys are enlisting. There's such a crowd in the dean's office, the dean's not there but they wouldn't leave, they make the clerk take down their names. The poor old clerk, it looks like he has to work all night: Lum Yum-chang, Chang Yum-yu, Yu Lum-chan —" she whooped.

"Are they really going into the army?" a senior exclaimed.

"They're joining the Volunteers and they're going to petition the Chancellor, they want to serve under their own professors and they want to be sure they'll be sent to the front."

"Serve under their own professors!" The seniors laughed. "Who's to get Eggleston? How did they get to be so fond of the professors all of a sudden?"

"Who did you hear this from?"

"Paula's Mr. Yip is here. He wants to join up. Paula won't let him."

"Who else has joined?"

"Everybody. They're still there."

"In the dean's office?"

"It's jam-packed."

"Ai-ya, I hope my brother is not going. I better telephone him." Angeline hurried out.

"I wonder if Y.K. has joined," the seniors speculated and "What about Gupta Singh?"

They all wanted to check with Mr. Yip who he had seen down there.

"Leave them alone," Tamara said. "After all he walked all the way up in the pitchdark to see her."

"You just butted in yourself."

"But isn't this crazy?" Lute whispered to Bebe, aghast. "Why do they do it?"

"Boys are like that," Bebe said.

As they came out of the refectory they passed Paula and Mr. Yip in the corridor talking except they were not talking much. Under the dim light bulb they stood side by side, backs to the wall, not looking at each other. Paula smiled at the girls. Mr. Yip smiled with eyes lowered. He was a small fair-skinned sulky-looking Malayan.

Sister Dominic peered down over the stair railing.

"Why don't you come up to the parlor? Paula, take Mr. Yip to the parlor."

Paula smiled up with folded arms. "He's going in a minute, Sister."

"Come sit in the parlor. There's nobody there. Nobody wants to go in the parlor. There's Lilypad and Mr. Tong," Sister Dominic jerked her chin toward the end of the corridor where the door stood open.

In the blackness outside a murmur of voices could be heard and the slight crunch of a shifted foot. For purposes of propriety Lilypad and her visitor were standing talking right outside the door. The hedge shut in the sound of their voices, husky and near. Lute had caught sight of Mr. Tong once before and had the impression of a homely man with glasses. But the whisper of northern voices in the night brought an irresistible wave of warmth and nostalgia that made her feel alone in a war far from home.

Later after a washroom conversation Bebe told her, "Lilypad says Mr. Tong asked her to stay with him in case the dormitory is not safe. This is too far out, there're only a few houses on this road and all rich people. There's talk of looters and looters are sure to come here first. She said her father had asked him to look after her but she couldn't make up her mind. People might talk."

"She shouldn't worry what people would say. Surely she can trust herself," Lute said, reminded instantly of all the popular novels set in the warlord era, the girl forced to take shelter with a man or the man with the girl, both observing the proprieties as best they could under the circumstances, constrained to show their feelings only by little things they did for each other. It seemed to her nobody should pass up an opportunity to be chaste and tender, brave and subtle all at once.

"His parents are here but his wife isn't. He got a job here and got his parents out first."

"If his parents are here surely that will make it all right."

"I don't know. This is China."

"That Mr. Tong looks harmless."

"Do you think she's in love with him?"

"Yes, maybe."

"She's so isolated here, that's why."

"A fellow townsman means a lot where she came from."

"They're both so — er —" Bebe made a vague gesture wrinkling up her face.

"So typical," Lute finished the sentence for her.

"So much of a period, Early Republic Chinese."

"Yes, down to her pigtails and blue cotton gown, like the girl students in my mother's time."

The next day all the higher grade Medical students were called up for hospital work including Paula and Mr. Yip, thus settling their argument. The day after even the lower grades were mobilized. Veronica and Angeline were first year Medicals. Bebe and Tamara were third year. Each first aid station would be manned by two boys and a girl. They would all report to the headquarters with their bedding rolls and await distribution. Angeline and Veronica looked grim as they packed but Veronica took one of her new gowns, a copper-colored brocade with green longevity patterns, thinly padded with silkworm fluff, as warm as fur but more supple.

"You're not going to take that?" Angeline shrieked.

"It may get very cold."

"What a pity. Look, Tamara, she wants to take this to the outpost."

"Well, you never can tell which two boys you're going to get. Who would you like best?"

"Speak for yourself, Tamara," cried Veronica.

"Ha, I know," Angeline said. "I know who. Veronica, shall I tell?"

"Don't you dare. Speak for yourself."

Many of the stations were near the front or at lonely outposts along the coast. Where the Japanese would land if they were to come in, Lute thought. If girls like Angeline and Veronica were to draw one of these places it would be like tethering a lamb to a tree as tiger bait. Bebe could take care of herself but there were times when stones and grass were crushed alike. She supposed Bebe also had those stories of mass rape in mind but they did not speak of it.

At the last minute Angeline's brother whisked her away saying she was ill. Nobody knew where he took her. He himself being a Medical senior was assisting at emergency operations at the Queen Mary's. Couldn't Bebe get away too? It was against all the rules of war as Lute knew them, to go out inviting danger, especially for a girl. She herself was fortunately not wanted by the university so there was no need for the escape to private life that she had at the back of her mind, staying with some people in town or renting an attic somewhere. By herself it was out of the question with just over ten dollars in the bank and only a few words of Cantonese. Bebe had more money and her father had friends here. The idea was never clearly formed in her mind because she never got to talk to Bebe about it. Bebe was not loyal to the British although she had never said so. She was proud of the India she had never seen, which had the best architecture she said, the barest and loveliest marble interiors and the most beautiful jewelry and women. She was just going into this like a girl scout and she had been a good scout once. But no girl could grow up in China without being influenced by the importance the Chinese put on virginity.

She rolled up some underwear and a toothbrush and comb in a blanket making a bundle. Lute helped to pack her other things into a trunk to be put away in the storeroom. There was no room for the bamboo hat with the painted veil.

"I'll put it in my trunk," Lute said.

"Well, goodbye. Take care of yourself." She went quickly, her face set.

After this Lute kept to her own cubicle and her side of the sea. As she went in and out she would not even glance in the direction of Bebe's dismantled room, the saloon swing door right opposite hers and behind the door the glassed-in silence and sunlight all day flooding the room with dust.

14

Only she and Lilypad remained. Once they were left alone together the distance between them became more apparent than ever. They were the only people within miles who spoke the northern dialect, yet they ate meals together in complete silence. Lilypad had sized Lute up as a marks-grubber with no feelings. Even the war had not wakened her. Lute had felt glad at first at what she thought would be an opportunity to know Lilypad better, then realized she could never talk to her without making her angry. Lilypad had come from the innermost interior, one of the oldest and now the poorest province, the mysterious northwest, the source of Chinese civilization turning into desert, so totally unknown to Lute she had no idea even why it was called mysterious, a journalistic euphemism for the Communist territory carved out of there, a nation within a nation. She did see mention of a Communist foothold in Kiangsi and Fukien, "a rash or eczema, a trivial affliction," the newspapers had called it. She did not know the exterminating expeditions had driven the Communists to the northwest where they were still being "mopped up". At the university here nobody

ever spoke of Yenan either. Actually the term Gungchandang, Share-property Party, had been familiar to her since childhood. In the novels the quickest way to get rid of a rival in love was to report him to the warlord as a Communist. As a child she had heard the amahs say in the backyard on a summer night:

"They're killing Gungchandang again. Cook was in the Old City today, he saw two heads hanging in bird cages on the electric poles."

The older women clucked.

"Who are these Gungchandang anyway? It's said that once caught they get their heads cut off at once."

"Well, share property. Share property is to share all property."

The others still did not quite understand. The idea of pooling all wealth might not seem a bad thing for the poor, but these were moral people. Inhibitions thirty centuries old rose up and blocked the mind.

A young one broke the silence. "Not just property, share wives too, they say."

Everybody snickered. Nothing difficult to understand there. In puritanical China that was merely the end of the world.

"Even in those days when the Long Hair were making trouble," Lute's old amah said, "the Long Hair killed everybody they saw, but even they didn't think of such a thing."

"Did you ever see a Long Hair?" Lute asked. The Taiping rebels wore their hair loose over the shoulders instead of in a pigtail.

"No, I didn't get to see them, but even in our time we scared children with 'The Long Hair are coming' so they would stop crying."

There seemed to have been many more Long Hair than there were Gungchandang. Lute had never known anyone who had even remotely known a Communist. The very word brought a ghostly chill wind every time it was whispered. To call a man a Communist was to "clap a red hat on his head," which head he was sure to lose. Now that the Japanese took Shansi the Communists were active in the countryside. They came and went, collecting revenues, plaguing Lilypad's father, a landowner. But she never once mentioned the Communists in speaking of the war back home. There was this taboo.

Lute realized the dormitory would not be kept open just for the two of them. Sister Dominic had not said anything. They were paid up to the middle of

January, still a month more to go. The convent was already filled to overflowing with refugees. She was not even Catholic although religion was not of prime importance. Their patrons ran to people of all faiths. Sister Dominic's favorite story was about Mr. Doraiswami the Hindu businessman who had invited her to tea in a new house he built. "It was a lovely house, oh I just love it," she said. "So I asked him for it, as a joke you know. And he gave it to me. He said all right, Sister, it's yours." The convent had turned it into a convalescents' home but she still referred to it happily as "my house on Blue Pool Road."

She beckoned to Lute coming upon her in the hall.

"I hear they are recruiting air raid wardens. Arts and engineering students can supply."

"What do they do, the wardens?"

"They will tell you. It's just a way of helping students who have no family here. Once you are a war worker you get rations. They will even get you a place to live," she added a little self-consciously with lowered voice.

"Really?" Lute was dubious, visualizing tiers of berths in an underground steerage, which they did not even have in England. Those pretty air raid wardens in *Picture Post* lived in their own homes or the subway terminal.

"Yes. They take care of the war workers," Sister Dominic said lightly but fixing her with those great black eyes with head down and jowls squeezed out.

Lute did not like to be a burden and was glad in a way there was this way out.

"Are you going?" she asked Lilypad at lunch. All student recruits would meet at the university gate and march to headquarters in Happy Valley for registration.

"Yes," Lilypad said after a slight pause with raised eyebrows and a faint smile.

"We'll go together."

She hesitated again before she smiled with a flash of surprisingly white teeth in the clay face. "All right."

Lute was well acquainted with what to wear in a war. Centuries of Confucian moralists had emphasized on teaching women rather than men how to conduct themselves in war time. Boil lotus leaves and apply the water to the face, it turns the skin sallow. Smear soot over it. Sew on pants so they could not be removed, the dead-end pants. Lute thought dead-end pants unhygienic. Besides the enemy was not yet in the city, and she could not sew.

Unobtrusive ugliness was the right note. She put on all her dresses one over the other, summer cottons, sweater and padded gown, bulging under her aunt's old mud-brown silk that went on top of everything. Her long straight hair, as fine as spider thread and as flat as a sheet of water, looked bad enough without anything being done to it.

She knocked on Lilypad's door. There was no answer. She went down the hallway calling "Lilypad". The entire floor sounded so empty she did not call again. She had not realized Lilypad disliked her so much she would rather go alone.

At the university gate she did not look for Lilypad in the crowd. There was no girl that she could see and not a single boy from her class. They were all Malayan Chinese in her class, trim in white ducks and business suits, apparently only playing safe in choosing Arts. One of them had married before he came out. When he went up the blackboard one day Ruthie had whispered:

"Moy Hop-hing is married."

Moy Hop-hing awkwardly kept a set face as if he had not heard. Everybody sputtered. Except for this one lapse the boys had always been gravely mature. Their unanimous absence today would seem to show a typical Chinese distrust of all public organizations.

By contrast the faces around her were boyish and unsure. They were the left-overs who were neither hot-blooded enough to enlist nor resourceful enough to find refuge with relative or friend. There was not much talking as they streamed down the long slope to town. She was conscious of their being a solid mass in the center of the road, an easy target if an airplane were to appear, followed by a belated warning blast of the siren as it often happened.

Heads snapped back for a second look at the dispirited mob of boys in sports coats. Once they were forced to the curb by a marching formation of Chinese soldiers in béret and khaki shirts. Who were they? In Hong Kong there had always been soldiers of all nationalities but never any Chinese troops. Lute would have thought they were Annamites from the béret. These men were short and dark but Annamites were even shorter and darker. She had never realized before how odd a Chinese soldier looked in Hong Kong. Were these the Chinese Volunteers? Somehow she would expect the Volunteers to be a more motley group. These little men cheerfully swung their arms and legs with the precision of chorus girls and were just as beautifully matched in height. But if they were regular troops where had they been hidden till now? Would they really go to battle for the British? There were also puzzled mutterings among the university boys. "Police," some said. Others said no.

Coolies were loading a truck in front of the government storehouse on Icehouse Street. A Malayan boy said to another with the rising inflections of Straits English that put a question mark after every sentence:

"Look at all these cartons, and inside how many more, stacked to the ceiling. Man, they're well-stocked. The British Volunteers get canned beef, canned ham-and-eggs. They get canned puddings, they get canned milk to put in their tea. The Chinese Volunteers get coolie chow and when they go to battle the Chinese go in front. Why? They don't want to use up the British troops. Man, the fellows are sorry now they enlisted. They said they never set eyes on a single can, so I said why not tell them no can do? No can do."

From downtown the long trek turned to follow the tramway to Happy Valley. Lute had always thought it was sinister to name the district after the Happy Valley Cemetery. Left to the Chinese themselves they would try to hush up a cemetery in their midst no matter how pretty it was, a bright green hillside sown thick with white tombstones, rising steeply from the thoroughfare. The entrance to the cemetery was flanked by a pair of antithetical scrolls written in that half-baked classical style called Hong Kong Chinese by mockers on the mainland:

> "This day my body returns to whence it came;
> Another year your corpus too will do the same."

Lute had never seen such ungracious un-Chinese sentiments. And sure enough the siren came on like Gabriel blowing his last horn making good the threat. The marchers scattered in a hurry. She followed a group into one of the defense structures at the corner of the road, a concrete pavilion piled with sandbags. Something familiar about the concrete screen half blocking the front haunted her until she realized it was like a spirit screen except for being blank instead of whitewashed and painted with the character Blessing. It seemed melodramatic to take shelter there, reminding her of the woman in Peking opera who stopped at a roadside pavilion in a rainstorm. She felt obliged to turn her back on the men decorously like the woman in the opera. One of the students exchanged a few words with the guard. The young guard with the Volunteer armband leaned on his bulwarks looking out. There was a mad gleam in his eyes that she thought was fright and the joy of great responsibility. War had not yet been spoiled for him by bloodshed. Hong Kong had never seen war, not even the Opium War that created the city. Bombs thudded close. A student asked where that might be. No, he did not know.

For a long time after there was no sound, nothing. The guard sat slumped miserably on a sandbag. She sat on another of those coarse brown ramie bags like rice sacks but cooler and heavier, getting more so as time went on. The novelty of that soft chill weight pulling away from her into the depth of the earth was the one real thing in this boredom of war that she had read about and was no more impressive than on paper.

Finally All Clear sounded. At the Civil Defense headquarters it was like school registration where each put down his name, faculty, class, name of dormitory and was given a helmet.

Some of the boys said, "Let's take the tram back," and the group broke up.

She climbed up the doubledecker tram that swayed along at its usual leisurely pace, bell clanging, looking levelly into all the upstairs verandas of the old arcaded shopping street exhibiting the same laundry, potted palms and rubber plants in the ubiquitous dark blue porcelain pots. Lute's guts crawled with it. Just as she feared, scarcely two blocks later the siren started to whoo-whoo. The tram stopped. Everybody scrambled downstairs. She joined a man and a woman in a doorway on a side street. More came flying, pressing them back against the old-style black folding doors with brass rings. She looked over the shoulders rounded by padded gowns. The unwashed winter hair and bodies smelled dandruffy. She could also smell the slightly cold moisture of cloth and wadding that had been worn day in and day out for months. She wished she knew what some of them were saying so excitedly laughing a little. It was strange not to understand when they felt so close. She could see into the deserted main street where the tram stood motionless and very large in the setting sun. The tram was a frame house painted a nice worn shade of green outside, and the inside a shiny rust red like watermelon seeds. Upstairs was flooded with sunshine, every lath distinct on the walls and ceiling. The rows of empty seats suggested a classroom in the summer vacation. A red window sill shone silken smooth where the sun touched it. I wouldn't mind living there, she thought. Like barracks and very hot in summer but still not bad. It had the deep peace of a long, wasted afternoon, that moment before the planes came.

The zooming went round and round like a dentist's drill. It would help to keep your eyes on something outside the dentist's window so she went on looking at the tram. She would live there if the city was destroyed. Round and round the buzz bored into head and gums. A bomb rumbled.

"*Mow dey*! *Mow dey*! Touch the ground! Touch the ground!" cried a pugnacious-looking black-browed young man in an open-collared shirt. There was one like this in almost any Cantonese gathering.

Everybody made room with difficulty to crouch down.

"Lower! Still lower," cried the young organizer.

Lute ducked her head and shut her eyes trying to fold her whole person under the dome of the helmet. The metallic hum of the drill turned all the roots of her teeth sour. Suddenly the drill skidded off its grooves squeaking on porcelain and nerves. The airplane came down grating on a rusty track slanting down crazily from the sky.

Boom! A jabber of voices followed, probably saying that was close, always with a trace of laughter. She knew so little about the Hong Kong people and now they were to die together.

"*Mow dey*! *Mow dey*!"

Boom!

"*Mow dey mow dey*!"

The next boom of sound blacked out all existence. Bodies were no longer jammed against hers in the pitchdark vacuum. She was afraid to feel, for then she would discover she was no more. If she tried to open her eyes she would find they were already open, but blind. Pain would burst upon her from a missing limb. Let it sleep, don't disturb it yet. An eternity of black space passed while she waited. She slowly looked up from under the helmet, checked and reclaimed all her parts. The others were also beginning to stir. A hubbub had risen across the street.

"Fell on the other side. Right opposite," the words were passed from mouth to mouth. "A big hole. Right on the other side."

A man was being carried over to them held up under his armpits and by his feet.

"Wounded," said the people in the doorway. "Somebody hurt. It's his leg."

"He ought to go in the house," said the public-spirited young man who had shouted *mow dey*.

The others made room for him to bang the brass rings on the folding doors.

"Open the door," he cried. "Open the door. Wounded man here."

The man now arrived in their midst seemed unused to so much attention. His young face was smiling apologetically. Lute marveled that at a time like this he still managed to be so Chinese. She did not see his leg, maybe she did not look very hard.

"Open the door!" Several people were helping to pound and shout.

"Tch, why don't they open?" the organizer said exasperatedly. "These people. No sympathy whatsoever. Hey, open up. Somebody wounded."

"They are afraid of looters," said another.

Finally the doors opened a crack. After heated parleys first with a pigtailed amah, then between the amah and her invisible master which also sounded like quarreling, the amah stood aside on her wooden clogs and let two men carry the wounded into the small courtyard. Lute had a glimpse of dark blue porcelain pots of palms and rubber plants on a rack and in a mass before the doors closed again on the rabble.

The bombing moved away. She took the same tram home. Walking up she suddenly realized that there was no one to tell it to. Bebe was gone. And not just in Hong Kong but in the whole world, who was there? She would like to tell her old amah if she was still alive. She had not been heard from ever since she went back to the country and Lute had not written her either, ashamed of not being able to do anything for her. She would tell Aunt Coral some day although she would not expect her aunt to be greatly stirred to hear that she had nearly got killed. Bebe would miss her if she had died but Bebe was always happy.

She told Sister Dominic at the door, "On my way back a bomb fell right across the street."

"Tut, tut," said Sister Dominic looking up from under knitted brows. "Well, when are they going to start giving you rations?"

"I don't know. I don't know when I'll start work yet."

"Lilypad has left."

"Oh? She's left?"

"Yes. Mr. Tong came to fetch her."

How geographically true to type we all are, Lute thought, Paula, Lilypad and I, as different as can be but all from the mainland. None of us wants to have anything to do with this war. Even the deviousness of Lilypad's departure was characteristic. She was still here when I was calling for her. She probably had already telephoned Mr. Tong to come for her when she said she was going down to register. Paula had let herself be drafted for the sake of her school record. I'm the only one stupid enough to volunteer against my will.

She reported at the university library, now the district civil defense headquarters run by the chemistry lecturer Mr. Lum, a small brisk Cantonese. He sat at a little school desk set in a corner of the big empty reading room, pecking at a typewriter with one finger.

"You're Miss Shen," he said in English, consulting his memorandum. "Good. Can you type?"

"No, but I can write very fast, I take good notes," she offered eagerly.

He shook his head. "Tch. That's a pity. You see I asked for a secretary and they recommended you, because you're the only girl and it's better for a girl to work indoors instead of poking around ruins rescuing people. But what I really need is a typist."

He put his hand on the telephone but did not pick it up. He tapped two fingers on his desk.

"I really don't know what to do." He murmured half to himself.

She waited placidly, determined not to mind his unflattering distress.

"Can't you type at all? With one finger?"

"Yes, but very slowly. I'd rather write."

He said nothing and turned back to the typewriter. After he had finished a sheet he handed her a notebook, a pencil and a clock.

"Make columns like this on every page. Write down the exact time of every air raid, the Warning and All Clear."

She could not see the point of this. The enemy would not be such fools as to come back tomorrow the same time. Waiting for a raid she browsed among the library shelves. How lucky she was to be stationed here, like a child in a cake shop. The library was conveniently near her dormitory too. One who does not die in a great catastrophe has blessings to come, said the proverb. Her heart pounded when she came upon a 17th century Chinese novel which she had always wanted to re-read. It was comparatively little known and she had never seen it anywhere ever since abandoning it on leaving her father's house. She had bought it with her own pocket money when the Commercial Press printed a modern edition in four volumes. Generously she had let her brother have Vols. I and II while she took Vols. III and IV. It being always on her conscience that she had not been able to do more for her brother, she liked to remember the few times she had been good to him. The fact was she had not minded starting from the middle. It was not unpleasant to grope around the many courtyards gradually making out the confusing faces. Sometimes she had formed ideas about some of the characters which turned out to be wrong when she got to read the earlier volumes. It only gave her the pleasure of getting to know them all over again. From the beginning she had again gone to the back with fresh enjoyment. And now it was like coming upon an old friend in a strange land. At first she stood reading in front of the bookshelves, then growing bold brought it to the table with the notebook and pencil ready at her right hand. In one long draught she took in the first volume without once lifting her head. She had just forgotten enough of it to give a tang to the taste of memory.

The siren started to roar and pant.

"You can go downstairs," Mr. Lum said. "But put down the time first."

"No, I'll stay here," she said.

"All right, but you really don't have to, everybody else has gone downstairs. I'm here to answer the phone."

She stayed but forgot to write down the time.

At noon a demure little woman with glasses brought Mr. Lum a covered dish in a shopping net, followed by an amah holding a small aluminum pot.

"This is my life," he said. "Miss Shen is here to help me."

Mrs. Lum nodded to her and cleared a space on his desk. The amah set the things out and filled his rice bowl.

"Have you eaten?" he asked his wife.

"Yes."

"You needn't have come," he said in a low voice with a slight frown and downcast eyes as he picked up his chopsticks.

She gave him a sulky look. He said no more. As he ate she came over to chat to Lute, starting in Cantonese, then changing to fluent Mandarin. After he had finished she helped the amah pack up and take the things away.

At half past five he told Lute she was off duty. The path was heavily shelled as she went uphill between the pines, azaleas and hibiscus bushes. The shrapnel whistled and held its high and level note. Now and then it fell hissing to the asphalt right and left but she was in too much of a hurry ever to see one. She climbed through a world of sound. Nothing else existed, only sound, and it was as hard work getting through as through underbrush. She could only see straight up, the tousled yellow head of roadside grass where the path entered the road. The minute she got on level ground she could breathe easier. There was not such a busy traffic of shells along the road. It was the same again the next morning, she ran downhill through the whistles and hisses clutching the luncheon sandwich made by Sister Celestine. The same again when she returned in the afternoon. She felt like a native clerk in some tropical country who had to go through uncleared jungle to get to the place he worked. It was a pleasant job, just a little troublesome to get to the office.

One day Mrs. Lum and the amah came in combined. Lute looked again. Yes, it was Mrs. Lum dressed in the amah's costume.

"Where's Ah Gum?" Mr. Lum asked.

"Looking after the house."

"Ai-ya, why didn't you send her? I told you not to come. What if you get hurt, and all by yourself."

She set out his food without a word. Then she sat down beside Lute to explain her costume which apparently embarrassed her a little.

"Everybody is borrowing clothes from amahs," she whispered.

"Is it because in case the Japanese come in?" Lute whispered back with a thrill of fear and recognition, all the ancient tales of war coming to life.

"Not only that. Even before that. The looters. The *hak sam*." Each sentence was accompanied by a slight nod that seemed confined to her small uplifted mouth, bringing it up and then down. *Hak sam* was Cantonese for black clothes. Lute had thought all Cantonese wore black most of the time but it seemed especially their gangsters.

"Really? Do you think there might be looting very soon?"

"Who knows? All the stores closed. Afraid of looters. No rice to be bought."

"Already?"

Mrs. Lum looked away. She was undermining office morale. She always seemed to get herself into these conversational traps. A need to explain got her into another such need.

"It's frightening waiting at home not knowing what's going to happen, and no man in the house. Mr. Lum had always been foolish," she said with wifely deprecation and a slight smile. "He didn't have to take this post."

"Did the university ask him to?"

"Of course they need men just now. But we're not British subjects. Nobody in the Chinese department is doing war work. But he," she jerked her chin at him with an artificial sneer, "he says he'll fight the Japanese anywhere, you can't pick and choose the place."

"All right," he frowned at her, having raced through his rice. "Now you can take the things home. Don't come out again."

"When are they going to give you rations?" Sister Dominic asked Lute.

"Any day now."

"Ma Mère wants us to close up and go back to the convent as soon as possible."

"They're talking about cooking for all the war workers, it probably takes some organizing."

"I tell you," Sister Dominic whispered with her air of producing a piece of goody just for you alone, "Go to the Methodist Mission, it's downhill, more convenient for you too going to work."

"I can't just live there?" She couldn't mean for free?

"Oh yes. Just tell them you are a university student and your home is not here. Angeline is there."

"Is she?"

"Yes. Go to the Mission and ask for Miss Muirhead. She will take you."

Over there I would just be a charity case, Lute thought. Where could I go from there if they told me to leave?

"What about our luggage?"

"You can leave everything here. The gardener would be here to look after the house."

"I'll go to the Mission and see what they say."

Miss Muirhead said severely that she could live there but no board. Lute assured her she would be getting meals at the university and moved in the same day bringing the last of her crackers. Angeline was a bit embarrassed with her in the beginning since she was supposed to be sick. Lute got a room to herself but Angeline shared a room with a Miss Eu for protection. Miss Eu was a little schoolteacher in her fifties with a look of professional Christian kindness. She was from Amoy so they were compatriots, Angeline being Fukienese transplanted.

"I'd die of fright if it wasn't for Miss Eu," Angeline told Lute. "She has been very good to me. At a time like this you feel better to have somebody around who knows things. Miss Eu has – seen things," she finished in a whisper looking away.

By that Lute understood that Miss Eu had frightened her still more with stories of rape. But in her quiet way Miss Eu had apparently made up her mind to risk her life if necessary to protect Angeline from the Japanese. Lute went in their room to exchange news the first day she moved in. Miss Eu sat and knitted and by an occasional word or glance showed her motherly feelings for Angeline. For Lute she had a quick smile when she came in, then chilliness. Lute got out in awkward haste. She soon learned that everybody kept their distance in this dingy old house. She never got to know who lived here and how many. Presumably all mission workers or refugees, no men of course. A Chinese rooming house was never as quiet as this. No one used the kitchen that she knew of. There was never any dispute about water which was now restricted, just a trickle for a few hours a day. They each kept to their own room. In case anything should happen to their neighbor, a shell wound, starvation, sudden illness, by then it would be too late to hold back if they had gotten too friendly. Being Christians made them scrupulous. Miss Muirhead never came upstairs but Lute ran into her in the hallway sometimes, a tall woman with mousy hair and a forbidding look. After the "Good Morning Miss Muirhead" Lute had to drop her eyes and pass her with just a faint smile acknowledging her ownership here. How embarrassing it was to be good and then having to draw the line somewhere. Lute wished she could tell her not to feel like that. It was already more than fair to let her live here when she wasn't even a Christian.

The plumbing consisted of a tap and a concrete tray set in the floor boards of a dark little room. Lute was just back one afternoon washing her stockings in a tooth mug to save water. Angeline burst in.

"Hey, did you hear, Mr. Blaisdell is dead. Did he teach you?"

"Mr. Blaisdell? Dead?" Lute exclaimed.

"Yes, he was killed."

"Killed fighting?"

"No, he was walking back to camp, the sentry challenged him but he didn't answer so the sentry shot him."

Lute remonstrated although she knew it was true, "But how did it *happen*? How could he have not heard?"

"He must have been thinking."

They continued to gape at each other.

Lute said to herself, "Please, whoever is god, if you are there, it was very kind of you to stop the examination but it's not necessary to kill the teacher too."

After Angeline was gone she cried as she went on washing her stockings. The tears came spasmodically like the water, in coughing spurts. What had he been thinking about when he was walking back to camp? Was it about the war? He might not have hated modern history as she did but it must have appalled him the way it surged up and had him surrounded, cut off from his books and antiques and cook boy and the white house that stood alone in a wild bay. Wasn't it enough to die, he must be made to look foolish too? Why couldn't he at least be killed in battle? Even if he did not believe in these things he might at the last, he was an Englishman.

Now he would never know her being behind in her lessons. But hadn't he known at all? Instantly his face came to mind. He was asking a question in class, skipping her to give the others a chance to answer, calling one name after another until he finally gave up and said resignedly, "Miss Shen?" But Lute also shook her head smiling like everybody else. An irritated expression leaped into his china blue eyes as he snapped out the next name. He knew. Even now she half shied away from the thought that was as cold and long as the shadow of a fish. She demanded loudly to herself: what did it matter now whether he had or had not known? For the first time she had an idea of what death is, making all relations null and void. It took two to make any relationship. Now it was all stray ends dangling on her side.

She went back to her room and hung the stockings on the back of the chair. Darkness was coming on. Without electric light each day closed so slowly and ominously. The Japanese had got into the habit of starting a bombardment around this hour. It was on. She sat in the half dark not listening.

Boom! This time quite loud though still not the loudest, somewhat muffled. Her sudden movement in the chair brought her heart to her mouth. Something ice cold had touched the back of her wrist. A wet stocking. She heard a stir, a slight hubbub somewhere in the house. She went out to the stairway. Angeline was down there talking to an amah.

"Angeline, what was that?"

"We're hit."

"Where?"

"They say a shell took off part of the eaves."

Several women came down to tell the story on their side of the house and question the amah in turn.

"Better stay downstairs," Miss Eu said.

Lute followed them into the unlit parlor. The women sat silent around the linoleum covered table as at a seance. She went out again to sit by herself on the staircase.

The doorbell rang.

"*Bing go?* Who?" the amah shouted close to the door. She opened a crack to check the answer, then turned and called out, "Miss Ng, your brother to see you."

Angeline came out of the parlor. Her brother stood just inside the door. He looked like her but more thick-set and almost thirty.

"Come with me, it's dangerous here," he said.

"Where are we going?"

"To my place."

"To stay?"

"We'll see."

"They won't let me."

"Never mind, just come. Don't take anything with you."

"Lute, do you want to come along?"

The brother nodded at Lute. "Come with us."

Lute hesitated only a second. She was lucky she could go.

"You won't need anything, it's not cold out," he said.

"It's very near," Angeline said.

"It's the lowest of the boys' dormitories," he said.

They walked fast three abreast on the side road heavily bordered with vegetation. Big scarlet wheels of poinsettia studded the high trees up and down all over, the flat redness unreal and staring in the grey dusk. The road turned into a path leading upward. That was when the shrapnel started coming, singing loudly as it sailed by in its leisurely long arc. The whistling creak, a magnified insect sound, was a steely falsetto meant to carry on all night although when you least expected it would swoop down several scales and break off abruptly. Angeline's brother took the girls by the hand and ran. Lute wanted to say half laughing, "Let's turn back quick," only there was no time to turn her head and speak. Her face was set in the half laugh, too much of a strain to keep up but still more strenuous to wipe out, as they rushed on over the bumpy old asphalt. It was like climbing a buff facing the wind with not a shred of clothing on, naked and tender, through a criss-cross of invisible flying things as thick as whipping branches. How did I get here? She wondered.

As the path rose the hill dropped away on one side. It was almost daylight here still, so she felt more exposed, colder and shorter of breath. Then she was jerked off balance. They had nearly fallen off the hill dragging each other down. Angeline was crouched on the ground talking Fukienese to her brother. People from other provinces called the Fukien dialect "bird talk". Her flood of chirps and twitterings added to the unreality of the moment. Lute stood by stupidly until she turned and called out:

"Help me get him up."

He was heavy and it was hard to know where to grip him without hurting, he was groaning so. But Lute's struggle to get him on his feet faded to a dream beside the acute consciousness of her own flesh that seemed spread out in all directions to catch the shrapnel, tenderly expectant. How she stretched herself out to stop them, she was a soft scallopy wall in the twilight, at places thinned out to a net, a mist, undulating every time the metal blew through. Now they were staggering on holding him between them. The side of her body pressed against him luxuriated in the safety, drugged with warmth. All the other facets of the body were wide awake waiting for the puncture, awash with cold as though just rubbed with alcohol before injection.

They tottered on. The path turned and leveled, crossed a lawn between shrubberies. The shells still followed them singing. Lute kept her eyes down, afraid to trip in the deepening darkness and having to get him up again. They came to a red brick portal and maneuvered the steps to the veranda.

"Anybody here?" Lute called out.

The house was in complete darkness. She could not spare the hand to open the screen door. She shouted again:

"Somebody wounded here!"

At this Angeline started to cry and again talked Fukienese to her brother. A student came out, then more came. They got him inside and helped him lie down on a blanket spread over a dining table. They made many phone calls and managed to get a car to take him to Queen Mary's. The car came about an hour later. Angeline went with them. Lute went home, the shelling was over then.

Angeline did not come back from the hospital that night but that was to be expected, transportation being hard to get. The next day Lute was back with her own air raids, the ones she was to record as the old imperial astronomers had the earthquakes, and in surroundings almost as handsome and remote, the Chinese section of the marble-paneled library, she imagined not unlike the Imperial Observatory in old Peking. She sat across the table from Mr. Lum and read her

17th century novel that she hoped to finish before she died. Boom! right in the house it seemed. The floor rocked and windows shattered. Politeness demanded that she look up attentively. Mr. Lum held still, listening to the faint hubbub of the watchers on the flat roof top. Other boys were yelling up from below.

He got up and Lute dutifully followed him out to the landing.

"What is it?" he called out to the boys milling in the hallway.

"I don't know," one of them said. "I was yelling up from outside but I couldn't make out what happened up there."

Mr. Lum went halfway up the staircase that led to the roof.

"What happened?" he shouted up. "Anybody hurt?"

A voice barked staccato Straits English.

"Good," Mr. Lum shouted back grinning. "Everybody all right? How's the anti-aircraft? ... Is that all? Good."

That was the first she had heard of an anti-aircraft gun on the roof. No wonder the bombs and cannonballs had been falling closer and closer. There it went again, she had not known what it was before, the anti-aircraft's ineffectual blap-pap-pap-pap, like an awning flapping in the wind. She was so exasperated she could cry. All it did was sit on top of her head attracting planes like flies. As in a dream she put on a hat and it turned into a hornets' nest. Everybody in Hong Kong had to take his chances but this was unfair. How like fate, to save you once, twice so you would feel magically immune, only to wipe you out carelessly the next instant. And to choose such an unlikely place for it, this big sunny house smelling of books, that reminded her of her home in the north as well as the house in Shanghai. The sunlight of other years enveloped her from harm.

"Did you put down the time?" Mr. Lum asked when they came back to the room.

"I forgot," Lute said guiltily.

He reached for the pencil and notebook. "You've got to remember. Every time you hear the siren. When did it go last? About half an hour ago?" He looked at the clock. It had stopped. She had forgotten to wind it.

Mr. Lum did not say anything. After a while he said:

"How would you like to work outside?"

"You mean, be a regular air raid warden?"

"Yes," he looked up from under his brows with a sprightly expression.

"I can try," she said hopefully, thinking to get away from that anti-aircraft gun.

"Do you know this district?"

"No."

"You can ask for directions if you get lost."

"I can't speak Cantonese."

He said no more about a transfer.

Thumm! The sound now had a metallic strumming somewhere in it. It was different from the first days at the dormitory. Thumm! Thumm! A deliberate pummeling right and left into the softness of earth, and then as if maddened by inattention, a vicious blow into the vitals, THUMM! The floor quaked but she did not. Death, ceasing to exist, what was it really? In terms of one's self it was difficult to think about. Confucius had said what was best translated into pidgin English, "Not know life, how know death?" In losing her life what was it she lost? A chance to live she supposed. But a chance to live was not the same as life. Nothing was quite like it. As a child she had wanted endless lives one after the other in the transmigration of souls and would not mind greatly if she had to be a beggar sometimes or a pig and get butchered, as long as she could be rich and beautiful too sometimes. Hadn't she tasted life and liked it or was it just blind greed? Hadn't she ever lived? The trouble was too many things had happened that had come of themselves, nothing that she had particularly wanted or had brought on herself. Is that the misfortune of most people not yet grown up? Too many things and yet nothing.

Mr. Lum had stopped pecking at his typewriter. He turned to the notebook.

"When was the All Clear?" He looked at his wristwatch and figured aloud to himself as he scribbled, "4:11 now. Say about five minutes ago, would make it 4:06."

15

In the Mission she used old picture magazines for blankets. They were cool and slippery but they kept her warm as long as they did not slide off. Every morning she went out the French window and did exercises on the veranda. Besieged Hong Kong was grey and flat in the dawn mist. A few cocks crowed thinly, so smothered it sounded like faint mewings. The city was nearer here than seen from uphill and appeared dingier, more broken up, like a sea of rubble blearily coming to life but still playing dead. It gave a feeling of such complete devastation it made her curl back into herself protectively, feeling virtuous because she was taking good care of herself with her deep knee bending and touching the toe ten times.

One evening she heard Bebe's voice calling her name. She ran out on the landing incredulously and saw Bebe come up holding a candle dressed in a wrinkled grey uniform.

"See how good I am, I walked all this distance to see you."

"Aw, but you shouldn't have. How did you know I'm here?"

"I telephoned the convent."

"Where are you stationed?"

"Downtown, past the Central Market."

"And you walked all the way?"

"There's no bus now."

"Aw, you needn't have come."

"I wanted to see how you are."

"You know I'd be all right."

"Have you had dinner?"

"I didn't eat all day today."

"Why, aren't you supposed to get rations?"

"It's not started yet, it's always 'any day now.' "

"It's the red tape. They don't give you food here at the Mission?"

"No, they made that clear when I moved in."

"If I had known I would have brought you some of my dinner."

"As long as you're here, will you tell me where to buy some crackers or peanuts, anything."

"All the shops are closed."

"I know but I thought you might know some place where you could still get something. I have two dollars here."

"Hang on to your money," Bebe said immediately, her business instincts outraged. "They charge fantastic prices."

"But it's very likely there still won't be rations tomorrow."

"Are you very hungry?"

"No, not particularly." She added hastily, "In fact not at all. It's like when you didn't have breakfast you're not hungry at lunch."

"Fasting is actually good for the system you know, as we do at Ramadan."

"I'm not worried. Nobody dies of starvation. At least it takes months."

"Well, if you can stand it," Bebe said after a moment's hesitation, "I think you should wait because I definitely know they are going to serve food to the ARP."

They sat talking in the room with the candle blown out.

"I have to stay here for the night."

"That's wonderful."

"Can I sleep here?"

"There's no blanket. You don't mind, do you?"

"I'll see if I can get you one. I was talking to Leela downstairs, the Indian girl. Did you know she's from the university too?"

"Yes, I was wondering why she didn't have to go to an outpost."

"She got a job at the switchboard. I didn't see Angeline. Isn't it terrible about her brother."

"I was there."

"Yes, Leela told me. Did you see the wound?"

"No, I'm glad I didn't."

"I guess you're right."

"I wish this was over soon."

"You'd rather have the Japs come in?"

"Anything as long as this stops."

"You can still get killed after the Japs come."

"Maybe, but this is certain. If it goes on long enough."

"I know what you mean," Bebe murmured quickly before she could come out with more of this kind of talk. "I've seen a lot at the outpost. Central Market was bombed you know. I was saying to myself: Now you're really seeing life. Maybe I'm morbid, as though only this is life."

"What did you see?" Lute asked guardedly.

She mumbled with an air of dismissal, "Horrible things. Armless, legless, bones out, intestines out —"

"Don't tell me, I don't want to know."

"All right," Bebe said shortly, she lit the candle. "Which way is Leela's room?"

"I don't know. Try the back."

"Leela!" she called.

She found Leela who knew of an unoccupied room where there might be beddings. She came back with a grey army blanket and blew out the candle as she entered the room.

"I'm going to bed. I have to go as soon as there's light."

"I'm sleeping early these days. You can't sit up in the dark."

They both felt a little embarrassed to get under the same blanket and tried not to crowd too close. Lute's bare leg happened to brush against Bebe's thigh, its cool hard smooth surface contrasting with the rough blanket and the bare mattress they slept on. The leg felt odd, being much shorter than her own. Somehow, maybe because she was hungry, it reminded her of frog leg, she had often had stewed frog when she was a child in Tientsin, the amahs always remarking while helping to pick it apart with chopsticks that it was a sin, frogs looked so human. Fond as she was of Bebe she felt a slight tremor of disgust. Bebe had no love for girls either but if the contact revolted her too she hid it as well as Lute and did not draw back perceptibly.

They did not talk however. There was a slight constraint until Lute heard from her breathing that she was asleep and fell asleep also from the warmth of the blanket and another body.

Bebe left at dawn. Nobody knew anything about rations at the office. After Lute came home she went to ask Leela if she had heard anything. The inmates at the Mission had become friendlier, at any rate more talkative after Angeline's brother died. The shock of the news, the indignation that anybody should have wanted to run away from a house where they themselves had remained, then to have this folly punished so promptly and drastically, all of this had stirred and opened them up. Leela was an Indian Christian who had lived here at the Mission of her church ever since she came to Hong Kong to study. She was squat, with pigtails and a chiseled brown face and wore cotton print dresses. Since the war she had learned to be a telephone operator. The professors in charge of war work kept the university lines busy. The medical professors had always been known for boorishness.

"The way they swear when they have to wait," Leela said. "I never heard such words before."

"If the professors are running the war why can't they get the students fed?" Lute asked.

"Who knows? Can you imagine what they will say if the operator cuts in to ask about her rations?"

Lute could understand how the British might want to hold on to their stores, not knowing how long the war was going to last. Besides nobody was starving that she could see. Everybody seemed to have his or her secret means of subsistence, maybe no more than a biscuit tin. Her own lack of it also had to be kept secret since speaking of it was the same as begging.

She had not been in touch with the M.H. Cheungs ever since the war because she did not like to trouble them. They had had enough of helping her mother, she did not want them to think they now had her on their hands too. They lived in an apartment in Causeway Bay. She called them that night. They should be able to tell her where to buy food.

Their Cantonese amah answered the phone.

"Master and Taitai are not here, they have gone to Repulse Bay."

"Repulse Bay Hotel?"

"Yes. Only I am here to look after the house."

Hadn't they had enough trouble in Repulse Bay? And why was Repulse Bay thought safe? Far out on the sea front, probably one of the first places for enemy landing and the hotel full of wealthy tourists inviting looters. Of course she knew nothing about these things. M.H. must have acted on a tip from some foreign friend. Perhaps in some way unknown to her the hotel was a sanctuary like the Foreign Legations of Peking.

She went to the bureau in the corridor and was glad the thermos weighed heavy in the hand. She took two and a half cups, careful not to drink it dry in case Miss Muirhead needed some hot water in a hurry. If she got angry she would not leave the thermos out any more. She washed the cup in the kitchen before putting it back. Dinnertime and no sign of food. The pots were clean, the stove was cold. The Mission amah sat under the center light bending over the small print of her Bible. The dimly lit room smelled unused and carefully swept. Lute thought, how orderly and immaculate and high-minded we are once we can do without food.

She went upstairs warmed and well filled by the hot water and not really worried. At bottom there was always the feeling that if anybody could be relied on in the matter of rationing it was the British.

"The British are good at this sort of thing," her mother had said once when she asked what if war came when she went to England to study.

The third day she did not eat she walked to office feeling light-headed and afloat, a little tired as after soaking too long in a hot bath. The asphalt road dipped and rose. She had to half slide, half scrape down a trackless unpaved slope, then walk up the flights of stone steps winding through trees, rather like the hills of Hangchow. The past felt near today because the present was so thinned out. Now stop this floating and weaving around, she told herself. Aunt Coral once said with a look of slight repugnance, "Nobody really gets drunk. It's just acting, letting yourself go under cover of drink." She spoke from experience since she was a drinker herself, though only at feasts. Lute guessed she was acting faint and weak just because it was time that she felt it. She felt all right really except for a slight stomach cramp in the night that was over in a minute. It must be she was so proud of knowing hunger at last the pride had drowned the sensation. Had she never felt hungry before? Yes, but that was just appetite. She smiled thinking of lunch in Tientsin timed by the cotton mill's noonday blast. "The tiger is roaring" the amahs had said.

"How is it so loud?" she had wondered.

"It's a very big tiger," they had said.

"How big? As big as a house?"

"Bigger."

Soon after the great long bellow her old amah came upstairs with the tray and righted the chairs that she and her brother had turned upside down to make a car to ride to war, a forerunner of the jeep. Childhood kept coming back this morning. At the back of her complacency was her mother's belief that starvation is a healthy thing, it's always safer not to eat than eat too much, and doctors say most Chinese have distended stomachs from too much rice.

"Mr. Lum, are we going to get rations today?" she asked at the office.

"I don't know, I didn't hear anything about it," he said.

She had finished all four volumes of the novel that she had feared she would not live to read through and could not find anything else as interesting from the shelves. There was nothing to take her mind off the empty blank inside her, not even an air raid.

At noon she was on the look out for a messenger boy from headquarters, perhaps with a burlap sack of bread loaves, she had no idea in what form the food would be. A cupful of rice would do, she could cook it in the Mission kitchen.

A student stuck his head in.

"No rations, Mr. Lum?"

"I know nothing about it."

"The fellows are asking."

"If it comes you won't be left out."

Mrs. Lum nodded to Lute as she came in carrying her pot in a shopping net, the rice bowl inverted over the lid. She set chopsticks before Mr. Lum and filled the bowl with fried rice. There were eggs scrambled into it, the dark red spots could be chopped sausage or ham. Lute had read that when a hungry man saw food there seemed to be a hand stretching out from his throat to grab it. She examined herself. No little hand. It was true that just now she would rather have fried rice than anything else in the world, preferably with eggs and ham or sausage. She was sure Mr. and Mrs. Lum as well as Miss Muirhead would give her food if she told them this was the third day she had not had anything. She would do that if she was really fainting from hunger but it had not come to that yet. She glued her eyes to a dull book and carefully set the expression on her face. But Mr. Lum was aware of her plight. He looked bad-tempered as he ate, no doubt reminding himself of her irresponsibility and utter uselessness.

Mrs. Lum sat down after serving him, sunk in gloom. She usually exchanged a few words with Lute so Lute asked in an effort to cover up the awkwardness:

"Have you heard any news, Mrs. Lum?"

"No," she said, unaccountably flustered. "I haven't, have you?"

"No, I just thought you seem worried."

"Oh, that of course. Can't get anything, everything running out. Milk has stopped deliveries." She stared into space. Trapped again she had to either give further explanations or seem silly. After a brief struggle with herself she lowered her voice embarrassedly. "Mr. Lum has to have milk every day. It acts as a laxative for him."

"That's terrible. To be without."

"I don't know what to do," she whispered looking at her husband pityingly, watching him eat.

"Have some more?" she murmured rising to refill his bowl.

He shook his head irritably and turned back to his work. She was a little guilty at letting out his secret. With closed face she packed up the things and went.

Back in the Mission Lute met Leela on the stairs.

"There is talk of surrender," Leela told her in a low scared voice.

At last the surgical knife to cut off all the misery. Lute had thought the British would never surrender, it would have to be the Japanese breaking in. No wonder Mrs. Lum had looked nervous when asked if she had heard any news. Of course she would not tell. Bad for morale.

"Is that why there was no air raid today?"

"Oh, they're still fighting. But there is talk that we are going to surrender. I don't know," she retracted.

"Are we losing?"

"No, they say the Japanese have landed in two places but we are holding them back. I don't know," she said resentfully, washing her hands of the whole business.

After Lute had thought it over she realized that the negotiations might take days, to be followed by a period of confusion right after the Japanese came in. But as long as they were going to surrender the British were certainly not going to start any new undertaking such as feeding the civil defense workers. In that case the rations were not coming over. What to do in the mean time?

She went to bed numbed by panic. Tomorrow she would go and forage for food before she got too weak for that. Go downhill, look for those small shops, see if they would let her talk through a peephole and if her two dollar thirty cents could still buy anything. On the road down she had seen a few shops in old garages cut out of the stone foundations of houses. There were no buildings on the other side of the road so the shop, a hole in a great stone wall, looked out to sea with its back to the hill, strategically impregnable as though foreseeing this day when it was in danger of being robbed of its stale cookies. She did not know enough Cantonese to reassure them and they distrusted people of the outer provinces but she would have to try. What if the ration came while she was absent from office? Go later? It would be more difficult than ever to get the storekeeper to open the peephole after dark.

In the morning there was a knock on her door.

"Miss Mew asks you to go down," a voice called out.

That would be the Mission amah who called Miss Muirhead by her Chinese name. Lute opened the door.

"What is it, do you know?"

The amah had gone on to other doors.

"Everybody is to go down," she said.

The Japanese had come in during the night? Or Miss Muirhead was going to announce the surrender and ask them to be prepared, gather together, sing hymns and pray while waiting for the Japanese. It seemed unlike Miss Muirhead to be so dramatic. We're being evicted, Lute thought. The old house is falling down after getting a corner blown off the other day. Fate has made the last turn of the screw, not really unexpected. She dressed and went down.

Some of the women were down before her. She followed them into the parlor and from there drifted over the adjoining room where all the others were waiting. The dining table was set and they were milling around smiling with the unmistakable air of guests reluctant to be seated. Lute hung back uncertainly. Leela came up to her.

"Come on. You're invited for Christmas breakfast," she said. The smile on her dark Greco-Roman face seemed sarcastic. She kept her hands in the pockets of the university blazer which she wore open over her cotton dress, showing the matronly little figure underneath.

"What? It's Christmas?"

"Didn't you know? It's Christmas today."

"Christmas already? I didn't even know." She had been counting the days of her starvation only.

"Come on. Everybody is invited," Leela said.

Miss Muirhead in a cashmere cardigan of the 1920s, practically new, was busy putting finishing touches to the table. There were no Christmas decorations but the cutlery and starry cookies and plates of porridge and jam, sugar and canned milk dazzled the eye. A silvery sunlight slanted in from a high barred window and shone on the dark green linoleum tablecloth. The guests had given in and loosely encircled the table, each standing more or less behind a chair smiling embarrassedly. To keep talking Lute asked Leela, then found she had to do it in a whisper:

"Is this Christmas Day? Then yesterday was Christmas Eve!"

Miss Muirhead straightened up and smiled at the gathering.

"We thought it would be nice to invite you all to Christmas breakfast, since today is the day that our Savior was born. We want to make it a happy day for all of you."

Her tone clearly implied this was only for today, no precedent to be made. This was a day with no past or future. But how was she to go back to the stark poverty of the empty kitchen and unlit stove, after this show of strength?

Everybody had sat down.

"Now let us pray."

Lute looked down in her lap as Miss Muirhead prayed aloud. The sunlight on the green linoleum with all the food and table silver on it swam in her head above the eyes like reflections of sea waves on a porthole glass. Don't eat much all at once or the stomach can break, she had heard this somewhere. After the prayer she toyed with her porridge and passed her cup for tea. The discomfort of the situation made self-control easy. She took a cookie every time the platter came her way and set them beside her plate to take with her. Angeline who sat opposite to her ate with that fixed look in her eyes she had, that made them small and hard. Pink circles appeared around the eyes as they filled with tears. Lute thought, it must be terrible, the first Christmas after losing someone. She did not know what to say to Angeline. They had scarcely spoken to each other since she came back from the hospital after her brother died. She sometimes acted almost as if it had been Lute's fault. Anyway Lute thought it was best that she keep away as she must remind her of it. Miss Eu sat next to Angeline, put milk and sugar in her tea and saw that she had everything.

They all rose to thank Miss Muirhead and wish her merry Christmas. Lute went to office. Mr. Lum was not yet there. She browsed among the library shelves. The alarm clock with which she was to time the air raids had stopped again, so she could not tell how long she had been there when she started to wonder why Mr. Lum was so late. It was not like him even if it was Christmas.

It suddenly occurred to her she had not seen a single soul upon coming in. She went out and looked down the stair well. Nobody was in the vestibule where some of the room doors stood open. The house seemed unnaturally quiet. She went up the stairs leading to the roof, stopped and listened. It did not sound like anybody was up there. She hesitated to go up and look. There was that anti-aircraft gun that had plagued her all these days sitting on top of her head attracting bombing planes. She ran up the last few steps. There it was, just her and it under the sun on the vast rooftop paved with concrete flags.

The silence in the house rose to a crescendo as she went down. We have surrendered, she thought, and I'm the only one here today. The Japanese may come in any minute and find me here with the anti-aircraft gun. She went round the vestibule downstairs looking into all the rooms just in case anybody was there. It could still be that nothing had happened. She would not be caught deserting her post just because her boss was late to office.

She went home happily. The war was over and nobody to tell it to, and merry Christmas.

In the afternoon Angeline came to her door.

"Hong Kong has surrendered, Lute. We're all to move into Stanley Hall."

"Really? They'll allow girls in there?"

"Yes, we can all go."

"Stanley Hall — that's higher than Cuninghame Hall," Lute blurted and was sorry at once. Already the pink shadows had appeared around Angeline's eyes.

"Yes. They're going to turn Cuninghame Hall into a war hospital. We're all going to be nurses."

"When can we move in?"

"Any time."

"Right now?"

"Sure."

16

Lute took a room for herself and Bebe, one in a long row on the second floor. The same evening the students got their first meal. The stock of rice and beans had been moved into Cuninghame Hall days ago awaiting orders to start cooking. Now that the Japanese had taken over all the stores, Dr. Mok the head of the new war hospital obtained permission to use what was at hand for student relief. Dr. Mok had taught anatomy at the university. The British faculty being interned, the Chinese doctor was in charge. He got some students to work under him, boys and girls from his home town in Malaya, following the age-old practice of giving jobs to fellow townsmen. The boys were in high spirits serving rice and beans to the waiting queue.

"The Japanese haven't come in yet?" somebody asked in the queue.

"They're very slow," said the boy passing out plates from behind the barrier of up-ended chairs.

"Don't worry, man," said another squatting monkey-like on a chair, dipping into the big enamel drum for beans, "the Japs want to put on a show, be kind to students."

"Wait and see. Wait till the soldiers come," Leela said at the head of the queue.

"What are you girls afraid of? So many of us here to protect you," said the boy with the dipper.

There were sniggers down the line while Leela blushed and muttered, "Yes, you people."

Lute went back in the morning to get her things from the girls' dormitory. As it was further uphill it seemed safe to assume the Japanese had not yet reached there. She turned into the familiar road with the mixed feelings of homecoming. The poinsettias were still on the trees, big red cartwheels with every spoke intact, as well-kept as though they had spent the last few weeks in a parlor. The craggy stone foundations that walled one side of the road showed no marks of gunfire. The same dark blue flower pots marched up the balustrades of every house on the way. The sea on the other side of the road remained distant and blue. She met no one but that was nothing unusual. There was something different though, a little disturbing until she was able to locate it, the absence of the sound of passing cars coiling up the hill. It deepened the silence and made the scene smaller, more shut in. It seemed even the birds did not chirp.

After the long climb up the steps she saw that the garage doors of the refectory were bolted. She went round the house and tried the side door at the gardener's quarters, also locked. She peeped into the small barred windows, filmed over. It was unlikely anyway that the gardener was still here. She went up the stoop to the front door just to make sure.

To her astonishment the door was merely pulled to. As she pushed it open there was a loud tearing noise. Several pigeons blundered out. She half ducked bewildered as the black and grey wings fanned her face with gusts of musty bird smell. When they were gone she went in expecting the ceiling had been blown off. It was still the same quiet foyer. Then she saw the stairway. An enormous train of brilliant silks swept down the winding stairs, lit up by the two-storey high domed window partly of stained glass. Satin, chiffon, sarong cloth, suede, lamé, swimming suits, embroidered dragons, the way they poured down took her breath away. She went up for a closer look and felt as helpless as if the plumbing had burst. The looters had been.

She hurried to the basement. Were her things still there? She turned on the light in the storeroom. There was a confusion of clothes and open suitcases on the floor. She waded over to the luggage rack. There was her battered old trunk with Aunt Coral's travel labels on it marked with all the countries of Europe. Nobody seemed to have touched it. She looked for Bebe's trunk. It had been pulled out on the floor but the lock was intact. She opened her own trunk, took out most of her things and wrapped them in a big bath towel. Pushing it back on the bottom rack she noticed something on the floor which she thought she might have dropped. She picked it up. It was a photograph of Angeline, round-cheeked and almond-eyed. Scrawled across it with a heavily pressed-down pencil but keeping clear of the demurely smiling face were these Chinese words: Younger Sister I love you. A looter had written it. Her first impulse was to laugh, to think anybody would loot in such a leisurely fashion, pausing to admire a pretty face and write this sentiment on the picture. Younger sister was a common word of endearment. But seeing how Angeline's brother had died for her sake it was almost as if he had spoken.

She could not help an eerie feeling here in this deserted vault under the dim light bulb. She thought she heard footsteps somewhere in the house. It was unlikely that she could hear anything down here if there was anybody upstairs. It might be the wind blowing the front door or pigeons bumping the window or she had imagined it. But the roots of her hair went cold. She dropped the photograph down among the litter, then bent down and put it carefully where she would not trample on it by chance and offend Angeline's brother. How did she know there weren't still looters in the house? Some of them might have come back for more. Also the Japanese might have come uphill. If they found her here she could be taken for a looter and shot.

She put the light out and went to the staircase carrying her bundle, stopped to listen and heard nothing. She went noiselessly up the cement stairs and peeked round the wall at the foyer. It was empty. She headed quickly for the front door. But a last look around her shoulder made her heart lurch up to hit her chin, almost knocking her unconscious. In the river of silk was a human figure she had not noticed before, curled up on the stairs with the black head bowed down, covered with ringlets and pompadour. In a consternation of horror, all booming icebergs inside, Lute watched the crouched figure in brocade move up a step and reach out for something. Then it turned and faced her.

"*Say lo*! you gave me such a fright," the girl cried out, her hand going to her heart, then reaching to clutch the railings. "I didn't know you were here."

"I didn't know either."

It was Veronica Kwok.

"I almost fell off the stairs," she said.

"You weren't here when I first came in."

"I only just came. Look what happened to my things." Veronica held out a silk print *cheongsam*, then grabbed a pink petticoat. "This looks like mine too."

"When did you come back?"

"This morning. Lucky I wore this to the outpost," she looked down at her padded brocade gown, "otherwise it would be gone too. Ha, you should have seen me chopping wood dressed in this, and starting the stove on my knees, cooking for the boys. How they laughed, they were always teasing me," she said happily.

Veronica used to look a little lost and disgruntled, tacked on to Angeline with whom she suffered by comparison. Now there was such pure joy in her face, part of Lute watched awestruck and humbled. It takes a wise woman to get such happiness out of a war.

"Did you see Bebe? Is everybody back from the outposts?"

"I don't know," Veronica said. "I got the third room from the end."

"Oh, you're next to me."

"I hurried up here because I was worried about my things, and look what I found." She dipped wildly into it wading upstream.

"Did you look upstairs?"

"All the cupboards are empty. Not a thing left. This is Angeline's. I'll bring it to her."

"There's more in the basement. I'll go down with you."

In the basement Veronica found her shoes and more of her clothes and stuffed them into a suitcase that had been broken into.

"We better not stay here too long," Lute said.

"Yes, we'd better go. I'll get the boys to come with me another time."

Coming out of the house she noticed Lute's bundle was wrapped in a bath towel.

"Hey, do you want a hot bath?"

"That will be wonderful, but where can you get hot water?"

"In one of the professors' house. Some of the boys went there to bathe."

Lute was confused. "There's nobody there?"

"All the British are in camp."

"But there's hot water in the tap?"

"Sure."

"Do you want to go?"

"I have no bath towel."

"You can use mine, it's clean."

"What about you?"

"I can bathe after you, it makes no difference."

Veronica still grinned at her uncertainly, tempted and impish. "You want to go?"

"I don't know. I do need a bath."

"All right, let's go."

So on their way back they stopped at one of the little faculty houses set back behind rhododendrons and mottled rust red hedges on a small lawn cut out of the hill. It was Professor Shackford's house. Lute had been here for English tutorials, those weekly sessions where the professor smoked a pipe beneath his large black moustache and tried to make the four of them talk. She liked him and had felt shocked when Paula said one day, "Shackford and his wife drink like fish. Everybody knows." Lute did hear titters the time he came to class more high-colored than usual, scarlet against the jet black eyebrows and moustache and the black hair that grew low on his forehead. She had come across Mrs. Shackford in their house, a chunky faded blonde in an old cotton print dress. Passing the students on the stairs she would drop her eyes half smiling and sidle by quickly in mock self-effacement. Lute had thought there was an odd look in her large blue eyes but without connecting it with drunkenness, a purely fictitious state according to Aunt Coral. But the Shackfords came to mind when she read some of Maugham's stories. They would put the drinking on the Hong Kong climate, near perfect as it is. Or the boredom, the wife having nothing to do in a small house tended by two, three servants. Were they bored with each other? Not having known them when they had been young it was hard to tell in what ways they had been disappointed. The professor was the dean of the faculty, as high up as he would go in Hong Kong. They had a daughter at school in England. But they were now in a concentration camp, passed out of Maugham's stories and the limits of her ken. The term concentration camp, seldom spoken and always whispered, was easy to dodge. It did not mean the same as in Germany. What the Germans did to the Jews the Japanese would not do to the British. They would be uncomfortable and undernourished but otherwise all right, surely?

Their door was not locked. As she went in with Veronica they felt like uninvited guests in the small cozy vestibule. This being war, houses were empty. Half stealthily and tittering they went up the polished stairs. There was the sound of running water and Malayan English. Lute was glad to hear the water coming on so big and strong after the war time dribble. The bathroom was on the first landing. Through the open door she had a glimpse of several boys waiting for the tub to fill.

"*Say lo*!" cried Veronica. "None of you bathed yet? How long do we have to wait?"

As they laughed and joked with her Lute went on to the next room. It did not seem right to talk to boys in a bathroom and a new note in their voices showed they felt it too and were tickled by it. She found herself in the same study where the tutorials had been held. The floor was white with papers strewn inches thick. It looked like all the drawers and files had been emptied in a rage. The looters had been here too. Yet the bookshelves that lined the walls were packed full of expensive-looking books, evidently untouched. The contrast between the neat shelves and the littered floor was strangely upsetting, unlike the work of human hands, as though a low tornado had come in on its belly. She looked around stunned. Who were these looters? Were they the servants and their kins? Or the *hak sam*, the gangsters in black? Or the occasional country women gathering wood on the hillside, a big conical hat emerging out of the mist like a mountain peak in old paintings? The university area was the one district where the poor were not in sight. The nearest general store and jumble of old tenements were a long way downhill.

The water was still running. Veronica's high-pitched voice came over clearly.

"*Ho sui eh*!" she swore. "I'll never bathe as long as there are peeping toms around. No thanks. After you. Gentlemen first."

Lute did not catch what the boys said with their strong Malayan accent half swallowed by guffaws.

"Charlie, you're as bad as the others," scolded Veronica, "and after we went through the war together."

Resigned to a long wait Lute put her bundle down on the desk, unwrapped it to free the bath towel and stuffed everything else into a pillow case. The sea of paper on the floor rustled at her every step. She was bemused by the two distinct strata of existence in the room. The anarchy underfoot mocked the dreamy peace in the top layer made up of rows of books, gold letterings on red and black, cloth and leather, and somehow deepened and sweetened the slumber in the upper berth. She remembered Professor Shackford explaining about coats of arms:

"Mr. Gilbert Wong, what would you have on your coat of arms, if you have to choose a coat of arms?" the last phrase fraught with sarcasm which the class did not miss. Everyone smiled at the idea of Gilbert Wong being created a British peer.

"A lion," Gilbert said smiling.

The class broke down. Even Shackford on the platform had difficulty keeping a straight face.

"What kind of a lion?" he asked. "The lion *couchant* or the lion *rampant*?"

He explained the French words and the class exploded again. It seemed the funniest joke Lute had ever heard just because it had to do with Gilbert Wong. Gilbert was the eager beaver of the class. He worked so hard to get higher marks than her, he had studied the next year's textbooks in the summer vacation. Mr. Bromley the lecturer on *King Lear* had been furious when he happened to see Gilbert's book, scrawled with penciled-in definitions of words he had looked up in the dictionary, with some of the meanings twisted.

Bebe had asked Lute indignantly, "Is it true you're friendly with this Gilbert Wong?"

"No," Lute had said surprised. "Why?"

"Some people say you're in love with him. They thought it was such a big joke."

It was Lute's turn to be indignant. "We're not even friends. He comes up and talks to me sometimes in the library. Maybe he thinks I have some tricks he can steal."

"It's different if it's any other boy. Because this Gilbert Wong is what they call a mug," Bebe spoke the lowest name she knew in a whisper.

No Chinese would have a sleeping lion on his shield. China had been called the sleeping lion and the name had always rankled. Gilbert had no choice. His round face reddened, he looked down through his steel-rimmed glasses and whispered, "The lion *rampant*."

In the uproar that followed, Lute had laughed until tears came, burying her face in her arms.

In this same room at a tutorial Professor Shackford had asked her who was her favorite writer.

"Aldous Huxley," she had said.

He had nodded and added after a moment, "The typical undergraduate taste."

She had wanted to ask what the adults liked. Now was the chance to find out. She went to the shelves to look and pulled out the first book that meant anything to her, Oscar Wilde's *Salome*. She had never seen these illustrations by Aubrey Beardsley. She riffled through hurriedly looking for the pictures. They combined the fairyland of the West that she had known as a child together with a reality that overwhelmed her. She could not let them go. I'll take them back to Shanghai, they'll be with me wherever I go, nothing shall ever happen to them. I'll just take the pictures, to save luggage space. It seemed to her less like stealing if she just took the pictures. Her intentions ought to be clear then: just to salvage what she could out of the war. She stopped to listen first. The water was no longer running. Somebody was bathing. Veronica was talking with the rest of them at the head of the stairs, nearer to her now but they could not see into the room. She hardened her heart and tore out all the illustrations one by one. The torn edges crinkled but they could be pressed down. Keeping an eye on the open door she slipped them quickly into her pillowcase so they lay smooth on top of everything else.

She put the book back on the shelf. Suddenly drained of all enthusiasm she could not bring herself to look over the other books. How much longer must she wait? Right now she would like to get in the bathroom for a minute. But even after the bather came out she would not like to ask those boys to let her in first. They would laugh behind her back. That would be just their idea of a joke.

More waiting. She finally pushed the door to without turning the knob so it just barely closed as though by accident. She squatted down behind the door and heard the water rain on the leaves of paper. Thieves always relieved themselves on the floor before they left the scene of the crime. For a moment she felt united with all the thieves of China throughout the ages. She got up quickly, tidied her clothes and opened the door halfway. The same voices were talking and laughing outside. She could not wait here any longer. The white littered floor had become oppressive, seeming to encroach on the orderly upper level. All the reminiscences were gone from the room. She went out.

"Veronica, here's the bath towel. I have to be going, so I'll go first."

She carried the stuffed pillowcase back to Stanley Hall. She had just started to put the things away, cleaning and lining the drawer where she was going to store the pictures, when a girl's voice called out on the stairs:

"Lute Shen? Somebody downstairs to see you."

Who would that be? Not the Cheungs, they would never venture out so soon after the war. A girl would come upstairs. It must be a boy then. Who? Nobody could have seen her just now in the professor's study? Veronica had spoken of peeping toms.

She took a grip on herself and hurried down. There was no one waiting on the porch. She did not know where the visiting room was. There was the ceremonial hall at back which seemed to be used as a recreation room on ordinary days. No one in there. She looked in the dining hall. Gilbert Wong rose to greet her looking very small in the huge empty room with most of the benches stacked on the round dining tables, legs up.

"Hello," she said smiling, wondering why he had come. Wasn't the competition over now?

Gilbert looked neat as always in his only suit, the pepper-and-salt yellowed with age.

"How are you?" he said. He came from Malaya so they had to talk in English.

"I thought I would come and see how you were," he explained after the greetings.

"That's very nice of you. Won't you sit down?"

"That was really unexpected, the war," he said smiling.

"Yes. A real surprise."

She did not ask where he was staying. He might not like to talk about how he had gone underground like all the rest of the boys in their class. She admired their sagacity but they would not know.

"I'm glad you're not hurt," he said.

"We're lucky."

"Yes." After a pause he said, suddenly grinning at her with a secret meaning that she failed to catch at first, "They're burning the records at the university office."

"What records?"

"All the files. Marks and — all the records on the students," he began a gesture and stopped.

"But why?"

"They want to destroy all the papers before the Japanese arrive."

"Oh," she said, unable to see why students' records should be military secrets.

"They're not going to leave a single copy of anything." He continued to grin at her like a bespectacled cat.

"Is there still time?"

"Oh yes, the Japanese are not here yet. The head clerk is making a big bonfire outside the building."

As he pointed she twisted around to look out the French window as though the flames might be visible from this distance. She quickly turned back again, aware that it seemed like she was hiding the expression on her face.

"Really?"

"It's true," he said earnestly. "Lots of boys are looking on. Would you like to go and see?"

"No, what for?" she said smiling. Something was missing in her heart, lost forever.

"A big fire. You want to see? Lots of people watching."

"No."

"I'll go with you."

She half wanted to go. A bonfire outside the administration building might be worth seeing.

"No, I'm not going down."

"Why? Why not?" He was still watching for any sign of pain in her expression.

"I just don't want to bother."

He grinned wider as if saying he understood. Now that he had delivered the blow they became much more relaxed and friendly.

"What are you going to do now? Are you going to stay here?" He sounded genuinely concerned.

"I want to go back to Shanghai."

He nodded approvingly. Going home was a safe and feminine thing to do.

"What about you? Have you got any plans?" she said warmly to show that she did not mind being told that her unprecedented marks were lost to posterity.

He hesitated, looked down and mumbled, "For the time being I'm staying with somebody I know, I keep accounts for his store. A relative."

"That's nice. Do you think you'll be going home later?"

He hesitated again before he mumbled, "There's no ship to Malaya."

"Of course." She did not know what it was that made her persist, raising her voice a little, "But you are going back eventually, aren't you?"

He wore the look of one who had difficulties he would rather not go into. She suddenly realized that since the war everybody seemed to have secrets, political, financial, amorous, connections and resources they were afraid to share.

"Oh yes," he ended by saying.

She in turn looked reassured while feeling ridiculous. Why was she so anxious for everybody to go home just because she herself wanted to? He must be as penniless as she was and probably had nothing to go back to. Maybe a job in a small town and a mother and grandmother to support. What aspirations had driven him to try so hard to distinguish himself at school? Whatever it was, perhaps she was glad that the war had smashed it to pieces as it had her own hopes of a fellowship at Oxford. Hers were not plans or dreams, just prospects. She was contemptuous of the dreams of youth and thought more of older people for having lived, no matter how they had lived. She had always felt a bond with her brother and the others who had only wanted to grow up and get married and own things. She was not sure that was all she wanted but she never laughed at them as she laughed at other young people with nobler dreams.

Gilbert's hair stuck up at the back of the head like her brother's when he had combed his hair with water. After sitting silent for a while he got up to go. They nodded goodbye smiling. A sadness gripped her throat as they wished each other luck.

17

"I was sweeping the courtyard when this Jap came in," Bebe said. "I've cut my hair like a boy's and borrowed a boy's shirt and trousers. But I saw this Jap look at me. He came at me and I threw down the broom and ran upstairs and he followed me up."

She spoke with the same mousy husky voice with which she had answered biology questions just before the examination. Lute could not bear the sound of it.

"I got to the top floor. There was a window open, I got on the window sill and yelled at him: you come up and I'll jump. He stood there for a minute, then he went down and went away."

"What language did you speak?" Lute asked. "He understood?"

"I suppose English. Maybe Cantonese, I don't know, it didn't make any difference. He saw me there half out of the window."

"Were you really going to jump?" Lute whispered in awe.

"I don't know," the small bleak voice answered. Then she craftily hooked an eyebrow in the Arab manner. "Anyway he believed me."

"But this is thrilling, like Rebecca in *Ivanhoe*," Lute said uneasily. It seemed wrong to accept this romantic view of a Japanese soldier and the first time she had come up against one too, in a sense of speaking.

"It was over in a minute."

"What was he like? About how old?"

"I don't know. Not old. They all look the same to me."

The thin faint windblown voice sounded as though she was again up there backed against the window. Lute could go on asking questions forever, it was such a great thing, but she did not. Talk would only degrade it, chip away the drama and wonder of it — to come face to face with the enemy which was more than most soldiers ever got to do in modern warfare, and then to defeat him in a combat of will.

The Japanese soldiers were now all over the compound. The girls walked warily among them not looking at them for fear of starting something. They did not look at the girls either. They went about in twos and threes scouting the land or hung around the piano in the ceremonial hall taking turns playing with one finger. They looked like chunky red-cheeked schoolboys.

"They've been told to behave here," one of the girls said.

Another said, "By the time they got to the center of town they were back into discipline."

Lute was a little amused by the moral zoning. She did not ask Bebe if she happened to see the one who had chased her upstairs. Anyway it would be hard to tell them apart.

"The bank is open," Bebe said. "Do you want to get your money out? I'm going down."

They set out on foot. It was Lute's first trip to town since the organized hike to ARP headquarters. The feeling that a lot had happened came over her as St. Matthew's Academy loomed in sight. The Academy's facade, a small Greek temple in concrete, had always been a landmark, the last stop before the bus reached the university.

"Look!" she exclaimed.

There were heaps of faeces on the immaculate white steps leading to the colonnade.

"Yes, I saw." Bebe turned her head away slightly.

"Was it the soldiers?"

"I suppose so. It's like this everywhere."

Bebe was too British to laugh. Lute was sputtering. Half of the old Chinese jokes were about excretion. She had to laugh although the little yellow-brown mounds so conspicuous on the steps seemed to be final desolation, the end of all civilization. In the shadows of the columns the stone pavings were spotted with bits of straw. There were also horse droppings, a more familiar public sight.

"It looks like they kept horses in there. I didn't know they still used horses in war."

"Some. Not many," Bebe said.

Halfway down the hill the road was blocked by wire fences and two sentries.

"We have to bow?" Lute whispered.

"Same as at Garden Bridge in Shanghai."

"I never crossed Garden Bridge."

"You were lucky you didn't have to."

They were coming to the barricade. Lute was careful not to look at Bebe in her humiliation as she herself bowed slightly in the Chinese way, not much more than a nod. The soldier stared back stonily. She was mortified as a woman bowing to men who made no acknowledgement but she would not have felt this so keenly if she were not with Bebe who was more thoroughly Westernized.

They had walked past when the sentry gave a grunting roar, an amplified "Hrrmph." They stopped and looked back. He barked out a question. Probably about who they were. While Bebe hung back prudently Lute answered in English, having heard that most Japanese learned English in school:

"We're university students."

Would it make him angry using the language of the previous conqueror?

"Hrrmph?" very loudly and incredulously.

Should she try Mandarin or Cantonese? Then she remembered that the Japanese were said to write Chinese characters. She made a gesture of writing. He handed her his pencil and paper pad. She wrote the Chinese words for college students. He nodded and let them pass. The Imperial Army loved culture.

The business section of town seemed unchanged except there was no vehicle traffic. Many people were out walking hurriedly. She had the impression it was such a cold day they had to walk briskly to keep warm. She had forgotten it never got that cold in Hong Kong. A man in Chinese cotton tweed blouse and pants lay stretched out on the sidewalk with a law-abiding air as though siestas were the accepted thing here.

"Don't look," Bebe said.

"Is he dead?" Lute said startled.

"Yes."

She did not look. All she had noticed were the neat stockinged feet in black cloth shoes sticking up close together. Not two steps away another man sat crouched before a small stove frying little yellow cakes. They were rice flour patties, stone hard and amateurish. The man that squatted before them with such concentration looked as if he had been a shroff or seal-carver or shoe salesman before the war. Who would buy these stodgy cakes? But people seemed to have forgotten how to eat in these eighteen days of war. Even Lute was tempted although she knew they were no good, still there was something fresh and exciting about those yellow patties sizzling in the black pan, and so close to death, the last call for dinner.

More bodies blocked the sidewalk, always modestly clothed and decorously stretched out on their backs, arms arranged at their sides, feet together. The crowd hurrying past neatly skimmed by them without a glance. The bizarre thought occurred to her that some undertaker had worked over them but did not take them away.

The Hong Kong and Shanghai Bank was a new building. Lute had seen it going up in scaffolds but the first she had heard of it was in the English class taught by Mr. Allenby, one of the young men that came down from Oxford or Cambridge to serve their apprenticeship in the Far East. He kept his hair a little long behind the ears and read Shakespeare like an actor of the old school, strutting, crouching, whispering lines to a pretty girl in the front row, his voice rising, breaking into a yell, fist crashing down on her desk. The class tittered.

"Ah, the temple of Mammon!" he declaimed one day, then opened his eyes wide and whispered, "Haven't you seen? The new Hong Kong and Shanghai Bank?"

The bank did not look particularly impressive to Lute from the outside, a tall white cube. The pair of stone lions in Chinese style were outsized Pekinese dogs. But the interior had smelled cleaner and mellower than any other place she had ever been, all marble space and distilled light and hushed echoes. She had a shock today going in. The air was so stale, hundreds of people must have slept in here with windows closed. The marble floor was smudgy and wet, dotted with the inevitable little mounds of faeces. They went along the cashiers' cages until they found one that had a man in it. The harassed-looking Eurasian motioned them to queue up at another window.

Bebe was only allowed to draw out a part of what she had in the bank. Lute took all of her $11.19.

"Leave a dollar, or you'll lose your account," Bebe said.

The remark struck Lute as funny in these ruins of the former civilization.

"Never mind," she said, "I'm going back to Shanghai anyway."

"How? We're cut off."

"Don't people come and go from occupied areas?"

"You can't go now anyway."

"Don't you want to go too?"

"Of course, but I don't know when we can."

"I don't even have the money for a boat ticket."

"I'll lend you."

"I was thinking I would have to ask you."

Coming out of the bank Lute said, "Let's go and see the Cheungs, I want to ask them about Shanghai."

"Oh, your relatives. Didn't you say they were in Repulse Bay?"

"They may be back by now."

"All right, let's go. You're not tired?"

"No, are you?"

"I'm not."

"I don't' want to go back yet."

"It's the city," Bebe said. "It's still here, isn't it?"

"Yes. I can walk around forever."

"I tell you, we're crazy."

They had drifted to the sea front. A red ricksha was out, green canvas top folded. A farmer was crossing the road carrying a flatpole on his shoulder with loads of vegetables dangling from both ends. The sentry posted in front of Star Ferry went forward to intercept him. Without a word he slapped the elderly farmer many times. The farmer had not tried to speak, knowing he would not be understood, but he kept smiling. He wore a knitted cap and a padded blue gown tied at the waist, with long narrow sleeves. The archaic clothes and humble mien made him look old but it was difficult to tell his age. A cold wind was blowing, the sun shone bright on the sea and whitened the embankment so that every detail in that instant stood out clear, the pudgy young soldier's arm working mechanically, slapping away, the other hand holding the rifle standing on the ground, the farmer smiling, his apple cheeks no redder on one side than the other, his eyes no less liquid and kindly, his smile no less warm.

"Come on," Bebe said.

Lute realized she was standing still. The shock had a physical impact on her and the bruise felt more sore in the winter cold. They walked on. She was angry but there was nothing to be said. They headed toward De Vore Road where they would follow the tramway to the Cheungs in Causeway Bay.

"It's open," Bebe was surprised when they passed a department store. "Shall we go in?"

"Yes."

A notice board set up at the entrance showed photographs under glass with a handwritten propaganda poster in Japanese. Lute could read the headline in Chinese characters.

"It's about Singapore."

"What does it say?"

"That it fell."

"I heard that."

They passed by without giving the pictures a glance. The news was no surprise, merely deadening. It explained why no help had come from Singapore and made the present situation more irrevocable.

The store had been forced to open to keep up the appearance of normalcy. The unlit counters looked half empty. Here and there a salesman lurked in the shadows. Not one salesgirl among them. Lute and Bebe were the only customers. Their footsteps rang out as they circled around. There was an art exhibit on the other side. That was a new thing. Department stores here never had picture shows. This was an exhibit of old Japanese prints. Lute had never seen any and was instantly taken and overwhelmed by their cruel beauty, very like the Beardsley drawings. It seemed to her it was the first time she saw the true old Orient as it had been lived, seen up close, the details rendered fondly, irreverentially, a woman scratching her hair, two women spreading a mosquito net, humpbacked laborers crouched on the scaffolding with almost a gleam of cupidity in their eyes trying to do a hard piece of work just right. The stylization was just an exaggeration grown out of love and time, the lines becoming distended from their own weight. It was not the same as the kind of distortion that took things apart and put them together again like a gifted child playing with a clock.

"But these are wonderful."

"Yes, they're very good."

They had to whisper, it was so deathly quiet in here, cold too. One or two men in black overcoats shuffled along the rows looking at the pictures glumly, keeping well apart. They must be Japanese. No Chinese would want to see Japanese pictures. Even these Japanese were probably exhibitors, not viewers.

After they got out in the street Lute burst out with "I love this. Much more than Chinese painting."

"Chinese painting is greater, more varied," Bebe said.

"Oh, I know they got it from us in the beginning, but we didn't have anything like this."

"They're more limited."

"We may have had the tendency, but they developed it."

"The Chinese went as far as you can go in some things."

"Not figures. We can't stand people unless they're just a dot in the scenery."

"You just don't like nature."

"I know it must sound terrible to be so fond of their things after what we just saw." She did not have to say the old man getting beaten.

"No, I don't think it's wrong to like their art, I just think Chinese art is greater."

Lute looked back at all the copies of copies of scholarly landscapes.

"Where did you see the good things? In foreign books on Chinese art?"

"No, I've seen them around," Bebe gestured non-committally. Didn't your family have things?

"I never saw any."

They found the Cheungs back in their apartment. It was an old house divided into flats. The Cheungs had furnished it inexpensively with secondhand furniture, not meaning to stay long.

"We were just wondering about you," M.H.'s wife said.

"I telephoned, you were in Repulse Bay."

"Hey-ya, don't speak of it," she shook a palm from side to side with revulsion. "It was said to be safer there with all the foreigners in the hotel —"

"Neutral nationals," her husband put in.

"Even if the Japanese came in they should have some consideration for face, we thought. And what did we find? British troops in the lounge setting up big cannons shooting out. Japanese outside setting up big cannons shooting in. Too late by then to go home, the roads were blocked. Everybody stayed downstairs in the lounge, still the safest place in the house. We ran from one wall to the other. Shells coming this way, we rushed to the other side. They coming that way, back we ran. Everybody standing plastered to the wall, like facing a firing squad only I dared not say so. Hey-ya," she sighed half laughing.

Their Cantonese amah brought tea trailing a pigtail over her rump. M.H. asked about conditions at the university.

"Ah, your friend speaks Chinese," his wife cooed and bent over to whisper to Lute, "She's cute."

"We both want to go back to Shanghai. There're no ships now, are there?"

"No. We want to go back too."

"Will you let me know when there are ships?"

"Of course, but the only thing to do now is wait, and you're all right, aren't you? The university is taking care of you?"

"Did you get any letters from Shanghai?" he asked.

"No, do you think the mail still works?" Lute said.

"Letters come and go from occupied areas to Chungking, Shanghai, everywhere," his wife said.

"Is it also like this in the European war?"

"No, it's only in China." He smiled ironically.

"All our post offices seem to have a kind of understanding."

"Then I'll write to my aunt," Lute said.

"Yes, it may get through," she said. "They must be worried about us in Shanghai."

She gave the girls a batch of preserved beancurd sticks to take home.

Paula Hu came to their room at night dressed in a pale green satin slit gown with a little organdy cape that matched.

"Do you think it looks all right?" she asked worriedly.

"Very nice," Bebe said. Lute noticed that her voice had turned small and sad again. "Is this what you wore to the Cuninghame Hall dance?" she bent to examine it close.

"Yes. Do you think the cape will make a veil?"

"Let's try it."

"Not enough ribbon."

"Paula is going to get married," Bebe said to Lute.

"Really? To Mr. Yip?"

"Of course to Mr. Yip!"

"Congratulations!"

Paula smiled and looked as though she was going to be shy and say nothing. But then she murmured in her hard matter-of-fact way although with her eyes down and cheeks slightly flushed, "We thought, might as well."

"The ribbon won't tie but you can use hairpins."

"Maybe I shouldn't wear a veil."

"You mean, for a registry wedding? I don't know."

"Maybe just the dress will be better."

"But you'll want to look a little special, won't you?"

"This color is not right anyway, it should be white."

"It doesn't really matter in a time like this."

"I'll just wear the dress."

"How's that? Just an eye veil."

"Doesn't it look funny with a Chinese dress?"

"I think this is very smart."

After Paula left Bebe said to Lute, "I really can't understand why she wants to get married now."

"I didn't know you can. Is the registry open?"

"It will be in a few days."

"Where are they going to live?"

"They'll have a room downstairs. She'll just move in, no party or anything."

It seemed to Lute part of the picture of desolation around them.

"She says they can have the wedding all over again later. But it won't be the same thing."

"Their families won't object?"

"I wonder what her father will say. I met her family last summer. Her father is a very sharp lawyer. Calculating. That's why Paula's like that," she whispered reluctantly.

"They knew about Mr. Yip?"

"Oh, they were very happy about it."

"Of course. A rich overseas Chinese."

"But where's his rubber plantation now? Singapore is gone. Nobody knows what's happening in Malaya."

"She really loves him then."

"She says there's no such thing as love."

"Well, she still wants to marry him."

"He's such a dope," Bebe said disgruntled.

"Maybe she feels in a time like this a girl is better off married."

"The worst is over. She's back from the outpost safe and sound."

"Mr. Yip was with her at the outpost?"

"Y-yes, why?"

"Do you think she could have, as a safeguard, when they didn't know what would happen when the Japanese came in —"

"You mean she gave herself to him?" Bebe said excitedly. "Do you think so really?"

"Well, if she was going to marry him anyway."

Bebe stared at her and started to laugh. "No wonder she's in such a hurry to get married, before he changes his mind."

"You said he's a dope."

"Not such a dope as that."

"Anyway she's smarter than he."

"If she's really smart she wouldn't have got into this."

They were on night duty the day Paula got married. She had asked Bebe to get their dinner for them. There was bound to be a lot of ragging if the bride and groom were to stand in queue tonight. They would have dinner in their room. They had bought things in town to eat with the rice and beans which they could warm in the hospital kitchen. Bebe and Lute were rolling bandages and cotton balls in the nurses' room when they came in.

"I've got your dinner here, but do sit down," Bebe said.

She beamed helplessly at Paula with nothing to say after asking about their trip to the Registry. The newly-weds sat down at the desk, Mr. Yip still in his overcoat. They looked expectant, keeping their eyes down and their smiles held back, as though waiting for a judgment or a piece of pleasant news such a lawyer was about to read out from a will. Paula had changed into a grey wool gown and cardigan. In the light of the table lamp her face had that skinned raw look that came after hours of crying, the sorrow and happiness shining through.

Bebe handed them two covered plates when they got up to go.

"Don't forget your meal tickets." She gave them back the little rectangles of unpainted wood with numbers written on them by which everybody got his meal.

She and Lute did not speak after they were gone. Lute knew she must feel lonely suddenly same as she herself. That bit of warmth and joy had made this broken-down warehouse kind of a place even colder and drearier.

"I never knew Hong Kong can be so cold," Lute said.

"They say it's the coldest winter since 1860 or something," Bebe said.

"My fingers are frostbitten."

"I wish I have a cup of hot coffee."

"Shall I go and heat the milk?"

"No, wait till they're asleep."

She did not want the patients to see. The patients got two meals of rice and beans a day same as the nurses. They were poor people wounded in the war, treated free here. Only the night nurses got an extra ration of milk and two slices of unbuttered bread each. To heat the milk in the kitchen they had to cross the length of the ward. Neither of them liked to do it but Lute always took it on, feeling she was the harder of the two.

Although she waited until after midnight most of the patients were still awake or had wakened immediately at the approach of food. There being no pillows the campbeds were pushed against the wooden pillars in the former dining hall, totem-like, the black eyes wide open. She walked brazenly down the aisle between the beds in the dimly lit raftered room. The milk bottles cradled in her arms one on each side seemed as indecent as exposed big pendulous breasts. The milk must be poisoned by all the eyes looking at it.

In the haven of the kitchen at the other end there was a gas range and miraculously gas. As nobody had to pay for it it was left burning day and night to save matches. But first she had to scrub the cheap brass pot, more dipper than pot, with edges that cut. It was hard to get the grease off in the icy tap water that turned fingers into carrots. Who was it that made these meat stews diligently supplementing the rice and bean diet? The students or the hospital chore men? Tomorrow she would have to scour the pot again in order to boil surgical instruments in it.

When the milk started to bubble she took the pot off the fire and carried it back through the ward slinging the empty bottles in her other hand trying not to let them tinkle. That was the worst moment, the scent of hot milk blowing from the open pot, the combined affront of sight, sound and heat ploughing a path through the cold stale air that smelled of dirty army blankets without bed sheets. All the heads were watching from the poles.

Back in the nurses' area she poured the milk into glasses. They ate the bread with it. The ward sounded restive. Coughs and whispers and campbeds creaking. But in their resentment not one of the men called for the nurses. The gangrene patient was the only one without pride. After a while he started to whine:

"*Gu-niang* ah! *Gu-niang* ah! Ah Miss! Ah Miss!"

"I'll go," Lute said.

She went out and walked over to the bed with the sweetish foul smell. The wound had gangrened. The thin comedian's face under the black mop of hair was twisted into a smile as if he had a horrible itch.

"*Gu-niang* AH! *Gu-niang* AH!" he continued to chant loudly, melodiously, smiling with eyes half closed letting himself be tickled.

She stood before him. "What do you want?"

For a moment he did not speak, seemingly taken aback, without opening his eyes. Perhaps he had not expected anyone to come so soon. But Lute in her guilt thought he was intimidated and her own voice echoed back curt and brutal.

"Bedpan," he said.

She went to the door and gave a shout, "Bedpan!" and turned to go before the chore man came in with the cracked enamel pan. The rule was the nurses were not to do these things. They were college girls and these were poor men. "Who knows, maybe there're looters among them," one of the girls had said. It was specially bad to be poor in Hong Kong where there was this saying:

> "We laugh at the poor
> But not at the whore."

It was not like the Shanghai war hospital where girl students had nursed wounded soldiers. Lute wished there was some such spirit here, some big wave of moral enthusiasm that would throw her out of herself, make her happy to carry bedpans and empty them too. As it was she did not know how to behave. It must be possible to be kind and gracious while observing social distinctions but it was beyond her.

"What did he want?" Bebe asked.

"Bedpan."

"He doesn't really want it, the chore man was complaining," Bebe said. "He just calls because he's in pain."

In a few minutes he was again singing out:

> "*Gu-niang* AH! *Gu-niang* AE!"

tenderly, resignedly with a sigh in his voice, not expecting anything, just calling for a woman in that sweet indefatigable tenor.

The two girls sat without moving. Finally Bebe got up and went out. Lute heard her ask "What do you want?"

18

Lute preferred night duty, there was more time to read or draw. Only it ended at six in the morning and at ten they had to get up for the first meal of the day. And even before then, just when they had got in bed and fallen asleep Veronica would be screaming next door:

"Ow! No! Charlie stop! No really. *Ho sui eh*, Charlie! Now stop it. Hey, no. No-o! Yeow!"

It sounded like cold hands in warm blankets. Charlie Fong never uttered a sound. Soft-faced and handsome, from Penang, Malaya, he was one of the boys at her outpost, the other was an Indian. Lute and Bebe never spoke or exchanged a look during the nerve-wracking yowling. But Bebe said when they were alone:

"Veronica is beginning to have breasts now. She used to be as flat as you."

"I didn't notice."

"I was thinking: a girl falls in love and she blossoms out, even grows breasts when she didn't have any, just at the right time, just when she needs most to be attractive. Isn't nature wonderful?"

From her readings Lute had a suspicion that Bebe was confusing the result with the cause. But with Bebe looking raptly at her she could only smile and murmur yes.

There was a heap of discarded books on the dormitory landing which had never been cleared away. Lute dug among them, mostly textbooks, some in Chinese, Confucius, Laotze and Mencius. She wished she could find *The Book of Change*, supposedly written by Wen Wong, the founder of the Chou Dynasty, 12th century B.C., when he had been in prison, already an old man and had thought he was going to be killed. It was philosophy based on the forces of *yang* and *yin*, light and darkness, male and female, how they wax and wane, grow and erode, with eight basic diagrams by which fortunes could be told with tortoise shells. She had never read it. It was the most esoteric of the five classics and not taught in the schoolroom because of its obscurity and more important, its mention of sex. Laotze was also not in her curriculum for unorthodoxy. She had only read him in quotations. Here was his book at last. He was the sage of hard times which happen to be most of the time, while Confucianism is only practicable in relative prosperity. As Confucius himself said:

"One learns etiquette and loyalty only when the granary is full."

She had known Confucius and Mencius by heart once without understanding much of it. She took them to her room. The pandemonium around her made her yearn desperately for some restraint or discipline although there was no going back to the past. That was not there any more. In fact there had been the same lawlessness in her father's house. Confucius was far away, his voice no longer disciplinary, turned sweet and nostalgic.

"What dialect did Confucius speak? Is it known at all?" she had asked Professor Chow.

The old man hesitated, and gained her respect and confidence by his moment of uncertainty. "Cantonese," he said surprisingly. "The words he spoke would be classical Chinese, but the pronunciation would be very close to the present Cantonese."

He spoke a poor Cantonese himself and used to make the students laugh. He also courted popularity by inviting the boys to peanut breaks between classes, though of course not the girls. It had been during one of these peanut and green tea sessions that the story got out about his trip to Canton with Mr. Blaisdell and their night in the nunnery. He was a *hsieu-tsai* of the empire, having passed the primary imperial examination, one of the last ever held.

"It used to be said that we have to fight our way out from within. 'Chinese learning as basis, Western learning for practical use.' With you people here it's the other way round," he said to the class. "When you're born in Hong Kong or overseas you have you groundwork laid in foreign learning. With you it's fighting from the outside in. Heh heh heh heh!" he laughed and everybody laughed once more at his favorite metaphor.

Lute thought, I know what's inside. There is nothing left. Anybody who says differently says so because his living depends on it. Nothing left on the outside either when they have finished fighting. The wall in between is the only thing that still makes us think there is something on the other side.

What puzzled her about Confucius was his obsession with ceremony, rather odd in such a balanced sensible man. But she was beginning to see what ceremony could do for living and for ruling, controlling people whether it was a family, a tribe, a kingdom or nation. She thought, I wouldn't even mind oppression if only there was some beauty in it. Beauty that you were used to had a sense of rightness that for most people passed for virtue. Oppression we had always had, in our best periods as well as our worst and the hand always falling heavier on women. That wistfulness that was so much a part of the beauty, didn't it come from oppression?

Confucius said, "When a ceremony is lost, search for it in the wilderness."

It might still be preserved in some out-of-the-way countryside. Japan had been a wilderness beyond the sea. The islanders had taken our things and kept them better than we did ourselves and added to them, while we had become a country with no ceremony. She remembered how comical it had seemed when her aunt shook hands with her on parting. Even bowing now was a Western importation. Our own bowing was accompanied with hand and arm movement different for men and women. Nobody did it any more. We even did the new bowing half-heartedly, self-consciously, slightly to one side just missing the subject of reverence. It was practically never done except at weddings, funerals and speech-making. At other times it looked affected and middle-class. We also laughed at the stiff low bows of some Europeans and the ninety degree ducking of the Japanese. Some of us still kowtowed, though less and less. Kowtowing was not graceful in tight slit gowns and Western suits. But Lute did not mind doing it.

"Isn't it unfair that you have to kowtow to everybody on your own birthday?" the Marquise had said to her once.

"I don't' mind, I like to kowtow."

The Marquise had laughed. "I never heard that before. She likes to kowtow."

She also found paints and brushes among the discarded books as well as a large roll of thick white paper that had probably belonged to an engineering student, too smooth for painting she thought, very like the kind of paper pinned on to mah-jong tables. But the water colors held. She transplanted sketches to the big sheets which she prized too much to cut down. Instead she fitted the figures together to save space filling every inch. One picture all in blues and purples reminded her of two lines from Li Yi-shan's poem which she had always liked:

"When the moon is bright on the sea the pearls have tears,
When the sun is warm on the jade mine the jade smokes."

A visual exercise she often did was to look at a room or a street with neon lights and say: what was this like to a Tang Dynasty man? And the scene changed, the lines and areas rearranging themselves to form different patterns as in an optical illusion. Now it was a middle Manchu dynasty man looking. The pattern shifted again. But in her paintings she did it without thinking. Bebe said she liked them.

"I've always liked this sort of thing," she added.

"What sort of thing?" Lute asked.

"You know. Morbid things."

"I didn't think of this as morbid."

"I like this, I really do," Bebe reassured her. "I didn't like your drawings before, I asked you to stop altogether, remember? I thought it would do you good."

"Yes, I'm glad I stopped."

Bebe pinned up the big pictures and swept her flashlight over them at night lying in bed in the blackout. The faces leaped to life in the spotlight. Going from one to the other was as bumpy and exciting as sailing the rapids.

"Frightening, isn't it?" she said.

"Yes."

"It's like sleeping in a temple with frescos of hell."

"I can look at them all night."

"I tell you, we're crazy."

All the students had to attend Japanese classes. A sandy-haired hulking young Russian came twice a week to teach them Japanese. Nobody took it seriously, the boys especially flaunted their inattention to show they were here under protest. But to Lute it was grist to grind on for the time being. She wanted badly to study hard and somehow make up for what she owed Mr. Blaisdell. The Russian knew he was unwelcome. He never went after his pupils for not studying. When he had to make a sentence he paused to think, chalk in hand, and generally ended up with "This is Teacher's coat," pointing to his own coat or "These are Teacher's shoes," pointing to his shoes.

"He probably never wore shoes before," Bebe said.

"I wonder what he did before," Lute said.

"He came from Harbin, that's how he knew Japanese."

The teacher wandered upstairs and knocked at the door.

"Good evening," he said in English.

"Good evening," Bebe said.

Lute recognized that bleak note in her voice, this time a substitute for chilliness.

He walked in and looked around. Pointing to the pictures on the wall he asked Lute because she was painting:

"You — this?"

"Yes."

"Oh. Mmm!" He stood looking at the pictures for the want of something to do. The girls smiled at each other behind his back.

"Won't you sit down?" Bebe moved over to her bed to give him her chair.

"You have not work today?" he asked.

"Oh, we're off duty," Bebe said.

"Oh yes."

"Is it a long way for you to come?" Bebe said. "How do you get here?"

"Oh yes. Very far."

"There's no bus now."

"No bus."

"You have car?"

"No gasoline. No use have car."

"Then how did you come? Walk?" she laughed slightly.

"No, I came with people," he said offhandedly.

"Oh."

He could only mean he came by Japanese army truck.

After a pause she made another try at conversation.

"Where do you work? I mean what do you do all day besides teaching here?"

"Oh yes I work."

"What do you do? Teach?"

"Yes teach."

"Teach Japanese?"

"Oh yes," he mumbled unwillingly.

She did not go on.

He reached over and took a framed picture from her desk. It was a portrait that Lute did of her in brassieres, on the cardboard backing of a writing pad that was the same golden mustard color as her skin. Bebe loved her own complexion. Every time she saw Lute without stockings she would poke a finger at her mauvish white leg crying disgustedly in bad Mandarin, "Dead man's flesh." She had been very pleased with the picture and had found a glass frame with a narrow gold border for it in the pile of cast-offs on the landing, so the crayon colors would not shed. It was a faithful likeness with sure lines, the thick black upslant of a downcast eye, the bud of a nose, the short hair just growing out into a feather cap, the breasts half encased in white cones forcibly pointing outward at forty-five degrees and the Indian black smudge at the dimpled elbow.

"This you?" he asked.

The girls sputtered.

"Does it look like me?" Bebe asked.

"Very good. You?" he nodded toward Lute. "Mmm! You very good. You sell?"

The girls looked at each other and laughed.

"Why, do you want to buy it?" Bebe said.

"Yes-I-want-to-buy," he said defiantly, casually in one word. "How much you sell?"

Bebe turned again to Lute, her mouth swollen with suppressed giggles.

"I don't' know," she turned back to him. "We never thought of selling it. Now where's my other needle? Lute, have you seen my knitting needle? Look under your paper. Never mind, I found it." He had to get up to let her reach behind him.

He sat down again on the chair a little too small for him, hunched to study the picture he held on his knee. His pale head seen sideways had much width.

"Well, where else do you teach?"

"Hm?"

"You said you also teach in other places?"

"Yes I work other place," he mumbled. To take the conversation off himself he asked with obvious effort, "Where is your home?"

"In Shanghai."

"And your friend?"

"She's also from Shanghai."

"Oh! Mmm! So you all from Shanghai."

"Are you from Harbin?"

"Yes I was many places." He suddenly flashed the picture at her. "How much you sell?"

She laughed. "He really wants to buy."

"How much?" he lowered his voice in a reasonable tone.

Bebe could not resist bargaining. "How much will you give for it?"

"Five dollar." He held up the fingers of one hand. "No frame," he added.

"Why, what's wrong with the frame? You don't like it?"

"No, no, I have. This you take. I not want." He shook his head and a hand sidewise Chinese fashion. "I have many. Many."

Lute saw numerous rococo-framed family photographs as in her Russian piano teacher's house and one of the ancestors displaced by half nude Bebe. It seemed to her his change to a businesslike attitude showed he had given up the idea of winning Bebe through her picture. Now he just wanted it for a souvenir.

"Well, do you want to sell?' Bebe asked Lute.

"It's yours really. I don't mind either way."

"It's your work. Don't you want to keep it?"

"Five dollar. No frame," he repeated firmly.

"What do you think?"

"Well, no."

"I'm sorry, we don't want to sell," Bebe dropped her eyes and mumbled very fast, the way she got past a sales clerk after being shown all the goods.

He stayed a little longer, then went. The girls were highly elated as artist and model.

"We better put this away," Bebe said. "With Japanese soldiers dropping in all the time."

They came in twos. The girls did not greet them and went on with whatever they were doing but were careful not to look unpleasant just so as to give them nothing to pick on. Lute covered her Japanese textbook with other books in case the soldiers should see it and try to start a conversation. The soldiers sat on the bed side by side and talked to each other laughing occasionally. As far as Lute could make out they were not talking about Bebe or her. They never even looked at them directly. They reminded her of the pair of geese in her garden in Shanghai who seemed never to see her no matter how she crossed their path, maintaining the dignity of one species forced to live alongside another. It was odd how much these Japanese seemed an entirely different kind of animal although they looked Chinese, just rosier and more thick-set. On the other hand the White Russian had no mystery for her. Young Russians that grew up in China were very much like herself except more Westernized, dispossessed, the old influences hanging in rags that shamed them and did not keep out the cold.

The utter strangeness of the Japanese made them unpredictable. The pair as alike as twins sat at ease on the little bed in the cold room, exuding a refrigerated sweaty smell from their uniforms down to the khaki-bandaged legs. They might be enjoying themselves in their own fashion but there was always the feeling that they were liable to break into violence any minute.

Lute gave a start when one of them leaned across and addressed a remark to her for the first time. He took a pencil from her desk.

"Can I have this?"

She was not sure that was what he said but he was gesturing with it toward his pocket. She nodded. He put it in his pocket. They both got up as at a signal and left the room.

Crossing the lawn one day she saw a student come up to two of the soldiers. She recognized P.T. Pan, Bebe's boy friend at one time. The same lock of hair still hung down his forehead. His small boy's face was white from the cold and he had both hands thrust deep in the pockets of his black overcoat. The soldiers stopped as he came toward them on the asphalt path. For a moment she had the impression he was going to pull out a gun and shoot them. He astonished her by speaking Japanese very fast, batting his eyes just as rapidly. She did not remember he had this nervous habit, probably the effect of learning a new language in such a short time. She was full of admiration. They had made so little progress in Japanese class. He addressed the soldiers earnestly, unsmiling, while they stood on one foot talking back freely but not entirely off their guard. It was hard to tell how well he knew them.

She saw him again one evening when everybody was milling around waiting to be let into the dining hall, in a room which might have been a sports store room but was now stripped bare. Large anatomical jars on a shelf held soya beans soaking for the night.

"Hello, Bebe. This is for you." He gave her a cube of butter.

She laughed with some constraint, her voice turned small and husky. "Why, what for?"

"Butter."

"Why don't you have it yourself?"

"No, I have lots."

"Come on. Where would you get them?"

"Honest, I can get plenty."

"Keep this for yourself."

"I have. Really. I can speak some Japanese so I help the soldiers buy things."

"*Jing yieh*, the best stuff," muttered one of several boys standing nearby.

The others snickered. P.T. Pan paid them no attention as he walked out. His eyes did not twitch when he was not speaking Japanese.

"Not staying for dinner," one of the boys said.

"No coolie chow for him, man," another said. "Eat downtown. Business hours right now."

With their chopped sentences and the barking straits accent Lute was never sure she had heard them right. *Jing yieh* was a common Cantonese phrase but the way they said it reminded her of a serialized novel in the local papers where it had stood for beautiful prostitutes without diseases.

They said no more, already slightly discountenanced by having said so much in the girls' presence. They swiveled about on one foot, hands deep in their pockets, shoulders high against the cold. Lute turned toward a window. Somebody had traced out "Home sweet home" with a finger on the dusty steamed-up glass. The words stood out in the dim electric light.

Bebe was talking to the boy with the blue-green sports coat. Lute recognized him by the coat because Bebe was always jokingly asking him for it.

"Isn't it a lovely color?" she turned to Lute.

"Lovely," Lute said.

"Did you see me try it on? It looked very nice on me. Don't you think so?" she turned back to the pleasant-faced boy.

He smiled sheepishly. "Sure."

"You should really give it to me. I love this color but you seldom get this deep shade. Have you ever seen a coat like this?" she asked Lute.

"No."

"It's warm too. Feel it." Gingerly Lute felt the piece she held out. "You're warm, aren't you? Well, if you should ever want to throw it away, remember me. With this you'll know I won't die of cold."

A curiously apprehensive look came into his face and he seemed about to speak. He's going to give it to her, Lute thought with alarm. It did not seem right, Bebe had so many clothes and this appeared to be his only coat.

He did not say anything and the moment passed.

"Well, how's the work? Are you still at the Bonham Road outpatients'?" Bebe asked.

She liked him, only there was not much to talk about aside from his coat. Lute supposed that she was flirting with him in a way, her acquisitive instinct and other instincts working together without her knowing it. What else was there, the way everybody milled around forever in this murky light like particles in the primeval brew out of which only the most elementary life would come. The male and female force, *yin* and *yang* in the beginning of the world. Lute had never remembered seeing Mimi Choy before, a large drab girl with a kinky permanent and the figure of a wet nurse. Now she suddenly became conspicuous and literally threw her weights around. She was leaning against a window ledge knitting a sweater. A boy was saying:

"Hey, is it true we're going to get salaries?"

"Who said?" demanded another in their choppy manner.

"T.F. said, according to Charlie. Wasn't it Charlie?"

"Where's T.F.?"

"Hey, where's T.F.?"

This last was addressed to Mimi Choy, who like T.F. had come from the same town as Dr. Mok and thus belonged to the inner circle. In his eagerness the boy had thrust his face toward hers. Mimi just gave him a long fixed look out of her slit eyes in the doughy face. Nonplussed the boy hesitated, then slunk away with a low laugh, fearful of being teased by his cronies.

"Hold this for me," Bebe said to Lute. "You're going to have it too.'

"Not butter with rice."

"Why not? That's how they have it in the Near East."

"Well, Bebe," Mimi Choy greeted her, favoring her with another of those long fixed looks.

"What's that you're knitting?" Bebe bent down to see.

On the other side of the room the boy was shaking his head muttering disclaimers.

"Sour grapes, man," one of his friends said. "Who do you think that was? The big wife no less.'

"Big wife. Who's the little wife then?"

"Where have you been, man? Don't you know?"

"No, who's the little wife?"

"Guess who. From your town."

"Not from theirs? Can't be, man. From Kuala Lumpur like me?"

"You still won't do, man, sorry. You're not as pretty."

"Ah, I know, I know who."

"Big wife, little wife and here comes the midwife."

"No need for midwife, he delivers babies himself," another still had time to whisper.

A short girl came in. She had a concave face and glasses with thin black rims. She went up to Mimi Choy to ask secretively in a low bark:

"Where're the keys?"

Mimi trained the mystifying gaze on her, this time perhaps indicating perplexity, denial of all knowledge or warning to keep mum. Whatever it was she did not get it across.

"The storeroom keys," the other girl insisted. "Dr. Mok wants them."

Mimi just looked at her unwaveringly with eyes too small for staring.

"Has T.F. got them?" the other girl asked.

Mimi picked up her ball of wool, stuffed it in her cardigan pocket and left, probably for Dr. Mok's office.

"Where's T.F.?" the other girl was still asking around when Paula and Mr. Yip came in. Paula made for Bebe and Lute and burst out challengingly:

"Have you heard? Shanghai has been taken."

"You mean the foreign settlements?" Bebe asked.

"Of course, the rest was gone long ago."

"When was this?"

"The same time as the war here."

Lute was thunderstruck. It meant a thousand times more than the fall of Singapore, and not just because it was home. For her family as for everybody else living there it had been the basis of life. The political immunity of Shanghai, the eternal city in a passive, feminine and sinister way. She had heard it said often enough: Shanghai is always Shanghai. This was a geological change, a coastline sinking, a world gone under.

"Was there a lot of fighting?" Bebe was saying.

"Don't know," Paula grunted.

"Maybe it's all in ruins," Lute said, seeing her aunt poking through the debris of the apartment building picking up pieces of the jigsaw tables.

"Who knows?" Paula stared into space, her face touched with red at the high spots as if frostbitten.

She heaved a close-mouthed sigh.

"Don't know what's going to happen," she said.

Lute wrote her aunt again that night. Since both cities had been occupied for months why no letters? The one comforting thing was that the Cheungs had not heard from Shanghai either. Not that she really thought anything might have happened to her aunt. Coral would always be all right. She still had two of her letters. One of them enclosed a clipping from a Shanghai newspaper that Coral said would amuse her. It was an item about the Tiger Balm Garden of Hong and the Peak tram and the Victoria University, "the most luxurious college in the Orient, so aristocratic you can ring for coffee in the library." Coral probably had not noticed what was at the back, a columnist talking about a tea called the green snails of spring for its spirally leaves:

> "The green snails of spring is grown on the Dungting Mountain. The majority of the tea pickers are virgin girls who wear aprons with pockets over the heart in which they keep their tea leaves. This is why it is said this tea has the fragrance of virgins' breasts.

Lute smiled again re-reading it. There it went, our national penchant for virgins, she thought with impersonal complacency even though she did not have those fragrant breasts.

Coral's letter said she had been quite cheerful lately. That was after she had written Dew about getting a lover. The other letter was earlier, just after Dew had left.

"I just finished straightening up the apartment," she wrote. "I spent a weekend in Nanking visiting your Aunt Chien and bought some fake antiques in the Temple of Confucius. Funny to think of buying fakes after all the antiques I have sold. But I like the colors and shapes of these bowls and plates, I put them on the table and sit looking at them, and am beginning to enjoy this half full life."

Lute winced at the last phrase. It was bland and casual, the way she always sounded but it was the first time she had ever said anything about being unhappy, in Lute's hearing anyway. No matter what she came to know about her mother and aunt, after a respite the cozy childhood impressions crept back again. Women have to have men's company just as an accessory to complete a smart appearance. She was prepared to be notified that her mother was going to marry Hennings and her aunt her new friend, but was not surprised when no news came. To her mind they would never change or grow old or be bothered by any of the fundamental things of life. Even though she had seen with her own eyes her aunt getting up by the alarm clock and making much of sleeping late on Sundays, she did not think of Coral's office job as a struggle for a living but more like a demonstration of her smartness. She would like to stay with her aunt when she got back but was not at all sure Coral would be glad to have her, she had seemed so happy to be alone at last. It would not matter where she stayed, the important thing was to hear from Coral, from Shanghai.

After light out she said to Bebe, "I still want to go back."

"There may be nothing left."

"As long as the same people are still there it will be the same again, and they'll never leave because no matter how bad things are it'll be still worse outside Shanghai."

"I hope my family's all right."

"Don't you want to be with them?"

"Of course, but if they're having a difficult time I don't want to add to their burden."

"It's funny, I have nobody there, my aunt doesn't really count, and yet I want so much to go back."

"What do you want to do there?"

"I'm going to try to paint for a living." If she could make a living by it she would love it almost as much as living.

"But Lute! Now is not the time to sell paintings."

"I know, but I can at least try. Here it's no use doing anything," Ruthie had taken her to clannish exhibits of the Lingnan school of painting – South of the Ridge, for which read Cantonese.

"They're both occupied cities."

"I just have a feeling Shanghai is going to be different."

"Well, Shanghai has always been lucky, up until this time."

"I told you, didn't I, about the picture I sold to the newspaper?"

"For tell dollars."

"I can always paint you. Somebody will always want to buy it."

"For five dollars without frame."

"I can raise the price when I get better known."

Bebe did not say anything. But after a moment she said, "I'll go with you."

When she spoke again her voice was sad in the dark:

"You know it does sound funny, but it's really true what I told you about my family being very happy, and yet in a funny way I don't want to go back."

"Why? I don't understand."

"Because I know it's going to be the same thing again," Bebe said fretfully as though cornered.

"What do you mean the same thing?"

"You don't know, you haven't been to our house. Oh, you'll love it there and you'll like my father and mother. I know I'll be happy to be back but I just don't want to."

"Is it because there're too many people?" Lute asked, conjuring up a large Indian family.

"No. No."

Lute still did not understand, unless it was just that she preferred to be on her own away from home so she could grow up. But how? Here? They had nothing here. She was not in love with one of the boys? Not Green Coat?

"You'd rather be here?"

"Oh, I don't mind it here. I'm terrible, I just don't care where I am, I'm always happy."

"But we don't know how long this will last. We're on relief."

"I know."

"We may be disbanded any time."

"I know. It's so silly the way Veronica acts with Charlie. Any time we leave that's the end of it. He's not going to marry her or anything."

"She seems very much in love."

"Just because she's in the mood. At first she liked Dutta, that's the other boy at her outpost. He just joked with her. With those Indian boys it never means anything. They all go home to marry."

"Don't they meet Indian girls here?" Lute said but not with Bebe in mind, never having seen her with any Indian.

"They only marry the girls their family pick for them. Girls that don't go to school."

"Did you hear those boys today? When P.T. Pan gave you the butter."

"No, what? What did they say?" Bebe said with controlled excitement, expecting something about herself.

"They seemed to be hinting that he takes Japanese soldiers to prostitutes."

"I won't be surprised," she said coldly.

"He knows prostitutes?"

"They all do. Those Malayan boys are bad."

"They were also laughing at Mimi Choy. Something about big wife, little wife."

"They're jealous. Mimi Choy and her gang have the run of the storeroom, canned meat, canned fruits and all."

"You make me hungry. I wish we were on night duty."

"I can do with the milk and bread too."

They tried to sleep.

"You know Mr. Lum?" Bebe said softly. "He teaches chemistry."

"I told you, I worked for him during the war."

"He's in Chungking now."

"What?"

"Don't tell anybody. He and his wife escaped the day after the Japanese came in."

"Really? How?"

"There's a way over the mountains. You have to have a guide."

Lute half whistled.

"He's nice. The boys like him very much."

"I liked them both."

"Now don't tell anybody. Some of the boys want to walk to Chungking."

"Walk!"

"That's what the Lums did, and they got there safely, they sent back word. The boys want me to go with them, but I told them I won't go unless they take you too. They said they would."

"I don't want to go," Lute said instantly.

"Come on, you're not as frail as that. I'll help you. They will too."

"No, it's not the hardship, I just don't want to go."

"Why? Would you rather live under the Japanese?"

"No, I just don't want to go to Chungking."

Lute always got indignant when people tried to silence her by clapping a big hat on her head, as the Chinese say. Ever since her stepmother with her handy principles, she had hated rationalizations so much, leaning over backwards to avoid it she never could find any reasons for her preferences, much less argue it out. There was nothing left but be stubborn. With Japan inching over all the time, patriotism had been a moral pressure that never let up ever since she was growing up even in the seclusion of home. The times demanded that here was something everybody should be dedicated to. Her instinctive reaction to anything universally held sacred was revolt, as when she had had to kowtow to Confucius on the first day of school. Patriotism was just another religion she could not believe in. It was a good thing, like all religions. But it had killed more people than all the holy wars put together. She was no pacifist, just too fond of being alive. As long as a person was still living something might yet be worked out. A country could win all the wars and still weaken and die through the loss of *yuan chi*, vital gas or vitality. Taoism's feminine way of meeting calamity, winning by losing, had passed beyond the academic into folk thinking. It might be that this skepticism and holding back had still saved China a great store of untapped energy in spite of the people being squeezed dry like sugar canes these many centuries.

But in an age of nationalism how was a people to have self-respect without it? No use saying that we had gone through this phase in the second century and again in the eighth century and were now looking ahead beyond our time. Nationalism was far from having run its course. Those that had it loved it, those that did not yearned for it. It seemed to be a thing no modern man was complete without. The shame of not defending ourselves must in the end take something from us as a people. What to do when the Japanese came? Act like Viceroy Yieh Ming-sheng in the Opium War? Viceroy Yieh had read Buddhist classics throughout the British attack on Canton. When the city fell he had sat in state waiting dressed in court garb. Captured and taken to India he had died years later without ever having spoken a word. The Chinese of his day made up this jingle about him:

"Ho would not fight, he would not dig in,
He would not surrender and he would not run."

Lute did not know. She never sat down to think things out. Anybody who thought he had it all figured out was almost always wrong. Better to leave it in loose ends. At the back of it was her lack of faith in Chungking even when the government was still in Nanking. Sun Yatsen had once said that the Chinese Republic had to go through three stages before the people were ready for democracy: the period of military government, the period of teaching self-government and finally the period of constitutional government. Lute did not believe this when she had first heard of it at twelve or thirteen. No doubt Sun Yatsen had meant it but it just would not be as he said. As it was the republic was thirty years old and still showing no signs of getting out of the first period. Even without the war with Japan the country would still be ruled by a generalissimo. Nobody would ever give up anything he had, as she should know just by looking at her parents.

"All the big universities have moved into the interior," Bebe said. "They'll let us in. They say once we're there everything is taken care of."

Bebe could never resist a bargain.

"How can they take care of all the students going there? From all over the country," Lute said.

"Mr. Lum will see that we get looked after and get into colleges. Maybe we won't even lose a year."

"Even Lilypad said you can't really study there."

"It's not all bombing. People live there just the same."

"It's not bombing I'm thinking of. There's politics in the air all the time, patriotism and slogans and all that, just what I hate."

"Don't blame me for patriotism. It's not even my country."

"But you want to go."

"I just thought it would be the right place to go if you want to finish college. We won't even have to pay."

"We'll be on relief just like here. All I want is to go home and make a living."

After a pause Bebe said, "Don't worry, I'll go back to Shanghai with you."

They fell silent and eventually slept. Lute in her defensive fury had never got round to wondering what was the real reason that Bebe wanted to follow those boys to Chungking, whether she had felt this would be life and perhaps she would fall in love there.

19

The Cheungs also had no idea what was happening in Shanghai.

"Strange there're still no letters," M.H.'s wife said. "There're ships now, don't they carry mail?"

"Are there ships?" Lute exclaimed.

"Only a few, and terribly crowded."

"Is it possible to get tickets?"

"No use trying. Do you know how long the waiting list is?"

"Can't I at least put my name on it?"

"Of course if you want to," M.H. sneered. "With so much black-marketing you don't know when it will ever be your turn."

"Ships are dangerous too," his wife said.

"Are they bombed?"

"And torpedoed," he said.

His wife jerked her head as though referring to somebody in the next room, "There's talk that Mei Lan-fang was killed on a ship that sank on the way to Shanghai."

"Mei Lan-fang is dead?" He was the famous Peking opera singer who had taken women parts for thirty years

and still stood for the loveliest girl as well as the handsomest man in the remotest corners of the country.

"That's just rumor. He's here," M.H.'s wife whispered with a lift of her chin and a half wink.

"I didn't know he's in Hong Kong," Lute said.

"He's been living here quietly," he said.

"The Japanese have got him now," his wife said.

"Why? He's not political, is he?"

"Times like these are hard on well-known people," his wife said. "The tall tree gets the wind."

"He's known as being patriotic," he said. "He's grown a beard to show he won't act again."

"Mei Lan-fang with a beard! — I wonder how long we have to wait to get on a ship."

"Don't worry, we're not the only ones stranded here," M.H.'s wife said.

"There may be more ships later on," he said.

His wife said, "There's this other way of going by the Shao Pass, but we can't make up our mind. That's a longer way."

"Is it by train?"

"Yes, and change at Canton."

"Will it be more expensive?"

"Not so much difference, except you don't know how long you will have to wait at Canton."

Lute fell silent. Bebe's money probably would not be enough to get both of them home with hotel bills and all and she did not want to borrow from the Cheungs.

"We don't know yet what we're going to do," M.H.'s wife said.

"Will you let me know whatever you decide?"

"Of course we will."

"How's your friend? The Indian girl," he said.

"Yes, how is she? We liked her very much, but you didn't tell her anything about M.H., did you?"

"No, I didn't," Lute said without comprehension.

"I know you won't," she said. "It just occurred to me. Although we haven't got any connection with Chungking, it's been so many years now since he's worked for the government, still his name is known, so it's best to be careful."

"I didn't tell anyone. Bebe only knows we're relatives."

"Of course, and I wouldn't be saying this to anybody outside the family. But you know what happened to this man we know? A Mr. Hsueh." She dropped her voice and leaned closer. "And he'd already left his job with the Chungking government. When the Japanese came into Kowloon they went in his house, shot him, shot his wife and son, raped the daughter and daughter-in-law, locked them in the garage. The two girls managed to get out, but without a thing. Not a thing left in the house."

She spoke matter-of-factly as though complaining about a common acquaintance for over-tipping her servants or similar indiscretions, in the full-bodied voice that matched her weight, the unhurried sentences in falling pitch bumping downstairs.

"But how did the Japanese single them out?" Lute asked.

"They were led there I'm sure. Some bad people of the district. What they call black clothes. The same people that did the looting. It's they that cleaned out the house. Here in Causeway Bay too. Our amah happens to be trustworthy. We were lucky to have her look after the house."

"What happened to the daughter and daughter-in-law?"

"I'm not supposed to tell, but it's all right to tell you. They came here to borrow money. Wanted to go to Chungking. That's how we knew."

She continued to glare at Lute minutes after the story was over. Her husband just looked grim. Lute could see they must be afraid for their own safety. She thought, they would not have been trapped here but for my mother. They had been on their way to Chungking.

Not being able to tell Bebe the story of Mr. Hsueh and his family she had it on her mind a great deal. There were the innocent-looking Japanese soldiers walking about the campus two by two. Did they see it as samurais sacking a castle, breaking into the Chungking official's house to rob, rape, and massacre? As if they needed any such excuse. There must be hundreds of these cases only she did not get to hear of them. But their carnival was over now, they had turned school police.

She decided to ask Dr. Mok if he might help them book passages. As head of students' relief couldn't his duties include repatriation? He lived in his office, a suite of rooms at the back of the hospital ward. Going down the passageway she looked in the first open door into a large room, half dark although it was still afternoon. The homey shabby sofas and armchairs had an air of peopling the room. Mimi Choy was fixing the table. She glanced up but paid no attention and continued with what she was doing at the table. It was Angeline Ng who came forward out of the shadows.

"Hello, Lute," she said, seeming frightened.

Lute had the ridiculous notion of being a ghost out of her past coming back to haunt her. Was she working here now?

"Hello, Angeline. May I see Dr. Mok?"

Angeline turned nervously to Mimi. Knowing Mimi Choy Lute could tell without looking that a minimum of movement took place on her heavy face to deliver the usual inscrutable message. Angeline wandered off uncertainly circling half the room before she said:

"Will you please wait a minute, Lute?"

She went in another door, closing it after her. Pointedly Mimi turned her back on the intruder and walked into a pantry or closet to tidy up the shelves. Lute had time to look around her. There was a cake on the pedestal table covered with a dark green tablecloth fringed with pompons. The cake was set out on a plate but still surrounded by paper lace that showed it was store-bought. Were there still such things in Hong Kong? No wonder the others were envious of these people and they themselves were as suspicious as a criminal gang. She did not want to be caught looking at it. Already the cake with its rococo icing added to the dreamlike feeling of her stage fright as she rehearsed in her mind what to say to Dr. Mok.

The girl that was called Midwife came in and saw Lute. Consternation rang like a gong behind her concave face. Lute could hear her saying to herself: what was she doing here? How did she worm her way in? Midwife looked around the empty room for enlightenment and seemed quite lost, like the middle bear who came back and said, "Who ate my porridge?" or was it "who sat in may chair?" But then she heard somebody moving around in the closet. She went in quickly. Lute did not hear any whisperings but in a few minutes she emerged reassured. She went about the room straightening things up ignoring Lute.

Lute was just thinking of sitting down, no matter how unwelcome, when Angeline came out.

"Dr. Mok will see you now, Lute," she said with that embittered long-suffering look she had.

Lute went in the small office. The desk light was on.

"Yes?" Dr. Mok looked up from his desk. He had an imposing face, pale and square with gold-rimmed glasses. His short stature did not show sitting down.

He waited for her to state her case, then said at once, "I'm sorry, I won't be able to do anything for you."

"We'll be very grateful if you will just try. There's just the two of us."

"I'm sorry, but I won't know how to — " he laughed slightly and finished in mumble, "book passages for you."

"I shouldn't have troubled you, but I thought since the organization is here to help us — "

"I'd gladly help if I can, but there's nothing I can do."

"But — won't it be to the interest of students' relief if some of us can go home, so there're less mouths to feed?"

He listened carefully as though for hidden nuances. Satisfied that there were none, he repeated:

"I'm sorry, there is nothing I can do."

Lute went out. Angeline had hidden herself away. Mimi and the other girl busied themselves about the room turning guarded rears to her.

When she told Bebe about it Bebe said, "I wouldn't have gone to him if I were you."

"Why?"

"I just wouldn't."

"He's very unpleasant but there's nobody else in charge."

"How is he to get us boat tickets?"

"He has connections. The Japanese know him, he represents the university, and isn't it supposed to be their policy to be nice to students?"

"If he has any pull he won't use it for a thing like this."

"I was trying to tell him it pays to get us off his hands, less mouths to feed."

"He's not feeding us. In fact we're his meal tickets, the more the better."

"I never thought of that."

"Who did you see there?"

"Mimi Choy and the other girl, and Angeline."

"Angeline was there?"

"Yes, I didn't know she's working there."

"You should hear all the talk going around."

"Oh. Is she the little wife?"

"That's the kind of thing they say. And 'Dr. Mok's harem.' "

"Angeline in a harem." Lute laughed. "But I can imagine he'll have designs on her. She's such a dumb beauty."

"Would you call her a beauty?" Bebe said surprised. She never called anybody that.

"Well yes, according to current Chinese standards."

"She may be dumb, but do you think she'd take up with Dr. Mok just like that?" Bebe flung her the question truculently.

"I don't know. She's so prim."

"Then there's Veronica. Those boys are terrible. The things they say," Bebe said with a helpless snicker.

"Do you think there's actually anything between Veronica and Charlie Fong?"

"I don't know," Bebe said huffily.

They had chatted in Veronica's room the other evening. Veronica and Charlie sat leaning against each other back to the wall, their legs pulled up on the bed, she with her shoes off. Lute recalled their placid young faces on top of the dark mound of winter clothing, with just one pale stockinged foot trailing out like a path into the heart of the mountain, and his hand holding the foot. Lute had been shocked and a little squirmy too, feeling the warm shiver of contact in the cold. She had kept her eyes on whoever was speaking, looking diligently from one face to another and not at the hand and foot.

"I just don't believe they can be that silly," Bebe said.

"You'll never believe it of anybody," Lute said. "Your future husband will find it very easy to deceive you."

"I don't know," Bebe said, not amused. "If I see you in bed with my husband I will certainly get suspicious."

"I've come to the conclusion that the more promiscuous or preoccupied you are with these things the more you'll suspect others."

"Then are you preoccupied?"

"No, if I'm suspicious it's only because I never used to suspect anybody and was proved wrong every time. Even now if you really ask me I still think in the end probably nothing has happened."

"I can understand too about Angeline, she needs somebody badly, some older person. Because of her brother. And here they take her in just like a big family."

"The strange thing is Mimi Choy doesn't seem to be jealous."

"She's acting like a real old-fashioned concubine, getting another one for him."

"The other girl, she can't be a concubine too?"

"She looks like a soup plate straddled by a pair of glasses."

"I must write that down."

"You save up everything," Bebe said happily.

"I may want to draw her."

"You're such a nice receptacle, a real spittoon."

"Where's my notebook?"

"What was it I said?"

"Tch, I forgot already. What did you say?"

"How am I to remember? What were we talking about?"

"About Angeline and Veronica."

"Now what was it? I thought it was very good," Bebe said.

"See, if you don't put it down at once it's gone forever."

Black oblivion was always waiting there for things to drop into without a sound. Anything she just narrowly failed to catch went over the brink. It was horrible to have that deep pool of nothingness right by your elbow all the time, a catch-all for any amount of waste and losses one could have in a lifetime. She must get back to Shanghai before too long. Here although she worked hard at painting she knew it still did not count. But even the worry was not a bad feeling compared to the vague sense of pressure she had had all her life of having to do something and not knowing what. Her mother and aunt had said there was no market for art in China. But then she was not an art student from Paris. She did not expect Shanghai to be like Paris. She would just go back and see what she could do. Paint beautiful women in the traditional manner where you literally draw every hair on the head. Anything to get started. She had no idea how, but was reluctant to grope around too much for the small hardening core of self-confidence somewhere at the back of her mind for fear of destroying it.

Dr. Mok was taking some Japanese officials over the grounds. They were here to inspect the hospital. The group of four including Dr. Mok were all short, all in black overcoats and walking briskly in close formation. She watched for a minute from the distance, then stiffened her scalp and advanced toward them.

"Excuse me, may I speak to you for a minute?" she addressed the nearest Japanese in Mandarin.

"Yes?" he said in English so she changed to English.

"I'm a student from Shanghai. I wonder if you can help me go home, it's very difficult to get a boat ticket."

"Ha ha," he said gravely. "You are from Shanghai."

He preferred Mandarin after all, so she repeated her problem in Mandarin. The others had stopped as he stopped. Dr. Mok showed no sign of recognizing her and continued to smile happily in honor of the occasion but she could tell he was listening hard to a dialect he probably did not speak. The Japanese finally nodded, put his hand inside his coat and produced a card which he gave her with a slight bow.

"Please come and see me at my office."

They marched away. She looked at the card. To her dismay the address was Japanese army headquarters. She had thought it would be the consulate or some other branch of the diplomatic service.

"You want to go?" Bebe said.

"We have to try every possible way or we'll never get those tickets."

"Of course if you want to go I won't try to stop you, but I wouldn't if I were you."

Lute was silent for a moment weighting the risks. "I think it's all right really," she said. "The headquarters is an official place. They'll want face. It's not like running into soldiers on the loose."

"The thing is if you accidentally run into soldiers, anything happens nobody can blame you. But this is different. You know what people will say."

She did not go but kept the card.

There was this old saying, the homing heart goes like an arrow. It flies so straight and fast glancing neither left nor right. To her Shanghai was home precisely because she had none. A fatherland means more to those who have nothing else to lean on or believe in.

Her day at the hospital had no meaning. Up at dawn to take over from the night shift, groggily she followed Bebe around the ward picking up the temperature charts while Bebe took the temperatures. Back in the nurses' room they worked out the graphs under the desk lamp, zigzags and curves that seemed as hypothetical as the price of eggs in arithmetic class.

The doctor made his round. It was never Dr. Mok these days, he left it to the young doctors that came over from Queen Mary's. They followed him wheeling the tools cart. Another girl, a higher grade Medical, passed the instruments. With infallible bad timing the chore man always happened to be serving breakfast just as the doctor came. Two pairs of chopsticks and two bowls of rice topped by a soya bean and beef sauce were set down on the little cupboards between beds. Nothing would keep the patients from their breakfast, they did not want their rice to get cold. A man managed to hold the bowl to his lips and work his chopsticks while the doctor was changing the dressing on his wounded arm. Bebe and the other girl pressed close to watch. Though without their clinical interest Lute also crowded up. The man twisted around smiling down tenderly and proudly at his wound as if it was his baby being admired. The morning sun touched the knotty crimson-painted post behind him and the side of his strong long face under the cropped head. All the while he transported rice to his mouth without breaking his Madonna smile. Lute could feel with distaste each mouthful of the hard-boiled, hard-packed mound of rice flecked with yellow husks and tooth-grinding gravel, the solid comfort of it going down mingled with the burning of mercurocrome on raw flesh, the cold morning air on bare back and shoulder, the moth wings of loosened bandage falling off, the self love and self pity when he looked at the healing wound, all of this making up a mixed taste and a rough lump in the throat.

Starting from April the nurses were getting paid in rice and canned milk aside from the board and lodging.

"We can sell it, you know," Bebe said.

"That's good, we need money."

"I'll try to find out where to sell it."

"Do you think," Lute hesitated, "in time we may make enough for black-market boat tickets?"

"I'm not going to pay for black market, that's crazy."

"The fact is I won't either."

"How much is it?"

"I don't know."

"We won't earn enough if we work here for ten years,"

The month's salary for the two of them made a ten catty sack of rice and a big carton of Carnation milk. After making inquiries Bebe came back saying:

"The whole lot for twenty-five dollars. But we have to deliver."

"Where is it?"

"In Wanchai."

"That's very far, isn't it?"

"I suppose. I've never been there."

"We'll have to carry it ourselves?"

"Can you lift this? See if you can."

"Yes, I can."

"We can make two trips and take turns carrying. — Well, do you want to sell?"

"Yes."

The next day they started out together. Lute cradled the rice sack and tucked an old jacket around it.

"With all the talk about war babies, this really looks like smuggling a baby out," Bebe said.

As they came to the barricade halfway down Lute remembered the farmer getting beaten for carrying vegetables to town. This was black market rice. If they should be questioned they were taking it to a friend but they should have got the story straight between them. She saw the sentry look at her bundle. They bowed and passed. He did not call them back.

"I'll carry it now."

"No, it's all right. I'll tell you when I get tired."

Since Bebe had supplied the brains and the connections she wanted to be fair and do more than her share of the labor. The sack had felt heavy to begin with but never really became insupportable. If only she could sling it over a shoulder or something. Any change would be bliss. But it was difficult to maneuver and Bebe instead of helping merely offered to take over every time Lute tried for a change of position. If she put it down Bebe was sure to take it. She had to stagger on hugging it leaning backward, the streets in a blur. Her face dragged. She could not feel her feet.

"I swear I don't know where we are," Bebe said with a nervous giggle. "I hope we find the place."

"I hope so too. It will be terrible to carry this back again."

Was that how the peasants sank to their position? By doing the heaviest work and still feeling humble and indebted. In the end she had to let Bebe carry it a few blocks, fortunately the last.

It was a small shop, the dark interior empty and bare as all shops had become so that it was hard to tell what they dealt in except for that dusty smell of grain about the place. A man weighed the rice quickly on a scales stick, took a peep inside the bag, paid Bebe ten dollars and hustled them out in no time, for fear of the transaction being discovered.

Wanchai was a slum district that was never mentioned without a suggestive snigger. Lute looked around her but was too tired to have any idea what it was like. Her arms hanging loose seemed to float with all the vacuously gnawing discomforts ascribed to the weightless state. But by the time they reached downtown she was revived. They were like miners fresh out of the mines. They wandered over to the smart shops in the arcade, all open half-heartedly. There was nothing to see, two cheap dresses in a dusty unlit shopwindow, yet they stood outside a long time looking at them. Who were these meant for? Soldiers' girls? They would be the only people buying dresses nowadays. Were they specially tailored to the Japanese taste for dowdy Western clothes? Or just dowdy leftovers from old stock?

A woman inside the shop who saw them staring so hungrily came to the door and said in Cantonese:

"What do you want to buy?"

"We're just looking," Bebe said.

"Come in, there's more inside."

"No, never mind."

She looked at them sizing them up. Girls hid themselves these days, they did not roam around town except to earn Military Yen.

"Come in. Young girls like you ought to wear nice clothes, not like these," she pinched Lute's dress on the shoulder.

Lute just smiled.

"She prefers Chinese gowns," Bebe said.

"She will look very nice in Western clothes."

"Maybe, but not these."

They walked off.

"What salesmanship," Bebe said.

"They're not like that in Shanghai."

It struck her that the people here were more crude in every way. They were the same coastal southerners as the overseas Chinese, more honest than the other Chinese but more disagreeable. In Hong Kong they were forced to be servile to the British which they did in an obvious manner. Now they were just as obviously adjusting themselves to a new master. In Shanghai everything was more subtle and less offensive. There it was an older people and older evils.

"Shall we go and see the stalls?" Bebe said.

"Yes."

"We might as well."

The side street off Central Market was a bazaar. Customers threaded through the little stalls, high boxes piled with fabrics. The street slanted down steeply to sea, making a deep blue gap. The blue T of the sea spread horizontally above the city to meet the brilliant blue air. All the silks and cloths looked brighter and the crowd bigger and happier against that blue.

"Why so many people here?" Lute said.

"And the shops not doing any business."

"Everybody must be economizing."

"There are bargains here but you can get gypped too."

Bebe stopped to examine a cobalt blue silk that looked like wet paint. "This will be very good for you."

"It is a lovely color."

"I wonder if it comes off. *Lug mm lug sigah*?" she asked the stall keeper.

"*Mm lug sig*," he said curtly with a slight shake of the head.

Bebe still fingered it doubtfully and crumpled it in her fist. Lute also handled it. It felt a little like wet paint too.

"It's sticky."

"It may be all right. I don't know," Bebe said.

"If only we can ask for half a cup of water."

"They won't get it for you."

"Buy or not buy, *dai gu*, big miss?" the man asked.

"I'm afraid the color will come off," Bebe whined plaintively.

"*Mm lug sig*," he said.

"I don't know," she said to Lute.

She looked at it some more front and back, finally wetted a fingertip in her mouth and rubbed on the cloth. Shocked, Lute stole an apprehensive look at the stall keeper. He did not flinch. Bebe examined her finger tip. He watched without much interest.

"I suppose it's all right," she said.

Lute bought enough for a dress. At another stall the same cotton print caught the eyes of both of them, a deep pink with pointillistic patterns of pale pink flowers and little green leaves.

"This is nice," Bebe said.

"I've never seen anything like this."

"Look, there's another one."

The same pattern on a purple ground. Another on bright green. Circling around the stall Lute found a black one. All with the same flowers and leaves drawn carefully by a peasant hand. Who made these? For whom? It was said that the country people had stopped making what the Chinese themselves disdainfully called *tu bu*, native cloth. Lute had thought they only came in blue and white.

Could this be a Japanese imitation of *tu bu*, catering to the country people's taste? The pointillistic design was suspect but the texture was so thick, tough enough to last a lifetime and too warm for summer. There was a clumsiness about it that was not like Japanese goods.

"Will the color come off?"

"No. Look at the back," Bebe said.

"I like the purple best."

"The green is also good."

"Yes, I love the green."

"Where's the first one we saw?"

"That's the pink. I still like that best."

"The black is also good in a different way."

"I can't buy them all."

"They each make a different picture."

"I was thinking this will be the nearest you can get to carrying a picture around all the time."

"You need the color."

"Don't you want any?"

"They're better for you."

"Now I'm sorry I got the blue silk."

After long and painful selection she finally bought all except the black.

"I tell you we're crazy," Bebe said.

The next day they came back for the black one. The first joy of acquisition had gone into Lute's head as if she had never owned anything before. At home everything had always been bought for her or it had always been there. What you came by that way was like a wife that a man's parents got for him, generally still welcome but hardly the same as one he took himself. But the things she had got from her mother burdened and depressed her. The night before she left Shanghai her mother had packed her luggage and shown her where everything was, saying repeatedly and again when Lute was taking her last bath and she herself was creaming her face:

"There it is, all there. Lose anything and you'll never have it again."

Lute lay in the warm water floating mistily in front of herself. She was glad to take the length of it and go and did not want the cheerless dowry. She was ready to get out of the bath but to dry herself on the bathmat with so little room she might jab her mother in the back with a wet elbow. She could hear the indignant little cry already.

"Are you happy now?" Bebe asked when the black piece had been wrapped up and handed over to her.

"Yes."

"Now you won't get any rest until you have them all made."

"I'm not going to make any clothes until we get back to Shanghai."

"You need clothes."

"Not here. Here we always have to put on our oldest clothes to go out."

As they made their way through the stalls they were surprised to see Lilypad Chen. The man with her must be Mr. Tong. They would not have recognized him by himself. They said hello.

"Hello," said Lilypad with a cynical smile on her dark yellow face between the sand-dusted pigtails.

"How are you?" Bebe said.

"Very well. How are you?"

The loose blue coat that Lilypad had always worn was parted in the middle by the big belly. Lute felt shocked laughter coming on like a sneeze. She forced it back and fixed her eyes on Lilypad's face even when Bebe was talking, afraid to meet Bebe's eyes which might touch off the laughter. But the belly was so big and long, like an insect's, it was difficult to focus on the face without the blue-framed abdomen swarming up into the corner of the eyes.

"Have you been to dormitory?" Bebe said.

"Yes, to get my things. Did you get your things back?"

"Yes, we were lucky we didn't lose anything."

Mr. Tong stood a pace behind, correctly keeping out of the conversation, half attentive, half looking about him. Lilypad did not introduce him which was not against Chinese etiquette. She soon nodded goodbye and they walked away. Bebe and Lute took the other direction. Bebe looked at Lute round-eyed and as if holding water in her mouth. At the end of the block she said sputtering:

"Did you see?"

"How can you help seeing?"

"And we were just talking about war babies."

"I wonder if they're still staying with his parents?"

"I didn't dare ask."

"The parents may be very pleased for all you know, especially with a grandson coming."

"You think they won't object?"

"It's her family's loss."

"So she's just going to be his concubine?"

"People don't say concubine any more."

But they had looked so much like just any married couple. Bebe and Lute never had the least doubt that it was a permanent union. Now that they had lost sight of the long ridge of abdomen ridiculously peeping out they could feel sympathy for a love that weathered through trouble.

"He can't get a divorce anyway," Bebe said. "His wife is where?"

"In Shansi."

"They're cut off."

"I wonder why they don't go to Chungking. There she'll be the Resistance wife."

"She can't go in this condition."

"Maybe there's also the question of money and what to do with the old people."

"They won't tell us anyway if they're going."

They passed a theater. A crowd was streaming in.

"You've never seen Cantonese opera?" Bebe asked.

"No."

"How I used to go every night. My Cantonese amah took me."

"Is it any good?"

"I like it. You want to see it?"

"I don't mind."

"Let's go in."

"All right."

"I tell you, we're spending money like drunken sailors."

"Will we have enough for boat tickets?"

"Which we can't get anyway."

"No, but what a cruel joke if one day we can and haven't got the money."

"We have enough," Bebe murmured with a closed face.

The show was not very good. Compared to Peking opera it seemed slipshod and flashy and Lute missed most of the plot and the jokes. Still she enjoyed it thoroughly, drinking in the sounds of the audience cracking watermelon seeds, coughing, spitting, stirring cozily in their return to normal times and their old haunts. It was her first look at China as an outsider through the tourist's eye she got from Bebe who had lived in China as a foreigner all her life. And for the first time she loved her country in an uninvolved way that was pure delight.

20

Bebe and Lute went out to collect the washed bandages that were spread on the hedges to dry. They were on night duty but it was still bright out. The days were getting long as the weather turned warm. Insects cheep-cheeped under the hibiscus bushes with big red flowers carelessly wrapped around themselves. The Number Four patient was leaning on the brick wall eating out of a can. He did not look up at the girls moving along the hedge rolling up the bandages. But when a boy walked past he ambled after him to the other side of the building. Number Four was the only one well enough to walk, a tall man slightly stooped in his hospital blouse of coarse white cloth with short sleeves jutting out at the elbow. There were several others that looked like him, tall and lean, the same cropped head and regular features but he had more identity than the others because he was around more. Lute had seen him fetching water to other beds or bringing something from one bed to another, his high-shouldered opium smoker's slouch seeming insolent on him with his powerful build. The pajamas

and slippers gave him a feckless appearance but perhaps he had always gone around like this as many Cantonese men did, on the street, in the teahouse.

He seemed to have stationed himself here waiting. The front door to the old warden's suite, now Dr. Mok's quarters, was just around the corner. She heard their voices talking, then no more. Maybe they had gone up the stoop into the house.

Suddenly the boy's voice came over:

"*Mo*! *Mo*! *Mo* eh!"

Have none?

"*Mo*!" again the way Cantonese shout at beggars. Then something else that she thought afterwards had sounded like "*Mung do mo*" as in "*Ng mung do mo*, not even five dollars" or "*Yeb mung do mo*, not even a dollar." At the time all she heard was the ringing crash and clatter of an empty can hurled on the ground. There it came rolling on the asphalt and finally stood still, the yellow pineapple slices on the label abnormally clear and brilliant in the strange yellow light of the summer dusk. She looked at Bebe and laughed.

"He's crazy," Bebe said. "That's the one that stole the scissors. Snitched it from the cart when the doctor was working at the next bed."

"The pineapples aren't stolen or he wouldn't be eating it here?"

"Paula saw him downtown buying *chiashiu*. He goes every day to get things for the other patients. You can spot him a mile away flapping around in that hospital blouse."

"An invalid buying barbecued pork!"

"Why isn't he discharged is what I can't understand."

"They're all Dr. Mok's meal tickets, you said yourself."

"Paula said to keep an eye on the things in the nurses' room, kidney dishes, enamel drums, even our own things. Don't leavc sweaters around."

When they came into the ward Number Four was just shuffling in through the French window nearest to his bed. He lay down at his ease with one leg resting on the other. With warm weather here all the French windows stayed open on to night. The glass panes had been painted dark blue for blackouts. Somebody had scratched little figures all over them with a fingernail, little people in white lines jerking stick arms and legs. Lute thought they looked demonical on the blue doors open against the black night filled with summer's tropical sounds. They made her think of the paper dolls used in old curses. Who did them? If these markings had been there all along she had never noticed them before. The patients could not reach the windows from their beds, unless it was Number Four again?

The gangrene smelled stronger in the heat, hanging like a curtain around the bed. His neighbors left and right suffered in silence. They were not here to be comfortable. They were not anxious to go home either. Two free meals a day meant something these days. When Lute went to heat her milk around midnight the chore man had closed all the French windows. The ward looked like a steerage. The mild yet peculiarly revolting odor of dirty army blankets thickly pervaded the room. In winter the smell had used to be iced and clotted, not everywhere. She held her breath when she passed the gangrene case. The waxen face was held tilted on the pillow, bushy black eyebrows clownishly slanting downward, eyes half closed, the mouth dropped open in a dreamy smile. He never stopped calling, as though sweetly sighing for some woman that was both mother and lover and yet was hard-hearted and never would come:

"*Gu-niang* ah! *Gu-niang* ah!

Nobody paid any attention any more when he called. He never wanted anything.

Somebody was already in the kitchen when she went in, an Indian. She thought he was the Dutta that Bebe had said was at the same outpost with Veronica and Charlie during the war. He was making *chupatti* in his own frying pan greasing it with some grainy fat spooned out of what looked like a big gasoline can with funnel and all.

She took the brass pot, scrubbed it and put on the milk. She could not understand why it took so long to boil. The fire was turned on its highest. She watched it fixedly but somehow had seen in detail how amazingly handsome he was, the thick straight profile under the lowering hairline, lots of eyebrows and eyelashes and green eyes very pale against the smoky skin. He was a big man, no longer a boy. Bebe had familiarized her with Indians but Bebe was not very Indian herself growing up in China with British schooling. Going up to the dormitory after classes she had used to pass the Indian barracks. Through the barbed wire fence she could see washings hung up to dry in the windows of the brown huts and sometimes a soldier napping on his bunk, hands under his head. A radio loudspeaker had Indian music on loud. All over the hillside the azaleas were either blooming or shedding their petals in slow magenta rain while the strange wriggly music blasted through the empty hills. But what puzzled her most about the Indians was the same thing in the Japanese. Both hung on to their past. While the Chinese had just wakened from a long dream feeling lost and dry in the mouth, the Indians seemed still deep in the throes of some magnificent nightmare, fingers and feet twitching, running in their sleep.

She kept her eyes on the brass pot sitting on the blue lotus of gas flames, watching for the first bubbles to appear around the rim of the milk's white disk. She had waited such a long time by the side of a stranger it was becoming unendurable. She had never looked at him except maybe to see how you toss *chupatti*, and was astonished and indignant when he laughed and came at her with mockingly wide open arms. She backed away and ducked, half smiling in order not to seem too silly. Still he came on. She backed and side-stepped, forced into a graceless dance with the same idiotic trapped feeling as when she stepped aside to let somebody pass who also stepped aside to let her pass, then both moved over to the other side each blocking the other's way.

"I'm not going to kiss you," he said as though that made it all right.

He had that cast of features more common among Western Asians that looked fiendish when they smiled. He got in a stroke at her cheek. She darted off but was called back by the hiss of milk boiling over. He caught her.

"You're very beautiful really."

He meant although not at first sight but she was too busy struggling to think. His arms were like an iron band around her, his wool jacket had a faint musty smell unrelated to anything she knew unless it was Bebe's sleeping bag because they were both Indians. He was reaching down to nuzzle the side of her face. With a violent push she twisted free, pitching herself sideways against the stove. He grabbed her with one hand thinking she would fall on the fire and she grabbed the brass pot, the handle burning her. He stepped back not knowing if she was going to throw boiling milk on him. But she just took the dripping pot and went quickly out of the room.

There was a stir in the long ward as she passed. The toasty smell of burned milk was enough to wake the dead. She thickened her skin and forged down the aisle between the beds, went round the white cloth screen into the little office. Bebe sat reading by the desk lamp. It seemed to Lute she had been gone an hour. She poured out the milk, there was just enough for one glass.

"I've had mine."

"I'll also have mine cold tomorrow."

"Yes, it's better cold."

"It's almost like summer now."

Lute sat down with a book and let the thundering happiness close over her head. Her heart swelled to bursting and somehow held a cupful of sweetness that thickened while it was slowly stirred as with a spoon. It was nothing and had meant nothing to him. That was clear even if she did not remember what Bebe had said about all the Indian boys going home to the girls chosen by their families. It seemed to her that the only real love was the kind that led nowhere, not with marriage and a lifetime's support in view, asking for nothing, not even companionship. Just now there had been a moment when she had been detached from life, they had each lived outside their own system for a minute. She had never thought of herself as living under a system. Actually it worked even here under these circumstances. Most of the girls kept away from the boys and the boys left them alone. The Chinese of their time no longer believed in anything except the virginity of their wives on wedding night. The code built around that single tenet still held.

There were footsteps outside. A man came round the screen. It was Dutta. She remained bent over her book but felt him look at her.

"Hello," Bebe said.

"Hello." He put the gasoline can on the table.

Bebe got up. "What's that?"

"I had some oil left over."

"What do you want done with it?"

"I thought maybe you can use it."

"Gasoline?"

"No, coconut oil."

"Oh. I was wondering where you could have got gasoline. Why, can't you use it yourself?"

"I have this left over, and here's some flour."

"But why?" Bebe murmured laughing a little. "Don't you want it any more?"

"I have no use for it." He reached for her necklace. "What is this? Jade?"

"No, no, not jade, I don't know, some sort of stone." Her answer was no more than embarrassed little protesting noises as though the rough cut green beads were extensions of herself that he had gotten hold of. Her hand hovered protectively in the air near her throat but she was half laughing with her head tilted back and her eyes half closed.

"What is it? It's not a chemical?" he said curiously, still bending over the few beads he was fingering.

"No, no, it's semi-precious, but I don't know what it is."

"It looks like jade."

"No, it's not jade, I don't know what it is, some sort of quartz." Her voice was husky and sad. All the barriers were down among these ruins and yet she still had to keep him out.

He let the beads fall back with a light clack and walked out, turning to wave at her briefly not looking at Lute.

"Now what to do with these things?" Bebe said.

"I don't know. Can you cook?"

"We can make cookies. Go ask Leela if she has a tin sheet or any kind of baking dish."

"You'd better go yourself to be sure you get the right thing."

"She'll know. Oh, and ask her for sugar."

"We don't have to do it tonight, it's so late."

"It's better at night, less people around."

Bebe always made her run her errands. She did not feel like going out in the pitchdark as though Dutta might be waiting outside. But how would he know she would be coming out at this hour? Besides he was angry with her.

She closed the front door behind her and turned on her flashlight to see the steps. With a jolt she found she was not alone. Flashlights were being snapped on and off. She could make out people coming and going around the dark bulk of a truck parked at a side door. It must be a Japanese army truck since nobody had gasoline except the military, yet she thought she heard English spoken in a stray word or phrase coming her way. They were still there when she came back with Leela.

"What are they doing there?" she wondered aloud.

Leela pulled at her arm and whispered, "Turn off your light."

They made their way to the front stoop in the dark. So it was the Japanese. Why were they here after midnight? What were they loading on the truck? Briefly she thought of mass executions, removal of bodies. The flashlights flickered on and off blocked by moving shadows. An occasional grunt or half shout gave directions to the carriers. Again she thought she heard that familiar bark of Straits English. Were some of the students helping them?

She asked in the kitchen, "Why do you think they came here so late at night?"

"Don't say anything, we're not supposed to know," Leela whispered mixing the dough.

"Why?" What were they doing?"

Leela looked around her first. "It's those boys. They're taking things out to sell."

"What things?"

"Rice. Cans. Everything."

"Dr. Mok knows?"

"Who do you think got them the truck?"

Lute said after a moment of silence, awed and half smiling, "I had no idea."

"Don't say anything. It has nothing to do with us."

"That's true. It's all supposed to belong to the Japanese army."

"It's been going on for some time now."

"Lots of people must know about it."

"I don't know. Maybe. Nobody said anything."

Leela stooped to light the oven, her pigtails hanging down next to the full bosom. The fire springing up shone red in her Greco-Roman bronze face. She was also Indian but entirely lacking in mystery to Lute. Maybe because she was a Christian. But mainly because she was a girl. She had come from somewhere in Malaya, Lute believed she had said and did not want to ask again. Was Dutta from Malaya too? They both spoke Straits English but she believed they also spoke that way in India. Perhaps Malaya got it from India.

Leela closed the oven and they settled down to wait.

"I don't know how it's going to turn out." Leela kept saying modestly. "I never made this before."

"Have you ever used coconut oil?"

"No, never."

"I thought it's for making soap."

"Maybe we cannot eat this."

"It doesn't matter. Of course you did all the work."

"It's no work, only I don't know if it will come out right. Where's Bebe? Isn't she coming?"

"She said she'd be here later."

"I wish she'd come. Maybe she knows how to make this."

Two Malayan boys came in to fry their leftover rice to take with them to work tomorrow. The one at the stove stood in his business suit blandly frying rice. The other watched through tortoise shell glasses, holding their lunch boxes. The smell from the oven was beginning to come out but they showed no signs of wondering what it was. The boys had got over the excitement of coeducation without education, moving in with the girls. The titillation had worn off. Whatever might happen had already happened, as with Charlie and Veronica. Others had split into small groups and kept to themselves. They were left out of everything, no girls, no making money by smuggling. The roar of the truck going away could be heard distinctly in the silent kitchen. The one with glasses grunted something in Fukienese. The other smiled Buddha-like, pressed down hard on his sheet of rice and flipped it expertly. Lute had the impression they knew what was going on. The smell of baking was now so strong it filled the small room like loud radio. Still nobody remarked on it. Leela stood against the sink with folded arms not looking at anybody. Lute felt odd to be in a kitchen at three o'clock in the morning with these faintly hostile people, as in a dream.

Leela waited until the boys were gone before she peered in the oven.

"When did we put this in? We really should have a clock."

"Shall I go and get the clock from the office?"

"No, never mind. When is Bebe coming?"

"She probably thought somebody should be there."

"I wish she were here. I never made this before."

She had just got it out when Bebe came in.

"Where were you all this time?" Leela said. "We were not going to leave any for you."

"Number Eleven died," Bebe said.

"Who? The gangrene case?" said Leela.

"Yes."

"But he seemed the same as ever! Still calling."

"Yes. He just died."

"Shall we go and help?" Leela whispered.

"No, it's all over," Bebe murmured coldly.

Lute could not think of a thing to say. Bebe must have been very busy attending to everything.

"Isn't there anything at all we can do?" Leela said.

"It's all finished. They've taken everything away."

Leela looked at her anxious-eyed. "What about the beddings?" she whispered.

"All cleared away."

Nobody spoke for a while. The cocks were crowing. Lute felt a hollow ache as though unplugged somewhere with wind blowing through. But mingled with the sense of irreparable loss was relief that it was all over and she had just missed it.

"Oh, you made the cookies," Bebe said.

"Be careful, it's still hot," Leela said.

"It's very good," Bebe said munching.

"Just delicious," Lute murmured.

It was hot and crunchy although it tasted a little of soap. They could not see the dawn's light in the kitchen but the cocks were crowing.

21

Lute went to the Cheungs again to ask about ships. It never was any use but there seemed to be nothing else she could do. Nobody answered the doorbell. She had walked a long way and did not want to go back just like that so she waited on the stairs until after dark. Finally their Cantonese amah came back and let her in.

"Master and Taitai are not here. They have moved to Hong Kong Hotel."

Hong Kong Hotel – last time Repulse Bay Hotel. What was the point now? And Hong Kong Hotel, wasn't it requisitioned? She had seen Japanese going in and out and sentries.

"Why? Do you know?" she asked.

"It's the Japanese," the amah whispered. "Some Japanese came here and said it would be safer for Master at Hong Kong Hotel. That's what Taitai told me, and that I'm to stay here and look after the house."

"Oh. The Japanese went with them?"

"Yes. All went in the car they came in."

At Lute's look of dismay she added, "The Japanese were very polite. Taitai told me not to worry, told me it's all right. But I don't know. People like us don't really know."

If she had told Lute in the hope of finding out more about her master, why the Japanese should want him, she soon gave up, Lute's Cantonese was so poor.

Lute went home dejected. It seemed like the Japanese wanted him for a puppet. If they held him in Hong Kong Hotel he was treated as an honored guest but was he still there? Nothing could really happen to him? They would not kill anybody who might be considered an elder statesman known internationally after forty years in the diplomatic service? She could not tell with the Japanese.

She had not known until now how much she had counted on the Cheungs as a last resort. If all else failed she might still ask them to take her and Bebe with them through Canton. She knew that relatives could not be depended on, unlike friends as Aunt Coral had always said. Still there was this old assumption that they were as good as family in times of need. Now they were gone, her last connection with home.

She thought often of Dutta. He had avoided looking at her while coming across her lining up for supper one day. At other times she had seen him looking at her across the dining hall. Uncannily she could always locate him immediately in a crowd. It was over and had been nothing, she had always known and yet would still feel slighted to be proved right. She was afraid he would approach her again and afraid he would not and ended being just afraid of him. She wished she was away from here.

Oddly enough by the time she got to climb the hill in total blackness she felt a little better, more assured. It had that effect on her because she had seen a snake here once: she had been walking up after class and suddenly found herself looking into the face of a small snake reared up about a foot high in the grass right beside the path. She stared long enough to make certain. If she had cried out she did not hear it. The minute she turned and ran the terror ballooned out over her shoulder, expanding behind her taking up all the space as fast as she could vacate it. The amahs had always told her not to run if she was frightened of a dog. Once you started running it would run after you. Worse still to look back as you run. Those who walked alone at night should never look over their shoulder. One look and they died of fright. All the terrors of childhood were at her heels as she clattered down the steps in between flying leaps as easy as in a dream.

Afterwards she avoided the path until she was forced to use it again and gradually stopped watching out for snakes. And having got over that she had come to like the hill. Since war came she had got to the point of going up in a blackout without thinking anything of it. She knew the steps as well as her own backyard and scarcely had to turn on the flashlight. It happened that she had never met anybody on the way at night. The hill became very small and comforting when you had it all to yourself and took it for granted. She was finishing a straight flight of steps with the mildly pleasant sensation of its getting shorter all the time. Then her feet got entangled in something and the next thing she knew, something was crawling up her legs. She kicked and backed down a step but the shock had deadened all sensations after the initial ones, so she had no idea what was happening.

It seemed to take a long time for her to click on the flashlight. There was a white pile on the ground, clothing or wrapping cloth. The itchy crawling up her leg continued in more places than one. She pulled up her gown and saw ants. She brushed them off in frantic slaps getting goose pimples all over. What on earth was this? She gingerly lifted the cloth on the ground. It was a blouse. Pieces of barbecued pork tumbled out. There was the grease-stained piece of paper it came in, black with those large ants of Hong Kong. The blouse had the hospital's blue stamp on it. She thought at once of Number Four. Where was he?

She turned the flashlight around. There were a few more of those small pieces of red-striped pork strewn about. Suddenly she had the feeling that eyes were watching her from behind the azalea and hibiscus bushes, the pines and cypresses, the windows of the professors' deserted houses behind the undulating lawns and from as far above as the abandoned Indian barracks over the shoulder of the hill, everywhere in the rustling cheep-cheeping darkness. She snapped the light off nervously, turned it on again to avoid stepping on the blouse so she would not get more ants on her and walked up as fast as she could.

She went straight over to the hospital to find out if Number Four was safe in bed. Veronica was on duty.

"No, he's not back yet," she said. "He's getting bolder and bolder."

"I saw something funny just now on my way back. There's a hospital uniform lying on the path and a package of *chiashiu* fallen all over the place."

"That sounds like him," Veronica said.

"I thought something might have happened to him."

"Drunk?" she whispered.

"But where is he?"

"Did you look in the grass?"

"Nobody there, but I didn't look everywhere, I was frightened. Do you think he could have been robbed and killed?"

"He has no money."

"He may have enemies."

"That could be," the other girl said, "if he's a *hak sam*. Some other *hak sam* may want to kill him."

"They say there're all sorts of people among these patients," Veronica said.

"When they found those scissors and scalpels under his mattress and still didn't throw him out, I was wondering if he's a *hak sam*, else why were they afraid of him?" the other girl said.

"Don't you think we should tell somebody, in case something has happened?"

Veronica and the other girl looked at each other. "Have you seen Mimi?"

"No. None of them has been around."

"You want to tell Dr. Mok?" Veronica asked Lute.

"Don't you think we should?"

"You go in, I'm not going in," Veronica leered.

Lute smiled back. Intrude on the harem at this hour? Besides it would be bad to be marked down as a troublemaker. "Maybe we better wait and see if Number Four comes back."

"He may still turn up," the other girl said.

In the morning Lute and Bebe followed the doctor around the ward pushing the medical tools cart. Number Four was not in his bed.

"Has he run away?" said the senior girl who passed the instruments.

"Just home to see his wife," said his neighbor and all the other patients laughed.

"*Sui* eh," the girl looked away with a snicker.

"Lute saw his uniform and *chiashiu* on the path last night," Bebe said.

"The pork was scattered all over," Lute said.

"It looks as if he did come back," Bebe said.

The patients did not understand the talk in English. Both the doctor and the girl showed puzzlement and gave a grunt that stood for no comment.

Lute wheeled the tools cart out on the lawn and boiled the instruments on an alcohol burner. It was pleasant out in the morning sun with a wind blowing the colorless flames about.

Bebe came out to tell her, "We have to count the instruments. They're checking to see if anything is missing."

"Why?"

"They thought Number Four might have taken something with him."

"He didn't run away. I was telling them."

"I know, I know," Bebe sounded bored and stirred the tools in the pot with a pair of forceps. "How long have you boiled them?"

"Two more minutes to go."

When the time was up by the clock on the cart Bebe picked them up and stood them in the jar. Lute emptied the hot water in the sewer. T.F. Lai from Dr. Mok's hometown walked past.

"Nothing's missing," Bebe called to him.

"You're sure?" he called back.

"Hey, T.F., Lute here saw a hospital uniform on the road here last night."

"What?" he said without comprehension but coming over to them.

"Last night when I was coming home I saw this uniform lying on the path."

"And the *chiashiu* Number Four was always buying," Bebe said.

T.F. stared down at Lute with knotted eyebrows tilted up, the slit eyes pulled up with them. Being tall and husky added impact to his look of shocked anger, his face flushed in red welts that also slanted upward.

"What's this? What uniform?"

He listened to the story once again. Then he also gave one of those universal no comment grunts and moved on.

"He had such an odd expression," Lute said afterwards.

"That's the way he looks," Bebe said.

That was true, Lute thought, he had looked just as angry dishing out rice and beans to the waiting queue. They were eating up what he could take out and sell.

"What are you trying to make out?" Bebe asked. "That they killed Number Four? For what?"

"Maybe he knew about the smuggling."

"But Lu-ute!" Bebe wailed. "Everybody knows. It's no secret."

"He might be the only one to blackmail them. We heard him the other day asking the boy for money and that wouldn't be the only time."

"I didn't hear anything about money."

"The boy kept saying there wasn't any."

"All I knew was he got into a pet and threw the can down."

"He must have threatened them."

"With what? What could he do?"

"They can get shot for stealing Japanese army stores."

For a moment there was a gleam of excitement in Bebe's eyes. Then she ducked her head with a cuddly animal movement and said huffily, "I don't know." She was always in a huff when confronted with sins, crimes, war, politics, any of those things she did not like. She started to straighten the trolley, burrowing into the lower rack the way Lute remembered her digging into her porridge when war had just been announced.

In the afternoon Lute sneaked down to the path while they were still on duty. She went below the intersection where she had seen the crumpled blouse. It was not there, and no barbecued pork, no wrapping paper, no ants, nothing. She looked around at the professors' quiet little houses. The azalea petals fell noiselessly, already inches deep around the magenta bushes and still coming down.

At night she listened for the truck. It did not come every night. When it came she heard every huff and puff and snuffle of the engine with uneasiness.

Bebe went with her to take over from Veronica one evening.

"Number Four's wife came today," Veronica told them.

"Why did she come?" Bebe asked.

"To see him."

"He never went back?" Lute exclaimed.

"That's what she says. She went around talking to all the other patients until T.F. threw her out, told her to make her husband bring back the things he stole."

"What things? We checked, didn't we?"

Lute turned to Bebe who fell into another of her seemingly offended silences, busy rearranging the books and bottles to make room on the desk.

"What was it he said?" Veronica asked the other girl. "Scissors and scalpels."

"That was the other time," the other girl said.

"I suppose after that anything missing they just blame it on Number Four," Veronica said.

"But nothing is missing, is there?" Lute said.

"He just said that to get rid of her," the other girl said.

"Why?" Lute asked.

"These people you know, with her husband gone she may put it on the hospital."

"Yes, these people are hard to deal with," Veronica said.

"What was she like? Like a gangster's woman?"

"I don't know," Veronica sounded surprised. "She looked poor, carried the child in a sling on her back."

"They're not supposed to come here," the other girl said.

"Maybe Number Four sent her," Veronica laughed.

"He ran out on her," said the other.

"I heard her hanging around outside crying."

Lute thought, he would not have dared send her. The poor people here were afraid of institutions. Even the poor mixed up with *hak sam* would be afraid. Had he just got tired of the hospital and did not want to go home either? No matter what had come over him that night on the hill no one threw away barbecued pork in these famished times. Unless he had been drunk and he had never bought wine or come back drunk. The picture of Number Four doing little chores for the other patients came back to mind. He was a man that poverty had brought up to be as careful with things as a woman.

What little she knew about it all fitted in. It might be that the pieces like her aunt's jigsaw tables could be put together to make about any shape you wanted. The mind was a tricky thing. What really convinced her was the ugly mood in the place. Dr. Mok's aides had enjoyed serving meals at first, now they were bad-tempered, passing a full plate to somebody they liked as a special favor, slapping a small portion on another plate and stinting on the sauce, thrusting it at the next in line as at a beggar. They were getting more and more impatient with these dupes they fed on. That was the way greed went. They were not selling the stores fast enough, they had to pay too much bribery, they were getting too small a share, somebody was taking a bigger cut than he admitted. If on top of all this an outsider no better than a tramp had dared demand a share, they could kill him. They owned this whole hillside. The university had carefully laid out these grounds to be a clearing in the jungle of humanity, gradually merging into the elegant houses on the hilltop, now all deserted. The English had gone to camp, the rich Chinese could not live so far up without gasoline to run their cars. After the Japanese troops were withdrawn the entire area was a vacuum. Number Four might be buried in a flower bed or just lying in the cellar of one of the empty houses. She would never find it, she would just get seen snooping around.

Was not the story worth anything? Like two boat tickets? There was this Mr. Nakamura, army adviser, who had given her his card. She had been thinking it over and felt certain she could go to the Japanese army headquarters and come out safe. Her lank hair and figure, British accent and old-fashioned Chinese air made her difficult to place, an intimidating thing in itself. If Nakamura did not seem anxious to help her get passages she would tell him about the missing patient. The loss of one more Chinese life after the war would not upset him but surely he would be interested in the theft of Japanese army property. Unless he was the one that got Dr. Mok his military truck.

If he knew nothing about this then she would be an informer. Dr. Mok and his boys might die for this. Although they themselves had killed she did not want any more killing through her doing. She would pay for that some day, somehow. That was a Buddhist thing that had gone into the unthinking part of the mind. The Chinese words for retribution were just cause and fruit, *ying guo*, as natural as any other cause and effect, and the intention to kill was the kind of thing always paid for in the end.

Dr. Mok was not in the next day. She tried again later the same day and caught him at home.

"Yes?" he looked up from his desk.

He seemed not to recognize her. It was possible he did not remember the other time she came into this office but she thought he was not likely to forget the girl who had intercepted the tour of inspection and spoken to the Japanese over his head.

"Good afternoon, Dr. Mok," she said smiling. "I came to see you before."

"Yes?"

"I asked you to help us get boat tickets to go back to Shanghai."

"I'm sorry but I can't help you."

"That's what you told me, Doctor, that's why I tried the Japanese officials that time they were here, and I was told to go and see someone at the army headquarters, but I couldn't make up my mind to go. I wouldn't know what to say if they asked questions about things here."

She had a sinking feeling as she waded into the middle of the speech. There was something familiar about the desk light and the blank face in front of her holding still, flat-eyed behind the glasses. She had to remember hard to keep to her carefully prepared words just as if she was again delivering her mother's speech at her father who listened dumbfounded, then bored, then angry. But she got over that feeling. For the first time in her life it was entirely her own idea, what nobody else would approve and she had never spoken so well.

"I don't understand what you're talking about."

"What if they ask about the army stores here, and the Number Four patient."

"I really don't know what you're talking about," he rose from his seat. "I'm a busy man so if –"

"But Dr. Mok, what shall I tell them if they ask how Number Four died?"

"I don't understand a word you say and I'm busy, I have other things to do."

"Dr. Mok, I came to you because you've been kind and helpful –"

"I've never helped you, I don't even know you," he shouted.

"You were kind enough to take on this job to help stranded students, and after all we're all Chinese, I wouldn't go to the Japanese unless I have no choice."

"I don't know who you are or what you want," he came at her around the desk. "Will you please go?"

It was particularly unnerving when a smooth inscrutable Chinese started to scream. But she had to make sure he understood, she would never get another such chance.

"We just want to go home. Two tickets to Shanghai, any class."

"Will you please go."

"We'll pay," she said on her way out.

Now she would have to tell Bebe.

"So I have to be careful from now on and always stay close to you," she concluded.

"Did you mention my name?" Bebe asked.

"I did before. They'd know anyway."

Bebe was silent and Lute suddenly realized that she was also in danger.

"It's not worth it, you know," Bebe said after a moment.

"I'm sorry to have got you into this."

"Never mind now, but how are we going to be on guard all the time?"

"I don't think they'd dare do anything."

"You thought they killed Number Four."

"He was frightened just now, he really panicked."

"Number Four must have frightened him too."

Lute reasoned that Dr. Mok and his boys were amateurs who had got into this deeper and deeper, started off by the easy money. It would not be so simple to arrange two more disappearances even if they were homeless girls and the compound was no longer patrolled by Japanese soldiers. But she did not want to inflict any more of her guesses on Bebe who so disliked these talks but had become a captive audience now that her own safety was involved. She was sorry about Bebe. Maybe not really sorry, they had become too close for that. And she did not think they would go so far as to kill Bebe too when she herself was clearly the only one that was making trouble.

For herself she willingly faced the risks. It would not be like dying in the war. This was her own doing. Though it was not an admirable thing she had done it was for her the beginning of life. When you did what was mapped out for you you won and lost in a dream. It all felt different the minute you did what you really wanted to do. Even the consequences were not so bitter when you were ready for them. She no longer wondered about life and death either as in the war. Life was here in her hands, she knew its worth because valuable or not it was all she had. Miserly about it as she was, the minute it came to face the end all the love and greed fell away and she was as calm and cold-blooded as a general disposing of ten thousand lives instead of just one.

She could still go to Nakamura tomorrow. Even if they had her watched and followed they could not waylay her in broad daylight? And halfway down to town there were Japanese sentries.

She did not go. For two days she put off going. She was acting too slow. She thought she had estimated Dr. Mok right but in real life you never could tell. You thought you knew but you did not really know.

Bebe took no precautions that she could see and made no comments about her locking their room door. At bottom Bebe did not really believe in any of it. Lute did not ask her to get any boys to help them. She never knew which were Bebe's friends who were going to walk to Chungking and could not tell whether the crowd had thinned out a bit at mealtimes but had the impression they had already left. Green Goat for one was no longer seen around. Bebe never spoke of the secret expedition ever since that night talking in bed. Was she sorry now not to have gone with them? Lute tried not to think of that.

T.F. Lai and the other boys of his group took turns at meals ladling out beans, scooping up rice and passing out the plates. Lute thought they paid her no special attention as the queue moved up. Dr. Mok being a doctor could easily give them some poison to put in her food but it would take some sleight of hand since it all came from big pots. Mimi Choy and the girl with the concave face continued to ignore her. The concave face was as transparent as Mimi was inscrutable. It would seem as though Dr. Mok had not yet told any of them. Angeline ever since her adoption by the gang had kept out of everybody's way, subdued and bitter-looking. Lute was surprised she came to their room just before bedtime.

"This is for you, Lute."

Lute looked at the unaddressed envelope. She opened it and took out a sheet of paper with the printed letter head of a Nam Him Shipping Company. She was so excited she could hardly read the typed paragraph:

"Bearer of chit may purchase one tourist class ticket & seven steerage tickets not later than May 20th.

Signed: On Fook Fat, business manager."

"Dr. Mok says it's for all the students from Shanghai who want to go back but there're only eight tickets, that's all he could get," Angeline said.

"Please tell him we're very grateful."

"I'll ask Paula and Mr. Yip if they want to go," Bebe said.

"Dr. Mok says you will have to settle among yourselves who is to go. He sent this to Lute because she was the one who spoke to him."

"I'll ask the Russian boys and there's that Jewish girl Luba," Bebe said.

"We don't have to pick up all the tickets if there aren't enough people," Lute said.

"Not pick up the tickets. Are you crazy? You can sell them black market."

"So you're going back to Shanghai," Angeline said wistfully. "I don't know when we can go home," she finished weakly as though aware what the others must think. Would she still want to go? What about Dr. Mok?

"Tamara said she would go back to Harbin through Shanghai. I'll ask her," Bebe said.

She came back with all six spare tickets spoken for. There were not any left to sell black market after all.

"They say since you got them you should have the tourist class ticket," Bebe said, "They say even black market only has steerage tickets. First class and tourist can't be had at any price."

Lute hesitated for a moment, the proudest in her life. "Would you like to have it?"

"You better take it, it's much more comfortable, unless you think it's too expensive?" Bebe asked hopefully.

"Well, it's still cheap, isn't it?"

"It's worth it. It's going to be hell in the steerage."

"Do you think you can stand it?"

"I'll be all right. It's only going to be for a few days."

The shipping company could not tell them how long it would take. The sailing was scheduled for the 23rd but the name of the ship was withheld.

Luggage was limited to what they themselves could carry. Bebe drew all her money from the bank. After paying for their passages she still had a hundred forty odd left in small notes. The bank refused to give her larger bills. She was lucky enough to get her money out at all.

"Will you carry it for me?" she said to Lute.

"Let's divide it."

"It's going to be terrible in the steerage. It'll be safer with you."

"All right, but I'm afraid to keep it in a purse. Can you sew it into my clothes?"

"Summer clothes will show."

"What about the suspenders belt?"

Bebe put a cloth lining on the stockings belt and spread the wads of banknotes in between. The rest she sewed into a pair of her own brassieres.

"This will give you a figure."

"With a stomach sticking out underneath," Lute said.

"The stomach will actually make it look sexier," said Bebe who had a bit of a stomach herself.

"Are you sure it won't fall out?"

"It can't."

"I'll be very careful, I'll never take them off no matter how long we're at sea."

"I know you're very good this way, you really hang on to things."

"My mother should hear you," Lute said happily.

22

There was no room in their luggage for the big peasant hat of split bamboo. She would have to wear it but it was curtained all round with blue cloth which would block the view. She slung the gaudily painted domed cartwheel on her back to leave her hands free for the luggage. The Russian boys in their party got a ricksha for each. She sat in hers with her arms around the trunk stood up on the foot rest. A great joy sitting four square inside her filled her up to the eyebrows. With the unseeing eyes of an office-goer she looked at Hong Kong passing before her on the bright hot morning. The long wall around the university was piled with bougainvillaeas. The cream stucco stepped wall had inserted rows of green glazed little pillars about a foot high. A tall tree at the crossroad was hung with pink flowers as flimsy as butterflies. The macadam road flowed down between hill and sea, the sunken rooftops on the sea side crowded with laundry poles with ends resting on the street. She had no feeling of seeing it for the last time. Like when she left Tientsin as a child she was just going somewhere, not leaving anywhere.

No porters were allowed at the pier. Her padded bosom and belly jutted through her cotton gown hoisting it up to her knees. She felt like a tourist who had blundered into a war. At the barricaded wharf the eight of them showed their papers to the sentry and filed in. They were the only people on the pier. The only ship reared up alongside very close. It seemed small and old, with a Japanese name painted on it.

"I'll find you later," Bebe said and followed Paula and Mr. Yip and the Russians dragging their trunks and canvas sacks down a short gangplank leading to a doorway low in the ship.

The soldier reached out for Lute's ticket, took a look and motioned toward the other end. She dragged her trunk bumpily after her. The soldier posted at the foot of the other gangway pointed a rifle at the trunk. She squatted down to open it for him to see, then pulled it up the wide gangway that went diagonally the entire height of the ship. No one else appeared to be coming up this way. It was a lonely struggle up and the linked planks felt so soft underfoot, the whole world seemed to be sliding away like an eroded mountainside of loose dry beige earth. She dared not look at the deep gulch between ship and pier. Certainly those soldiers would not jump in to fish her out.

There was nobody on the top deck. She looked through a window into a dining room. Glass vases in the center of long tables covered with white tablecloth, Western style. This must be first class. She could not drag the trunk around looking for tourist class. There must be a steward around?

As she loitered undecided a group of people came round the deck. Something immediately marked them as Japanese on an inspection tour. They came close-packed, dark-suited, of uniform height and many more of them than in the hospital compound but less grim, though equally brisk. As the path narrowed they broke rank to let a gold-braided sea captain emerge from their midst to lead the way. After the captain came M.H.'s wife in a silk print gown, white lace gloves and high-heeled sandals, and after her M.H. in summer suit and dark glasses carrying a cane. They saw Lute at the same time.

"Ek," M.H.'s wife made the smiling little noise.

"Ek, how are you?" M.H. said. "This is really unexpected."

"I'm so glad," Lute said.

"We never thought to be on the same ship," his wife said.

"Tickets are very difficult to get," he said.

"Oh yes, I had such trouble," Lute said.

"How did you get it?" he asked.

She hesitated a moment, too full of her triumph to pass it off lightly but it was not possible even to hint of it with all the Japanese listening in. "It's through the people in charge at our place," she mumbled.

"You're really lucky," M.H.'s wife said.

Lute pressed back against the rails to let another Chinese woman pass who was as well-dressed as M.H.'s wife, maybe younger, a big woman, rather handsome, she did not really see. But there was something about the Chinese man behind the woman that made her take a good look at him. He was tall and immaculately dressed in a grey suit that somehow seemed borrowed. His pallid face was a squarish moon with almond eyes and a straggly moustache. He sidled by self-effacingly and as if afraid to be touched.

"That's Mei Lan-fang," M.H.'s wife whispered to Lute after he had passed with three Japanese in obsequious attendance.

"Really?"

Lute could hardly believe she was on the same boat as Dr. Mei Lan-fang, considered the most beautiful Chinese alive, awarded an honorary degree by the University of California after the American tour of his Peking opera troupe. Both the female impersonator and the diplomat were taken by the Japanese in protective custody and shipped back to Shanghai where they were best known and could be put to the greatest use. The woman with Mei would be his concubine the Manchu who had also used to be a Peking opera singer.

"I didn't recognize him," she whispered. "With his moustache."

"Yes," M.H.'s wife said too quickly with a smile.

So the moustache was an issue and a forbidden subject. Lute remembered now, he had grown a beard as a patriotic gesture to show he had retired for good. Beard and moustache are the same word in Chinese, to tell one from the other it must be qualified. Judging by the moustache he had not yet capitulated. It looked like M.H. was also still being wooed. They really should not be standing here talking although those Japanese that had not gone on ahead showed no impatience, just leaned on the rails talking softly to each other looking at the sea.

"Which way is your cabin?" M.H. asked delicately instead of saying steerage.

"I don't know. I'm in tourist class."

"Tourist class?" M.H. was so astonished he forgot his tact. "Tourist class tickets are impossible to get."

Lute smiled. "I know."

He glanced at her sharply, taking in the big beach hat, the tight dress, the new bust and belly. Lute noticed it and suddenly understood why his wife had been looking into her face with eyes that would not quite focus, the same as when she herself had tried not to look at Lilypad's belly. She was as horrified as they were and wanted to laugh at the same time.

M.H. made a slight bow of leave taking, suddenly formal, his face stiffened with fear. Whether her Japanese friend was high or low, great or small, even a bee's sting has poison.

"See you in Shanghai," Lute said. Once there they would find out how she had got her ticket. Relatives knew these things.

"We'll be seeing you," M.H.'s wife said irritably going ahead of him.

He turned on a warm slick smile bobbing his head at Lute and hooding his eyes keeping them on the ground, looking suddenly like any old Chinese man but not M.H. Cheung, American-returned student and thirty years a diplomat. He followed his wife through the gangway. The Japanese closing in blocked them from view.

Tourist class was one large room with partly raised floor covered with tatami. The crowd sitting on the tatami were Shanghai people. It was like home already to hear the buzz of talk. Unused to sitting with their legs up they seemed to be all stocking soles. The two nearest women looked like well-to-do housewives. They observed her more openly than their husbands, unable to place her. It was her bizarre hat. She took it off. The Shanghai voices and the inevitable picnic baskets and shopping nets with the thermos bottle were vastly reassuring. They lacked only watermelon seeds to make this an excursion train to Hangchow. The tatami gave a lurch under them. Cries of joy and relief swept through the cabin. They were on their way.

Bebe came just when Lute was beginning to wonder whether they would let her into the upper deck, whether she ought to go look for her.

"It's hot here, isn't it?" Bebe said looking around.

"How is it down there?"

"Terrible. Let's go out."

"Do you think it's all right to leave my things here?"

"It's all right. Isn't your hair hot? I'm going to make pigtails."

She braided her own hair and Lute's. They went on deck and walked about. The South China Sea was just as blue as when they had come to Hong Kong together. To Lute it already seemed smaller and homier now that she was going home. They took turns sitting on a metal stump to rest their feet and watch the passers-by. They did not see anybody from first class or steerage. None of the ladies on the tatami showed up either. Were they busy guarding their belongings or was it to keep out of the way of the Japanese? There were one or more Japanese officers on board, Lute could not tell whether it was the same man waddling about purposefully in baggy khaki pants and riding boots. The Chinese could easily forego fresh air, they stayed in with their women and luggage. They were in a sense on a pirate ship.

"Bebeshka! Lunch!" Tamara shouted down below from the hatchway.

Lute went back for hers. Chinese meals for eight were being served on different parts of the tatami. She joined her group in the awkward picnic struggling with her slit gown and kneecaps. The dishes showed Japanese frugality, just pickles and a watery soup but plenty of hard-boiled rice. She heard no comments, everybody had come prepared for hardship. The two couples had got acquainted. Mr. and Mrs. Ong were older and richer. Mr. Ong with his large ochre face and important-looking stoop seemed to hold himself back with the natural caution of a man of substance. His lean wife had long hair that she wore in a bun. Mrs. Yu the younger wife was boyishly pretty with a bird's round black eyes. Not long after dinner she came back to the cabin and said to her husband:

"There're fried rice cakes to be had."

"Where?" he asked, his lantern jaw hanging slackly.

"At the stern."

"How much?" he whispered with half his arm down in the pocket in his long gown.

She went off with the money and came back with a large bowl of rice flour cakes sliced and fried with shredded pork and long greens. She brought a spare pair of chopsticks. Her husband tried a few pieces and she had the rest. Mrs. Ong looked amusedly at the heaping bowl and asked:

"How much is it?"

"Two fifty," she murmured a little guiltily.

"Hong Kong money?"

"Yes. There's also fried rice," she offered helpfully.

Later in the afternoon she was eating a big bowl of fried rice when Lute came back for a handkerchief. Did she have worms or was she pregnant? She was so small and slender in her black gown. She did not love her husband and ate to make up for it. No, it was probably just the war. Famine always followed war. Just the preoccupation with food made you hungry all the time. Then there was the sea air. When Lute walked around with Bebe they always turned back self-consciously before they reached the concession frying rice and rice cakes under a khaki tarpaulin roof.

Before the light came on the steward closed all the windows and drew the blackout curtains amidst shocked cries.

"So hot, we'll die!"

"How can we pass the night like this? We'll choke."

"Actually we don't have to have the light on," Mrs. Yu said, bringing on a pause. Everybody was afraid for his own valuables and could not trust the others in the dark.

"It's the custom on board ships to keep the light on all night," Mr. Ong said with studied carelessness.

"But how are we to get through the night?" Mrs. Yu balled up a handkerchief and stuck it on to keep her collar away from the nape of her neck.

"They're afraid the light can be seen from airplanes," her husband explained to her.

"Ai-ya, say no more, don't let's run into a bombing," she said.

"Yes, that will smash the eggs," Mr. Ong said shortly.

There was a moment of silence in which Lute felt a common wish rising like steam or incense smoke or a prayer and part of herself going up with it. She remembered the rumor about Mei Lan-fang being drowned with a bombed ship. Having this said about him would seem to ensure that it would never happen. It was a good thing to have such a celebrity on board. Just as a lottery ticket ending in several round numbers never would win, so it was unlikely that it just happened his ship would get struck. Nobody else seemed to know he was here, otherwise the news would be all over the boat in no time and they would be talking of nothing else.

She had been wondering how there would be room to lie down when you could not even sit and stretch your legs. But they managed and without anybody giving directions fell into a grouping in accordance with the Chinese instinct for propriety, Lute in between Mrs. Yu and Mrs. Ong, their husbands on their other side and the two men with other men on their other side. Lute tried to take up as little room as possible, curled up cautiously around her new bulges which she realized was rare among Chinese girls and must attract a lot of attention. Could they tell it was false? And guess what was inside? She had to be specially careful when the money was not her own. The heat was bearable once you were resigned to it, like sweating out a fever. There was no room for turning and tossing, yet a scraping noise on the tatami persisted like the rustling of live crabs in a steaming pan.

She woke when the steward came to open the windows. Everybody sat up to catch the dawn breeze. Mrs. Ong patted her bun, not a hair astray. She was wiry and smart with a pair of tiny eyes, very like an aunt of Lute's, one of Autumn Crane's sisters. Evidently Lute had also struck her as familiar. While waiting their turn to wash in the basins of warm water the steward brought, she said smiling:

"I can tell from the way you sleep that you had a good upbringing."

"No," Lute automatically mumbled smiling. Sleeping postures had been one of the few things her old amah had been particular about, with the idea that it had to do with chastity. Sleep like a bow and never on your back. The poor old amah had not succeeded in making a lady of her. One amah could not make a lady. Was she still alive? What could she do for her anyway? Back after three years and still no money to send her. But it seemed enough if both were to hear that the other still lived. She also yearned to see her aunt and would not even mind to come face to face with her father and stepmother again with nothing to show. She had learned things in the war and forgotten much too.

The ship stopped on the third evening.

"We're in Amoy," the word spread.

"How is that?" Mr. Yu half whispered slack-jawed. "After all this sailing, only just got to Amoy?"

Mr. Ong shook his head. "At this rate we don't know when we'll ever be in Shanghai."

There were groans all through the cabin. Room had to be made for the new passengers from Amoy. Some of the newcomers camped outside the window to sleep in the open. Lute walked past them the next day, young men with hair in their eyes sitting on a bundle or leaning on a bedding roll. They wore their hair long in imitation of the Formosans who had got the mop style from the Japanese. Formosa having once been colonized from Fukien it was difficult to tell the people apart but these must be small Fukienese traders running the blockade. The Formosans ranking as second class Japanese would not have to camp out in the gangway.

Normally it took four days to reach Shanghai. On the fifth day there was a hubbub on deck. Lute heard Bebe calling for her. She rushed out to join her at the rails.

"Look, look."

She saw nothing but the duck egg green sea crinkled with fish scale waves. It was a sunless day.

"Look up!" Bebe yelled.

She pressed against the rails and poked her head out. Two distant peaks hung high in the sky, brilliant green mountains veined and whittled down to the slim sculptured shapes you only see in Chinese painting, out off at the waist by mist. Were these among the three mountains of the immortals in the Eastern Sea? They were incredible the way they hung suspended in that white sky. Everybody stared as though they might vanish any minute.

"That's Formosa," she heard somebody say.

"Formosa has such high mountains?"

"In the south they have."

"Where is this? Tainan? We're not going to stop here?"

The crowd watched until the peaks rising and rising were lost to sight.

"Isn't it like Chinese painting?" Bebe said to Lute.

"Yes. I never knew there are really such mountains."

"You know what I mean now about Chinese painting."

"Yes."

At supper Mr. Yu demanded slack-jawed, "Now how did we get to Formosa? We're way out of the way."

"We're certainly making a big turn," Mr. Ong said.

No one remarked that it was to dodge airplanes and submarines. It was bad omen to talk about it. Everybody not thinking about this one thing that was constantly with them gave the life on board a glassed-in make-believe quality almost like luxury as though they were playing house on the sea or dining alongside an aquarium with the giant octopus sucked to the glass, its eye that was hard to locate ignoring them just as they paid no attention to it.

The Formosan coast appeared, long slopes cutting across pale blue water, of a mildness reminiscent of the south of the Yangtze. At dusk the ship stopped outside Keelung. For refueling or to get supplies? But the port was nowhere in sight, they must have dropped anchor way out in the sea. Lute saw no steamer or sampan come near. The ship stood quietly in the mist. Leaning at the rails she heard snatches of Fukienese shouts that seemed to have come from down below but could see nothing. She could just make out the ghostly outlines of two fishing boats hanging around a little way off, each with a red lantern that bobbed up and down. The boats floated on their own shadows, a thick brush stroke of dark grey at the waterline, the only fluid thing in the evening's pale grey void. She watched its heavy reptilian movement under the boats, stretching, contracting, stretching, contracting. The mist even smothered sounds. Only now and then came a lapping of water.

Strange that she should come here where her grandfather had lost the battle. Chinese for Keelung originally meant chicken cage but like many other place names had been changed to more respectable words of the same sounds, so Keelung now meant Foundation Success. But in her grandfather's day she believed it had still been Chicken Cage. His betrayers the Fukienese were on this ship too, still more or less the only seafarers of the country. She wished she knew something about nautical history so she could conjure up the old warships with swarms of supplementary sailboats getting in the way. The soldiers with a big circle sewn on their uniform with the appliquéd word *yung*, brave, worn over the heart and another on the back. The sailors in equally colorful uniform. Their war cries. The flaming cannon blasts in the rain. She supposed it was always rain or fog along these shores. Trying to see through the curtain of time she only felt the curtain blowing softly against her face.

"What are you looking at?"

She turned and saw a Japanese officer standing beside her. Why, she understood him perfectly and he had spoken in Japanese. She could not resist answering, there was a sentence very like it in the textbook.

"The red lanterns are beautiful."

"Yes. Beautiful," he said.

They stood looking at the fishing boats. He was in his late twenties or maybe younger, shortish with a pale clean-cut profile. His heavy uniform with the baggy pants smelled of perspiration. For a while she felt he was just a man who had lived strenuously.

"Do you like Japanese man?" he asked.

At her blank look he repeated the question in the same grave tone but more slowly, "Do — you — like — Japanese — man."

"My friend is calling me." She had had time to think.

"Ha," he acknowledged with a slight nod.

She ran off to the lower deck.

All the portholes were closed again after the lights came on. Even with the windows open it had been unbearably hot because neither the ship nor the air was moving. Lute sweated so much in the night she got worried that the banknotes on her would be as soggy and useless as money left in clothes that had gone through a washing. Finally dozing off she was wakened by a jolt of the tatami and groans of relief all round. It was dawn and they were on their way again.

It took eight days but finally the Shanghai voices were babbling, "*Daw leh daw leh*! We're there, we're there!" A crowd of porters waited at the foot of the gangway across a low fence, arms waving. The pier was not cleared. It was always different in Shanghai. The porters' uniform consisted of a large red sleeveless jacket with a number on it that made them look like sandwich men. They were all laughing and shouting in broken Shanghai dialect, having come from the north of the Yangtze. What made them so happy? They had no reason to be. Yes, it was the same people, they were still here. In other parts of the country no matter how good the people were they did not laugh like this. These round faces of the lower Yangtze just seemed to light up more easily and open up wide like a box. Lute found herself also laughing as she tried to rein in her trunk so it would not go crashing down the ramp, then struggled to pass it over the fence to be fought for as though it was a great prize, feeling a little like the girl in the old stories who threw down a multi-colored silk ball into the street to marry whoever it hit. She wished she had many more pieces of luggage for the others, so many she would not mind losing a few.

She waited for Bebe outside the wharf.

"Come to my house," Bebe said.

"I'd better go to my aunt's first."

"You can telephone from my house to see if your aunt is home."

They each took a ricksha. She was not worried about Coral. She was the one person you could depend on. In an hour she would hear her voice on the phone, surprised and smiling, not overly astonished.

The warehouses and shanties fell back from the wide streets in that strangely withdrawn way they had in this characterless district that you never got to see except when you were either coming or leaving, always an emotional journey. The city seemed deliberately to hold itself back unwilling to say goodbye or welcome. She remembered the other time she had come here at eight years old, having to tilt her head back to see through her long fringe, looking so hard and getting no impressions except of herself in the new blouse and pants with large butterflies all over, looking like a country child riding in the old horse carriage. Why was it every time she returned to Shanghai it felt like a triumphant entry?

"You're in Shanghai now," Bebe turned round and called out.

Lute grinned back. There was the old saying, to be rich and influential without returning to your native land is like wearing brocade to walk in the dark. She did not come back rich and influential, just older and more sure of herself, which was not much except that everything counted more here because it was home. She loved the plain act of living and this piece of ground had been fattened by all the years off her own life and the lives of all those she knew best. Here the weave and tangle of people's ups and downs were the thickest and gave life a different feel than anywhere else.

As they got into the city the streets remained faceless in the grey glare of macadam. The houses were the most frustratingly nondescript collection of grey bricks and khaki concrete, old business buildings with Moorish arches, alley gates with old Chinese horned edifices. The truth was even the heart of town was elusive, nowhere was characteristic, not the wide streets lined with poplars or plane trees, said to be like France nor the functional apartment buildings further out with the look of northern Europe. There were also the new boxlike "Spanish style" alleys, the gasoline stations that were red-and-gold pavilions, the huge old silver stores with calligraphic signboards crowned by carved filigrees like a bride's headdress, among new shops that were all window, with a single dress and smart lighting, and everywhere the dingy accumulations of various foreign period architecture brightened by gonorrhea posters in red or black slapped all over. Unlike Hong Kong this was not a place to look at, just a world to live in. To Lute it had promised everything ever since she was a child. Now it would all be hers since she had fought so hard to get back, risked her life for it although what happened in Hong Kong already had no reality, just a story she would laugh over with her aunt. Shanghai came mixed and indistinguishable with her own hopes, a thundering chorus in an unknown language but with her it was always the feelings without words that sang the loudest.

The ricksha jogged on in the wake of the puller whose golden shoulders jerked left and right under the blue rags. They had turned into Nanking Road. The three department stores loomed ahead, grey fortresses with watchtowers confronting each other. Then the bright green Race Course burst in sight and the Victorian Romanesque clock tower on the lawn. As the scene grew familiar, there was a slight stir among her senses as if just coming to life again while previously she had only been in heaven.

"It hasn't changed, has it?" Bebe called out.

"No."

This song had been sung all over town the summer she came here from Tientsin:

"The sun,
The sun,
The sun it remembers
Having shone on Sister Gold's face
and Sister Silver's clothes,
and shone on poor Autumn Scent too."

It was summer again and the same time of the morning as when she had ridden in the other time in the open carriage by her old amah's side. The sun was hot along her arms and legs in the unshaded richsha and like two hot irons on the dress over her thighs. I'm here, she said. The sun remembered her.